Billy the Kid and Other Plays

Chicana & Chicano Visions of the Américas

BILLY THE KID AND OTHER PLAYS

RUDOLFO ANAYA

With an afterword by
CECILIA J. ARAGÓN and
ROBERT CON DAVIS-UNDIANO

UNIVERSITY OF OKLAHOMA PRESS : NORMAN

Publication of this book is made possible through
the generosity of Edith Kinney Gaylord.

The play Billy the Kid was previously published in The Anaya Reader (Warner Books, 1995).
Who Killed Don José? was previously published in The Anaya Reader and New Mexico
Plays, edited by David Richard Jones (University of New Mexico Press, 1989).

Library of Congress Cataloging-in-Publication Data

Anaya, Rudolfo A.
    Billy the Kid and other plays / Rudolfo Anaya ; with an afterword by Cecilia J.
Aragón and Robert Con Davis-Undiano.
        p. cm.—(Chicana & Chicano visions of the Américas ; v. 10)
    ISBN 978-0-8061-4225-8 (pbk.)
    1. Mexican Americans—Drama.   2. New Mexico—Drama.   I. Title.
    PS3551.N27B55 2011
    812'54—dc23

                                                                2011025941

Billy the Kid and Other Plays is Volume 10 in the
Chicana & Chicano Visions of the Américas series.

The paper in this book meets the guidelines for permanence and durability
of the Committee on Production Guidelines for Book Longevity of the
Council on Library Resources, Inc. ∞

To all the actors, directors, and stage crew
who have brought these plays to life. I love you all!
And to the readers who may get the urge to stage them,
I say, "Break a leg!"

CONTENTS

COMMENTS FROM THE PLAYWRIGHT

Although I consider novels my principal genre, I have always been fascinated with the stage. In my secret, imaginary life, I have seen myself as an actor. I did play the role of a shepherd in a fifth-grade Christmas play long ago. I described that scene in my novel Bless Me, Ultima. Alas, that was the beginning and end of my acting career.

As a university student in the 1960s I didn't take drama classes, but I did read a lot of plays. Later, my wife, Patricia, and I regularly attended local theater, and to our joy we once enjoyed a production of Hamlet at Stratford-on-Avon. Once upon a time we also enjoyed a few Broadway plays. If there is a destiny to every life, then mine was fulfilled when I finally connected the theatrical dots by writing my first play.

The year was 1979, and José Rodríguez had just organized a community theater, La Compañía, here in Alburquerque. José asked me to write a play for a special performance he was planning. He had read my novella, The Legend of La Llorona, and recognized its dramatic potential. So I wrote The Season of La Llorona, and with his guidance my first play was produced.

The Malinche/Cortés story is a play within a play. I suppose the classic emotions of fear, pity, and eventual catharsis fit Malinche's tragic story, and other storytellers have also been intrigued by this powerful story. In 2001 Daniel Steven Crafts, a composer, came to me and asked me to write a libretto based on the story. I did, he composed the music, and we now have the opera La Llorona, waiting to be produced. A few other writers have since used Malinche as La Llorona in their stories. The story of Cortés and Malinche has evolved through these different genres.

The Season of La Llorona also says volumes about storytelling in our New Mexican culture. Our cuentos (folktales) number in the hundreds and are the basis for our oral tradition. My plays are inspired by this tradition, and it is through story that La Llorona takes on aspects of historical reality. In telling the story of La Llorona, the grandfather tells the tragic story of Cortés and Malinche. Cortés first uses the native woman Malinche to conquer the Aztecs, then deserts her. Malinche, to save her sons, kills them. In my story, Malinche thus becomes the first Llorona, the Crying Woman, of the New World.

After La Llorona I wrote a script, Consuelo Goes to School, for an educational company in Los Angeles. Rudy Vargas directed it, and while working with him I followed him around East LA, learning a lot about film and the city. I met Jesús Treviño, who was to become the most accomplished Chicano movie and television director of his generation. I was flying high with the homeboys, rubbing elbows with the most talented artists of the Chicano movement.

My connection with LA continued. Years later, I sat in the audience for the premiere stage performance of *Zoot Suit*. Then more good news: In 1982 *American Playhouse*, through the Corporation for Public Broadcasting, sponsored a script development project. I entered the program and was selected to write an original screenplay. I used the folksong "Delgadina" as the basis for *Rosa Linda*. The screenplay wasn't accepted—but what the hell, I was learning. The subject of the story is incest, and the producers weren't ready for it. Later I wrote *Rosa Linda* as a play; it's weathering in a file cabinet in my writing room. Some day . . .

I became an abuelo in the mid-1980s when granddaughter Kristan came along. Only I could put her to bed at night, because she claimed I told the best stories. I told her many of the folktales I had heard as a child, and I composed dozens of my own originals. One, *The Farolitos of Christmas*, seemed good enough to write down as a children's book. Later Ramon Flores, director of La Compañía, asked me for a Christmas play, so the children's story became a play. How our luminarias became farolitos is the plot that reflects a larger picture—cultural evolution.

In the 1940s New Mexican cultures were a-changing. In the background lurked World War II and the building of Los Alamos Laboratories. The first atomic bomb was detonated in our southern desert. The landscape and the traditional cultures of New Mexico began to shift. The forces of assimilation affected every aspect of Hispano/Nuevo Mexicano culture. So from the storehouse of our Nuevo Mexicano folk songs, I added traditional Christmas music to the play. The community was hungry to see aspects of their culture on the stage, and *The Farolitos of Christmas* always played to packed, appreciative audiences.

I was a drop in the bucket in the Chicano Theater movement that came alive during the Chicano movement of the 1960s and 70s. In California, the master, Luis Valdez, organized the most important theater of our time, Teatro Campesino. Other Chicano theaters sprang up throughout the Southwest. Latino USA was marching onto the stage sporting a new language, Spanish mixed with English, and new themes. In New York the Nuyoricans created a fascinating, new beat—salsa on stage. Latino plays were ready for the movies; *Zoot Suit* led the way.

Me? I was still loyal to my native earth, and if my themes and characters didn't fit Broadway, I didn't care. My gente loved my plays. That's what mattered.

In 1987, Jorge Huerta, the dean of Chicano Theater, was invited by La Compañía to Alburquerque to direct *Who Killed Don José?* I was in heaven. I was learning more and more about community theater and appreciating the talented actors who lived and breathed in our city. The stage became a mirror for the people; audiences laughed when Don José talked about implanting chips in his sheep, the better to breed them at the right time.

The play touches on the new world of chip technology, and some of its characters worry that if we New Mexicans didn't join, we would be left behind. The play also serves other themes, alluding to our once-productive sheep industry and its historical importance, as well as down-and-dirty New Mexican political intrigue, passion, murder, and greed. It's the whole kitchen sink, set in a ranch just outside Santa Fe. I felt blessed, marching those characters onto the stage to strut and fret, and all from the depths of my quiet writing room. (Playwrights also need a room of their own.)

Workshopping the play with Jorge was a joy, a gratifying experience. I learned that regional plays can also shine with universal truths. Don't let New York tell you otherwise. A case in point is my play about the dance-drama of the matachines, one of the oldest in New Mexico, performed on feast days in the open-air, earth-packed plazas in both Indian pueblos and Hispanic villages. The dance has its roots in Mexico, where it is still performed. I have always been fascinated with the spiritual nature of the dance and have observed it many times, my favorite being at Jemez Pueblo on December 12. The Bernalillo matachines also have continued the tradition of the dance.

I asked myself, why can't the dance move from the village plaza and onto the stage? Didn't the ancient Greek chorus take its dithyramb out of the olive groves into the amphitheaters? So I wrote *Matachines*, using the dance-drama as the basis for the play, hoping to capture some of the spirituality of the dance. If our young people won't go to the village dances, I thought, maybe they'll come to the theater.

That's the question. Will our young Nuevo Mexicanos continue to attend the fiestas, the dances, the ceremonies? Will the folkways of our traditional cultures thrive, or die? Will the young speak Spanish? Will commercial interests grow so strong that they will erode the old village cultures? At the root of the play lies misguided passion, the lustful lover hiding behind the mask of El Toro. The mask hides the reality. Will we, too, hide behind masks as we assimilate into a culture of crass materialism? Would our departed ancestors recognize us?

If the centuries-old fiestas of our pueblos and villages disappear, can drama on stage substitute for ancient ceremonies that should not be forgotten? A few of our stories have been turned into movies, a powerful medium. But only live stage allows us to be in close contact with the characters and their conflicts. Live actors create a magical connection with the audience. Being only rows away from the actors, we feel intimately their desires and fears, and all the other primal emotions they may portray. Plays mirror the joys and foibles of human nature, and the action happens in front of our noses.

Of course, eventual catharsis depends on the script and how the actors play the play, but there's an added dimension to community theater: those are friends on stage, family members. Fellow students. Teachers. The plumber who always dreamed of acting. With community theater we can watch folks we never realized had talent, playing roles we never imagined! We recognize the players, much like Greek audiences must have recognized who was playing their Medea or Oedipus—and that's presentation of illusion that's hard to beat. The invisible curtain slips away, and suddenly it's our story being acted out on stage. Our joys, our despair. That feels good.

I struggle with questions of cultural survival, and answer those questions by sticking close to my region—its people and traditions. Plays present not only illusion, but also the reality of place. And I know it's possible to share our plays and stories across frontiers, not only being observant to the spirit of our place but also learning about those other regions where spirit also abides. We write locus in quo, the place in which we reside, but we share our plays across borders and break down walls, renounce old fears and prejudices. Isn't that what sharing and learning are all about? "Arms and the man, I sing"—love and revolution, two great themes of stagecraft. I love my characters, but do I make revolution? Isn't writing from my place revolutionary? I lead you into my world, as other plays lead me into the places they portray.

As I approached midlife, I thought I'd best deal with it by writing about the new journey. Of course I insisted that I myself never experienced midlife crisis! Not me! But the playwright does become his characters; the characters reflect the playwright. (I think someone already wrote that.) So how do we accept the changes brought on by time? Is the play a comedy or tragedy? Or comic-tragic? Or just plain fun?

Cecilia Aragón first directed Ay, Compadre! in Alburquerque. At the end of the play middle-aged ladies in the audience would flock to me, hugging and kissing me. "You told it like it is," they crowed. I loved it. My playwriting was paying rewards.

Ay, Compadre! is my most produced play. It went to Denver and LA. Some told me it should be the basis for a sitcom. But even in comedy, questions arise: Can we Spanish-speaking, culturally different Latinos move out of the barrio? Do we have to? If we do move, will we be happy? As our families move away from the center, we lose touch, we assimilate, we pay the price.

My concerns seem old-fashioned. Of course Latinos are moving into the mainstream society, working and surviving in it. Still, because New Mexico is such a distinct culture with centuries-old roots, Nuevo Mexicanos worry, perhaps more than others, that we will lose the language and values of our ancestors. Our culture is not reflected in the school curriculum, and many of our kids suffer for it. That's a reality we know.

Other realities concern the plethora of fascinating historical characters who have strutted across the stage of our harsh but beloved land. Such a character is Billy the Kid, loved by some, hated by others. Recently the governor of New Mexico was asked to grant The Kid a pardon. He didn't. Nevertheless, Billy remains the best-known historical figure from our state. You say "New Mexico" and many will answer, "New Mexico? Yeah, Billy the Kid." The myth goes on, due in part to too many bad movies.

My grandparents and parents were born in Puerto de Luna, a small farming village on the Pecos River in east-central New Mexico. I grew up in Santa Rosa and would often visit my grandfather in Puerto de Luna. In the 1800s, as legend tells us, Billy also went to Puerto de Luna, to gamble at the card tables and dance with the pretty girls. So I grew up hearing stories about El Bilito. At about age seventeen, my grandfather Liborio Mares might even have run into Billy at one of the famous Puerto de Luna dances. The Nuevo Mexicanos told many stories about Billy. He spoke Spanish, was respectful, didn't drink, and didn't smoke. He wasn't like the other gringo americanos.

After the Civil War a tremendous land grab was on in New Mexico. The Lincoln County War is part of that history, and Billy was caught in the middle. Texans and easterners were moving into the state, the old Spanish/Mexican land grants were being taken over by foreigners, and the way of life of the Nuevo Mexicanos was being forced to fit into an English-speaking world. The history is complex, but knowing the history of the time helps to establish a more-correct context for Billy's brief life. Directors need to do research in order to set the stage.

I feel empathy for Billy, a kid born in Brooklyn whose family traveled west and wound up in New Mexico. Billy's mother warned him, he who lives by the gun, dies by the gun. The pistol shot that ended his brief life exploded with fire in that dark room. Billy may have died instantly, but his flaming spirit rose to live in posterity, well beyond the time of the Lincoln County War. I only hope all my characters are filled with the same fiery passion I found in Billy. The violent times helped mold who he was. I think he got a raw deal— several raw deals. I don't condone the murders he committed; I just wonder what the time did to his psyche—a time when everyone was armed and greed ran rampant.

Sounds contemporary, doesn't it?

You be the judge. We go to plays and come out discussing the plot, the acting, the director's role, the characters we liked or didn't like, the stage setting, our emotions. Did the play "work"? Did we fear for Billy? Pity him? Or have we too grown so jaded that we care little when Billy dies? Can we still create theatrical heroes and heroines in our time? Some in the world of the absurd say no.

When the play doesn't work, maybe the playwright's at fault. I can accept that. Still, I keep inviting everyone to attend and support community theater. Get involved, write it and act in it. It's fun, communal, interactive, and you grow as the play grows. If the community can attend local sports events, why can't it attend the theater?

A great example of community theater in action is *Angie*, one of my favorite plays. Cecilia Aragón, then a doctoral student in drama at the University of New Mexico, first produced it in 1998. She formed her own theater company, La Casa Teatro, and produced four of my plays in the 1990s. She didn't just stay in the academic ivory tower—she got out in the community and took theater to the people. Those were great years for me, and for all who enjoyed acting in or attending the plays.

As with my other plays, *Angie* coincides with events in my career as a writer. In my early sixties I had the first inkling of the changes we experience as we get older. Angie is crippled and winds up in a nursing home. She is taken away from her home, the center of her life and her storehouse of memories. In the novel *Bless Me, Ultima*, the boy Antonio dreams a lot; Angie's memories are analogous to Antonio's dreams. Both child and elder share the world of dreams and memories.

In my recent novel *Randy Lopez Goes Home*, the role of memory also plays an important part. What do we remember? Why? And who remembers us? One of the characters in the novel suggests that we compose our memories as we go along. We are constantly writing stories in our minds, second by second. In my novel *Tortuga*, even the children in a vegetative stage are dreaming. The dream/memory should not be destroyed, because it is linked to a greater, universal dream, something like what Jung proposes with his collective unconscious. There seems to exist a shared biologic memory that stretches across human evolution. If that is so, do universal, shared dreams and memories activate the substratum of my plays? Is memory the dark matter every play needs to succeed?

Angie needs to return home because that's her place of power, where she can enter the world of memory. Will she ever be able to make the nursing home her new casa, the home that holds her memories? Casa is an important value, and a constant theme in my plays. New Mexico is my casa, and so it is the source of the themes and characters I write. Are soul and dream/memory born from the place?

Angie's young lover, long dead, enters her memories, but so do family, friends, furniture, photographs, foods, smells. Everything is wrapped in memory and can only exist therein; especially for the very old, little seems to exist outside memory. I hope Angie teaches us something of the tremendous power inherent in memory, and thus how we might better care for our elders.

Like Athena springing full-grown and armed from the forehead of Zeus, every play strives to be full-grown and armed. But plays do not come full-grown. There's the workshop, the rehearsals and readings, and even after it's performed, the playwright, directors, and actors keep tweaking here and there. Actors always want more lines. One learns from the collaborative process.

Mostly, it has been Chicano theaters that have produced plays written by Chicanas or Chicanos. Mainstream theater has not shown much interest in our work. That said, I wish to thank the following directors who have produced my plays: Ricardo Lopez in Los Angeles; Pedro Garcia in McAllen, Texas; Tony Garcia at Su Teatro in Denver; Elisa Alvarado in San Jose, California; Marcos Martinez at Nosotros Theater in Los Angeles; Teatro Milagro in Portland; and Debra Gallegos in Denver. The list goes on; I've had a good run.

But why are these plays produced only in Chicano theaters? The question deserves an answer.

One important exception is the Vortex Theatre in Alburquerque, which in 2010 produced my play *Bless Me, Ultima*, based on my novel of the same title. Under the guidance of David Jones and with the excellent direction of Valli Rivera, the play toured seven cities and broke every attendance record in the state. People will attend theater, especially when it speaks to their sense of community. The play is not included in this volume, but it is available from me.

The play's the thing. Here are mine; you be the judge. Enjoy. You might get interested enough to act in one or direct one. Build community. Bring talented people together. That's what has happened with these plays, and with this collection.

There are so many other people to thank. I thank Professor Robert Con Davis-Undiano, series editor for the Chicano & Chicana Visions of the Américas series at the University of Oklahoma Press, for publishing this collection, and also for outlining some major themes that appear in my plays. His insights and those of Professor Cecilia Aragón outline other dramatic inferences and thus provide a wider context for the plays. I also thank Emily Jerman, my wonderful editor at University of Oklahoma Press.

The Season of La Llorona

CHARACTERS

ALFREDO, son

MOTHER

MARGARITA, daughter

ABUELO

MALINCHE

FIRST SON

SECOND SON

BERNAL

CAPTAIN

DRUMMER

PRINCESS

MOCTEZUMA'S GHOST

FATHER

Halloween evening. Alfredo and Margarita, in their early teens, are seated at the kitchen table, carving a pumpkin into a jack-o-lantern. Both are dressed in Halloween costumes. Mother is at the stove baking biscochitos. The kitchen is warm and cozy. Outside the wind howls.

ALFREDO: Yummy, the biscochitos smell good. Can I have one?

MOTHER: "May I?"

ALFREDO: Yes, you can have one too.

MOTHER: Very funny. And, no, you may not have one. These cookies are for the trick-or-treaters.

MARGARITA: Next to Christmas, Halloween is my favorite time.

ALFREDO: Mine too. I like to scare people—

MARGARITA: I love the costumes.

ALFREDO: I like the candy. Mom, can we go now?

MOTHER: You *may* go as soon as your father gets home. I don't want you going out alone.

There's a knock at the door.

ALFREDO: I'll get it!

MARGARITA: Maybe it's trick-or-treaters . . .

The wind howls. Abuelo enters, holding a mask over his face.

ABUELO: Trick or treat!

ALFREDO: ¡Abuelo!

ABUELO: Gotcha! (*He hugs Alfredo.*)

MARGARITA: Grandpa! (*She runs to greet him.*)

ABUELO: ¡Mira que bonita mi princesa!

MARGARITA: Mother made my costume.

ALFREDO: I got mine at Walmart.

MOTHER: Papá. What are you doing out?

ABUELO: Oh, I just came to check on things. . . . I wanted to see my goblins. (*He picks up Margarita and kisses her.*)

MOTHER: Alfredo, get a chair for Abuelo.

ALFREDO: Are you going trick or treating with us, 'Buelo? (*The kids help him take off his jacket.*)

ABUELO: Estoy muy viejo, está muy frio. . . . I came to borrow sugar. Your grandma is baking cookies for Día de los Muertos.

MOTHER: Día de los Muertos . . .

ABUELO: Sí. In two days the spirits come to visit. Tonight is the season of la Llorona.

MOTHER: (*to herself*) . . . the season of la Llorona . . .

MARGARITA: Come help us with our jack-o-lantern, Abuelo.

MOTHER: Hijita, pour your Abuelo some coffee.

Abuelo sits at the table and munches on a cookie.

ABUELO: Mmm. I love biscochitos.

MOTHER: If you eat them hot, they'll give you empache.

ALFREDO: What's empache?

ABUELO: Food sticks to your intestines. Stomach ache. (*mischievously*) The best way to get rid of it is to eat another cookie.

MOTHER: ¡Papá! Don't spoil them.

ABUELO: Pues, what's an abuelo for?

MARGARITA: Grandpa, who's la Llorona?

ALFREDO: She's the old bogey woman who lives by the ditch. She chases kids.

MARGARITA: You mean Doña Lupita?

ABUELO: No, she's not la Llorona. Doña Lupe is a little loca en la cabeza, but she's harmless. The real Llorona is the crying woman we hear late at night—

MARGARITA: Why is she crying?

MOTHER: She cries for her children. (*She picks up a carving knife and cuts into the pumpkin.*)

ALFREDO: Why?

MARGARITA: Is she real?

ABUELO: You mean I've never told you the story of la Malinche? You should know about her; she might appear on a night like tonight.

ALFREDO: Why tonight?

ABUELO: Pues, la Llorona loves Halloween. She hears the boys and girls running in the streets, and she comes out to look for her children.

MARGARITA: (*puzzled*) But we're not her children.

ABUELO: Oh, she will take any malcriado she catches.

ALFREDO: What happened to her kids?

MOTHER: (*stares at the knife*) Something terrible . . .

Margarita draws close to her mother.

MARGARITA: Do you know the story?

MOTHER: (*nods*) Let your Abuelo tell it.

ALFREDO: Come on, 'Buelo, tell us.

ABUELO: Not tonight. You might get susto.

ALFREDO: Tell us! Please, 'Buelo.

Abuelo looks closely at Mother.

MARGARITA: (*to Mother*) Do you feel okay, Mom?

MOTHER: Yes . . . I just thought of my son, Miguel.

ABUELO: Miguelito. Que descanse en paz.

MOTHER: It's been two years since he disappeared.

Mother holds her apron to her eyes. Margarita hugs her.

MARGARITA: I remember our little brother.

ALFREDO: We used to play games.

MOTHER: (*pensive*) It was a night like tonight.

MARGARITA: Don't be sad, Mamá. We're here.

Mother hugs her.

MOTHER: Yes, you are here . . . mis hijos.

ALFREDO: Did la Llorona take Miguel?

MOTHER: (*angry*) Don't say things like that!

Alfredo is startled.

ABUELO: (*calmly*) No, la Llorona didn't take Miguel. Sit by me. I'll tell you a story.

MOTHER: I pray every day he will return to us. There will be a knock at the door, and he will be standing there . . . (*She looks at the door.*)

ABUELO: Hija, we have to let go of our grief.

MARGARITA: Tell us the story of Malinche, 'Buelo.

ABUELO: Not tonight. Let me tell you about the time Pedro de Ordimalas went to visit the devil.

ALFREDO: You already told us that story.

MOTHER: Tell them. The children should know.

ABUELO: Are you sure?

Mother nods.

ALFREDO: Yeah, tell us about la Malinche.

MARGARITA: Who was she?

ABUELO: La Malinche, a beautiful princess who lived long ago. She helped the Spaniards conquer Mexico. Now her spirit roams the land, crying for her sons. Some say she carries a bloody knife.

MARGARITA: Oh, sounds scary.

ABUELO: Maybe tonight's not the night . . .

MARGARITA: Yes, Grandpa. I love scary stories!

Outside the wind howls mournfully.

ABUELO: Listen! That's la Llorona crying for her children.

MOTHER: The sound of lost children . . .

MARGARITA: Is she real?

ABUELO: Oh yes, she's real to us. But the americanos don't believe in her.

ALFREDO: Some of the kids saw her by the river.

ABUELO: Malcriados see la Llorona. So be good.

MARGARITA: That goes for you, Alfredo.

ALFREDO: I ain't afraid of nothing.

MARGARITA: You are!

ALFREDO: I'm not!

He pushes her. Mother grabs Alfredo.

MOTHER: (*nervously*) Behave, or you're grounded!

Mother regrets her outburst.

MOTHER: I'm sorry. . . . I'm tired. Sit and listen to the story. I'll make hot chocolate.

MARGARITA: All right! Go on, Grandpa. How did Malinche become la Llorona?

ABUELO: Pues, some people say it's a true story, others say it's just make-believe. Who knows? But it's certainly a sad story. La Llorona cannot rest until she finds her children.

Sound of wailing wind.

ALFREDO: Is that la Llorona?

MARGARITA: Shh, be still.

ALFREDO: I just want to know if she's real?

ABUELO: Oh, yes. Late at night she walks along the river. A horrible sight to see. Her long hair falls to her waist. Some say she carries a sharp dagger. Her eyes glow red from crying. Don't stay out late at night because she might GET YOU! (*shouting*)

The children jump.

MARGARITA: Grandpa!

ALFREDO: Didn't scare me.

MARGARITA: Go on, Grandpa.

ABUELO: In the land of the Aztecs, long, long, ago . . . (*An Aztec flute is heard as the lights dim.*) This happened years after the Spaniards had conquered

Tenochtitlán, the capital city of the Aztecs. The Spaniards were led by a captain, a conquistador. He was able to conquer the Aztecs by turning other tribes against them. And he fell in love with a young Indian woman who understood many languages. The Aztecs named her Malinche, but the soldiers called her Doña Marina. She was young, beautiful, and very intelligent.

The light in the kitchen dims as the focus moves into the story. Malinche stands at the altar of the god Huitzilopochtli. She is beautiful—dark and striking.

MALINCHE: God of the Aztecs, the empire has fallen.

In the background, Popocatepetl flashes fire and thunders.

MALINCHE: The people are enslaved, thousands die of foreign diseases. I brought the Spaniards to Tenochtitlán. Am I to blame for the devastation? Will history call me the traitor of the Mexicans? I cannot sleep, I walk the streets at night. . . . I am the cause of so much misery.

Her two sons enter.

FIRST SON: Mamá. The volcano speaks and makes fire.

MALINCHE: The gods are angry. Let us dance. Let us ask forgiveness from Huitzilopochtli, the god of war. Let us dance for our fallen prince, Moctezuma.

They begin to dance but are interrupted by Bernal, the Captain's guard.

BERNAL: ¡Hola, Doña Marina! Con permiso.

MALINCHE: What news?

BERNAL: El capitán has just arrived.

MALINCHE: Home from another conquest.

BERNAL: As you know, he has met with el Conde de Aragón.

MALINCHE: A conniving man who seeks only gold. Go, my sons—let me greet your father in private.

Bernal and the sons exit. Drums announce the entrance of the Captain.

CAPTAIN: Mi amor.

MALINCHE: Mi esposo—

They embrace.

CAPTAIN: It has been too long since I held you.

MALINCHE: I have missed you.

CAPTAIN: I have good news to relate. El Conde de Aragón assures me— (*He pauses, looks at the statue.*)
Still praying to the heathen idol.

MALINCHE: Our war god is a powerful god.

CAPTAIN: He didn't do Moctezuma much good—

MALINCHE: Moctezuma was a man of peace, not a warrior! He would have been an ally—instead he was murdered!

CAPTAIN: I was not responsible for his death! You know I loved Moctezuma and respected him. But, amor, I didn't come to argue. The past is history—

MALINCHE: A history that lives in my blood.

CAPTAIN: I, too, grieved Moctezuma's death. If he had lived there would have been peace between us. Instead the Jaguar warriors chose to fight us. We had no choice but to fight back.

MALINCHE: And to destroy.

CAPTAIN: There's still time for peace. Moctezuma loved you like a daughter. On his death he gave you his obsidian knife, a symbol of power. If I possessed the dagger, the tribes would see me as his heir.

MALINCHE: You know Moctezuma's knife belongs to my sons.

CAPTAIN: It should be mine, your conquistador. (*He holds her.*) You are the fruit I desire.

MALINCHE: I remember the night we first made love, on the beach of Veracruz.

CAPTAIN: You were a witch who captured my heart.

MALINCHE: You had just arrived, a time before the conquest. (*pauses*)
Can you give up your wars of conquest?

CAPTAIN: No, amor. It's my destiny to subdue this land and teach the natives the Holy Faith.

MALINCHE: I think it's gold you desire.

CAPTAIN: I desire you, amor. Without your help I could never have conquered the Aztecs. Your advice has always been true. You have never lied to me.

MALINCHE: I paved your way, and now I feel a guilt so heavy it suffocates me.

CAPTAIN: Guilt is for the weak, amor. (*He turns away from her.*) Where are my sons? The lands I conquer will someday belong to them. The names of your sons will be known in history. Our destiny will be fulfilled.

MALINCHE: This is the pledge you made to me the night I entered your tent. The night my sons were conceived. When they were born you promised—

CAPTAIN: (*angry*) I'll keep my promise! My sons will make fine Spanish officers. (*He calls.*) ¡Hijos míos! ¡Vengan acá!

MALINCHE: I haven't raised them to be Spanish officers. They follow the way of Moctezuma.

Sound of a conch shell and Aztec drums.

CAPTAIN: (*laughs*) The way of the Aztec is dead, amor. Now is the time of the conqueror. I admit, I've been neglectful. I've spent too much time in the field. But now I must look to their future. . . . Ah, here they are!

The two boys enter. Bernal and an Indian drummer follow.

FIRST SON: (*excited*) Mother, come dance with us!

MALINCHE: What bad manners! First greet your father.

FIRST SON: Father, welcome home.

SECOND SON: Our gods have returned you safely.

CAPTAIN: Hijos míos. How you grow. But why are you naked? Do you want my friends to say I cannot clothe you as proper gentlemen?

FIRST SON: We were practicing a dance.

CAPTAIN: A dance?

SECOND SON: Mother taught us.

MALINCHE: It's part of their training—

CAPTAIN: (*laughs*) Dancing? They should be practicing swordplay, not dancing.

SECOND SON: The dance of the Jaguar prepares us for war.

FIRST SON: Show him, mother.

CAPTAIN: (*sits down and speaks sarcastically*) Very well, let me see the dance.

MALINCHE: Now is not the time—

CAPTAIN: No, I insist! Dance for me!

Malinche nods. The drummer begins, and the three dance toward the statue of Huitzilopochtli.

FIRST SON: God of war, give us the strength of the Jaguar!

SECOND SON: Help us defeat our enemies!

The boys begin a mock battle with their war clubs. The Captain frowns, stands.

CAPTAIN: Enough! It's a dance for the idol!

SECOND SON: It's a war dance.

CAPTAIN: My sons don't dance for the heathen idols! And these clubs are no good against the steel of Toledo!

He grabs the clubs, dashes them to the ground, and brandishes his sword.

CAPTAIN: This is the weapon you must learn to use!

FIRST SON: These are the war clubs of Moctezuma!

CAPTAIN: And little good they did him. Bernal! Have they practiced their swordplay?

BERNAL: Sí, mi capitán. Son excelentes con la espada.

MALINCHE: Yes, they know how to use the weapons of the conqueror.

CAPTAIN: Show me. Anda, Bernal—put them to the test.

BERNAL: Con mucho gusto. Adelante muchachos, con las espadas.

He hands them their swords. The boys show off their swordplay until Bernal stops them.

BERNAL: ¿Qué le parece, mi capitán?

CAPTAIN: Sí, como dices, excelentes. ¡Bravo, mis hijos!

MALINCHE: Now leave us. Your father and I have much to discuss.

The Captain picks up the war clubs.

CAPTAIN: And take these useless clubs with you!

Bernal and the boys exit with the drummer.

MALINCHE: Don't admonish the boys. If you must be angry, be angry with me.

CAPTAIN: I can't be angry with you, amor. I grow jealous when I see your beauty wasted on your god.

He holds her, kisses her shoulder. The Princess appears at the garden entrance and watches for a moment.

PRINCESS: (*to herself*) So the conqueror of the New World grovels at the feet of his whore. My work will not be easy. (*calling out*) ¡Buenas tardes!

CAPTAIN: Ah, la Princesa. Please enter.

PRINCESS: I don't want to interrupt . . .

CAPTAIN: Not at all, we were expecting you. My dear, you know la Princesa de Aragón.

MALINCHE: (*coldly*) We've met.

CAPTAIN: She and her father are returning to Spain.

MALINCHE: (*to the Princess*) Are you pleased?

PRINCESS: Yes. I'm not suited for this savage country. My father and I leave for Veracruz tomorrow.

MALINCHE: Did he find the gold he sought?

PRINCESS: Yes. Thanks to an arrangement with our capitán.

MALINCHE: What sort of arrangement?

CAPTAIN: A way to exploit some gold mines. But let's not talk business. Come, join us in a refresco?

PRINCESS: No, I must take my leave . . .

MALINCHE: From our savage country?

CAPTAIN: She means—

PRINCESS: I mean your ways are strange. This morning my Indian maids baked cookies in the shape of skulls. Am I supposed to eat them?

MALINCHE: Tomorrow we honor our dead.

PRINCESS: It's horrible. I saw the natives taking human skulls from burial crypts and placing them on altars.

MALINCHE: It's our custom to clean the burial places on el Día de los Muertos. We take flowers and food to our ancestors.

CAPTAIN: When I first came to this land I thought those skulls belonged to sacrificial victims. No, as Doña Marina says, it's a way of honoring the dead.

PRINCESS: I don't understand.

MALINCHE: On Día de los Muertos, the spirits of our dead ancestors return to be with us.

PRINCESS: It's so uncivilized—

MALINCHE: What could be more uncivilized than the conquest of our people?

PRINCESS: Yes, well, it is the destiny of Spain to rule this New World and Christianize it. (*She walks seductively toward the Captain.*) I do have one good thing to say of this Aztec land.

MALINCHE: And what is that?

PRINCESS: I have had the honor, and pleasure, of meeting the conqueror of the New World. All of Spain is talking about his exploits. Everyone in court wants to meet this gallant conquistador, and the king has promised to make him a lord when he returns—

MALINCHE: But he has no intention of returning.

CAPTAIN: Perhaps the time is right . . .

PRINCESS: Yes. Think of the honors you'll receive. All of Spain bowing at your feet. You must seize the time or it will pass.

MALINCHE: He also has enemies in court.

PRINCESS: Enemies who can be bought with gold. My dear capitán, you will have the civilized world in your hands. What do you have here? A country full of savages. (*She looks at Malinche.*) Oh, I forget—

MALINCHE: That I am savage?

PRINCESS: No. A . . . a native.

MALINCHE: I am the daughter of a proud people!

PRINCESS: I see no pride in their dark faces, only resentment.

MALINCHE: Because we are the slaves of the church and the encomienda!

CAPTAIN: The natives are paid for their work, and protected—

MALINCHE: And they die by the thousands. No, my dear conquistador, forced labor by another name is slavery.

PRINCESS: But the heathens, or the "natives" as you say, are being civilized.

MALINCHE: And dying of diseases brought by your people to our land.

CAPTAIN: La Princesa is not responsible—

MALINCHE: Who, then, is to blame for the suffering of my people?

CAPTAIN: You know other native tribes helped us conquer the Aztecs. They were tired of paying tribute—

MALINCHE: Now we pay to a new master.

PRINCESS: My father says that turning one tribe against another was the strategy of a genius. And you must admit, Christianity is the salvation of heathens. (*She turns to the Captain.*) But I haven't come to argue. I must take my leave. (*She holds out her hand for him to kiss.*) Will I see you again?

CAPTAIN: Yes, as we agreed.

PRINCESS: Then it's settled. Adios, Doña Marina.

She bows, goes out. The Captain paces.

MALINCHE: Do you intend to return to Spain?

CAPTAIN: It has been on my mind, but I had not seriously considered it until—

MALINCHE: Until *she* came?

CAPTAIN: Her father tells me the king of Spain is ready to grant me a title.

MALINCHE: What of your enemies?

CAPTAIN: Gold will buy their silence. Once my reputation is restored I can claim the title I've always wanted, Conqueror of the New World!

MALINCHE: Your true desire?

CAPTAIN: Yes! To be recognized for my exploits as a conqueror, with a title and a commission from the king!

MALINCHE: And to continue waging war on our neighbors?

CAPTAIN: There is so much that needs to be done. There are vast empires in the land of the Maya, and to the north in the land called Aztlán. I want to rule this vast New World as a king!

MALINCHE: What of your sons?

CAPTAIN: I know the wars have kept me busy. But I am proud of my sons. They will make fine Spanish officers.

MALINCHE: Soldiers to help you rule your empire?

CAPTAIN: Yes. It's time for them to see my homeland.

MALINCHE: Take them with you? You can't mean that.

CAPTAIN: Why not?

MALINCHE: Because our warriors would rather die than be taken as slaves across the sea.

CAPTAIN: My sons aren't slaves.

MALINCHE: Why are you concerned for them *now*?

CAPTAIN: Because I'm afraid if they remain here . . .

MALINCHE: Go on. What do you fear?

CAPTAIN: They're on the wrong path!

MALINCHE: Because they follow the Aztec way?

CAPTAIN: Yes! Running around half naked! Dancing pagan dances! I feel them turning against all I stand for.

MALINCHE: They can be of both worlds, yours and mine. Why fear that?

CAPTAIN: No, they must be of my world. My people will accept them only if they act like true Spaniards!

MALINCHE: I refuse to let them go!

CAPTAIN: You have no say in this!

MALINCHE: I am their mother! And you have been so busy with your wars they hardly know you!

CAPTAIN: They pay little attention to me because you've filled their minds with stories of your heathen gods.

MALINCHE: They honor the ways of my ancestors—

CAPTAIN: Honor? In Spain they will learn what *true* honor means.

MALINCHE: I will not part with them. They're all I have. Go to Spain, but leave my sons with me.

CAPTAIN: They must go with me—la Princesa understands this.

MALINCHE: She's not their mother! She has no love for them!

CAPTAIN: She can be very helpful once they're in Spain.

MALINCHE: (*whispering*) I sense something evil in the air. . . . (*She softens, changes her approach.*) You are the father, and I trust you have their best interests in mind.

CAPTAIN: Now you're being sensible.

In the background, the volcano belches fire. Malinche glances at the statue.

MALINCHE: The wars of conquest have changed you.

CAPTAIN: War hardens the heart of any man.

MALINCHE: Is your heart so cold you would take my sons from me? Allow them to stay, and when you return they will be here to greet you.

CAPTAIN: Will they submit to my rule?

MALINCHE: Yes, as I did once submit . . .

CAPTAIN: Will they denounce the pagan gods?

MALINCHE: The Aztec priests say that to give up our gods means the end of our world.

CAPTAIN: Nonsense. This is the beginning of our history.

MALINCHE: A history made by force.

CAPTAIN: Conquerors must use force. It is the only way to rule.

MALINCHE: Is there no love in the conqueror's heart?

CAPTAIN: Love is temporary. What I create will last forever.

MALINCHE: Then your mind is firm?

CAPTAIN: Yes, my sons must become part of my history.

MALINCHE: And what of me?

CAPTAIN: Bernal has always admired you, so I have promised him—

MALINCHE: You dare to pawn me off like a slave!

CAPTAIN: Your law allows me to give you to anyone I desire!

MALINCHE: Why do you betray me?

CAPTAIN: We were not married by the church—

MALINCHE: That has never mattered. Now you use the law to achieve your desire.

CAPTAIN: The conqueror makes his own laws!

MALINCHE: Do what you want with me, but don't separate me from my sons!

CAPTAIN: I have decided. Tomorrow we leave with la Princesa.

MALINCHE: She's behind this! Promising the royalty you seek!

CAPTAIN: Yes!

She grabs at him, pleads.

MALINCHE: Then go with her, but I beg you . . . on my knees I beg you! Don't take my sons from me!

CAPTAIN: It's settled! I have decided!

He pushes her away, exits.

MALINCHE: His heart has turned to stone. (*She pauses.*)
    Why did I think there could be love in the heart of a conqueror? He used me, and now he betrays me! As I betrayed Moctezuma! Oh, my conquered people! Beware the promises of the master! (*She pauses again.*)
    I bore his children and mixed my blood with his. . . . Yes, it is true, I helped him conquer the Aztecs . . . I became a traitor to my people. Now he wants to take the fruit of my womb from their native land. (*She moves to the statue.*) Moctezuma, great leader of your people! Return and see the devastation! Return and help us in our hour of need!

From the shadows the ghost of Moctezuma appears, holding fire in his hands.

MALINCHE: Prince of the Aztecs!

Moctezuma holds out the fire.

MALINCHE: The fire does not burn your hands. (*Malinche cowers.*) I am afraid. (*Hesitantly she takes the fire.*) Have I forgotten? You once taught me to hold the fire of life. . . . Yes, I too can hold the sacred fire . . . the fire of the sun lit in Teotihuacán at the beginning of time. . . . Now your spirit burns through me like a river of fire. . . . Help me! Liberate me! Liberate my sons!

She turns and lights the incense at the altar of Huitzilopochtli. When she exits, the Captain enters and stares at the altar.

CAPTAIN: Again she lights the incense to her heathen god.

He attempts to put out the burning incense, but burns his hand.

CAPTAIN: Damn this fire of magicians! It cannot be extinguished! (*He draws back.*) I hate this idol. . . . Why can't I bring myself to smash it in a million pieces? Is it because of her, my Doña Marina? Or is it because I fear the god's wrath? What if there is some spirit lurking in the cold stone?

No! Nonsense. She believes, but I do not. It is the one true God who must rule these lands, not the many idols they adore. We must teach these simple people the way. . . . Ah, but they resist, and the way is paved with slaughter. I am sick of the blood that stains my hands. (*He looks at his hands and raises them to the statue.*) If you are a god, wash away the smell of blood!

The ghost of Moctezuma appears. The Captain draws back in fear.

CAPTAIN: Dear God! Can I believe my eyes? The spirit of Moctezuma walks! It cannot be, I saw you die. Speak, speak! Why do you return from the land of the dead?

(*The Captain draws his sword.*) Is it really you, or a magician's trick? (*He runs the sword through Moctezuma, but the ghost remains standing.*) The sword draws no blood! It is a ghost!

(*The Captain kneels.*) Oh dear, dear spirit of my departed friend, why do you haunt me? I did love you like a brother. I did not wish you dead . . .

The ghost withdraws as the Princess enters.

CAPTAIN: Together we could have ruled this land. . . . Together we could have ruled an empire.

PRINCESS: My lord.

He doesn't respond.

Malinche enters and hides behind one of the palms.

CAPTAIN: Moctezuma! Great leader of your people! Return! Speak to me!

PRINCESS: (*to herself*) He doesn't hear me. He speaks to the air. . . . Or to a ghost. This land is full of spirits . . . they will destroy us. I must save myself—
(*She starts to exit, then pauses.*) No. I will not return to Spain empty-handed. I came with a purpose, and I will carry it through. Only the whore Malinche and her bastard sons stand in my way. But what if somewhere at sea they drown. . . . That's easily arranged.

CAPTAIN: (*softly*) He will return . . . Moctezuma will return . . .

He rises slowly. The Princess goes to him.

PRINCESS: My lord?

CAPTAIN: (*turns*) What? Who goes there? (*Raising his sword.*)

PRINCESS: (*frightened*) It's me, my lord! Why raise your sword?

CAPTAIN: Ah, mi dulce Princesa. I thought you were a ghost.

PRINCESS: No, not a ghost. Touch me, my lord, and feel the flesh you pressed last night still warm with love.

CAPTAIN: But, just now, there in the shadows—I swear I saw Moctezuma walking . . . (He looks into the shadows.)

PRINCESS: I see nothing.

CAPTAIN: Nothing . . . an illusion . . .

PRINCESS: You saw Moctezuma?

CAPTAIN: I saw his ghost. Is it guilt that brings such visions? He was a kind and loving man.

PRINCESS: A savage cannot be kind and loving.

CAPTAIN: You didn't know him. He was the most honest and trusting man I ever knew.

PRINCESS: I find that hard to believe . . . but I didn't come to discuss Moctezuma. What did you tell your Indian mistress?

CAPTAIN: Doña Marina? Is it she who sent the ghost?

PRINCESS: Why all this talk of ghosts? Did you tell her our plans?

CAPTAIN: Yes.

PRINCESS: (embracing him) You are ready to sail with me?

CAPTAIN: Yes . . . but she will fight me if I insist on taking my sons—

PRINCESS: But we agreed—if you leave them they will oppose you when you return.

CAPTAIN: Yes, I feel it in my blood . . .

PRINCESS: Are you afraid of her?

CAPTAIN: Afraid? Nonsense. I fear no one. . . . Still—

PRINCESS: What?

CAPTAIN: She is a woman of great power—

PRINCESS: You are afraid of her, aren't you? (She laughs scornfully.) You, the conqueror of the New World, afraid of his Indian whore. Oh, you would be laughed out of court if this were known.

CAPTAIN: (*angry*) You don't know her as I do! She possesses supernatural powers.

PRINCESS: What kind of powers?

CAPTAIN: She was raised to be a priestess . . . one of those magic people we call brujos. She speaks many languages, and the Aztec priests consider her a leader.

PRINCESS: She doesn't impress me—

CAPTAIN: I have seen her hold fire in her hands, and it did not burn her.

PRINCESS: I don't believe it. It's simply one of their heathen tricks.

CAPTAIN: No! It's true!

PRINCESS: (*shivers*) I don't like this land. . . . There's too much magic in the air . . .

CAPTAIN: I conquered them, and still they resist. They have a profound, inner strength—

PRINCESS: You must destroy that power.

CAPTAIN: There are revolts everywhere . . . first here, then there. It spreads my army thin. If these natives only knew how tenuous is our hold.

PRINCESS: Do you mean they could still overthrow you?

CAPTAIN: Yes . . . if the right leader came along . . . someone related to Moctezuma.

PRINCESS: But he has no heirs.

CAPTAIN: My sons.

PRINCESS: Are they related to Moctezuma?

CAPTAIN: Not by blood, but he honored and respected Malinche. Before he died he gave her his obsidian knife. That knife is a symbol of his power.

PRINCESS: You must destroy the knife.

CAPTAIN: She keeps it hidden, saving it for her sons.

PRINCESS: All the more reason to take them to Spain!

CAPTAIN: (*distracted*) Yes, this is what I must do . . .

PRINCESS: I will help you, and when we're married I will call them my sons.

She puts her arms around him. Malinche rushes out.

MALINCHE: You lie! You plot their death!

She rushes at the Princess.

CAPTAIN: Keep back!

MALINCHE: Can't you see she lies!

PRINCESS: She heard!

MALINCHE: Yes, I heard, and I will die before I give up my sons!

CAPTAIN: They're my sons, too!

MALINCHE: And you would make them slaves?

CAPTAIN: You don't know what you're saying!

MALINCHE: It's already too late! Spain will enslave all of our sons!

The Princess takes hold of the Captain's arm.

PRINCESS: Don't listen to her. She's insane with jealousy.

MALINCHE: (*laughs*) Yes, betrayal makes my blood run hot!

PRINCESS: I fear her. Call the guards.

MALINCHE: They cannot save you when Moctezuma seeks revenge!

CAPTAIN: He's dead!

MALINCHE: But not his spirit! He haunts you! He befriended you, and you killed him!

CAPTAIN: He was killed by his own people!

MALINCHE: You betrayed him!

CAPTAIN: Silence!

He pushes Malinche aside. The volcano erupts violently, with flashing fire and loud thunder.

PRINCESS: ¡Dios mío! The volcano!

They turn to see the flashes of light.

MALINCHE: Moctezuma returns!

CAPTAIN: Nonsense! He's dead!

More thunder and flashes of light.

CAPTAIN: I rule this land! I have been to the bishop, and he has given me custody of my sons!

MALINCHE: No!

CAPTAIN: Yes. And once in Spain I plan to be truly married. By the laws of the church.

MALINCHE: Marry her! I care not what you do. But don't take my sons!

She reaches out, imploring, but he turns away.

CAPTAIN: My mind is firm. ¡Vamos!

He starts away with the Princess.

MALINCHE: They will never reach Spain!

CAPTAIN: What?

MALINCHE: She plans to drown them at sea!

PRINCESS: She lies!

CAPTAIN: (*to Malinche*) How dare you! You must apologize!

The sound of a drum is heard.

MALINCHE: Wait! Here come my sons. Ask them if they wish to leave their mother. I . . . I will abide by their choice.

PRINCESS: I cannot wait while she plays games with you. I will sail with or without you, my lord. But remember, the door to court will not be open again.

She exits.

CAPTAIN: (*shouts*) ¡Princesa!

The boys enter and Malinche embraces them.

FIRST SON: The volcano boils with fire! It speaks!

SECOND SON: A storm stirs up the lake!

FIRST SON: Our world is ending!

CAPTAIN: The end of the world? Nonsense! Come now, there's no time for play. You must prepare for a trip.

FIRST SON: A trip? Where?

The boys step back.

CAPTAIN: To Spain.

SECOND SON: A visit?

CAPTAIN: Yes, a visit to my homeland. You will meet the king—

FIRST SON: (*to Malinche*) Will you come with us?

CAPTAIN: No, she will stay here. What she has been teaching you is nonsense—

FIRST SON: She teaches us the true path.

CAPTAIN: And what path is that?

SECOND SON: The path of our leader, Moctezuma—

CAPTAIN: He's dead!

SECOND SON: Killed by your orders!

CAPTAIN: How dare you! (*He raises his hand to strike, stops, turns to Malinche.*) This is what you teach them? That their father is a murderer! Come now, this is no time to argue. You must prepare for the trip! Quickly!

FIRST SON: We go only if she goes.

Malinche embraces her sons.

CAPTAIN: You will come with me!

He steps forward and holds out his hand, but the boys cling to Malinche.

FIRST SON: We will not go without our mother.

CAPTAIN: You will do as I say!

He grabs the boys, who struggle.

MALINCHE: Don't you see, they won't go with you.

CAPTAIN: They will do as I say!

The Captain pushes Malinche away.

CAPTAIN: Bernal! Pull her away!

Bernal rushes in and holds Malinche.

MALINCHE: Please! Let me speak to them. They'll understand.

CAPTAIN: Understand they must go with me?

Malinche nods, the boys go to her.

MALINCHE: Yes.

CAPTAIN: You agree?

MALINCHE: Yes.

The Captain looks at her suspiciously.

SECOND SON: (*to Malinche*) Will you betray us?

FIRST SON: And send us to our deaths?

MALINCHE: (*lovingly*) No, my sons, I would never betray you . . . but there is a solution—

CAPTAIN: What do you propose?

MALINCHE: Allow me only an hour with them. This is my last request.

CAPTAIN: Only if you agree to cut the cord that binds them to you.

MALINCHE: Yes. I will do as you say.

CAPTAIN: I see you've come to your senses. I grant you one hour, no more. But Bernal remains with you. (*He nods at Bernal, turns, and exits.*)

MALINCHE: Oh, cruel, cruel man. I will have eternity with my sons, not an hour. (*She turns to Bernal.*) Leave us.

BERNAL: Kind lady, I am ordered to stay.

MALINCHE: If you have any love in your heart for me, allow me time alone with my sons.

BERNAL: Only for you do I disobey mi capitán.

He withdraws. Malinche turns to her children.

SECOND SON: You taught us a time to resist would come! It's here!

FIRST SON: We're ready.

They pick up the Aztec war clubs.

MALINCHE: Some will die in battle, but our people will live on.

FIRST SON: We will defend our homeland against all enemies.

SECOND SON: Better to die here than in a foreign land.

MALINCHE: Yes. Now you know why death is preferable to enslavement. You are the fruit of my womb . . . fruit of this earth. . . . In my dream you came to me, destined to be rulers. . . . And now you are despised mestizos in your own land. No, I will not part with you. I will not give up the dream of your true destiny. You are the sons of Moctezuma.

Come, let us dance and call forth the spirit of Moctezuma!

The drummer enters. The boys follow Malinche's dance toward the statue. Moctezuma appears.

MALINCHE: Great leader of the Aztecs, give me a sign. Tell me what I must do.

Moctezuma places the knife on the altar and steps into the shadows.

MALINCHE: (*shocked*) The obsidian knife! Is this your answer? Dear Prince, can I obey? Will my sons be . . . Yes. In my heart I know what I must do. Once I was the consort of the Spaniard . . . now I am free to wage war. My sons will be the first warriors to fall in battle.

(*She turns to her sons.*) My sons, you know how much I love you.

FIRST SON: And we love you.

SECOND SON: We are ready.

MALINCHE: (*to herself*) Then I know what I must do. Many years hence, I will be called the cruelest of women . . . but I will know your spirits rest in our earth . . . not in foreign soil.

(*to her sons*) Come now! Dance for Moctezuma!

They exit dancing. The light dims, the wail of the wind raises. Thunder and light flashes. The Captain enters.

CAPTAIN: The sun sets in a sea of blood, thunder shakes the earth. Where is Malinche? My sons? Bernal! Bernal!

Bernal enters.

CAPTAIN: Is there any sign of Doña Marina and the boys?

BERNAL: No, mi capitán. The day has turned to night, the volcano erupts with fury. All of nature turns against us—

CAPTAIN: Ay, and spirits walk the land. Have you searched by the lake?

BERNAL: No, your Excellency.

CAPTAIN: Go there!

Bernal bows and exits. The Princess enters.

PRINCESS: Have you found her?

CAPTAIN: She's vanished.

PRINCESS: Calm yourself—she can't escape. The causeways out of the city are guarded.

CAPTAIN: That means little to those who can fly.

PRINCESS: Fly? You jest.

CAPTAIN: No, I have seen their magicians fly . . . and I swear, she, too, can fly.

PRINCESS: Superstitions, that's all.

CAPTAIN: You don't know her as I do. I'm afraid of what she might do. When I told her I was taking the boys I heard a threat in her voice that frightened me.

The wind moans, birds screech, there is thunder and flashes of light. The Princess trembles and goes to the Captain.

PRINCESS: What a fearful wind. . . . I'm afraid.

CAPTAIN: This is not nature's storm, but voices from hell.

PRINCESS: I hate this land of spirits.

Bernal enters, stumbling.

BERNAL: Blood! Blood! The lake is red with blood! The devil rides the waves! All hell is loose. By the lake the crying woman weeps, her hands red with blood!

PRINCESS: Dear God, he's seen a ghost!

CAPTAIN: What is it? Report!

BERNAL: Oh, kind sir, have mercy on me. Don't ask me to report, for I have seen the queen of hell, the devil's bride, her gown red with blood, she runs along the shore crying for her sons!

CAPTAIN: Make sense!

BERNAL: The devil rides the waves, the lake is on fire!

PRINCESS: He's gone mad.

The Captain grabs Bernal.

CAPTAIN: Compose yourself! What did you see?

BERNAL: A most terrible sight . . . a lake of blood!

CAPTAIN: (shouting) Why do you tremble? Have you seen the devil?

BERNAL: Worse, my lord! I would walk with the devil, yes, I would gladly walk with him into the pit of hell—but not with the woman at the lake!

CAPTAIN: What woman? Make sense!

BERNAL: What I saw made my blood run cold.

The wail of la Llorona is heard.

PRINCESS: Dear God! Who cries?

BERNAL: It's her! It's her!

CAPTAIN: The cry of a woman mourning in grief.

BERNAL: Blood on the hands of the mother . . .

CAPTAIN: Good lord! Tell us what you found!

BERNAL: The lake churned with blood! The sky turned dark! Even the animals seemed to cry at the sight. And she, the bloody dagger still in her hand, ran along the edge of the lake, crying for her children . . .

CAPTAIN: My sons?

BERNAL: She murdered them . . .

The Captain is stunned; the Princess makes the sign of the cross.

CAPTAIN: Murdered them? No, no, you lie!

BERNAL: (sobbing) I swear, my lord, I saw her! She killed the children and threw them in the lake, and when she realized what she had done, she ran along the bank, crying for them. Her foul deed has driven her mad.

Again the piercing cry of la Llorona.

CAPTAIN: No . . . no . . .

BERNAL: She cries in vain! The boys are dead! (*Bernal rushes out.*)

PRINCESS: (pointing) It's her!

Malinche enters. Her gown is covered with blood, her hair is disarranged. She holds the bloody dagger. The Captain and the Princess draw back from the terrifying sight.

MALINCHE: The lake has swallowed my sons . . .

CAPTAIN: You sacrificed your sons. ¡Dios mío! (*makes the sign of the cross*)

MALINCHE: They rest in the arms of Moctezuma . . .

CAPTAIN: Why? Why?

MALINCHE: Better they die as warriors than live as slaves.

CAPTAIN: Warriors of Moctezuma . . .

MALINCHE: Their bodies rest in our sacred lake . . . but I cannot find their spirits. I search in vain . . .

PRINCESS: (*horrified*) She's mad! Let us away! (*She exits.*)

CAPTAIN: Did I cause this madness? If so, the conquest was not worth the lives of my sons. God forgive me. (*He exits.*)

MALINCHE: Forgiveness? When Moctezuma returns there will be forgiveness. . . . When he returns, my sons will be at his side.
(*She goes to the altar.*) The spirit of Moctezuma awakens. I am not the first nor the last mother to sacrifice her children. When love turns to rage, then our children will die . . . our hands will be stained with blood. Before you judge me, remember the treason that drove me to this dark deed.
(*She exits, crying.*) Hi-i-i-jos. . . . Hi-i-i-jos míos . . .

Slowly the light shifts back to the kitchen.

ABUELO: Some say la Malinche became la Llorona, the crying woman. She's still wandering the earth in search of her children. They say she always appears near water, along a river, a lake or an irrigation ditch.

MOTHER: She's a spirit who cannot rest.

ABUELO: Until she finds her children.

MOTHER: (*excited*) Or they find her!

ABUELO: (*puzzled*) Then she would rest. . . . But we can't change the story.

MOTHER: (*disappointed*) No . . .

MARGARITA: I feel sorry for her.

MOTHER: Yes. . . . She did a horrible thing. But we must forgive her . . . as we ask for forgiveness.

ALFREDO: We heard her by the river! Last summer!

MARGARITA: We were coming home, it was dark, and suddenly there was this awful cry.

ALFREDO: Maybe she is real.

MARGARITA: Isn't Malinche the virgin girl in the dance of the Matachines?

ABUELO: Yes. She dances for Moctezuma, the Monarca. She brings him back to life. The dance reminds us the spirit of Moctezuma will someday return to help the people.

Outside the wind howls, and there is a cry in the dark and a loud knock at the door. The children jump with fright.

MARGARITA: Who's there? (*She draws close to Abuelo.*)

ALFREDO: La Llorona!

MOTHER: (*softly*) Miguel . . . my son.

She starts to the door; Abuelo stops her.

ABUELO: No!

MOTHER: Miguel . . .

ABUELO: Alfredo! Answer the door!

Alfredo opens the door.

MOTHER: ¡Madre María!

A figure clothed in a sheet jumps in and cries BOO! Alfredo turns and runs to his grandfather. The figure pulls off the sheet, revealing Father.

MARGARITA: Papá!

FATHER: Trick or treat!

MOTHER: ¡Ay, que susto!

FATHER: ¿Qué pasa?

MOTHER: You scared us!

FATHER: I'm supposed to scare you. It's Halloween.

MOTHER: You're worse than the kids.

FATHER: Just having fun. Did you see Alfredo jump ten feet?

ALFREDO: I knew it was you.

FATHER: Of course you did. Mi'jo es puro macho. ¿Como está, Papá?

ABUELO: Bien, bien.

ALFREDO: He told us about la Llorona.

FATHER: Pues, I just saw her by Walgreens. There are ghosts and goblins everywhere. Are you ready?

ALFREDO AND MARGARITA: (in unison) We're ready! ¡Vamos!

Father looks at Mother.

FATHER: Are you okay?

MOTHER: I'm frightened. . . . No, just cold. Maybe you shouldn't go. It's so cold . . .

FATHER: Amor, you worry too much. Mi hijo es puro Azteca.

ALFREDO: Right on!

FATHER: ¿Y mi'jita?

MARGARITA: I'm Malinche!

FATHER: You look like a princess. Come on, it's candy time! (*He calls to Mother.*) Keep the coffee warm. ¡Volvemos pronto!

They go out shouting joyfully.

FATHER: ¡Ajuá! Trick or treat!

MOTHER: ¡Ay, que hombre!

ABUELO: He likes to have fun with the kids.

MOTHER: I know. It's just that the story sent shivers down my spine.

ABUELO: Long before Malinche the Aztecs already had a goddess who cried in the streets for her children.

MOTHER: Every mother fears for her children . . .

ABUELO: Sometimes too much fear is unnatural.

MOTHER: And too much grief.

ABUELO: She thought it best for her to end their lives. The Indian population of Mexico was devastated by the conquest. Enough to drive anyone insane.

MOTHER: She saw Moctezuma's ghost . . .

ABUELO: People hear voices . . .

They stare at each other. The howl of the wind rises, carrying with it the cry of la Llorona.

ABUELO: Bueno. I better get going. Will you be all right?

MOTHER: Yes. I need to finish carving the pumpkin.

She picks up the knife. He puts on his jacket.

ABUELO: Grandma baked biscochitos in the shape of skulls for el Día de los Muertos. That's what she's giving the trick-or-treaters. Ha, I wonder what the gringitos will say when they get cookies in the shape of skulls?

MOTHER: Día de los Muertos . . . Halloween . . . la Llorona. They seem to fit?

ABUELO: Yes, cultures affect each other. One day the Anglos will have their own Llorona. Buenas noches, hija.

MOTHER: Sí . . . sí . . . buenas noches. . . . Say hi to Mamá.

ABUELO: I will.

Abuelo exits, and Mother goes to the table.

MOTHER: I hear the children running in the street. Miguel, my son, runs with them. I cry at night. I long to hold him in my arms. La Llorona took my child, my son. . . . Why? Why?

She raises the knife.

MOTHER: Is it possible? Every woman can be a Llorona?

A shock of recognition shows on her face, she drops the knife with a clanging sound. The light dims, the wind howls.

END

The Farolitos of Christmas

CHARACTERS

JUAN GARCIA
DON VICENTE
MARÍA GARCIA
LUZ GARCIA/*GILA*
RAMÓN/*SAN MIGUEL*
FATHER RAEL
DOÑA JOSEFINA, the storekeeper
DOÑA GREGORITA
DON MANUEL/*BARTOLO*
MISS LORRAINE BLOOM
KIDS/*PASTORES*:

    REINA/*ESTRELLA*
    RITA/*LUNA*
    ANTONIO/*VERLADO*
    CARMEN/*ALBA*
    ANDRES/*FUENTE*
    ENRIQUE/*BATO*
    RUBEN/*MANZANO*
    LORENZO/*COSME*
    ELISA/*SONRISA*
DON PACO/*DEMONIO*
ESTEVAN/*FELETO*
MARCOS/*TORINGO*
CAPTAIN JIM RILEY
MÚSICOS

ACT ONE

Scene One

The village of San Juan, New Mexico, during the summer of 1944.

In the yard of the Garcia house stand Juan, María, Luz, and the elderly Don Vicente. Luz proudly holds her father's suitcase; María holds his jacket. Juan Garcia is dressed in a U.S. Army uniform. He steps away from the woodpile, axe in hand.

JUAN: I hope the war's over before you use up the wood.

DON VICENTE: We will pray for your safe return, hijo.

MARÍA: We have enough to last till Christmas. By then, con el favor de Dios, you'll be home.

JUAN: Wish I had the time to cut more, but my leave was short.

Don Vicente puts his arm around Luz.

DON VICENTE: We can take care of it, eh mi'jita?

JUAN: You have a good helper, Papá. (*He hands the axe to Luz.*) Hear that, hija? You have to help your abuelo. And your mamá. (*Juan puts his arm around María.*)

LUZ: I will, Papá. I'll pray for you every night.

MARÍA: And pray the war will end soon.

DON VICENTE: It's a bad thing. The war takes our sons away. Only old men, women, and children are left in San Juan.

JUAN: It has to be done, Papá. I volunteered to do my part. It's going to be over before I get to Paris.

MARÍA: Here comes Ramón.

Juan kneels in front of Don Vicente.

JUAN: Bendición, Papá.

Don Vicente blesses his son.

DON VICENTE: Que Dios te guarde, que la manta de la Virgen te cubra, y el Santo Niño cuide tus pasos. Santo Niño, I make a promesa to you. I will light the luminarias de Navidad for you. Please return my son home safe.

Juan stands and embraces his father.

JUAN: Gracias, Papá.

Ramón, in uniform, enters the yard.

RAMÓN: ¿Listo, Juan?

JUAN: Listo. (*Juan turns to María. They hug and kiss. Juan turns to Luz and sweeps her up in his arms.*) Take care of your mamá and abuelo.

LUZ: I will, Papá, I will. I'll help Abuelito keep his promise.

There is a last embrace and the final adióses. Juan and Ramón exit, waving. María cries, Luz comforts her.

LUZ: Don't cry, Mamá. Papá will come back.

DON VICENTE: We will pray to the Santo Niño.

They exit.

Scene Two

The store.

Father Felix Rael, the young village priest, has just purchased candles. Other villagers stand around.

FATHER RAEL: Thank you, Doña Josefina.

DOÑA JOSEFINA: Padre, how are the plans for los Pastores?

FATHER RAEL: It's hard with so many of the village men gone or leaving. It looks like we will have to depend on a few adults and the children to carry on our traditions this year.

DOÑA GREGORITA: Well, Padre, you know I can help. ¡Puedo hacer todo! I can go to that new teacher Miss Bloom and get the children from school. (*addressing Doña Josefina*) Y comadre—you can help me with costumes; and I can come over to the church later and see what I can start there; y también I can—

FATHER RAEL: Gracias, Doña Gregorita . . . pero . . . well . . . I'll let you know if I need help. We have almost everything already. All I need is a Gila.

DOÑA GREGORITA: I can do that, too!

FATHER RAEL: I was looking for one of the children to play Gila. But thank you.

DOÑA JOSEFINA: Mi comadre wants to do everything. (to Doña Gregorita) Let the Padre plan los Pastores. (turns to Don Manuel) Manuel. ¿Qué miras?

DON MANUEL: There goes another one of those army trucks to Los Alamos.

FATHER RAEL: They have built a whole new city up there.

DOÑA JOSEFINA: ¿Pero qué estarán haciendo?

DON MANUEL: Bombs.

DOÑA GREGORITA: Yes! They're building bombs . . . dicen que es "top secret."

DON MANUEL: My compadre Emilio got a job as a janitor.

DOÑA GREGORITA: I hear María, la nuera de Don Vicente, went up there looking for work.

DOÑA JOSEFINA: How is Don Vicente doing?

FATHER RAEL: (exiting) Not well, I'm afraid. I'm on my way to see him now. Adiós.

DOÑA GREGORITA: I'll go to the church later to see about los Pastores, Padre.

DON MANUEL: ¡Adiós, padre! Keep warm!

DOÑA JOSEFINA: I'll see you at confession!

DOÑA GREGORITA: Pues, he's good-looking!

DOÑA JOSEFINA: ¡Ay, Dios!

Scene Three

Outside the Garcia house. It is now December. The woodpile by the side of the house is nearly gone, and red ristras of chile hang on the outside wall. A blustery wind blows down from the Sangre de Cristo Mountains.

Father Rael stops to greet Don Vicente, who is chopping wood. Coughing fits make Don Vicente stop frequently.

FATHER RAEL: Buenos días le de Dios, Don Vicente.

DON VICENTE: Buenos días, Padre. ¿Cómo está?

FATHER RAEL: Bien, gracias. But it's you I'm worried about. You weren't at mass this morning.

DON VICENTE: Es este resfrío. No puedo hacer nada. I feel like an old man.

FATHER RAEL: You shouldn't be cutting wood on a cold morning.

DON VICENTE: Estoy bien. ¿Y los Pastores?

FATHER RAEL: I think we have enough people. I'll have to use some kids. Don Paco wants to play the Devil.

DON VICENTE: He will make a good one.

FATHER RAEL: He also wants to make the luminarias this year.

DON VICENTE: No! I light the luminarias!

FATHER RAEL: But you're ill, Don Vicente.

DON VICENTE: I have cut wood for the luminarias all my life. Since I was a boy I helped my papá.

FATHER RAEL: Things change, Don Vicente.

DON VICENTE: Sí, todo cambia. Each day the trucks go by. So much noise the cow gives no milk.

FATHER RAEL: Top secret, they say.

DON VICENTE: (coughs) One night I had a bad nightmare. I saw they were building a bomb. Big as a house. Big enough to destroy the world.

Don Vicente shakes his head, and Father Rael makes the sign of the cross.

FATHER RAEL: A lot of our people are working up there. I heard María has applied for work.

DON VICENTE: I don't want her to go, pero qué le vamos hacer? I lost the apple crop to the bad freeze.

FATHER RAEL: Times are difficult. The war is changing everything. I am afraid even our village traditions will change.

DON VICENTE: Los Pastores de San Juan will never change.

FATHER RAEL: Even los Pastores will change, Don Vicente. You know los Montoyas moved away.

DON VICENTE: I was sorry to see them leave.

FATHER RAEL: The family moved to Los Angeles to work in the shipyards. Now I have no one to play Gila.

DON VICENTE: Ay, California, the land of milk and honey. Everyone is leaving for California, but one day they are going to return and find their land is gone.

FATHER RAEL: What good is land if you can't make a living on it? Anyway, I am left without a Gila, and you have no wood for las luminarias.

DON VICENTE: Don't worry, Padre, I will cut the wood. (*Don Vicente coughs. He looks pale and weak. Father Rael shakes his head.*)

FATHER RAEL: Take care of yourself, Don Vicente. That cough doesn't sound good. Say hello to María and Luz.

DON VICENTE: Come in and have some coffee.

FATHER RAEL: Gracias, but I don't have time. The pastores start their practice today. And I have to find a Gila! Adiós.

DON VICENTE: Adiós. (*He lays the axe aside.*) Ah, this priest. Always in a hurry. The whole world is in a hurry. California. Bah! You have a job today and broke tomorrow.

He picks up a few pieces of wood and walks into the house, still muttering.

Scene Four

In the Garcia kitchen.

MARÍA: Papá, what were you doing out in the cold?

DON VICENTE: Making leña.

MARÍA: You know the doctor said no heavy work. You could get pneumonia. Get your nephew to cut the wood.

DON VICENTE: I can do it. (*coughs*) Father Rael came by.

MARÍA: What did he say?

DON VICENTE: They have enough vecinos to do los Pastores, but no Gila. Don José took his family to California. (*He empties the wood into the wood box and opens the stove to put in a log.*) And Don Paco wants to play the Devil. He will make a good one. ¡Es muy diablo! (*He laughs.*)

MARÍA: And the luminarias?

DON VICENTE: I will do them . . .

Luz enters the kitchen. She carries a crumpled letter from her father.

DON VICENTE: As I have every year since—

LUZ: —you were a boy.

DON VICENTE: Buenos días, mi'jita.

LUZ: Buenos días, Abuelo. How are you?

Luz goes to him and helps him sit in the comfortable chair by the woodstove.

DON VICENTE: Bien, bien.

María shakes her head as she serves him a cup of coffee.

MARÍA: His cold is worse, and he's out in the cold, cutting wood. Luz, how many times are you going to read that letter?

LUZ: I know it by heart.

DON VICENTE: Not good news, eh?

LUZ: He doesn't think he'll be home for Christmas. . . . I wish . . .

María and Don Vicente pause to look at Luz.

LUZ: I wish there was some way he could be here.

MARÍA: We all do, mi'jita. Now hurry and eat. Reina will be here soon.

DON VICENTE: The radio says the war might end before Christmas.

LUZ: That would be the best Christmas present.

Don Vicente nods.

DON VICENTE: In the meantime, I have to cut wood for the luminarias.

MARÍA: Papá, there are only old men and children left in San Juan to be pastores. Those who haven't gone to California are working in Los Alamos. No one has time. I think Father Rael should forget the whole thing.

DON VICENTE: No! We can't!

MARÍA: But you're not well enough to cut wood. I'm not going to let you.

DON VICENTE: I promised.

MARÍA: Promises sometimes have to be broken. So we won't have the luminarias this year. We have more important things to worry about.

There is a knock at the door. Reina enters. She is Luz's age and lives in the Indian pueblo next to San Juan.

LUZ: Reina, come in—I'm ready.

REINA: Good morning, Luz.

DON VICENTE: Buenos días, Reina.

REINA: Buenos días, Don Vicente. Are you feeling better?

DON VICENTE: Gracias, mi'jita, it's just a little cough.

REINA: Luz, my mom made a decoration for the Christmas tree. (*She holds a tin star.*)

LUZ: It's beautiful, Reina.

DON VICENTE: Crismes tree?

LUZ: We have one at school, Abuelo. Today we're going to decorate it. Mamá, can we have a Christmas tree this year?

REINA: We're going to have one.

MARÍA: Oh, Luz, that's just one more expense.

DON VICENTE: Why do you need a Crismes tree? You have the nacimiento.

LUZ: I know, Abuelo, but all the kids have Christmas trees now.

MARÍA: We'll see. On the way home stop by the store and buy some coffee, please. (*María takes her purse from the table, but she finds no money.*) Tell Doña Josefina to put it on our bill.

LUZ: She told me to remind you we still owe her for last month.

MARÍA: She knows we'll pay her.

LUZ: When?

MARÍA: Soon. Now hurry to school so you won't be late. (*As María hands Luz her jacket, she looks at the worn jacket.*) You need a new jacket.

LUZ: Maybe Santa Claus?

MARÍA: Maybe. Now run.

Luz gathers her books and kisses her mother and Don Vicente. The girls say goodbye and go out.

DON VICENTE: Santo Clos. Crismes trees. One of these days the children are going to forget the old ways.

MARÍA: Not Luz. She won't forget.

Scene Five

At the children's school.

On a desk stands a small, undecorated piñón tree. Miss Lorraine Bloom, a young, first-year teacher, talks to the class.

MISS BLOOM: How many of you have decorated a Christmas tree before?

Half the kids raise their hands.

MISS BLOOM: What other Christmas traditions are there?

RITA: We go to church.

ANTONIO: We have a nacimiento.

CARMEN: We do, too.

REINA: We have the deer dances.

ANDRES: We take food to the old people.

LUZ: We have the Pastores.

MISS BLOOM: The Pastores?

ENRIQUE: Shepherds. It's a play for Christmas.

RUBEN: All the villages have them, but San Juan has the best.

RITA: The men dress as shepherds. They are going to Bethlehem.

CARMEN: One lucky girl gets to be Gila.

LUZ: On their way to church they stop at our house, where my abuelo lights the luminarias.

MISS BLOOM: What are luminarias?

LUZ: Piñón wood that my abuelo stacks in neat piles. Then he lights them for the pastores, to guide their way. Sometimes they perform the play right in front of our house.

MISS BLOOM: Bonfires—that's lovely.

REINA: You're new, Miss Bloom, but you can come.

MISS BLOOM: I will.

ANTONIO: Enrique is Bato, one of the shepherds.

ENRIQUE: (proudly) My father taught me all the lines.

MISS BLOOM: Wonderful. It looks like I have quite a bit to learn about Christmas in San Juan.

LUZ: Please come. Our house is right across from the church.

RUBEN: Everybody knows where Don Vicente lives.

LORENZO: And Luz's mom makes the best posole. Yum . . .

MISS BLOOM: Sounds like a feast.

ELISA: It is a fiesta.

CARMEN: The whole village comes.

MISS BLOOM: I'll be there. Now, how about we decorate our Christmas tree?

ENRIQUE: Miss Bloom, you sure picked a skinny tree.

The boys laugh.

MISS BLOOM: I found it in the forest. It wasn't easy to cut.

ENRIQUE: Next time, tell me, I can do it.

The boys show off their muscles.

MISS BLOOM: I will.

RITA: It's a beautiful tree, Miss Bloom. We'll help you decorate it.

REINA: My father cuts tin, and I brought a star.

MISS BLOOM: It's beautiful, Reina.

LUZ: I brought a popcorn string.

The other girls take out the simple ornaments they have brought.

ENRIQUE: I can make a stand for it. So it will be straight.

MISS BLOOM: You're very helpful, Henry.

ENRIQUE: Enrique.

MISS BLOOM: En-reek-que.

ENRIQUE: Is it true the janitor's going to dress like Santo Clos?

MISS BLOOM: Yes, Mr. Martínez has volunteered to be Santa.

ENRIQUE: He's got a fat panza like Santo Clos!

Enrique makes a circle on his stomach, and the boys laugh.

LUZ: Don't be funny, Enrique.

MISS BLOOM: Maybe Enrique would like to recite the part of los Pastores he knows.

ANDRES: Extra points, Enrique.

ENRIQUE: Ah, there might not even be any Pastores this year.

MISS BLOOM: Why?

ENRIQUE: Cause the men are in the army. Father Rael can't get enough people to play the parts.

LORENZO: Enrique's father is going to be the Devil.

RUBEN: And make the luminarias.

LUZ: My abuelo makes the luminarias!

MISS BLOOM: But it sounds as if there will be no Pastores.

LUZ: We will have the Pastores!

MISS BLOOM: But if the men are gone . . .

LUZ: We'll do it some way.

MISS BLOOM: Why is it so important, Luz?

LUZ: It just is.

REINA: Her father's gone. He's in the army.

ELISA: And her grandpa's sick. He can't cut the wood for the luminarias.

MISS BLOOM: Can someone help him?

Luz shakes her head.

ENRIQUE: He can't cut the wood for the luminarias, and he won't let my father do it.

MISS BLOOM: Why?

REINA: Don Vicente has always cut the wood for the luminarias. And he'll do it this year, wait and see.

The children nod sadly.

MISS BLOOM: I see, it's a tradition.

CARMEN: It's more than that—he made a promise.

RITA: When we make a promise to the Santo Niño, we have to keep it.

MISS BLOOM: Yes, but . . .

The bell rings and the kids fly out, the boys first.

MISS BLOOM: Don't forget Monday's homework! And we finish the tree! (*She turns to Luz.*) I'm sorry your grandfather's sick, Luz. Is there any way I can help?

LUZ: No, thank you. Goodbye.

REINA: Goodbye. See you Monday.

Luz has forgotten her jacket.

MISS BLOOM: Luz, your jacket. (*Miss Bloom hands the jacket to Luz.*)

LUZ: Thank you, Miss Bloom.

MISS BLOOM: Goodbye, girls.

LUZ AND REINA: (*walking away*) Bye, Miss Bloom.

Scene Six

In front of the Garcia home.

REINA: Shall we go by the church and watch the pastores practice? (*points to the pastores practicing in front of the church*)

LUZ: I don't feel like it.

REINA: Why are you sad, Luz?

LUZ: Enrique's probably right. Maybe there will be no Pastores this year, and no luminarias. . . . My abuelo is very sick.

REINA: I wish there was something we could do.

LUZ: Pray he gets better.

REINA: Did you know Consuelo's family moved away?

LUZ: Yes.

REINA: She was going to be Gila. Now they don't have a Gila.

LUZ: I'd love to be Gila.

REINA: You have to be older than twelve.

LUZ: But they have nobody else. Maybe Father Rael would let me be Gila. I know the lines by heart. Did you know my mother was Gila? That's how she met my father.

REINA: And Enrique is Bato.

LUZ: Reina, I'm not interested in Enrique.

REINA: He likes you!

LUZ: Does not!

Luz chases Reina offstage.

Scene Seven

In front of the church.

Don Vicente stands with some of the village elders, including his neighbor Don Paco, who holds the Demonio costume. It is afternoon and the sun warms the front of the church where they gather to talk. Don Vicente coughs.

DON MANUEL: Bad cold, compadre?

DON VICENTE: It's got me. I'm weak as a lamb.

DON PACO: Too weak to make the luminarias, Don Vicente. But being a good neighbor, I will cut the wood.

DON VICENTE: No! I can make the luminarias.

DOÑA JOSEFINA: You better try some Vicks.

DOÑA GREGORITA: Yes, take care of your cold.

DON VICENTE: I don't want to take care of it, I want to get rid of it!

Luz and Reina enter. Luz runs to Don Vicente.

LUZ: Abuelo, buenas tardes. Can we stay and watch los Pastores?

She hugs Don Vicente and says "Buenas tardes" to the other elders.

DON VICENTE: Sí, mi'jita, but keep your jacket on. That cold wind from the mountain tells me it's going to snow for Christmas. (*He touches her jacket.*)

DOÑA GREGORITA: Now the women want to work in Los Alamos. It's good pay.

DON PACO: Women should stay home and take care of the children.

DON VICENTE: My son is at war, so María tries to help. The way we used to live is changing, compadres. The winds of war will blow over San Juan and change everything . . .

Father Rael and the pastores enter.

FATHER RAEL: Ah, here come the rest of my pastores!

Father Rael flourishes as the pastores enter. They are a sorry lot of old men and women in disarray, some dragging their costumes. The youngest boy is Enrique, who holds a guitar. Don Vicente shakes his head in sadness.

DOÑA JOSEFINA: Those pastores look like they're ready for the grave.

DON MANUEL: Come and join us!

FATHER RAEL: It's the best I could do.

DOÑA JOSEFINA: I can't—I got arthritis.

DON MANUEL: You got flojeras.

FATHER RAEL: Let's not argue. We do the best we can. Maybe if we sang "Jingle Bells" when we get to the church it would help.

DON VICENTE: No, Padre, los Pastores don't need "Chingle Bells."

FATHER RAEL: Okay, okay. But we do need a Gila.

He looks at Luz and Reina.

REINA: Luz knows all the lines.

FATHER RAEL: Do you, Luz?

LUZ: Sí.

FATHER RAEL: Thank you, Lord, I have found our Gila!

DON PACO: She's too young.

FATHER RAEL: She's almost as old as Enrique.

Luz looks at her grandfather.

LUZ: Abuelo, may I?

Don Vicente nods.

FATHER RAEL: Gracias a Dios.

LUZ: (*hugging her grandfather*) Thank you, Abuelo.

ENRIQUE: She doesn't know Gila's part!

LUZ: Yes, I do.

ENRIQUE: Okay, try this. (*He recites dramatically.*)
>Gila dispon un bocado
>Danos pronto que cenar.
>Porque ya el hambre me apura,
>Y no me puedo aguantar.

LUZ: (*thinks a moment, glances at her grandfather, then responds strongly*)
>Y si me apuran tantito,
>Los dejaré sin cenar.
>Porque vengo muy cansada,
>Y no puedo apurar.

REINA: (*claps*) I told you she knew all the lines.

FATHER RAEL: Muy bien, Luz.

DON VICENTE: She knows los Pastores by heart.

FATHER RAEL: Now we're in business! Let's start practice. The pastores are on their way to Bethlehem. Let's start with Bato's song. Ready, Enrique?

BATO
>(*singing*) Amigos, pastores,
>Ya es tiempo de ver
>A la Virgen María,
>Y el Niño en Belén.

TODOS LOS PASTORES

> (singing) Belén, Belén que debemos cantar
> Alabanzas al Niño,
> Que nacío en Belén.

TORINGO

> (singing) Amigos, pastores,
> Ya es tiempo de amar
> Al recién nacido
> Que está en el portal.

GILA

> (singing) Por la calle arriba
> Viene la custodia.
> Los ángeles todos
> Cantando la Gloria.

FELETO

> (singing) Anoche, estando sentado,
> Calentándome en la lumbre,
> Oí estar cantando a lo alto
> De aquella cumbre.

MANZANO

> (singing) Que noche tan linda y bella.
> Compañeros, no atendéis alzar
> La cara y veréis por el oriente
> Una estrella.

BATO Y TORINGO

> (singing) De la real Jerusalén
> Sale una estrella brillando,
> A los pastores guiando,
> Para el portal de Belén.

FATHER RAEL: ¡Muy bien! Gila, sing the line that starts with "Cielos soberanos."

GILA

> (singing) Cielos soberanos,
> Tenernos piedad,
> Que ya no suframos
> La nieve que cae.

FATHER RAEL: Now all of you answer Gila.

TODOS LOS PASTORES

> (*singing*) Todos los pastores
> Vamos caminando,
> Que este es el camino
> Que hemos de ir llevando.
> Por aquellos llanos,
> Y por las espinas,
> Divirtiendo a Gila
> Por estos caminos.
> Entre esta fresnera,
> Buscando el ganado,
> Dos mil maravillas
> Miro entre estos prados.
> Camina Gilita,
> Ya vendrás cansada.
> Breve llegaremos,
> A nuestra posada.

FATHER RAEL: Very good! Bartolo, how about your part? Try your lines.

BARTOLO: (*acting lazy*) I'm too lazy.

All laugh.

FATHER RAEL: Show us how lazy you are. Sing "Jesús que largo es el mundo."

BARTOLO

> (*lazily*) Jesús, que largo es el mundo. Ya
> No podía llegar. Que me tiendan
> Diez saleas, para poderme acostar.
> Si a mí me dan que cenar, tráigamelo
> Aquí a mi cama. Y si no, déjenme
> Dormir, más que nunca me den nada.

FATHER RAEL: Bartolo is a lazy shepherd. The pastores are like us—each has a fault. The Devil finds the weakness and uses it to keep the shepherds away from Jesus. The Devil wants to rule the universe. How about it, Don Paco? Give us that first speech of the Devil.

Don Paco has slipped on his devil's cloak. He grabs his pitchfork.

DEMONIO

> Guerra, guerra, tiemble mi furor, cielos y tierra.
> Oh infierno, que tirano, cuando a la ocasión pudiera
> Lo marchito y anhelo. Que yo mando ese sol,

Mando esa luna, mando ese cielo estrellado.
El sol se verá eclipsado, sólo porque yo mando.
Ya de esta entrada he logrado con vos amigos
Pastores, y quiero que a mis funciones vayan,
A ver que primero, que soy un rey,
Que vengo en trajo de pobre y traigo feria
Para que dejen todas sus habitaciones.

Everyone claps at Don Paco's dramatic speech.

FATHER RAEL: Muy bien, Don Paco. The Devil tempts the pastores, but San Miguel appears to defeat the Devil and guide the shepherds to Bethlehem. San Miguel!

San Miguel appears in full angelic costume.

SAN MIGUEL

Acompañemos, pues, a la iglesia con
Santo júbilo, y con alegría celestial.
Arrodillemos con ellos al pesebre
De Belén y en unión de María y de
José, cantemos con los pastores
Himnos de alabanzas y cánticos de amor.
Ofrezcamos nuestros corazones
Al Divino recién nacido, y
Preparémosle una morada que
Él se dignará santificar, pidiéndole
Estas gracias con actos de penitencia,
De amor, y de adoración.

DEMONIO

Oh, Miguel, suspende tus dulzuras.
Lo primero que tengo que borrar es
El mundo. Mando el sol, mando la
Luna, mando ese cielo estrellado.
El sol se verá eclipsado porque
Yo lo mando. Oh, infierno, que tirano
Has puesto en penas tan cruel. Mira
En que angustias se halla el príncipe
Lucifer para dar batalla al hombre
Y a este triunfo de Miguel. Yo haría
Todo un infierno. Oh, de aquel espeso
Monte, oh, de aquel oscuro seno,

Donde mi amor siempre se despensa y
Cual falto, lo marchita y anhelo. Yo
Soy para no cansar al hombre de mayor
Ciencia que hoy al mundo ha imaginado,
Y así es que de todo reino. Como es
Dudable que a un Jesús, como es posible
Que a un niño que ha nacido en un
Portal. Oh, prodigioso misterio,
Quieres quitarme el imperio por
Darle aumento a mi mal. ¡Pero viva
Lucifer! ¡Que antes que la luz del
Día se acerque al oriente dorado,
He de hacer que en esta noche sea
Este Mecías destriunfado, a pesar
De un rubio cielo, de nadie será adorado!

SAN MIGUEL: ¡Diablo, fiero! ¡El niño Cristo será el rey! ¡Afuera contigo!
¡Afuera!

*There is a brief scuffle, then San Miguel chases the Demonio off stage. The children give
chase and shout "¡Diablo Fiero!"*

FATHER RAEL: Wonderful! Enough practice! We meet again tomorrow!

*The old men laugh and the crowd slowly disperses, talking about the Pastores. Luz says
goodbye to Reina and turns home.*

Scene Eight

*Luz arrives home in time to see her mother escorted to the door by U.S. Army Captain Jim
Riley. He is thirty-five and very attentive to María.*

MARÍA: Thank you very much, Captain Riley.

JIM: Call me Jim.

MARÍA: Thanks for the ride, Jim.

JIM: I made you miss your bus by keeping you working late. I was glad to bring
you. This is a nice place you have here.

MARÍA: It's home.

JIM: How are you liking your work up on the hill?

MARÍA: I like it. But everything is so secretive. Seems like every time I turn around there's a security check. If you hadn't helped me I think I would have given up by now.

JIM: You're the best file clerk I have. In a month there's a secretarial opening . . .

MARÍA: I don't think I can handle that.

JIM: Sure, you can. You're learning fast.

MARÍA: It's changed my life. Now I work in Los Alamos, and I have a paycheck. But it's also changing the village. A lot of the families have moved to California.

JIM: Too bad to change a peaceful place like this, but it has to be done. Any word on your husband?

MARÍA: He writes often . . .

JIM: It's hard to be alone on Christmas.

MARÍA: Do you have children?

JIM: (taking out his wallet) A boy, thirteen. Loves baseball. Here's his picture.

MARÍA: He's handsome.

JIM: Takes after his old man. That's my wife, Carol. I won't see them this Christmas. Looks like we're both in the same boat.

MARÍA: Come and have dinner with us on Christmas Eve.

JIM: That's very kind of you—may I call you María?

MARÍA: Yes.

JIM: "Mrs. Garcia" sounds so formal.

Luz enters.

MARÍA: Luz, come and meet Captain Riley. This is my daughter, Luz.

JIM: Hi, Luz. Glad to meet you.

LUZ: Hello, Captain Riley.

JIM: Call me Jim. Well, I've got to be going. Bye, María.

MARÍA: Bye. Thanks again.

JIM: My pleasure.

Jim goes out, a car is heard leaving.

LUZ: Is he your boss?

MARÍA: Supervisor.

LUZ: You like him?

MARÍA: He's a very kind man, and he's lonely without his family.

LUZ: Are you lonely?

MARÍA: I miss Juan. Working helps.

LUZ: You like working?

MARÍA: Yes. We need the money. I'll be able to buy you a new jacket for Christmas. (*She touches Luz's old jacket.*)

LUZ: I don't need a jacket.

MARÍA: It's old and worn.

LUZ: I wish you didn't have to work.

MARÍA: Why?

LUZ: It just seems different. Dad wouldn't like it.

MARÍA: I know. If he was here maybe I wouldn't have to work. But we need the money. Your abuelo's sick, and you need clothes. I know some of the people gossip and say the women shouldn't be working, but I have to.

LUZ: I don't care about their mitote, as long as we stay together.

MARÍA: Of course we're going to stay together. I know I haven't seen much of you this week, but there's so much to learn at work. I've had to work late. Guess what? I might even try for the job as a secretary.

LUZ: And guess what?

MARÍA: What?

LUZ: Father Rael said I could be Gila.

MARÍA: That's wonderful! (*embraces her daughter*)

LUZ: Enrique is Bato.

MARÍA: Sounds like Father Rael is hard at work.

LUZ: And the luminarias?

Both glance at the low woodpile.

MARÍA: Your grandfather's very sick. I won't let him cut wood.

LUZ: Don Paco wants to do it.

MARÍA: He's always wanted to have the honor.

LUZ: But it would spoil Abuelo's promise.

MARÍA: (*shrugs*) His health comes first.

LUZ: I wish Father was home so it could be a real Christmas.

MARÍA: It will be a real Christmas! As long as we're together, it's Christmas. Come on, let's see how Don Vicente is doing.

They enter the kitchen, where Don Vicente dozes in an old chair near the stove.

Scene Nine

LUZ: Abuelo.

Luz goes to her grandfather and takes the newspaper from his lap. He awakens.

DON VICENTE: Hijita. María. Quizás me dormí. The Allies are advancing on Germany, and I was thinking about Juan, and I fell asleep.

MARÍA: How's your cough, Don Vicente?

DON VICENTE: Oh, I took the doctor's medicine, but what does the gringo doctor know? I need a tea of osha . . .

MARÍA: I'm going to fix you some right now, then supper.

DON VICENTE: How was school, mi'jita?

LUZ: Fine. Miss Bloom is teaching us how the americanos celebrate Christmas, and we tell her how we celebrate la Navidad. I told her all about los Pastores.

DON VICENTE: That's what I was dreaming. Los Pastores was coming out of the church, and we were lighting the luminarias.

LUZ: We don't have the wood for the luminarias.

DON VICENTE: I can cut the piñón . . .

LUZ: Maybe Estevan can help.

DON VICENTE: No, I made a promise, mi'jita. I promised the Santo Niño to light the luminarias for your father's safe return.

LUZ: I can help.

DON VICENTE: Sí, you can help. Just the two of us. Oh, the letter.

MARÍA: From Juan? Gracias a Dios.

He rises slowly and goes to the cupboard, where he takes out a letter and hands it to María. She opens it quickly.

MARÍA: November? He wrote this a month ago.

DON VICENTE: ¿Qué dice?

LUZ: Read it.

María reads aloud.

MARÍA: "My beloved family. I am in the hospital. I have a wound in one leg, but it is not serious. The doctors say I will soon be well. I pray all of you are well. My love to all. Juan." Oh, dear God, he's been wounded.

DON VICENTE: ¿Pero cómo?

LUZ: But he says not serious.

DON VICENTE: I knew it was not good. I promised the Santo Niño I would make the luminarias, and I haven't. Now my son is wounded. (*He starts out the door.*)

MARÍA: Don Vicente! You can't go out in the cold.

LUZ: ¡Abuelo!

Don Vicente stumbles to the woodpile, where he picks up the axe and starts splitting wood. After a few swings he falls back coughing and exhausted.

MARÍA: You'll only make your cold worse. Come inside!

LUZ: I'll help you, Abuelo!

Luz picks up the axe and swings at the tough piñón wood. Her frustrations come out, but she is no match for the heavy work. Exhausted, she falls back into her mother's arms. She weeps.

LUZ: Father's wounded, and there's not going to be a Christmas.

She sobs. María holds her and sings "A la Rú." Don Vicente stands by, helpless.

MARÍA

Duérmete, Niño lindo,
En los brazos del amor,
Mientras que duerme y descansa
La pena de mi dolor.

A la rú, a la mé,
A la rú, a la mé,
A la rú, a la mé,
A la rú, a la rú, a la mé.

No temas al rey Herodes,
Que nada te ha de hacer;
En los brazos de tu madre,
Y ahí nadie te ha de ofender.

A la rú, a la mé,
A la rú, a la mé,
A la rú, a la mé,
A la rú, a la rú, a la mé.

END ACT ONE

ACT TWO

Scene One

Outside the Garcia house.

Don Vicente enters the house and kneels at the altar of the Santo Niño. Luz pauses at the door and hears his prayer.

DON VICENTE: Santo Niño de Atocha, escúchame. ¿Por qué no cuidaste a mi hijo? Te rezo cada noche, Santo Niño, y todavía he gets wounded. Please give me some strength so I can keep my promise. When he is safe in this home, I will pray to you and bring you a candle.

He rises slowly and turns the statue of the Santo Niño to face the wall. He walks outside and stares at the woodpile. Luz watches as he picks up the axe. Don Paco appears.

DON VICENTE: (*to himself*) Ah, necesito fuerza . . .

DON PACO: Buenos días, Don Vicente.

DON VICENTE: Buenos días, Don Paco.

DON PACO: You need som help.

DON VICENTE: No, I don't need "som help."

DON PACO: You're ill, vecino. I will do the luminarias and put them here in front of my house. (*points to his house*)

DON VICENTE: Don Paco, you make a good Devil, but not a very good neighbor. I can cut the wood.

DON PACO: But you're sick!

DON VICENTE: I'll find a way. Con el favor de Dios.

DON PACO: Bah!

Don Paco whirls and sees Luz. He scoffs and marches off. Don Vicente remains standing in front of the woodpile. Luz slips away to the church.

Scene Two

In the churchyard.

LUZ: Padre.

FATHER RAEL: Luz, how are you?

LUZ: I need your advice.

FATHER RAEL: Of course, child.

LUZ: Can a promesa be broken?

FATHER RAEL: Well . . .

LUZ: A promesa to the Santo Niño?

FATHER RAEL: Your grandfather's promise?

LUZ: You know?

FATHER RAEL: We all know. But we don't want to interfere.

LUZ: But what can I do?

FATHER RAEL: I don't know, child, I don't know . . .

Luz walks away dejectedly. Father Rael shrugs and goes into the church. Luz walks to the woodpile, takes the axe, and continues to Reina's house.

Scene Three

LUZ: ¡Reina!

REINA: Hi Luz. What are you doing with the axe?

LUZ: Help me cut wood.

Reina hesitates, then puts on her gloves.

REINA: Let's go.

LUZ: In the summer I saw an old, dead piñón in the forest. We can cut it to make the luminarias.

Before they leave the village they encounter Enrique and his gang of boys.

ENRIQUE: Are you going to cut a Christmas tree for La Bloomers?

The boys laugh.

LUZ: Mind your own business.

ENRIQUE: Give me the axe. It's too heavy for you.

LUZ: I can handle it.

RUBEN: Girls can't cut wood.

REINA: We can do anything you can.

ANTONIO: You might cut your toe. Then you couldn't be Gila.

Boys laugh.

LORENZO: Hey, Enrique likes Gila.

ANDRES: Oh, Gila, Gila, give me a kiss.

ENRIQUE: Hey! I was just trying to help.

LUZ: Let's go, Reina.

Luz and Reina go offstage, followed by the boys.

Scene Four

María and Jim arrive at María's home.

JIM: I'm glad you let me bring you home.

MARÍA: This time I didn't miss my bus.

JIM: I volunteered. I enjoy talking to you.

MARÍA: And I enjoy your company. I didn't know you were a farm boy from Kansas. I guess for you the war is as big a change as for us?

JIM: I know what you're going through. If you ever need any help around here, I'll be glad to help. There's not much to do up on the hill. Play pool, watch movies. On weekends I take walks in the mountain.

MARÍA: Thank you, Jim, but the village is small. People wouldn't understand . . .

JIM: I guess I hadn't thought of that. I've been lonely, and talking to you has been a big help. (*He takes her hands.*) Think you'd like to go into Santa Fe for dinner one night?

María shakes her head.

MARÍA: Jim, I can't.

JIM: Not even once?

MARÍA: I . . . I can't.

JIM: Well, you can't blame a guy for trying.

MARÍA: We can be friends. Someday your family will come to see you and you can bring them to visit.

JIM: Yes. Thanks, María. If I don't see you before Christmas, have a very Merry Christmas.

MARÍA: You too, Jim.

Jim exits. María gazes after him, then enters the house.

Scene Five

MARÍA: Buenas tardes, Papá. How are you?

DON VICENTE: Lo mismo. I slept all afternoon . . .

MARÍA: That's what you need—rest. The doctor said a cold like this can turn to pneumonia. You have to be careful. Where's Luz?

DON VICENTE: No sé.

MARÍA: It's cold out.

DON VICENTE: We will get snow for Navidad.

MARÍA: Maybe she's at Reina's. I'll go look.

María puts on a scarf as Luz enters. Luz is muddy, wet, frozen. She still holds the axe.

MARÍA: Dios mío, where have you been? You're frozen!

LUZ: *(to her grandfather)* I tried to cut wood.

DON VICENTE: *(taking the axe)* ¡Mi'ja!

MARÍA: Take your jacket off; you're wet. Do you want to catch a cold like your abuelo?

LUZ: The luminarias, Abuelo. We only have two days.

MARÍA: Stop this nonsense! There will be no luminarias!

LUZ: There would be if father was home!

MARÍA: But he's not! We have to take care of things! And that means no foolishness.

María turns to the stove. Don Vicente sits in his chair by the stove and reads the newspaper. Luz answers Reina's knock at the door and together they huddle at the kitchen table. They have spread out altar candles.

LUZ: Last night I had a dream. I saw rows of candles, and los Pastores.

REINA: Don Vicente, maybe we can use candles as luminarias . . .

They look at Don Vicente.

DON VICENTE: No, mi'jita. The wind would blow them out.

LUZ: What if we put them in cans? (*She rushes to pantry and returns with a can.*)

DON VICENTE: Then the light of the candle could not be seen. Thank you for helping, mi'jita, but I think your mother is right. I cannot make the luminarias this year.

All sit dejectedly.

LUZ: What can I do?

REINA: I don't know, Luz, I don't know.

LUZ: We have to find a way to help Abuelo. (*She looks at her grandfather.*)

REINA: It's time for practice.

Quietly they put on their jackets and walk to the church. The pastores are waiting to rehearse.

Scene Six

FATHER RAEL: Here comes our lovely Gila.

LUZ: Buenas tardes, Padre.

FATHER RAEL: Why so sad?

LUZ: It's nothing.

LORENZO: Her and Reina tried to cut wood in the forest.

Reina nudges the boy.

REINA: Tattletale.

FATHER RAEL: It's too cold to be cutting wood.

ENRIQUE: Girls don't know better.

Luz scowls at him.

FATHER RAEL: I have the thing to cheer you up. I composed a new song for Enrique and Luz to sing.

DON PACO: A new song?

FATHER RAEL: Yes, a duet.

DON PACO: What's wrong with the old songs?

FATHER RAEL: Nothing, but times change.

DON PACO: You goin' sing "Chingle Bells?"

FATHER RAEL: No, it's something I made up. Here. (*He hands music to Enrique and Luz and takes up his guitar.*) Go ahead, try it.

ENRIQUE: I got to sing this?

FATHER RAEL: Sure, it's a little love story.

REINA: Between Bato and Gila?

FATHER RAEL: It's natural. After they give their gifts to the Christ child, they should be together.

Some of the pastores nod. They like the idea.

ENRIQUE: No.

FATHER RAEL: It's just a play, Enrique. Come on, try it.

ENRIQUE: Okay, okay.
>   (*singing*) Ya hemos visto el Cristo
>   Que vino a darnos luz,
>   Y a salvarnos del demonio
>   Con su Santa Cruz.

FATHER RAEL: Now you, Luz.

LUZ
>   (*singing*) Y hora regresamos
>   A cuidar nuestro ganado,
>   La noche esta fría
>   Y el lobo muy hambroso.

FATHER RAEL: Take her hand, Enrique.

Enrique takes Luz's hand.

ENRIQUE: Gila, mi corazón está lleno de amor . . .

LUZ: También el mío . . .

ENRIQUE: ¿Y tú te vas en este rato?

LUZ: ¿O me quedo con Bato?

Enrique and Luz look tenderly at each other for a moment. The other pastores clap.

FATHER RAEL: Wonderful!

DON PACO: I don' like it!

FATHER RAEL: It fits! Bato and Gila are together. Now if we could only do something for Bartolo.

Bartolo snores loudly.

TODOS LOS PASTORES: (*singing*) ¡Levántate Bartolo!

BARTOLO: Déjenme dormir.

TORINGO: ¡Levántese Don Bartolo! ¡Basta de tanta flojera!

BARTOLO: En préstame tus saleas, pa ponerme cabecera.

BATO: En Belén está la Gloria, Bartolo, vamos allá.

BARTOLO: Si la Gloria quiere verme, que venga la Gloria acá.

FELETO: Levántese, Don Bartolo, vamos a Belén corriendo.

BARTOLO: Yo estoy muy bien acostado, usted no me moleste.

VERLADO: Levántese, Don Bartolo, mire el campo hecho una flor.

BARTOLO: Permita Dios que se vuelva, de semitas y alberjón.

MANZANO: Levántese, Don Bartolo, corre leche en los arroyos.

BARTOLO: Si quieres que yo la beba, tráeme dos jarros de apuro.

VERLADO: Del cielo bajó aguardiente, vino blanco, y buen mescal.

BARTOLO: Con cien botijas de vino, no tengo ni pa' empezar.

FUENTE: Una mulita y un buey, verás a Dios adorar.

BARTOLO: La mula me patalea, y el buey me va a cornear.

ESTRELLA: En Belén hay chocolate, Bartolo, que se derrama.

BARTOLO: Si quieres que yo lo beba, tráemelo para mi cama.

VERLADO: Levántese, Don Bartolo, que ya Dios le perdonó.

BARTOLO: Más que nunca me perdone, estando durmiendo yo.

GILA: ¡Lavántate, flojo! ¡Es tiempo de ir a Belén!

Gila grabs a broom and whacks Bartolo. The pastores shout "¡Flojo! ¡Flojo!" and rush Bartolo. They pick him up and cart him off stage.

FATHER RAEL: (*enthusiastically*) We're ready! The pastores are ready for la Navidad!

Scene Seven

Inside the Garcia house.

María is at the table making biscochitos. Luz kneels in front of a small Christmas tree she has decorated. She has placed a small nacimiento at the foot of the tree. Don Vicente sits in his chair.

LUZ: There, that's perfect.

MARÍA: It looks beautiful, mi'ja.

LUZ: Can I help you?

MARÍA: No, gracias. I'm almost done with the masa for the tamales.

LUZ: Hmm, lots of food.

MARÍA: The pastores are always hungry.

LUZ: We have everything, except the luminarias.

There is a knock at the door. Luz goes to the door, and Father Rael enters.

FATHER RAEL: ¡Mere Crismes! ¡Mere Crismes!

LUZ: Buenas tardes, Padre.

MARÍA: Father Felix, come in. Have a biscochito. I'll warm you some coffee—

FATHER RAEL: No, gracias. I'm in a hurry. . . . Ah, everything smells delicious. ¿Cómo 'stá, Don Vicente?

DON VICENTE: Mejor. Tomorrow I can make the luminarias . . .

Father Rael glances at María, shrugs.

FATHER RAEL: (*eating the cookies*) Don't worry, Don Vicente. Don Paco has volunteered to make the luminarias. (*He turns to Luz.*) And you don't have to cut trees in the forest.

LUZ: I was only trying to help. (*Luz goes to sit by her grandfather's side.*)

MARÍA: (*whispering to Father Rael*) He made a promise to the Santo Niño.

FATHER RAEL: I know, but there's nothing I can do. . . . I have to go. Thank you for the biscochitos. Adiós, Don Vicente. Oh, I almost forgot why I came. Luz, can you be at the church at five?

LUZ: I'll be there, Father.

FATHER RAEL: Good. Adiós. ¡Mere Crismes!

The priest goes out in a rush.

DON VICENTE: Mere Crismes, Padre. (*He rises and goes to the window.*) That man is always in a hurry.

MARÍA: He has a lot to do.

DON VICENTE: Yes, to visit each kitchen to eat biscochitos. (*turning to Luz*) Sing for me, hijita. Sing Gila's song.

LUZ

> (*singing*) Por la calle arriba
> Viene la custodia.
> Los ángeles todos
> Cantando la gloria.

DON VICENTE: Muy bonito.

LUZ

> (*singing*) Cielos soberanos
> Tenernos piedad.
> Que ya no sufrimos
> La nieve que cae.

DON VICENTE: Yes, it's going to snow. It's going to be cold, just like that first Navidad when the pastores journeyed to Belén to take gifts to the Christ Child. El Diablo tried to stop them by telling the Hermit to steal Gila away for his wife.

LUZ: But I shout so loud the pastores awaken and give the Hermit a beating.

DON VICENTE: San Miguel conquers the Devil, and the pastores arrive in time to see the birth of Jesus.

MARÍA: A beautiful story. I remember the year I played the part of Gila.

DON VICENTE: And Juan was Bato.

MARÍA: We fell in love . . .

DON VICENTE: If Luz marries Enrique, Don Paco will be my compadre. That man drives me crazy.

LUZ: Don't worry, Abuelo, Enrique thinks girls can't do anything.

MARÍA: Well, I do. I'm out of sugar. Put your coat on and run to the store.

LUZ: Shall I put it on the bill?

María takes out her purse as Luz puts on her coat.

MARÍA: No, now we pay for what we need. No more credit.

Scene Eight

The store.

Miss Bloom is making a purchase. Doña Gregorita is in line behind her. Luz has just entered the store.

DOÑA JOSEFINA: 90, 95, one dollar. Thank you Miss Bloom.

MISS BLOOM: Gr-aw-see-oz. Fa-leez Naw-va . . . Oh . . . Merry Christmas.

DOÑA JOSEFINA: I hope you will be coming to see los Pastores, Miss Bloom.

MISS BLOOM: Oh yes. I can't wait to see the children. I'm not able to make it back home for the holidays, and watching the children get ready has helped make San Juan feel like home. Good-bye, ladies.

DOÑA JOSEFINA: Good-bye, Miss Bloom. (turns to Doña Gregorita) Qué muchacha tan amable.

DOÑA GREGORITA: Ay, comadre, las vísperas de Navidad, y yo todavía ni los tamales prepare.

DOÑA JOSEFINA: Ya la gente no tiene tiempo pa' nada. Everybody wants to work in Los Alamos.

DOÑA GREGORITA: Did you hear about María?

DOÑA JOSEFINA: ¡Sí! The captain brings her home in the army car every day. You can't trust those soldados—

They see Luz.

DOÑA JOSEFINA: Shhh.

DOÑA GREGORITA: Hokay, hokay. (*louder*) Put the arroz on my account.

DOÑA JOSEFINA: On your account? Ya está como los gringos. ¿Qué account?

DOÑA GREGORITA: Pues on account de que I don' have any money!

They laugh.

DOÑA JOSEFINA: ¡Buenas noches! Keep your biscochitos warm!

DOÑA GREGORITA: Buenas noches, comadre. I'll bring you tamales!

Doña Gregorita goes out with her package.

DOÑA JOSEFINA: Promises, promises. . . . Buenas tardes, Luz. ¿Qué necesitas?

LUZ: Azúcar, por favor.

Doña Josefina hands Luz a brown paper bag. They go to the large container that holds the sugar.

DOÑA JOSEFINA: How's Don Vicente?

LUZ: Better, gracias.

DOÑA JOSEFINA: ¿Y tu mamá?

LUZ: Bien, gracias.

DOÑA JOSEFINA: Anda. Detén el saco.

Luz holds the paper sack while Doña Josefina pours the sugar. A bright light shines on the sugar as it is poured.

LUZ: It looks like starlight . . .

DOÑA JOSEFINA: Your mamá is baking biscochitos?

LUZ: (*stares in amazement at the sugar*) That's it!

DOÑA JOSEFINA: ¿Qué?

Luz takes the bag, stuffs the dollar bill into the startled Doña Josefina's hand, and rushes out.

LUZ: (*shouts*) The sugar in the bag! ¡Gracias!

DOÑA JOSEFINA: ¡Ay, que muchacha!

LUZ: (*shouting*) The bag will hold the candle!

Scene Nine

The Garcia home.

Luz bursts in the door, breathless and eager to share her idea.

LUZ: Mamá! Abuelo! I saw it! I saw it!

MARÍA: What is it?

DON VICENTE: ¿Qué pasa, mi'jita?

LUZ: The bag! Glowing with light! The sugar was like snow! It was all lit up!

MARÍA: Calm down. Tell us.

DON VICENTE: Maybe she saw Santo Clos.

LUZ: Look! (*She empties the sugar on the table. She takes one of the small votive candles and puts it in the bag.*) See! The light of the candle will shine through the bag! Light it, Abuelo! It will shine!

Don Vicente scratches his head, then lights a match. He lights the candle in the bag.

LUZ: See!

MARÍA: It shines.

DON VICENTE: Let's take it outside . . .

Carefully Don Vicente carries the small farolito out into the dark. It shines even more.

MARÍA: It's very pretty . . .

DON VICENTE: And the wind doesn't put the candle out.

LUZ: It's a farolito!

DON VICENTE: Yes, it is a lantern. A farolito de Luz. The candle will burn all night.

MARÍA: I have dozens of candles.

LUZ: And I have dozens of bags I had saved to sell back to Doña Josefina!

DON VICENTE: We can use sand to keep the bag in place.

LUZ: We can put them along the road!

MARÍA: On the wall . . .

DON VICENTE: The farolitos of Christmas. Lighting the way for the pastores.

MARÍA: Hundreds of them.

LUZ: It will be beautiful, Abuelo.

DON VICENTE: You've done it, mi'ja. You've kept my promise. Juan will return . . .

Scene Ten

Outside the Garcia home, the following morning.

Luz, Reina, and Don Vicente are outside filling bags with sand. Some already line the wall. Enrique and his friends appear.

ENRIQUE: Buenos días, Don Vicente.

DON VICENTE: Buenos días te de Dios, Enrique.

ENRIQUE: Looks like snow.

DON VICENTE: Yes, that storm will bring snow by night.

ENRIQUE: (to Luz) What are you doing?

ANTONIO: Looks like they're collecting sand.

LUZ: We're making farolitos.

ENRIQUE: What?

ANDRES: There's a candle in each bag?

LUZ: Farolitos to light the way for the Christ child.

ENRIQUE: Like luminarias.

DON VICENTE: Smart boy.

REINA: For the pastores.

RUBEN: Will it work?

CARMEN: Sure, it will work.

ENRIQUE: You're going to light them?

DON VICENTE: I told you he is a smart boy.

RITA: We can decorate the house with farolitos.

ELISA: And the walls.

LUZ: They glow in the dark, Enrique.

ENRIQUE: Yeah, it might work. Can we help?

LUZ: Yes. Everybody can help.

LORENZO: Aw, I thought we were going rabbit hunting?

ENRIQUE: Not now. We have to help Luz. Before the snow comes.

LORENZO: All right.

The boys join in. María comes out to see. The word spreads, and villagers come to see, including Miss Bloom, Father Rael, and Indians from the pueblo. Don Paco appears dressed as the Demonio.

DON PACO: What are you doing, Don Vicente?

DON VICENTE: Making farolitos.

DON PACO: Bags with sand? A candle? These are not luminarias! I will make the luminarias!

DON VICENTE: Sorry, Don Paco, but the job is done.

DON PACO: You're changing the tradition, Don Vicente.

DON VICENTE: No, not changing it, just adding to it. Luz made the farolitos, and isn't la Navidad for the children?

FATHER RAEL: Amen.

DON PACO: I don't like it.

LUZ: We've kept our promise to the Santo Niño.

DON PACO: (*sputtering and turning on Enrique*) Why are you wasting your time filling bags with sand? Get home and chop wood for your mother!

ENRIQUE: But, Papá, it's a great idea!

DON PACO: ¡Anda! ¡Vamos! This is nonsense! Bah!

Don Paco and Enrique go off. Those left laugh and join in making the farolitos.

Scene Eleven

Outside.

An air of excitement fills the village. Neighbors rush back and forth, visiting, smiling, and pointing at the farolitos the children are placing everywhere. Father Rael and the children are busy setting the manger at the door of the church. The stage goes dark as the farolitos are lit.

DOÑA GREGORITA: ¿Qué es esto?

FATHER RAEL: Farolitos for los Pastores!

DOÑA GREGORITA: Is this your idea, Padre?

FATHER RAEL: No, the honor belongs to Luz.

The kids cheer. All turn to see Don Vicente emerge from the house, carrying the statue of the Santo Niño. María walks beside him.

DON VICENTE: I brought out the Santo Niño so he can see the farolitos.

LUZ: You kept your promise, Abuelo.

DON VICENTE: Yes, he is very happy with the bright lanterns.

LUZ: If only Father was here.

DON VICENTE: We will pray. Mira, los pastores.

The pastores appear in full dress. Villagers may accompany the procession.

BARTOLO: ¿Qué son esas luces?

LUZ: Farolitos para el Niño.

BARTOLO: Qué maravilla.

ENRIQUE: You did a good job, Luz.

LUZ: Thanks, Enrique.

FATHER RAEL: Christmas lights for the Baby Jesus.

Don Paco, dressed as the Demonio, jumps forward.

DEMONIO: Bah! I can't see anything! I told Don Vicente I would make the luminarias! These little candles in bags will never be part of our tradition! (*He spills one with his pitchfork.*)

FATHER RAEL: I think you're wrong, Don Paco. I think in a few years you'll see them all over the village, maybe even in Santa Fé.

Luz straightens the farolito.

DON VICENTE: (*speaking sternly*) The children can make them, Don Paco. So be
a good devil and fight San Miguel, not me.

DEMONIO: (*getting the message*) San Miguel! Where are you? I'm going to stick
you with my horca!

SAN MIGUEL: (*jumping forward*) ¡Aquí estoy, Diablo! ¡Listo para hacer lucha!

*There is a short scuffle, and San Miguel drives the Demonio out of the theatre. The people
laugh and cheer.*

DEMONIO: ¡Ay! ¡San Miguel! ¡No me pegues! ¡No me pegues! I'll be a good
boy! I promise!

*Father Rael places the crib of Jesus near a farolito. Each pastor kneels and lays a gift next
to the crib.*

TODOS LOS PASTORES
> Voy para Belén
> Siguiendo la luz,
> De mi dulce bien
> Mi dulce Jesús.

BATO
> (*speaking*) Ya estamos en el portal,
> Ya vemos la luz que sale.
> Quien habrá quien se la iguale,
> Toringo, llega adorar.

TORINGO
> Voy para Belén
> Con gusto y amor,
> Al recién nacido
> Le llevo un colchón.

ALBA
> Voy para Belén
> Con gusto infinito,
> Al recién nacido
> Le llevo un gallito.

LUNA
> Voy para Belén
> Con gusto infinito,

Al recién nacido
Le traigo un guajito.

MANZANO

Voy para Belén
Con gusto y morada,
Al recién nacido
Le llevo una almohada.

VERLADO

Voy para Belén
Con gusto y esmero,
Al recién nacido
Le llevo un cordero.

BATO

Voy para Belén
Con gusto, Gilita,
A llevarle al Niño
Esta fresadita.

COSME

Voy para Belén
Por esta sombrita,
A llevarle al Niño
Esta canastita.

GILA

Voy para Belén
Con gusto y esmero,
A llevarle al Niño
Pañal y fajero.

TODOS LOS PASTORES

Voy para Belén
Siguiendo la luz,
De mi dulce Bien
Mi dulce Jesús.

FATHER RAEL: (*with tears in his eyes*) Gracias a Díos.

DOÑA GREGORITA: Now we eat!

MARÍA: Yes, the posole is ready! Come in, everybody. Come and join us.

DON VICENTE: Entren, entren . . . todos mis vecinos. You, too, Don Paco!

Everyone laughs and enters the house to eat. Luz and Enrique remain outside.

LUZ: Thanks for helping with the farolitos.

ENRIQUE: It's a great idea. They're going to burn all night. My father, he's a little old-fashioned. (*He steps closer to Luz with each line.*)

LUZ: So is my abuelo.

ENRIQUE: They want to make sure we keep our traditions.

LUZ: We will.

ENRIQUE: Yes. Ready to eat?

LUZ: You go. I want to look at the farolitos . . .

Enrique enters house. María comes out.

MARÍA: Mi'jita, you'll get cold. Come in.

LUZ: I was enjoying the farolitos, and wishing . . .

MARÍA: It is a beautiful sight.

They are interrupted by the sound of a car. A man with a flashlight appears.

LUZ: Someone's coming.

JIM: María.

MARÍA: Who is it? (*pauses*)
Captain Riley. We're glad you could come.

JIM: I was on my way up to the labs when I met someone on the road.

Juan Garcia enters on crutches.

MARÍA: Juan!

LUZ: Papá!

Luz and María rush to embrace Juan.

JIM: I thought you'd like to see him.

MARÍA: Thank God you're home! Your leg?

JUAN: It's almost well. I'm glad to be home. To see my family. Mi'jita.

LUZ: We missed you, Papá. I'm so glad you're home!

JUAN: And I missed you, hijita. Missed all of you.

MARÍA: This is a miracle! But how did you get here?

JUAN: I got a ride from Santa Fé. (*Juan looks at Jim.*) Turns out he's your boss.

JIM: I was down there on business, and look who I meet.

MARÍA: Bendito sea Dios. Thank you, Jim. Come in and join us.

JIM: Glad to be Santa Claus and deliver the guy, but I can't stay. I'm delivering a package that's needed at the labs. Next time.

JUAN: Gracias.

JIM: Hey, these lanterns are beautiful. You do this every year?

LUZ: We will.

JUAN: I could see them a mile away.

JIM: Well, merry Christmas! I've got to get to the lab. Good night! (*Jim goes out.*)

JUAN, MARÍA, and LUZ: ¡Feliz Navidad! ¡Feliz Navidad!

JUAN: Jim's right. We could see the lights—what are these, candles in paper sacks?

LUZ: Farolitos. Abuelo and I made them. He kept his promise.

JUAN: Promise?

LUZ: His promise to the Santo Niño, that you would come back to us.

JUAN: It worked. I'm home. (*looks at Luz*) Don't catch cold, mi'jita.

Juan takes his jacket off and places it around Luz. The three embrace. Don Vicente enters.

DON VICENTE: ¡Hijo!

JUAN: Papá.

DON VICENTE: (*embracing Juan*) Gracias a Dios. You're home! You're safe! Your leg?

JUAN: I'm fine, Papá.

DON VICENTE: Gracias al Santo Niño.

MARÍA: We're a family again.

LUZ: And that's the best feeling in the world.

They stare at the farolitos for a moment, then enter the house to warm greeting from all.

END

Who Killed Don José?

CHARACTERS

MARÍA
TONY, a car dealer
DON JOSÉ, the patrón and María's father
DIEGO
DOÑA SOFÍA, the housekeeper and Diego's mother
ANA, lady friend of Don José
RAMÓN, the computer man
THE SHERIFF, the law of Santa Fe County

ACT ONE

It is a cold and windy October night in Santa Fe County. The spacious living room of Don José's ranch is decorated in old, territorial New Mexico style, including large fireplace, brick floor, Indian rugs on the walls, table with drinks, and comfortable sofa and chairs, all covered with well-worn Chimayo rugs. Outside the wind moans, dogs bark, and the distinct bleating of sheep can be heard.

Someone knocks on the door. María enters from the left and opens the door. Tony, about thirty-five, a car dealer in Santa Fe, enters. He wears a three-piece suit and is slick and confident. When María opens the door, he leaps forward.

TONY: Trick or treat!

MARÍA: Tony! You scared me!

TONY: Who were you expecting? Dracula? (*He embraces her.*) How about a treat?

MARÍA: How about you behave? (*She feels the bulge in his pocket.*) Hey, Señor Werewolf—what's this?

TONY: My trusty .38.

MARÍA: A gun?

TONY: A pistol. Come on, get your dancing shoes on! We're going dancing!

MARÍA: (*pulls back*) I didn't know you carried a gun.

TONY: I've sold a lot of used cars—a man needs protection. Hey, if it'll make you feel any better, I'll leave it in the car. (*Tony takes the pistol from under his jacket.*) It's a beauty, huh. Pearl handle. Got it from a guy who had to leave town in a hurry.

DON JOSÉ: (*offstage*) María! Did you get the door?

MARÍA: Yes, Dad—I got it! (*to Tony*) He doesn't allow guns in the house!

TONY: No guns. Why?

MARÍA: Since his father was shot. It's a rule.

TONY: Okay. I'll put it away—

MARÍA: No. Hide it. Dad would have a fit. (*She takes the gun, looks around.*)

TONY: Hey, what are you doing?

MARÍA: Getting rid of this. (*She goes to the telephone table. She opens a drawer, takes out the telephone directory, and puts the pistol in the drawer.*)

TONY: That's a joke—Don José afraid of guns. Ha!

MARÍA: He's not afraid of anything. He just won't allow them in the house.

Offstage, Don José sings "Rancho Grande."

TONY: But my—

MARÍA: Shh. He's coming.

Don José appears from a door, stage left. He is fifty, silver-haired, handsome. He has made a good living raising sheep. He is wealthy, traditional, well-mannered, and sophisticated. He wears an elegant smoking jacket.

DON JOSÉ: Oh, Tony. I thought it was somebody important.

TONY: Don José, anytime you need a job as a salesman, let me know. You always have a joke.

DON JOSÉ: (*frowns*) What brings you out on a night like tonight?

TONY: This beautiful daughter of yours. She's swept me off my feet.

DON JOSÉ: (*whispers*) Qué lástima.

TONY: We're invited to an important party, lots of wealthy people. They're important people to know.

MARÍA: I didn't know you were coming by, Tony. I had planned to stay home with Father—

DON JOSÉ: Don't worry about me, mi'jita. But you've been dancing every night for a week. Wouldn't you like a change of pace . . . and partner?

MARÍA: I *am* tired—

TONY: María's the best dance partner I've ever had.

DON JOSÉ: Life is just a dance, huh, Tony?

MARÍA: He is a great dancer. And he's helping me look for a car—

TONY: If a man wants to get ahead in this town, he needs to know the score.

DON JOSÉ: I don't know if I can live through this.

MARÍA: You will, Dad. . . . Aren't you going to offer Tony a drink?

TONY: Treat me right and I can get it for you wholesale.

DON JOSÉ: *(weakly)* Drink, Tony?

TONY: Double scotch, si voo play. For example, I see María in a Seville. And for you, Don José, I have just the thing. A gold El Dorado just came in. It's got style. A man like you should drive an expensive car.

DON JOSÉ: *(pours and serves drinks)* No, gracias, my old truck runs just fine.

MARÍA: Maybe you should treat yourself to a new car, Dad. You've been working too hard.

DON JOSÉ: Yes, you're right. Since you got home I've hardly seen you. We need to take time, just the two of us! To ride on the rancho like we used to. . . . This new plan has taken all my time.

TONY: Maybe your father can't afford a new car, María. I can get you credit, Don José.

DON JOSÉ: That'll be the day!

MARÍA: Dad!

TONY: What's the matter, don't you trust me?

MARÍA: Of course he does.

TONY: My father trusted you, Don José. Remember?

DON JOSÉ: *(grows pensive)* Don Estevan, que descanse en paz.

TONY: Hey, that's the past. Come on, let's go party!

MARÍA: Will you be all right?

DON JOSÉ: Sí. Sí. I was just thinking.

MARÍA: You seem to have something on your mind.

DON JOSÉ: Didn't I tell you? Ramón's delivering my computer tonight.

TONY: A computer?

MARÍA: He's going to put the whole ranch on a computer program—even the sheep.

TONY: I don't believe it.

MARÍA: When most people are planning to retire, he's starting a new project. I tell him to sell the ranch and move to Santa Fe, or Albuquerque, but no, the ranch is too important.

DON JOSÉ: Retire? Leave the rancho? My friends? My workers? No, impossible!

MARÍA: You can't be responsible for them all your life.

DON JOSÉ: ¿Por qué no? Our family has been on this land for many genera-
tions. Your grandfather taught me to love the land and take care of the
workers. He was a real patrón.

MARÍA: But times have changed.

DON JOSÉ: So we change with them. Use computers.

TONY: Let me get this straight. The computer's going to take care of your sheep?

DON JOSÉ: Every single borreguito. I'm moving into the future.

TONY: Just be careful you don't move too fast, Don José.

DON JOSÉ: The computer age is here whether we like it or not. If we don't
change now, we get left behind.

TONY: But nobody's making money in sheep anymore. You should get into
politics. That's how you make money.

MARÍA: You could get elected. Or appointed to a position.

TONY: (chuckling) Yeah, Goodwill Ambassador to Australia. They have sheep
there!

DON JOSÉ: Appointed? No. It's men like me who put governors in office in
this state. I still deliver a large part of the vote in this county. Politicians
come to me for votes and advice—I don't go to them. And after they're
elected, they are surrounded by the sheep they appoint. At least here on the
rancho my sheep are honest.

TONY: Can't argue there.

DON JOSÉ: My work is here. New opportunities are coming to this state—
technology, bullet trains, new investments . . .

TONY: A man can still get rich, if he's in the right place at the right time.

DON JOSÉ: We have to create our own future. (takes María's hands) That's why
I need you here.

MARÍA: I'm not sure how a degree in music can help.

DON JOSÉ: Just being here is enough. One day you will take over the rancho.

MARÍA: Someday. Right now I want to travel, see Europe, maybe study there—

DON JOSÉ: There's time for that, too. Just as soon as my plan is in place, we can take a trip together. Vas a ver.

MARÍA: I'd like that.

TONY: Anything beats raising sheep.

DON JOSÉ: You know what your grandfather used to say.

MARÍA: ¿Cada borrega es un mundo?

DON JOSÉ: Be serious, mi'jita. It is our sacred duty to protect this land. Now, excuse me. Ramón will be here soon . . . and maybe other guests. (*He kisses María on the forehead and goes out, whistling "Mary Had a Little Lamb."*)

TONY: I think your father's getting senile.

MARÍA: No, he's just set in his ways.

TONY: He could get a real deal for this ranch. Especially now—

MARÍA: Father won't sell. This land is his life. It can be confining and slow, but it's home. I've been out riding every morning since I've been back. I had forgotten how beautiful it is.

TONY: You can't bank beauty, honey. You gotta have money to buy the good things in life.

MARÍA: I do want to travel, but right now I want to be near Dad.

TONY: And I want to be near you.

MARÍA: It's been fun, Tony. But there's more to life than dancing.

TONY: Hey, we're meant for each other. I've always had my eyes on you. I remember the first time I saw you. I made up my mind then, someday we would be together.

MARÍA: You never said anything.

TONY: You were the daughter of the great Don José. I was a poor man's son. I could just watch you from a distance. Now I know better.

MARÍA: (*teasing*) I bet you do. Tony, the lady's man.

TONY: Don't believe Santa Fe gossip. I'm on one track, and that's you.

They are interrupted by Diego singing in the kitchen, "Yo no soy borreguero, soy capitán, soy capitán . . ."

TONY: Who's that?

MARÍA: Diego. He's been drinking—

TONY: Is he still around?

MARÍA: He's part of the family. He'll always be around. Anyway, if we're going dancing I'd better change. Be a few minutes.

TONY: Don't keep me waiting.

MARÍA: I bought Los Lobos's new album. It's in the library down the hall. I'll be a few minutes.

TONY: Great!

María goes out. Tony finishes his drink.

TONY: I could get used to this. Don Tony. Ha, ha . . .

Tony exits, chuckling. The voices in the kitchen grow louder. Doña Sofía and Diego, her son, enter. Doña Sofía is in her late sixties. They carry a small computer table, which they place in the middle of the room. Diego is drunk. He is a typical ranch hand, dressed in Levi's, boots, work shirt, leather vest. Offstage we hear salsa music.

DOÑA SOFÍA: (scolding) ¡Malcriado! ¡Sinvergüenza! How many times do I tell you, ¡no tengo dinero! If you want to waste your life drinking, use you own money, borracho! Ay, qué martirio es ser madre.

DIEGO: I ain't drunk, jefa, I just had a few beers.

DOÑA SOFÍA: Sí, a few beers. I know. Drinking con esos sin oficio—

DIEGO: They're my friends, jefa.

DOÑA SOFÍA: ¡Ándale! ¡Ayúdame con la mesa!

DIEGO: What is the table for?

DOÑA SOFÍA: For la computadora—

DIEGO: ¿A puta dora? What's that? A high-priced woman? (He laughs.)

DOÑA SOFÍA: No, it's a machine. A Japanese machine Don José bought. He said it can do anything. I just hope it can wash the floors.

DIEGO: Come on, jefita, just lend me few pesos. I'll pay you back next week.

DOÑA SOFÍA: You already spent your paycheck?

DIEGO: ¡Qué paycheck, ni que nada! Don José pays me cacahuates! The foremen of the other ranchos make good money, but they got cattle. And me? Stuck with these borregas of Don José. I'm sick of them!

DOÑA SOFÍA: Sí, sick enough to take one every week?

DIEGO: The coyotes take the sheep, not me.

DOÑA SOFÍA: Then get poison for the coyotes.

DIEGO: I bought some today. (*He lifts a bottle of whiskey at the bar and stares at it.*) When I put the poison, olvídate!

DOÑA SOFÍA: I know you take good care of the sheep, mi'jo, pero no importa. Someday soon this machine is going to replace you. You won't have work.

DIEGO: No work? What are you saying, jefa?

DOÑA SOFÍA: The machine, it takes care of the sheep—

DIEGO: ¡Chale! No pinche máquina can take care of sheep! You crazy?

DOÑA SOFÍA: (*pensive*) Máquinas del Diablo, that's what they are. Japanese machines to do our work. Con rázon que hay tanta gente sin trabajo.

DIEGO: I got a job!

DOÑA SOFÍA: You? You're a pendejo who can't even take care of your money. You have to give Don José credit, he takes good care of his sheep. ¿Y por qué no? They made his family rich. (*She goes to the fireplace to stir the fire.*)

DIEGO: Yeah, but they don't make *me* money! I know a man who's selling a ranchito, jefa. If I only had some lana I could buy it. Raise cattle up in Mora, get out of this pinche rancho!

DOÑA SOFÍA: A rancho in the mountains . . . Sí, that would be nice.

DIEGO: But I need the money!

DOÑA SOFÍA: You'll get the money.

DIEGO: From where? From you? Ha! If Don José is as tight as a coffin, then you're as tight as a grave!

DOÑA SOFÍA: ¡Malcriado!

DIEGO: So I take a couple of sheep a month, sell them to buy beer. Como dicen los politicos, those are my "fringe benefits"! (*He laughs.*)

DOÑA SOFÍA: ¡Cállate! Estas paredes tienen orejas.

DIEGO: Ah, nobody's listening. So, tell me how can I get some lana. Did you find a treasure?

DOÑA SOFÍA: No te importa—

DIEGO: (*grabs her arm*) Anda, ¿qué sabes?

DOÑA SOFÍA: I shouldn't tell you anything.

DIEGO: Come on, jefa, what are you hiding?

DOÑA SOFÍA: Shh! Last week I was cleaning Don José's room. He had all his papers out of the safe.

DIEGO: Yeah?

DOÑA SOFÍA: I found a very important paper.

DIEGO: What?

DOÑA SOFÍA: Don José's will.

DIEGO: His will?

DOÑA SOFÍA: ¡Sí. His will. That's where he puts down what he gives to people when he dies.

DIEGO: I know what a will is, jefa. But why should I care? The old bastard wouldn't put me in his will if it killed him. Ha, you get it? If it killed him!

DOÑA SOFÍA: He's tough, like an old ram. Like his father, Don Andrés. They shot him, or he would still be alive.

DIEGO: Don José's like an old coyote.

DOÑA SOFÍA: But a kind man, in his own way. He put you in his will.

DIEGO: Me? In the will?

DOÑA SOFÍA: ¡Sí! When Don José dies, you get a share of money. Enough to buy that rancho you want.

DIEGO: Are you sure?

DOÑA SOFÍA: I can read! That's what it says in the will!

DIEGO: Damn! That's good news! So that old sonofabitch is gonna cut me in. I don't believe it.

DOÑA SOFÍA: It's true.

DIEGO: I can buy a rancho! Be my own boss.

DOÑA SOFÍA: No seas loco. You don't get a penny until Don José dies.

DIEGO: Yeah. The will. He has to die . . .

DOÑA SOFÍA: That's the way it is.

She sees the telephone book and goes to place it in the drawer. She sees the pistol. She nervously picks up the pistol, stuffs it in her apron pocket, places the telephone book in the drawer.

DOÑA SOFÍA: Don José is as healthy as a goat. He's going to live a long life—

DIEGO: Unless he has an accident in his truck.

DOÑA SOFÍA: What do you mean?

DIEGO: Or somebody puts coyote poison in his drink—

DOÑA SOFÍA: ¡No digas eso! The devil will hear. It can come true.

DIEGO: Yeah, he could choke on his drink!

DOÑA SOFÍA: Don't be crazy. If Don José dies, it has to be a natural death.

DIEGO: (*puts his arms around her*) Pero que truchas, jefita. You're not so dumb. You go sniffing around and you find the will. Qué suave. I gotta think about this. I need a beer.

DOÑA SOFÍA: No more beer.

DIEGO: Enough money to buy my own rancho . . .

They exit. The telephone rings.

DON JOSÉ: (*offstage*) Doña Sofía, answer the phone! María, the telephone! (*He walks in.*) Women! When you need them, they're never around. (*He picks up the phone.*) Hello. Sheriff? Yes. Yes. Oh, I understand. But I have nothing to say to you. . . . No, no deal! Tell that to your friends. I don't care what you say, there's nothing to talk about. ¡Buenas noches!
(*He slams the phone down. There is a knock at the door.*) Ramón?

Don José opens the door. Ana enters. She is forty-five, a very attractive woman, well dressed. The small bell hung on the door tinkles when it's opened and shut.

DON JOSÉ: Ana! Come in. It's good to see you.

ANA: Why haven't you called?

They kiss. He takes her coat.

DON JOSÉ: You know I've been busy.

ANA: Have you heard the news from Santa Fe?

DON JOSÉ: Yes!

ANA: As of today, your land is worth millions.

DON JOSÉ: Just as I planned.

ANA: And the land the Santa Fe Corporation bought is worthless.

DON JOSÉ: Serves them right, the gang of crooks. They stole the foundation money and bought the wrong piece of real estate. Instead of going through their land, the bullet train is going through my ranch. And the attorney general is already investigating them.

ANA: Then it's true—you have information from the foundation files!

DON JOSÉ: How did you know?

ANA: I have friends. A very important file is missing. They know you have it, and they want it back. They're ready to murder—

DON JOSÉ: Murder me? I don't think they'll do anything as long as I have this. (*He takes a disk from his jacket pocket.*)

ANA: Is that it?

DON JOSÉ: Yes. This is what they want. As soon as I get my computer, I'll be able to read it, then I'll know who in the gang is involved. In the meantime it's my insurance.

ANA: While you have it, they won't touch you?

DON JOSÉ: They can't. It's this file they want, not me. As long as I have it, I'm safe.

ANA: What's in it?

DON JOSÉ: Bookkeeping entries and other information they don't want exposed.

ANA: How did you get it?

DON JOSÉ: By accident.

ANA: You stole it?

DON JOSÉ: I paid for it.

ANA: But it can only mean trouble, José.

DON JOSÉ: Yes, I know. And that's why I won't turn my back on their crooked deals! They stole from the people of this state. It's not right—every new investor that lands here takes a piece of our pie! Only the crumbs are left for the people. The foundation was set up for the good of the entire state, not just for the politicos who have their fingers in the pie!

ANA: (*sighs*) I agree. But I'm worried. Don't say I didn't warn you . . .

DON JOSÉ: Thank you, Ana, but I'm safe, as long as I have this. (*He slips the disk into his pocket.*)

ANA: You're being too complacent.

DON JOSÉ: Me, complacent? Never, my dear. I know New Mexican politics too well.

ANA: Did you know they've talked about hiring someone to kill you?

DON JOSÉ: I don't believe it.

ANA: It's true! I was there!

DON JOSÉ: Where?

ANA: At the Bull Ring in Santa Fe. Everybody was there, even the governor. All the Santa Fe Corporation investors were waiting for the foundation board vote. When it was announced and they knew they had lost millions, they got together in a back room to decide what to do.

DON JOSÉ: And?

ANA: As Vicente Silva used to say, your life ain't worth a plugged nickel.

DON JOSÉ: I need a drink. How about you?

ANA: Yes, por favor.

DON JOSÉ: (*goes to the bar*) You're serious, aren't you?

ANA: Dead serious.

DON JOSÉ: Who was there?

ANA: All of them. The people you call the High-Tech Mafia.

DON JOSÉ: So you think they would do it?

ANA: Of course they would. They not only lost their money, but like you said, the attorney general is asking questions.

DON JOSÉ: Damn!

ANA: (*offering a toast*) To Don José. You are a genius.

DON JOSÉ: There was never any doubt. I just don't plan to be a dead genius. But who would they get to do their dirty work?

ANA: You're worried, huh? The great Don José is afraid—I never thought I'd see the day.

DON JOSÉ: Don't play games, Ana. This is serious. Do you know?

ANA: (challenging him) It could be me!

DON JOSÉ: You?

ANA: Why not? You know I can shoot the head off a rattlesnake at fifty feet. (She pulls a pistol from her purse.)

DON JOSÉ: Ana, be careful!

ANA: You know I always carry a gun. What if it's me? It could be my revenge.

DON JOSÉ: Revenge for what?

ANA: For all those years you kept me waiting!

DON JOSÉ: Don't tease me, Ana. Tell me who they hired.

ANA: On one condition!

DON JOSÉ: What?

ANA: Marry me.

DON JOSÉ: You're impossible!

ANA: I don't think so. You're in trouble, and I'm the only person who can help you. I'm simply collecting for all the years I've waited.

Don José smiles, holds her, kisses her. She responds.

DON JOSÉ: Tell me.

ANA: Marry me.

DON JOSÉ: Tell me.

ANA: Marry me.

DON JOSÉ: My dear Ana, you drive a hard bargain. Let's see if I understand your proposal. My future in a coffin, or my future in marriage. I'll have to think about it.

ANA: ¡Cabrón! I'm crazy to love you.

DON JOSÉ: I'm irresistible.

ANA: You're egotistical!

DON JOSÉ: Ana, we've been good friends, good lovers all these years. Let's not spoil it.

ANA: It may already be spoiled.

DON JOSÉ: What do you mean?

ANA: You're a dead man!

DON JOSÉ: Come now, Ana, don't be so melodramatic. I admit, there's a few things that I hadn't planned on. I need your help.

ANA: Uh-huh. The only time you show affection is when you need my help.

DON JOSÉ: I haven't told María anything about the foundation vote or my plans for the ranch. I was going to tell her tonight, until Tony showed up.

ANA: So tell her.

DON JOSÉ: It's not that simple. The Sheriff just called me.

ANA: Ah-ha . . .

DON JOSÉ: I think he's going to drop by tonight. I know the Sheriff is involved with that bunch of crooks, but how deep is he in? Deep enough to murder? No, I don't think so. But I can't be sure.

ANA: You can't be sure of anybody. You've made enemies.

DON JOSÉ: All great men make enemies. Especially in this state. You make a name for yourself, and the zopilotes are there, pecking at you.

ANA: That's politics— (They hear the sound of laughter offstage.) Who's that?

DON JOSÉ: María and Tony Montoya.

ANA: Tony Montoya, from Tony's Cadillacs. I thought your daughter had better taste.

DON JOSÉ: She does, but she's been lonely . . . I've been busy. Anyway, she's buying a car from him.

ANA: I bought a car from him, and it was a lemon! And he wouldn't fix it. I don't like that man.

DON JOSÉ: I have to talk to María, now. Excuse me, amor.

ANA: I need to freshen up a bit. Damn wind.

DON JOSÉ: Thank you, Ana. (*He takes Ana to the door, kisses her, then calls.*) María!

Enter María and Tony.

MARÍA: Tony was showing me a new step. What's up?

TONY: We're going to be *the* couple at the party tonight.

DON JOSÉ: Wouldn't it be less painful if you just bought the damned car?

MARÍA: Papá, be nice. What do you want?

DON JOSÉ: Look, I have something to tell you. I wanted to wait until tomorrow, but I think you should hear it now. Stay. Have a drink. Tony?

TONY: Why not? Double scotch, si voo play.

DON JOSÉ: Good. Sit down, sit down. I'll get us a drink.

MARÍA: No, you sit—I'll get the drinks.

DON JOSÉ: A lot has happened today. I have very good news!

TONY: The price of mutton just went up?

DON JOSÉ: Much better!

TONY: The price of wool went up?

DON JOSÉ: How about . . . Don José, the millionaire.

TONY: That would impress me.

MARÍA: What's the joke?

DON JOSÉ: It's not a joke, María.

TONY: You struck oil!

MARÍA: Daddy, quit teasing. What's the secret?

DON JOSÉ: I want to relish the story. Where do I begin?

MARÍA: Just get to the point.

DON JOSÉ: Bueno. As you know, there are plans to build a bullet train to run from Los Alamos to Sandia Labs in Albuquerque, and from Santa Fe all the way to Las Cruces.

TONY: That's the buzz in town. If you ask me, this bullet train idea doesn't look too good for the car business.

DON JOSÉ: Good or not, it's here. And I just found out that the right-of-way for the corridor is going right through my rancho. This has just become the most valuable land in the state.

MARÍA: That's wonderful!

DON JOSÉ: Now I have the money I need to carry out my plan.

MARÍA: What plan?

DON JOSÉ: Your grandfather, que descanse en paz, always said, "Hold on to the land. It's our salvation."

TONY: Hey, who cares about salvation? You scored, right where it counts—making money!

MARÍA: Is that all that matters to you?

TONY: Hey, baby. Your daddy can write his own ticket. This is better than winning a Las Vegas jackpot. Better than the Mega Lottery! This really calls for a Fleetwood 60 Special!

DON JOSÉ: Not now, Tony. (*He turns to María.*) I wanted to be the one to tell you the news. I didn't want you to hear about this in Santa Fe.

MARÍA: I understand. And I'm happy! . . . But you look worried.

DON JOSÉ: No, not worried. But I have to be careful. A lot of people wanted . . . (*They are interrupted by a loud knock at the door.*) Ramón . . . I hope.

Don José goes to the door. Ramón, the computer man, enters. He is a handsome young man of twenty-five. He rolls in a computer on a small dolly.

RAMÓN: Buenas noches, Don José.

DON JOSÉ: Ramón. Entra, entra.

RAMÓN: Sorry I'm late.

TONY: What the hell—

MARÍA: Ramón!

RAMÓN: María! I didn't know you were home.

MARÍA: I've only been here a week.

RAMÓN: And you didn't call?

DON JOSÉ: She's been too busy buying a car.

RAMÓN: I see.

MARÍA: Can I help?

TONY: Watch out, it might bite.

RAMÓN: Speaking of bites, how's the car business, Tony?

TONY: We have the best in town. Remember that when you think of getting rid of that junk heap you drive.

DON JOSÉ: (helping with the computer) Get her up here. Careful, careful. Ah, what a beauty!

TONY: I see you're still selling video games.

RAMÓN: Not video games. Computers. You know, information systems.

DON JOSÉ: And he who controls information, controls power.

RAMÓN: There you are, Don José. Turn it on!

DON JOSÉ: The program disk?

RAMÓN: Right here.

DON JOSÉ: Ah, this is what I need.

RAMÓN: (turning to Maria) So how are things?

MARÍA: Fine. I finished my degree.

RAMÓN: Congratulations. The last time we talked you said you might go to Europe.

MARÍA: Someday. I want to study more. And you?

RAMÓN: I keep busy. The computer business is booming. I'm expanding every day.

MARÍA: I remember we agreed that computers and music were compatible.

TONY: How cute.

RAMÓN: This one does everything but play the piano.

DON JOSÉ: Don't mention music—he's liable to take you dancing.

TONY: María's the only dance partner I need.

DON JOSÉ: Look at that, it works like a charm. It's already asking me what I want to do.

TONY: What do you know? It works!

MARÍA: It's the fanciest computer I've ever seen.

DON JOSÉ: This is not just any computer, this is the latest Japanese model.

RAMÓN: State-of-the-art!

DON JOSÉ: Yes sir, state-of-the-art.

RAMÓN: Hot off the boat from Japan.

DON JOSÉ: But those boats won't be sailing for much longer. As soon as I build my factory, we'll be making these computers right here on the ranch!

MARÍA: Factory? Here?

DON JOSÉ: That's the plan. To build the biggest and best computer plant in the Southwest! Right here! El Patrón Monolithic Systems! It's going to revolutionize this state!

TONY: Are you serious?

MARÍA: So that's it! It wasn't just for the sheep.

DON JOSÉ: That's only the first step. We're going to build computers. Better than Intel!

RAMÓN: The El Patrón A.T.M. 1000! ¡A toda maquina!

DON JOSÉ: I want to train my workers here! I want my plant to become a model factory! This state is ready for it, and we're right in the middle of the whole chingadera!

MARÍA: Daddy!

DON JOSÉ: Excuse my language, but I get excited when I think of what can be done here. Don't you see the possibilities?

MARÍA: Yes, yes I do. I can't believe you learned to run this thing! I'm impressed.

DON JOSÉ: Nothing to it. It was harder learning to speak English when I was a kid.

RAMÓN: He's a whiz. He was computer literate in a few weeks.

TONY: Computer literate? Don't make me laugh.

RAMÓN: You need brains to run this machine, Tony.

TONY: Be careful, Ramón.

RAMÓN: Sorry, Tony, but you wouldn't understand Don José's plan—you're only interested in selling Cadillacs and making money.

TONY: So, I make a good living. I like to deal with people who can afford nothing but the best—nothing wrong with that. This whole thing sounds like a pipe dream.

DON JOSÉ: A dream that can become a reality. I will build the factory, train my workers, and help some become engineers.

MARÍA: We need Chicano engineers and technicians.

RAMÓN: Yeah, if Los Alamos won't do it, we'll have to do it ourselves.

TONY: Train cowboys and Indians to build computers? I don't think so.

DON JOSÉ: Why not? To survive we have to adapt. And in today's world that means build a better computer.

RAMÓN: The El Patrón model is going to make IBM look like second class. What we have here is pure Chicano ingenuity!

TONY: What are you going to build them with, baling wire? (*He laughs.*)

RAMÓN: No, Mr. Repo Man. We build them with the best know-how we have!

MARÍA: I think it's a great idea.

DON JOSÉ: It is. Ramón has a program that can inventory every borrega on the ranch. Instead of the borreguero, we now have the computer.

RAMÓN: A small transistor is implanted in each sheep. The computer records their location, their pulse, whether or not they need food or water. Maybe we can get it to tell the ewe and the ram the precise time for mating.

DON JOSÉ: (*smiling*) Imagine the wear and tear it will save on my prize rams.

TONY: Sounds like you've been watching too many science-fiction movies. You really think you can train people who have been sheepherders all their lives to build computers?

DON JOSÉ: We can start.

MARÍA: Sounds like the future has come to New Mexico.

RAMÓN: Our job is to make it user friendly.

TONY: Hey, I like that: "Tony's Cadillacs, User Friendly"!

DON JOSÉ: Ramón has some very interesting theories.

TONY: I bet.

MARÍA: I want to know more.

DON JOSÉ: We can always use a partner.

MARÍA: We?

DON JOSÉ: Ramón knows what I want to do. If anything happens to me, the project keeps going.

MARÍA: What could happen to you?

DON JOSÉ: Believe it or not, mi'jita, I am mortal.

MARÍA: You're going to live to be a hundred.

DON JOSÉ: I hope. But a man never knows. I want to make sure what I start continues.

TONY: Sounds like you need professionals for the job, not amateurs.

DON JOSÉ: Ramón knows the business.

TONY: So, he's a real Chicano success story. But can he handle it? What if it goes to his head?

RAMÓN: What do you mean, Tony?

TONY: You know the old saying—power corrupts.

DON JOSÉ: Power only corrupts the corruptible.

TONY: The idea's crazy. A Silicon Valley, here. There's only coyotes and sheep. It'll never fly.

DON JOSÉ: Oh, it will. We're going to put a computer in every kitchen and every classroom!

RAMÓN: Not cowchips, microchips!

DON JOSÉ: It means a revolution: work, education, and opportunity for everybody!

MARÍA: It's what you always wanted, Father. Count me in.

DON JOSÉ: As your grandfather used to say, "¡Sí, se puede!"

RAMÓN: Right on!

TONY: I think you all have computer fever.

RAMÓN: Why not? We can make them work for us. Hey, I have one more delivery to make. May I use your phone?

DON JOSÉ: Help yourself. It's on the table.

Ramón goes to the phone.

MARÍA: The phone book!

RAMÓN: No, the phone. I have to call in. Do you mind?

MARÍA: No, of course not . . .

Ramón picks up the phone.

RAMON: That's strange, the line is dead.

DON JOSÉ: What?

RAMÓN: The line is dead.

TONY: Maybe the wind knocked it down.

RAMÓN: But you have lights.

DON JOSÉ: Maybe I should check it out.

MARÍA: Dad, it's just the wind.

RAMÓN: Yeah, no telling where the problem is. Well, I'll just head on back.

MARÍA: So soon?

RAMÓN: I'm done here. How's the computer working, Don José?

DON JOSÉ: Like a '57 Chevy.

MARÍA: Won't you stay and have dinner with us?

TONY: Hey, I thought we were going dancing!

MARÍA: That can wait. I want to hear more about this project.

DON JOSÉ: ¡Eso es!

RAMÓN: I have another delivery to make tonight, but I could be back in an hour, if that's okay?

MARÍA: Perfect. We'll wait.

RAMÓN: By the way, did you call the Sheriff?

DON JOSÉ: The Sheriff? Why?

RAMÓN: He passed me on the way out here.

MARÍA: He didn't come here.

RAMÓN: (*puzzled*) But you're the only ones on this road. If he had turned back I would have seen him.

MARÍA: That's strange.

DON JOSÉ: Maybe not.

RAMÓN: Well, I gotta go. See you later.

MARÍA: We'll wait for dinner.

RAMÓN: Thanks. It's good to see you, María. You're looking great.

MARÍA: You too, Ramón.

RAMÓN: (turning to Don José) Any questions, Don José?

DON JOSÉ: No, todo está bien.

RAMÓN: Bueno, may your monitor glow brightly.

DON JOSÉ: May the force be with you. Keep your floppy disk dry.

MARÍA: I'll see you out.

RAMÓN: My pleasure, señorita.

TONY: I'll go with you.

RAMÓN: Tony, three's a crowd.

TONY: I know, but I have to protect my business interest.

MARÍA: What do you mean?

TONY: I wanna look at that wreck Ramón is driving. Maybe I can do something for him.

RAMÓN: Always looking for a sale, huh?

TONY: Business is business.

RAMÓN: Buenas noches, Don José.

DON JOSÉ: ¡Buenas noches! Drive carefully. The Sheriff may be on the road.

They go out. Don José looks around suspiciously. He goes to the fireplace, takes the disk from his pocket and stuffs it into the toy lamb on the mantel. He is interrupted by Doña Sofía and Diego.

DOÑA SOFÍA: Diego, ¡Escúchame! ¡Ay, hijito!

DIEGO: No more lecture, jefa! I want my lana.

DOÑA SOFÍA: Don José, please don't listen to him. He's been working too hard.

DON JOSÉ: Uh-huh. Working at a six-pack.

DIEGO: No, taking care of your pinche borregas!

DON JOSÉ: An obvious case of sheep stress syndrome.

DOÑA SOFÍA: Maybe he had one drink . . . no más uno.

DON JOSÉ: Un barril—

DIEGO: I ain't drunk!

DON JOSÉ: Okay, you're not drunk. ¿Qué quieres, Diego?

DIEGO: ¡Mi dinero! That's what I want!

DOÑA SOFÍA: Diego, por el amor de Dios—

DON JOSÉ: ¿Dinero? It's not payday!

DIEGO: Don't act dumb, patrón. I want my share!

DON JOSÉ: Here, sit here.

DIEGO: I don't want to sit! I want my share of the money! Then I quit!

DON JOSÉ: What money? Quit? Not take care of the flock?

DIEGO: To hell with your flock!

DOÑA SOFÍA: Don José, he doesn't mean that. When he drinks, the devil makes him say things.

DON JOSÉ: I understand. But I'm disappointed. A good shepherd never leaves his flock. Abel didn't leave his sheep—

DIEGO: Yeah, and he got killed!

DOÑA SOFÍA: Diego, por favor.

DON JOSÉ: Yes, Cain killed Abel.

DIEGO: Yeah, Cain was smart. He got what he wanted. Now I want my part—

DON JOSÉ: Part of my sheep?

DIEGO: No! Screw your sheep! I want my part of the will!

DOÑA SOFÍA: Diego!

DON JOSÉ: What do you know about the will, Diego?

DIEGO: I know you have one.

DON JOSÉ: So, I see . . . I see your mamacita is watching out for you.

DOÑA SOFÍA: Patrón, discúlpeme. It was an accident.

DON JOSÉ: Don't apologize, Doña Sofía. Diego, that will won't be changed. You'll get your share—when I die.

DIEGO: Sí, when you die. You may be the patrón, Don José, but la muerte don't give a damn about that.

Diego advances toward Don José but is interrupted by María coming in the front door.

DON JOSÉ: María. Just in time.

MARÍA: It's cold out there.

DON JOSÉ: Where's Tony?

MARÍA: He said he was going to check the telephone line. What's going on?

DOÑA SOFÍA: Señorita. It's nothing. Diego's not feeling well. He works too hard.

Don José makes a sign, tipping a bottle.

MARÍA: Oh, I see. Saturday night, huh?

DIEGO: (turns meek) Ah, María, I just had a couple of beers. I ain't drunk.

DON JOSÉ: No, he ain't drunk. Just abusive. Do me a favor, get some coffee in him.

MARÍA: Come on, Diego, let's drink some hot coffee and talk. Okay?

DIEGO: Don't forget, Don José—I get what's mine.

DON JOSÉ: I won't forget, Diego.

DOÑA SOFÍA: I'll put lots of sugar in it, Diego. Just like you like it.

DIEGO: Okay, jefita.

MARÍA: Sure. Just like old times.

DON JOSÉ: Just like old times.

All exit to the kitchen. Ana enters from the opposite door but sees the Sheriff peering in the living room window. Ana hides in the closet as the Sheriff stealthily enters and goes to the computer. He ejects the disk and inspects it.

SHERIFF: Program disk. There's got to be another.

The Sheriff puts the disk in his pocket and is searching the table when Don José enters.

DON JOSÉ: Sheriff!

SHERIFF: Don José! Sonamagon, you almost gave me a heart attack!

DON JOSÉ: What are you doing here? Who let you in?

SHERIFF: I knocked . . .

DON JOSÉ: We were in the kitchen.

SHERIFF: I thought maybe because of the wind you couldn't hear me.

DON JOSÉ: So you made yourself at home.

SHERIFF: Pues, like your people always say, mi casa es su casa.

DON JOSÉ: I think that rule of hospitality should be "mi casa es mi casa"! But being the good caballeros that we are, we even treat our enemies with courtesy.

SHERIFF: Don't think of me as your enemy, Don José. Think of me as a collector.

DON JOSÉ: I see. All in friendship, huh?

SHERIFF: Sure.

DON JOSÉ: In that case I should offer you a drink.

SHERIFF: You know I don't drink on duty. But it is cold out there. A shot of whiskey, por favor.

DON JOSÉ: So you came to collect . . . some information.

SHERIFF: You're a smart man.

DON JOSÉ: And if I don't have it?

SHERIFF: Let's not play games. Look, some of your old friends are very angry. But we're friends, right? They asked me to talk to you. Man to man. I don't want to see you hurt, Don José. Hell, we've known each other too long. We went to school together. My father knew your father. I'm not the kind of man who wants to see an old friend get hurt. Not if I can help it.

DON JOSÉ: And it can be helped—if I turn the information I'm supposed to have over to you . . .

SHERIFF: Yes.

DON JOSÉ: Instead of the attorney general?

SHERIFF: (grimaces) Please, Don José. Don't mention the attorney general. He's like the others—he just wants to get in the papers so he can run for governor. No, Don José, we got to keep this to ourselves. (*Diego shouts in the kitchen.*) Who's that?

DON JOSÉ: Diego.

SHERIFF: Diego. He was in Santa Fe this afternoon. Drinking. Telling everybody that one of these days he was going to give you a dose of coyote poison.

DON JOSÉ: It's been a bad night for the patrón.

SHERIFF: Diego could be a suspect.

DON JOSÉ: A suspect? To what?

SHERIFF: To your murder, Don José. Those old friends of yours would like to see your hide hanging in the Santa Fe plaza.

DON JOSÉ: That would be quite a sight. I'd find out who my friends really are. They'd come to the rosary. Imagine all the beautiful women crying by the side of my coffin.

SHERIFF: I didn't come to talk about your funeral, Don José. I came to get the evidence.

DON JOSÉ: But what you call "evidence" is my insurance policy. As long as I have it, I'm safe.

SHERIFF: Insurance? Wait a minute. Could it be that Don José is going to practice a little blackmail?

DON JOSÉ: Let's just say I know Santa Fe politics. My father always said, "If you want to live to a ripe old age in New Mexico, never turn your back on a rattlesnake . . . or a politician."

SHERIFF: A wise man, your father. As I remember, he died in Doña Carmela's bed. Shot by her husband.

DON JOSÉ: Don't believe Santa Fe gossip, Sheriff. You know in Santa Fe the mitote is about two things—love and politics.

SHERIFF: And money.

DON JOSÉ: No wonder the women in Santa Fe are lonely.

SHERIFF: God save us from the politicians, Don José.

DON JOSÉ: My father didn't trust sheriffs, either.

SHERIFF: What? . . . Enough jokes. Now— (*María calls for her father.*) Who's that?

DON JOSÉ: María. I don't want her to know you're here.

SHERIFF: You mean, you don't want her to be involved.

DON JOSÉ: She doesn't know anything. I don't want her hurt.

SHERIFF: I can understand that. But she'll be fine if I get what I came for, the foundation file.

DON JOSÉ: You'll get it. But leave, now!

SHERIFF: No, I won't leave—I'll be waiting outside. Get rid of her so we can talk.

DON JOSÉ: Yes, yes—go!

SHERIFF: I'll be watching.

The Sheriff goes out the front door. María enters from the kitchen.

MARÍA: Dad! Come quickly! Diego has a gun!

DON JOSÉ: A gun?

MARÍA: There was a gun! He grabbed it and ran. We've got to find him.

DON JOSÉ: Yes, yes, I'm coming!

María goes out. Don José starts to follow her but stops. He looks at the computer. The CD tray is still open.

DON JOSÉ: The program disk—it's missing. What in the devil did I do with it . . . (*He sits and rummages at the desk. At the same time the lights go off.*) Damn! The lights! (*Don José's outline appears in the glare of the monitor screen. He senses someone in the room.*) Sheriff? Is that you?

There is a gunshot, a flash of fire, a moan as Don José falls to the floor. A woman screams. The shadow of a running figure runs across the monitor screen, footsteps sound, the woman screams again. A moment later the lights come on. María appears at the door. She sees Ana standing over the crumpled body of Don José, holding a pistol in her hand. The Sheriff rushes in. María screams, runs to her father. Doña Sofía runs in from the door to the kitchen. Tony follows her. He stops, slowly removes his gloves.

MARÍA: He's dead! Oh my God, he's dead!

TONY: Dead?

DOÑA SOFÍA: ¡Dios mío! ¡Dios mío!

MARÍA: (*to Ana*) You killed him.

ANA: No. I didn't.

SHERIFF: Don't nobody move!

TONY: Listen!

All pause and turn to the voice that comes from the computer. The screen is flashing wildly. A computerized voice begins to sing.

COMPUTER VOICE: Mary had a little lamb . . . little lamb . . . little lamb. . . . Mary had a little lamb . . . whose fleece was white as snow . . .

END ACT ONE

ACT TWO

The living room. It is dark and somber.

Ana sits with a drink. María paces slowly, then goes to the window and looks out.

MARÍA: Such a dark and lonely place . . .

ANA: Sí, the llano is lonely at night.

MARÍA: This morning I rode out on horseback, as far as the mesa. The sun was coming up. There is nothing more beautiful than morning on the llano. There are autumn colors everywhere. I thought, "How beautiful life is on the rancho, how peaceful." *(María sobs. Ana reaches out.)* And now . . .

ANA: María . . .

MARÍA: I just can't believe he's dead. This morning, at breakfast, he was full of life, giving the men orders about bringing the sheep down from the mountain. And he was singing, the song he sang every day, "Allá en el Rancho Grande."

ANA: He was always singing that silly song. I think the rancherita he was singing about was you. He loved you. He missed you when you were gone.

MARÍA: And I was gone too long. I think now of the time I could have spent with him . . . here.

ANA: This land was his blood. "Soy puro Nuevo Mexicano," he used to say. He could taste the earth . . . taste the rain, the wind . . .

MARÍA: Now he's gone. I feel so empty. The ranch is empty.

ANA: And I . . .

MARÍA: I had a premonition this morning. I saw him walking outside, and I felt a shiver. I felt something was going to happen. For a moment there was a shadow. Now I see only darkness and emptiness.

ANA: You have to give yourself time.

MARÍA: This morning there was meaning and promise—now there's nothing.

ANA: I know how you feel, but you're alive. You'll have to think of the future. We have to find out who did this.

MARÍA: Father would want me to be strong . . .

ANA: Of course he would. He would want you to continue his plans.

MARÍA: Yes, you're right. Ana, I know you didn't—

ANA: Kill him? No, of course not. I loved your father.

MARÍA: But the sheriff—

ANA: The sheriff has his own motives. He wants to settle this in a hurry, so right now I'm his suspect. But I'm not worried.

MARÍA: What was really going on? Why was Father so secretive and worried?

ANA: I can tell you the little I know. It seems that for months a group of men have been taking money, illegally, from the foundation. Your father found a file that showed these entries. It may also have named names.

MARÍA: So they killed him?

ANA: They were desperate. Millions are missing. You see, if the foundation had bought the bullet train land, they would have replaced the money, and no one would have been the wiser. They would have made a fortune, using the foundation money, and they would be clean. It didn't turn out that way. Now they're trying to cover their tracks, but it's too late.

MARÍA: Father knew. Others may know.

ANA: Maybe. Anyway, it goes all the way to the top.

MARÍA: To the governor?

ANA: I don't know. The information is in the file. In fact, it may even point to the murderer.

MARÍA: We have to find it!

ANA: Both the program and the foundation disks are missing. I've looked— they're not here.

MARÍA: Are you sure?

ANA: Yes, someone took them.

The Sheriff and Tony enter from the kitchen. The Sheriff carries Ana's pistol in a plastic bag.

TONY: I brought you some coffee.

MARÍA: Thanks. What happens now?

SHERIFF: As soon as the coroner comes I'm taking Ana in and booking her. Murder one.

ANA: What's my motive, Sheriff? Or do you need a motive?

SHERIFF: I know your motive, Ana, but I don't need it. When I came in and flipped on the lights, you were standing over the body, with this pistol in your hand. I got you where I want you.

TONY: You couldn't get her the last time, Sheriff.

MARÍA: What last time?

TONY: When Ana's husband was killed, five years ago. He was found dead. Shot. A lot of people thought you did it for the insurance money.

ANA: You lie! It was suicide and you know it!

SHERIFF: I still think it was murder, but I couldn't pin it on you. This time the evidence is clear. We saw you right over his body, holding this.

TONY: Her husband had lost everything in a deal with Don José. So there is a motive, Ana, since you ask. Revenge.

ANA: You're crazy! ¡Estás loco!

MARÍA: Revenge? Now?

SHERIFF: Why not? I know Ana. I know what she's capable of.

TONY: Yes, you do, don't you, Sheriff? Isn't it true, Ana, that the Sheriff was in love with you, but you wouldn't have him?

SHERIFF: Shut up, Tony!

ANA: That's ridiculous.

TONY: Sheriff, everybody knows she turned you down. Why so sensitive?

SHERIFF: I said shut up!

MARÍA: And now you're trying to get even . . . is that it?

SHERIFF: I'm not interested in the past. I'm interested in what happened here tonight. Ana shot Don José.

ANA: I didn't kill him.

TONY: I think you're right about that, Sheriff.

MARÍA: Well, I don't believe it.

SHERIFF: What?

MARÍA: I don't believe she shot my father.

SHERIFF: God almighty! The woman was standing over the body when the lights went on, and you can't believe it? You're still in shock. The evidence is all there!

MARÍA: No, that's not true.

SHERIFF: What's missing? You came in here and saw her over the body. The pistol in her hand. Right?

MARÍA: Yes.

SHERIFF: Go on. What did you see?

MARÍA: Blood . . . It was horrible.

SHERIFF: What did you say?

MARÍA: I said, "You killed him."

SHERIFF: There you have it.

MARÍA: Then there was the eerie song from the computer. He was trying to tell me something.

SHERIFF: Nothing to that. I don't know much about these things, but this one has an audio component. It can be set to play at any time.

TONY: Voices from the dead, María?

ANA: José had a reason for everything he did—

TONY: Come on, Ana! Quit putting crazy ideas in her head! You did it! Quit the games!

ANA: I'm not admitting anything. (*She turns to the Sheriff.*) And I'm not afraid of you. I know about you and your little group in Santa Fe. You want to blame me to cover up your tracks.

SHERIFF: You don't know what you're talking about! This time I got you! I'm going to see that justice is done!

ANA: Justice? Don't make me laugh. What you were doing here tonight?

SHERIFF: What? Oh, I was just driving by, doing my rounds. Lucky I decided to stop.

ANA: Lucky? I saw you sneak into the house. I was in the closet. I heard you arguing with José.

MARÍA: In the closet? Why?

ANA: I came to warn José. I went to the bathroom, and when I returned I saw the Sheriff at the window. I know José didn't trust him, so I hid.

SHERIFF: Don't believe a word she says. She murdered him, and now she's making up stories. Just like when she shot her husband.

MARÍA: Why are you here, Sheriff?

SHERIFF: Okay, I'll level with you. I came because your father called me. He knew he was in trouble. When he heard Diego shouting, he asked me to stay and keep an eye on things.

MARÍA: But you made it look as if you had just gotten here.

SHERIFF: I had to, but don't go getting crazy ideas. I was here for a reason. Don José needed help. He had received a threat because of the information he had from the foundation.

ANA: Why would he tell you about the information he had?

SHERIFF: Everybody in Santa Fe knew José had won the right-of-way. That's why he called me. I had just gotten here when we heard a commotion in the kitchen. He asked me to stay outside. He needed protection—

ANA: That's a lie. He didn't ask you for protection. I heard what you said. You were desperate for that information!

SHERIFF: Believe what you want—it's my word against hers. A sheriff with a very good reputation, and a woman who's been at the scene of two murders.

TONY: It's a tie.

MARÍA: When you came in, what did you see?

SHERIFF: I opened the door, flipped on the lights, there was Ana.

ANA: And you. You also have a pistol.

SHERIFF: You're the only suspect, Ana. Know why? Because ballistics is going to show that the bullet came from your gun.

MARÍA: Ana? Did you—

ANA: No, María. My pistol wasn't fired. That's easy to check. Smell it.

MARÍA: Sheriff? She's right. Smelling it will tell us if . . .

ANA: Make my day, Sheriff.

MARÍA: Sheriff? Check her pistol.

SHERIFF: This is evidence. I'm not going to allow any tampering—

MARÍA: Sheriff, I insist!

TONY: Let it go, María.

ANA: Go on, Sheriff, what are you afraid of?

Sheriff angrily removes the pistol from the plastic bag, smells it.

SHERIFF: No powder smell . . . Damn! It's fully loaded.

TONY: It can't be!

ANA: I told you!

SHERIFF: I don't like this.

TONY: Maybe she used another pistol . . . and hid it.

MARÍA: Where? How? There wasn't time.

TONY: All she needed was a few seconds.

MARÍA: Why would she have two pistols? She didn't kill my father, I'm sure. Somebody else did.

TONY: She had the gun, she was standing right over him when he came in. What more do you want?

SHERIFF: I want a gun that's just been fired, that's what. Are there any other guns in the house?

MARÍA: Yes. Tony's!

SHERIFF: Tony?

TONY: I carry a pistol, Sheriff. I have a license.

SHERIFF: I'm going to have to ask you to hand it over, Tony.

TONY: I don't have it on me.

SHERIFF: Where is it?

TONY: When I got here, María took it.

SHERIFF: Took it? Why?

MARÍA: Father never allowed guns in the house. So I put Tony's pistol in the telephone table.

SHERIFF: Mind getting it for me?

MARÍA: Here . . . (*She opens the drawer of the telephone table.*) No, it's gone.

TONY: Gone?

SHERIFF: Let me see . . . nothing here. Are you sure you put it in here?

MARÍA: I'm positive! Dear God, could it have been the pistol used to—

TONY: Somehow Ana got ahold if it.

SHERIFF: Yeah. No telling how long you were in that closet. No telling what you heard. Come on, Ana, I'm gonna take you in. You have a lot of questions to answer.

ANA: I'm not going anywhere with you! (*Doña Sofía enters, holding a pistol.*)

DOÑA SOFÍA: Is this what you're looking for, Señor Sheriff?

SHERIFF: Doña Sofía! Be careful, that thing can go off.

DOÑA SOFÍA: I know it can go off. I know how to use a pistol. (*She advances on the Sheriff.*) I've lived on a ranch all my life.

MARÍA: Doña Sofía, don't—

SHERIFF: I'm warning you, I'm a law officer.

DOÑA SOFÍA: Law officer? You're a crook! Don José knew about you! Maybe you killed the patrón, and now you want to blame my son Diego!

SHERIFF: Diego—

DOÑA SOFÍA: You leave him alone! He didn't do anything! Don José promised him the money.

SHERIFF: What money?

DOÑA SOFÍA: The money in his will. Now that Don José is dead, Diego can get his money. That's all he wanted.

SHERIFF: Put the pistol down, Doña Sofía. We have to talk about this.

DOÑA SOFÍA: No!

MARÍA: Doña Sofía, don't make any trouble for yourself. Give the Sheriff the pistol.

DOÑA SOFÍA: There's already trouble. Your father is dead, but I'm not going to let him hurt Diego.

SHERIFF: I won't hurt him. I just want to talk to him . . . (*pointing*) There's Diego! (*Doña Sofía turns. The Sheriff grabs the pistol.*)

DOÑA SOFÍA: ¡Hijo del diablo!

TONY: Good trick, Sheriff.

SHERIFF: Don't move! Stay where you are. (turns to Tony) Is this yours?

TONY: No. Mine has a fancy pearl handle.

SHERIFF: (to María) Do you recognize this?

MARÍA: No. It's not Tony's.

SHERIFF: So where the hell did this come from?

DOÑA SOFÍA: It's mine. It belonged to my husband. I kept it hidden. . . . Ay, Dios. I wish I had never touched it.

SHERIFF: I have to warn you, anything you say may be used against you.

DOÑA SOFÍA: Used against me? ¡Qué me importa! I will do anything to protect my son.

SHERIFF: Including murder?

DOÑA SOFÍA: All my life I've taken care of Don José. ¿Y qué gané? My son is in trouble. With the money from the will, we could have bought a ranchito, away from the máquina del diablo who is taking away our work.

ANA: What will, Doña Sofía?

SHERIFF: Don José's will?

DOÑA SOFÍA: Sí. Don José put Diego in his will.

MARÍA: How do you know?

DOÑA SOFÍA: I read it, that's how I know!

ANA: You read his will?

DOÑA SOFÍA: Sí. I found it by accident.

TONY: I bet.

DOÑA SOFÍA: I was cleaning his oficina . . . there were all his papers. And his will.

SHERIFF: And Diego is mentioned in the will?

DOÑA SOFÍA: Sí. I told him.

MARÍA: Oh no.

TONY: Sounds like she's handing you a new suspect on a platter.

MARÍA: You don't have to say anything to the Sheriff—

DOÑA SOFÍA: Ay, hijita, I have nothing to hide. I only want to protect my son. I know he drinks, but he works hard. You know he works hard.

MARÍA: (goes to Doña Sofía) Yes.

DOÑA SOFÍA: And he's always wanted his ranchito . . . up in the mountains. . . . Díos mío, this is not the time to think about that. The patrón is dead . . . un momento estamos aquí, y el otro, adiós. Doña Sebastiana viene por todos. Y tu, hijita. You lost your father.

MARÍA: (crying) Sí, así es la vida . . .

ANA: (goes to María) Dear God, it's you we should be worrying about.

SHERIFF: This is a whole new ball game.

TONY: And how?

SHERIFF: (to Doña Sofía) You knew Diego would get some money when Don José died?

DOÑA SOFÍA: Sí.

SHERIFF: Did you kill Don José?

DOÑA SOFÍA: (softly) No.

SHERIFF: Did Diego?

DOÑA SOFÍA: No! I'm telling you, no! He wouldn't kill the patrón.

SHERIFF: He had a motive—

DOÑA SOFÍA: It was my fault. I saw the gun there, I put it in my apron. Maybe it was the devil who told me to take the pistol. Sí, fue el diablo.

MARÍA: Don't blame yourself. I put the gun there.

DOÑA SOFÍA: You? But why?

MARÍA: It was a mistake, a terrible mistake.

SHERIFF: Did you take the pistol into the kitchen?

DOÑA SOFÍA: Yes.

SHERIFF: (to María) I'd like to know exactly what happened in there.

MARÍA: I took Diego in there. He had been drinking.

SHERIFF: Then?

MARÍA: When he saw the pistol he grabbed it and ran out.

SHERIFF: Where was the pistol?

DOÑA SOFÍA: On the table, where I put it.

MARÍA: I ran in here to get Daddy, then back into the kitchen and out the back door. I called Diego, but he was gone. Then I heard a shot . . .

SHERIFF: He grabbed the pistol, came in here, and shot Don José. Open-and-shut case!

TONY: It makes sense.

ANA: If Diego ran out the kitchen door, there wasn't time for him—

TONY: You're making excuses, Ana.

SHERIFF: I agree. He's the prime suspect.

ANA: Something's not right. . . . Doña Sofía, did you take the pistol with the pearl handle?

DOÑA SOFÍA: Sí. That was the gun.

ANA: (to Tony) That was your pistol?

TONY: Yes. Now Diego has it. Like I said, open-and-shut case.

ANA: I don't believe—

TONY: Believe what you want! Diego took my pistol.

SHERIFF: Quit meddling in this, Ana. I'll do the questioning. And Diego has a hell of a lot of questions to answer. You ought to be glad. This might let you off the hook.

ANA: I'm not on a hook, Sheriff!

DOÑA SOFÍA: Yo tengo la culpa, toda la culpa.

MARÍA: Don't say that, Doña Sofía. We'll find out who murdered Father.

DOÑA SOFÍA: It was the devil—

SHERIFF: The devil doesn't kill people, Doña Sofía, guns do. I can't arrest the devil, but I'm going to have to arrest Diego.

DOÑA SOFÍA: Arrest me! I'm to blame. Don't hurt my son.

SHERIFF: You may be an accomplice, Doña Sofía, but right now it's Diego I want.

TONY: He's probably halfway to Juárez by now.

SHERIFF: I don't think so. I'm going to look around. I don't want anybody to leave this house. ¿Comprende?

ANA: We comprende, Sheriff.

The Sheriff goes out the front door.

DOÑA SOFÍA: Ay, Dios, what a terrible thing that has happened. This ranch has always been so peaceful. And now this. These máquinas coming. Look what it has done to Diego. My son, who was never greedy, who was always happy, and now he's accused of murder.

ANA: No se apene, Doña Sofía. Things will work out. A while ago the Sheriff was blaming me for the murder.

DOÑA SOFÍA: You? Why you? You two were friends.

ANA: Yes, we were.

DOÑA SOFÍA: More than friends.

MARÍA: The Sheriff needs a suspect.

DOÑA SOFÍA: Ay, the Sheriff can blame my son, but who blames the Sheriff? Listen. Don't trust him. I have good ears. I heard somebody out there. Like a coyote, sniffing around. It was him, it was the Sheriff!

TONY: She's got a point. I did some snooping around outside. The Sheriff parked his car down the road, where it couldn't be seen. Another thing: I checked the telephone wire. It's been cut.

MARÍA: Are you sure?

TONY: Positive. And there's a clear set of prints out there. Boot prints. The Sheriff wears boots . . .

MARÍA: So does Diego. You don't.

TONY: Nope, these are my dancing shoes.

DOÑA SOFÍA: Don't trust the Sheriff, that's all I can say. The Sheriff used to be a good man, but now he works for those bad politicos in Santa Fe. . . . I think I'll make some coffee. (*She exits.*)

MARÍA: I feel sorry for her. She's always had problems with Diego, but he never threatened Father.

TONY: He did tonight, and it looks like he killed him.

ANA: We don't know. There are too many unanswered questions.

MARÍA: I'm not going to rest till I find out who murdered Father.

ANA: If we could only find the disk with the information.

MARÍA: The disk . . . the answer has to be on the disk. The song?

ANA: "Mary had a little lamb . . ." What does it mean?

MARÍA: That's what he used to sing to me. Except he would say, "María had a little lamb." (She goes to the fireplace and picks up the lamb.) He gave it to me. It was my favorite toy, my security blanket. It could have something to do with . . . (removes the disk from the lamb) What's this?

TONY: What?

MARÍA: A disk?

ANA: (taking the disk) That's it! The foundation file!

MARÍA: Are you sure?

ANA: Yes. He showed it to me.

MARÍA: Can we play it?

ANA: We need the program disk.

MARÍA: Ramón!

ANA: Call him!

TONY: You can't. The phone's dead, remember?

MARÍA: I'm sure some of the answers are on it. Why would he hide it?

ANA: He knew there was going to be trouble. The answers are in here!

TONY: I can take it into town, get somebody I trust to play it. I could be back in an hour. (He reaches for the disk.)

ANA: I won't let it out of my sight.

TONY: Would you rather the Sheriff got hold of it?

MARÍA: I'll keep it. Ramón can help.

TONY: Hey, I'm just trying to help. I got an attorney in town who can do anything. I don't blame you for being cautious, but you're getting carried away, aren't you?

MARÍA: You think so?

TONY: Diego, the Sheriff, or . . . you don't have to look any further, but I'm not getting mixed up in this. Right now all I want is some fresh coffee. (*He goes out.*)

ANA: I bet he's a Scorpio.

MARÍA: What do you mean?

ANA: Capable of murder if you get on his bad side.

MARÍA: And you?

ANA: I'm a Scorpio . . . and I know I'm capable of murder. I admit it, I have to get what I want.

MARÍA: I don't believe you.

ANA: You're right—I could never hurt José. I've always loved your father, but our lives took different paths. The past few years, seeing him, they were the best years of my life. Oh, he could get on my nerves, with that bossy way of his. But inside he was a kind, considerate man.

MARÍA: He loved you.

ANA: Yes. We were two of a kind. (*There is a pause, a moment of understanding.*) And you, what's with you and Tony?

MARÍA: Nothing. I've been dating him, that's all.

ANA: He's gotten serious. Now a lot of people are going to get serious about you.

MARÍA: Yes . . . that's probably true. I haven't had time to think—I feel confused.

ANA: It's the shock. . . . Your father . . . and you could be in danger.

MARÍA: Why? You mean there may be more than one person involved?

ANA: Yes.

MARÍA: So I can't trust anyone.

They are interrupted by the Sheriff entering, leading Diego.

SHERIFF: You can breathe easy, Ana. I got my man. He confessed.

MARÍA: Diego?

SHERIFF: Found him hiding in the barn. Didn't even put up a fight. Came right out and said he killed Don José.

MARÍA: He couldn't have. Diego, tell me what happened?

DIEGO: I don't remember . . .

SHERIFF: Tell 'em what you told me.

DIEGO: The Sheriff said Don José is dead.

MARÍA: Yes.

DIEGO: That was the shot I heard. Chingao, I knew it was a bad thing when I heard it.

MARÍA: Tell us what happened.

DIEGO: I ran out of the kitchen, then I heard a shot. I got scared, so I hid in the barn.

SHERIFF: There you have it.

ANA: Did you kill Don José?

DIEGO: No—I don't remember. I had a pistol . . .

SHERIFF: Don't confuse him! A few minutes ago he told me he did it. That's good enough for me.

ANA: You want to wrap up things in a hurry, don't you, Sheriff? Any suspect will do.

SHERIFF: You're not out of this yet, Ana. How do I know you two aren't in this together? Diego's got problems, but you're not free yet.

MARÍA: Diego, where's the pistol you took from the kitchen?

Diego shrugs, then reaches in his jacket pocket, takes out the pistol and points it at the Sheriff.

DIEGO: Stay back, Sheriff!

SHERIFF: Damn! I forgot!

MARÍA: That's it! That's Tony's gun!

SHERIFF: Stand back, you two. Come on, Diego, hand it over.

DIEGO: No! Don't move! I'm getting out of here!

SHERIFF: You shot Don José, didn't you!

DIEGO: No! No!

SHERIFF: You're in a lot of trouble, boy. This only makes it worse. Now give me the gun.

DIEGO: No! I'll shoot!

MARÍA: No, Diego! Don't make things worse! Give the Sheriff the gun! Please!

ANA: Listen to her, Diego.

DIEGO: It wasn't me, María. I didn't kill the patrón. I was drinking, I got crazy, I heard the shot, but I didn't kill him. I'm not going to prison. Don't move, Sheriff!

Tony enters from the kitchen.

TONY: You found Diego, huh?

Diego turns and, while he is distracted, the Sheriff grabs the gun from him.

SHERIFF: Hold it!

TONY: What the hell?

SHERIFF: Thanks, Tony. I've got him.

TONY: That's my pistol.

SHERIFF: You sure?

TONY: Yes, I'm sure. The pearl handle . . .

MARÍA: Yes. It's the one I put in the drawer.

SHERIFF: This is the one Doña Sofía took into the kitchen. Diego picked it up, came around, and shot Don José. I'm taking you in on a homicide charge, Diego. Anything you say may be used against you . . .

The Sheriff reaches for his handcuffs. As he begins to draw them out, a floppy disk falls from his pocket.

MARÍA: (picking up the disk) What's this?

SHERIFF: Here, give me that! (to Diego) You stay put! Don't move!

ANA: The program disk.

MARÍA: Are you sure?

ANA: Positive! It's marked—

SHERIFF: I said give it to me.

ANA: How did you get it, Sheriff?

SHERIFF: Evidence, that's how. Now hand it over!

MARÍA: Father wouldn't have given it to you.

ANA: No, he wouldn't. With this we can play the foundation disk!

MARÍA: Can you?

ANA: I think so. (*She goes to the computer.*)

SHERIFF: Hold it! You can't do that!

MARÍA: Why?

SHERIFF: You're tampering with evidence—

MARÍA: But it could reveal the murderer.

TONY: Listen to the Sheriff.

SHERIFF: That's right, listen to me. Things are getting out of hand. I can't let you play around with evidence. Hand it over.

MARÍA: Don't give it to him, Ana! We don't trust you, Sheriff. If you want it, you're going to have to arrest us all!

TONY: Hey, I don't want any part of this. Give him the damn thing.

SHERIFF: You don't trust me? I'm the Sheriff. The law in this county. Your father trusted me.

MARÍA: And he's dead.

SHERIFF: You're not suggesting that I—

ANA: Listen!

VOICE OF DON JOSÉ, on the computer

María, listen carefully. I have recorded everything you need to know on this disk. If anything happens to me, go ahead with my plans. We must use this opportunity to provide work and education for our people. There are men in this state who only want to exploit the people. They must be stopped. You must not trust—

The Sheriff flips off the computer.

SHERIFF: That's enough!

MARÍA: Sheriff!

SHERIFF: This has gone far enough.

DIEGO: Don't hurt her!

SHERIFF: You stay where you are!

ANA: What are you afraid of, Sheriff? That we will find out it was you who killed José?

SHERIFF: You're crazy! I have enough evidence on you and Diego.

MARÍA: We have a bit of evidence on you, Sheriff.

SHERIFF: Evidence?

MARÍA: Why did you hide your car when you came tonight?

SHERIFF: Hide my car? I told you, Don José suspected something. He told me not to let anybody see me.

MARÍA: Did he tell you to cut the telephone line?

SHERIFF: I didn't cut the wire!

MARÍA: There are boot prints there. Tony found them. You're wearing boots.

SHERIFF: Tony? You believe Tony?

MARÍA: Why not?

SHERIFF: Your father didn't trust him.

TONY: Of course he trusted me. Why wouldn't he?

SHERIFF: Because of the past . . . a past he thought you couldn't forget.

MARÍA: What about the past?

TONY: Don't listen to him, María, he's going to dream up wild stories. I had nothing against your father.

SHERIFF: She doesn't have to believe me. You tell her, Ana, about Tony's dad.

MARÍA: What?

ANA: Yes, you have reason to hate Don José, because of your father—

TONY: Hey, you know the Sheriff, he wants to involve everyone. Don't you see what he's doing? He needs one of us as a suspect to save his neck! What are you saying, Sheriff, all of us pulled the trigger? We all killed Don José? Ana, Diego, me? It makes me laugh.

MARÍA: Tell me what happened.

ANA: Years ago, Tony's dad and Don José were partners in a business deal. For whatever reasons, the deal went sour. Tony's dad lost everything. He was sued by his creditors, and he died within a year. Some people say he put a curse on Don José.

MARÍA: Are you saying Tony has wanted revenge . . . all these years?

TONY: I told you it was a crazy story. Look, if I had wanted revenge I would have taken it years ago. Why tonight?

ANA: No, it doesn't make sense . . . unless . . .

MARÍA: Unless you were hired by the group that wants the information.

SHERIFF: It's possible, isn't it, Tony?

TONY: (laughs) You're making quite a story out of this. But what kind of evidence do you have?

MARÍA: There's only one way to find out. Switch the computer back on. Let's see what Father found in this file.

ANA: He said it would name names.

SHERIFF: Now I'm curious. Why not? Let's see whose names come up.

The Sheriff turns to the computer. Tony grabs the pistol in the Sheriff's holster. The Sheriff whirls, still holding the pearl-handled pistol. For a moment they face each other. Tony laughs.

TONY: There are no bullets in that pistol, Sheriff.

The Sheriff fires. There is a click.

SHERIFF: Damn! So you're the one!

TONY: Don't you think that's a good touch, Sheriff, to bring an empty pistol?

MARÍA: Tony. You . . .

TONY: Don José caused my father's death, and I've never forgotten. I vowed revenge!

MARÍA: You planned it—

ANA: He had a second pistol—

SHERIFF: And a pair of boots he put on to cut the wire.

ANA: You almost had a perfect alibi.

TONY: (*takes the disk*) You've got it all figured out, haven't you? Now I'll take this . . . and the score is even.

MARÍA: Why, Tony? Why?

TONY: I vowed at my father's deathbed to kill Don José. Now it's done.

SHERIFF: But it wasn't just for revenge, was it, Tony? Your name is on that disk, isn't it? You're part of the group that stole the foundation money.

TONY: Part of the group? That shows how little you know. I am the brains of the group. Taking the money from the foundation was my idea. A brilliant idea, until today, when the decision was made to use Don José's land. We lost everything. And to top it off, he found the file.

MARÍA: You'll never get away with this.

DIEGO: You killed the patrón!

Diego lunges forward. Tony hits him with the pistol. Diego falls.

TONY: No heroics, okay? I'm going to get out of here, and anybody who gets in the way gets shot!

ANA: What are you going to do? Murder all of us?

SHERIFF: Tony, you could stop now, take your chances with the law. Don't make it worse on yourself.

TONY: Worse? No, it's going to be beautiful. I have plenty of money to get out of the country. Enough to live like a king in Mexico. Let the others answer to the D.A.—I'll be gone. (*Tony grabs María.*) And I'm taking you with me! In case anybody tries to stop me.

MARÍA: (*struggles*) No! Let me go!

ANA: María!

SHERIFF: Don't do it, Tony!

MARÍA: (*struggling*) No! No!

Tony forces María to the door. As he opens it, Ramón rushes in and grabs Tony. The gun goes off. The Sheriff helps Ramón subdue Tony. The Sheriff takes the gun.

SHERIFF: Hold it!

MARÍA: Ramón!

RAMÓN: What the hell's going on here? Why the gun?

MARÍA: He murdered my father.

RAMÓN: What? Tony?

MARÍA: Yes, he killed him. He was trying to get away.

SHERIFF: Now he's going to jail.

RAMÓN: I knew he was a big talker, but murder?

SHERIFF: Yes, murder. And he gave himself away. You're smart, Tony, but not smart enough.

MARÍA: Diego, are you okay?

DIEGO: Yeah, I'm okay, it's just a scratch.

SHERIFF: I'm sorry about your father, María. But we got his murderer. I'm taking him in. Come on, Tony, let's go. Remember, anything you say can and will be used against you . . .

The Sheriff and Tony exit. Doña Sofía enters.

DOÑA SOFÍA: Dios mío, ¿qué pasó? Diego, you're bleeding.

DIEGO: It's nothing, jefa.

MARÍA: He's all right, Doña Sofía. He needs a bandage.

DOÑA SOFÍA: Ven, ven . . . I'll take care of that.

DIEGO: I'm okay, jefa. I could have gotten that cabrón.

Doña Sofía and Diego exit.

RAMÓN: Somebody tell me what happened.

MARÍA: Father had information that involved Tony in the foundation robbery.

RAMÓN: And he killed him?

ANA: Apparently the file names the group who took the money.

MARÍA: Tony was the head of the group.

RAMÓN: And Don José found out about it. . . . . María, I'm so sorry about Don José. How can I help?

MARÍA: You have already. If you hadn't gotten here when you did, I hate to think of what he would have done.

RAMÓN: Don José was a great man. . . . I can't believe he's dead. What can I say? I'm sorry.

MARÍA: Thank you. Daddy wasn't perfect, but he did want to help the people.

ANA: He was an honorable man . . . a good man.

RAMÓN: Yes, he was. María, can I get you anything?

MARÍA: Yes, something to drink.

RAMÓN: Water?

ANA: I think at a time like this, José would have said a brandy.

RAMÓN: Brandy? Sure.

Ramón goes to the bar.

MARÍA: I have so much to think about. Father would have wanted me to continue with his plans.

RAMÓN: You're right.

MARÍA: What was your arrangement with Dad?

RAMÓN: I was helping him on the computer end, you know, doing research, finding the best experts to bring on board.

MARÍA: Do you want to continue?

RAMÓN: Of course. This is an important project. But it's up to you. You're in charge now.

MARÍA: I would appreciate your help.

ANA: Then let's toast the success of Don José's project.

RAMÓN: And la patrona.

END

Matachines

CHARACTERS

CRISTINA
LORENZO, Cristina's boyfriend
DON PATRICIO BERNAL, Cristina's father
TERESA, Cristina's younger sister
RITA, Cristina's older sister
ANDRES
PRIEST
JUAN, Lorenzo's brother
ZONZO
DON CORNELIO AND DOÑA FRANCISCA, los Abuelos
OTHER DANCERS AND MÚSICOS
BRUJA, the witch
SHERIFF

ACT ONE

Scene One

It is a hot afternoon in late July in the small New Mexico town of Plaza Vieja.

The scene opens in the backyard patio of Don Patricio Bernal's home. An adobe wall runs along the background; to the right, a door leads into the house; to the left, a large gate faces the street. Backstage is a tall, stately cottonwood, its leaves covered with chalky dust. The patio includes a table, benches, tomato plants, and flower beds; all bear the trace of the white dust.

The dancers who will play roles in the Matachines dance gather each afternoon in the patio to practice the dance. The Matachines dance, an old tradition, is held in the village of Plaza Vieja each August 10 for the feast of San Lorenzo.

Cristina enters, carrying a box with flowers and a sword. She wipes the dust off the table.

CRISTINA: ¡Polvo maldito!

She is dressed in summer wear. She holds the sword and dances, a light airy dance. Lorenzo appears at the gate, pauses, then whistles.

CRISTINA: Lorenzo!

LORENZO: Hey, I like that. (*He goes to her and they kiss, softly.*) Mmm, you feel good.

CRISTINA: That's far enough.

LORENZO: I can't help it—I want you. What's this?

CRISTINA: Dad's sword . . . You've been drinking. (*She places the sword on the table.*)

LORENZO: Just a beer.

CRISTINA: Uh-huh. One?

LORENZO: Honest.

They kiss again.

LORENZO: Let's make love!

CRISTINA: Not until we're married—

LORENZO: So, let's get married. We can do it now.

CRISTINA: You got the job!

LORENZO: Simón, cara limón.

CRISTINA: I knew you would. When do you start? (*She embraces him.*)

LORENZO: Tonight. They need a night watchman.

CRISTINA: But if you're working, you can't take classes.

LORENZO: Forget the university. I got the job, that's what counts! Let's set the date.

CRISTINA: Right away?

LORENZO: It's what we want, isn't it?

CRISTINA: Yes, but I thought we'd get our degrees first.

LORENZO: That was yesterday. Look, I've been without a jale all summer. I can't buy anything, or take you out.

She takes the box of flowers to a bench.

CRISTINA: That doesn't matter.

LORENZO: It matters to me! And—

CRISTINA: What?

LORENZO: I know about the other guys.

CRISTINA: What guys?

LORENZO: Juan saw you at the drive-in.

CRISTINA: Lore! Those are guys from high school! They're just friends.

LORENZO: What about Andres?

CRISTINA: I don't pay attention to Andres!

LORENZO: Yeah, but he sure watches you.

CRISTINA: Are you jealous?

LORENZO: He's always hanging around.

CRISTINA: Oh, my jealous San Lorenzo. It doesn't fit you.

LORENZO: I'm not a santo! I'm a man. And I don't like the way he looks at you!

CRISTINA: He likes Rita, not me.

LORENZO: Let's get married right away. I can start at the U next year. Right now I need the money.

CRISTINA: Next year? I enrolled yesterday.

LORENZO: You what?

CRISTINA: I called and they signed me up—

LORENZO: Why?

CRISTINA: I need something to do, Lore. The summer's been boring.

LORENZO: (surprised) Boring?

CRISTINA: You know what I mean. I want to get an education while I can. I don't want to depend on Father forever.

LORENZO: You don't have to—I got a job. We can get married, start a family.

CRISTINA: Settle down and have kids? I don't know.

LORENZO: What do you mean, you don't know? We planned.

CRISTINA: Things change . . . I've changed.

LORENZO: What are you talking about?

CRISTINA: I've had the time to think about my future.

LORENZO: Your future's with me.

CRISTINA: I want an education. Maybe go into teaching.

LORENZO: So where do I fit in?

CRISTINA: I love you, Lore, but I don't want to rush into marriage.

LORENZO: I want to take care of you.

CRISTINA: You men are all alike.

LORENZO: What do you mean?

CRISTINA: Papá says he'll take care of me, you want to take care of me . . . I want to take care of myself!

LORENZO: What's wrong with a man taking care of the woman he loves?

CRISTINA: Give me time, Lorenzo—there's so much to learn. I want to see the world.

LORENZO: See the world? What's gotten into you, Cristina? What's the matter with Plaza Vieja? At least here it's safe—

CRISTINA: Safe, secure, unchanging, and boring.

LORENZO: You never complained before.

CRISTINA: I'm not complaining. I . . . Let's change the subject. (*She hands him the sword.*) Teresa's going to decorate it with flowers.

LORENZO: What for?

CRISTINA: For you.

LORENZO: For me? . . . A Monarca with a sword. Hey, I like it. I'll cut off the Toro's you-know-what.

She takes back the sword and places it on the table.

CRISTINA: It's not for that! Some people say the palma the Monarca holds used to be the war club of Moctezuma.

LORENZO: The Aztec king?

CRISTINA: Yes. Anyway, I want us to be the best Monarca and Malinche ever!

LORENZO: I'll dance circles around you, woman! (*He takes her in his arms.*)

CRISTINA: Promise?

LORENZO: I promise . . .

They are about to kiss when they are interrupted by Don Patricio, Rita, and Teresa. Don Patricio carries folding chairs. Teresa carries a pitcher and glasses, which she places on the table. Rita tosses a pack of cigarettes on the table.

DON PATRICIO: Buenas tardes, Lorenzo.

LORENZO: Buenas tardes, Don Patricio.

TERESA: Hi, Lore.

Rita kisses Lorenzo.

RITA: How's my favorite Monarca?

LORENZO: Great. I got a—

Teresa sits at the table and prepares to decorate the sword.

DON PATRICIO: Where are the others?

LORENZO: They're at the—ah, pool hall.

DON PATRICIO: Que muchachos, always late. We need to practice. Everything must be just right for the dance.

RITA: What for? People don't keep their promises.

DON PATRICIO: Some people don't, but I do. I believe in San Lorenzo . . . I can talk to him. (*He looks at the tree.*) Just like I talk to your mother. . . . Ah, in the old days it was an honor to dance the Matachines. People came from everywhere. Now everybody is too busy.

LORENZO: Too many video games.

TERESA: Cruising and drinking.

RITA: Hey, some of us work. But if I had a Monarca like Lore I'd dance all night.

CRISTINA: Watch it, Rita, your claws are showing.

Andres enters at the gate. He carries a sorry-looking rag of a Toro costume.

LORENZO: Well, speak of the devil.

Andres ignores him. He has eyes only for Cristina.

ANDRES: Buenas tardes, Don Patricio.

DON PATRICIO: Buenas tardes, Andres.

ANDRES: Hi, Cristina. You're looking good.

CRISTINA: Hi, Andres. We were just talking about the promesas we make to San Lorenzo.

ANDRES: For me, action speaks louder than promises. (*He kisses her cheek; Lorenzo draws her away.*)

RITA: I made a promesa last year . . . and I went to mass every single day. But he hasn't delivered.

TERESA: What did you ask for?

RITA: (*going to Lorenzo*) A handsome young man to love.

ANDRES: The santo isn't into your kind of love, Rita.

DON PATRICIO: Paciencia, mi'ja. San Lorenzo does answer our prayers. When you mother died I prayed to him to help me raise my daughters. I did pretty good, que no?

LORENZO: You did great, Don Patricio.

ANDRES: Hey, what's this? (*He reaches for the sword; Teresa pulls it back.*)

TERESA: Not for you!

LORENZO: It's for the Monarca.

ANDRES: What's the plan? Kill the Toro?

Lorenzo takes the Toro costume from Andres.

LORENZO: Hey, you finally got the Toro costume?

RITA: A cowhide? It's not your style, Andres.

ANDRES: Damn right, it's not.

LORENZO: It even smells bad.

ANDRES: I'll get me a new one—

DON PATRICIO: We don't need a new one.

LORENZO: (*flexing his muscles*) The Toro isn't as fancy as the Monarca. You watch, Don Patricio, Cristina and me are going to be the best Monarca and Malinche ever. Aren't we, baby?

CRISTINA: Lorenzo feels good because he got the job.

DON PATRICIO: Ah, qué bueno.

ANDRES: What job?

LORENZO: Night watchman at the plant. Minimum wage, but it's a job. I even wear a uniform.

RITA: I bet you look handsome in a uniform . . . (*She slides her hand along his back.*)

DON PATRICIO: There's so little work in Plaza Vieja. I don't like that damn factory on the hill. A lot of people are getting sick from the chemicals in the air. It gave me emphysema. But what can we do? We need jobs so our young men can stay here.

ANDRES: Minimum wage. What a joke.

LORENZO: It's a jale, ese!

DON PATRICIO: (*sneezes*) Polvo maldito. It kills everything. Even my tomatoes. When I was young the valley was green with vineyards.

RITA: I bet the abuelos made a lot of fine wine—

DON PATRICIO: Sure. The old Spanish friars brought the first vines to Plaza Vieja. My grandfather's wine was so good it went straight to the archbishop in Santa Fe.

TERESA: The dust is killing mother's tree.

DON PATRICIO: Que descanse en paz. She would not like the change that's come to Plaza Vieja.

RITA: We can't live in the past, Papá.

DON PATRICIO: What's wrong with the past? At least we had a little respeto. Kids obeyed their elders. Now you tell a mocosito what to do and he sues you.

LORENZO: Huh, huh. (takes Cristina's hand) Cristina and I have something to tell you. We want your permission to get married.

DON PATRICIO: I thought you two had big plans to attend the university.

CRISTINA: He means permission for later on . . .

DON PATRICIO: Of course you have my permission.

ANDRES: Aren't you moving kind of fast?

LORENZO: Why not? I'm a working man, ese, not hanging out at the pool hall like you.

ANDRES: Hey, if I knew a job would get me Cristina I'd hold down ten.

TERESA: He likes you, Cris.

DON PATRICIO: Calla, muchacha. Why don't you go make ice tea?

ANDRES: (to Cristina) Are you sure he's the right man?

LORENZO: Funny, Andres, real funny.

TERESA: If you get married will you ever go to college?

DON PATRICIO: She doesn't need college. A girl should be settled down.

CRISTINA: I'm not a girl anymore, I'm a woman—

RITA: Our hijita? A woman?

CRISTINA: Yes. And I want to have a career.

RITA: Is that what you want? A career?

CRISTINA: I want to be able to take care of myself.

TERESA: What do *you* want, Rita?

RITA: (*looks at Lorenzo*) Some romance, real romance. A nice-looking guy to sweep me off my feet. I'm tired of the pendejos who come into the grocery store. Love, that's the medicine I need.

DON PATRICIO: (*hugs her*) We do love you, hija.

TERESA: I think Rita means Lore.

DON PATRICIO: She loves Lorenzo like a brother. Now stop your tonterias— (*He coughs.*)

CRISTINA: You need to see your doctor. (*gets him a glass of water*)

DON PATRICIO: Gracias, mi'jita. You see, Lorenzo, if she marries you, I'm going to lose the daughter who takes care of me.

LORENZO: You won't lose her—you'll gain a son.

ANDRES: Not a good bargain . . .

DON PATRICIO: Yes, and grandchildren. Ya era tiempo. (*He puts his arm around Lorenzo's shoulder.*) You see, San Lorenzo does answer our prayers.

RITA: He didn't answer mine.

ANDRES: Nor mine.

CRISTINA: (*to Rita*) You can make a new promesa.

TERESA: Yeah, maybe San Lorenzo didn't like the deal you made him the last time.

DON PATRICIO: A que muchacha. Promesas to San Lorenzo aren't *deals*. If you pray to him he will answer.

ANDRES: Maybe you need to try something new.

RITA: Like what?

LORENZO: (*to Andres*) Like magic?

ANDRES: Why not?

DON PATRICIO: No magic. Pray to San Lorenzo. . . . Vamos a comer. I want to give you some consejos. Pero tengo mucho hambre.

They laugh and go into the house. Andres and Rita remain.

ANDRES: Damn him! I hate his guts!

RITA: Why, because he has Cristina?

ANDRES: Yes!

RITA: You love her and I love Lorenzo, and neither of us can have what we want.

ANDRES: Yes, we can.

RITA: How?

ANDRES: I've been talking to my tía.

RITA: About?

ANDRES: About this fire burning in me. God, I've wanted Cristina as long as I can remember. All through high school all I could do was watch her. And she didn't even know I existed.

RITA: Why does it hurt so much to want someone? (*She goes to the table and takes a cigarette.*)

ANDRES: I gave her a ride home once. After a baseball game. It was raining. When I dropped her off she kissed me . . . (*He rubs his cheek.*) I can still feel her lips . . .

RITA: But she chose Lore.

Andres picks up the Toro costume and slams it on the ground.

ANDRES: He gets to be the Monarca, wear fine ribbons, dance with Cristina, and I get the two-bit part of the Toro, dressed in a smelly cowhide.

Rita laughs.

ANDRES: Don't laugh!

RITA: You're angry.

ANDRES: Damn right, I am!

RITA: There's nothing you can do.

ANDRES: Yes, there is!

RITA: What?

ANDRES: How bad do you want Lore?

RITA: When I saw him dancing, I knew I wanted him. I began to dream about him, and now—it's like you said, a fire burning in me.

ANDRES: Then do something about it.

RITA: What?

ANDRES: I'm going to see my tía tonight. Come with me.

RITA: Your tía, la bruja?

ANDRES: She's not a bruja! She helps people!

RITA: Yeah, I've heard about the potions she sells.

ANDRES: Hey, if you need love medicine, my tía can help.

RITA: How?

ANDRES: She promised to make me a toro costume. One everyone will notice.

RITA: What can she do for me?

ANDRES: I don't know. Come with me, ask her.

RITA: She's a powerful woman, isn't she? When she comes into the grocery store you can hear a pin drop.

ANDRES: Yeah, people don't mess with her.

RITA: I heard of a girl she helped. . . . Maybe people call her a bruja because she's different—

ANDRES: You have no choice. If you do nothing, it's going to be Cristina in Lore's bed, making love, when it could've been you—

RITA: Shut up!

ANDRES: Let's do something, Rita. Or we lose what we want!

RITA: Do you really think she can—

ANDRES: Yes.

RITA: I don't want to be sorry later.

ANDRES: You won't. Can you go tonight?

RITA: Yes. I'll go. What do I have to lose?

ANDRES: Now you're with it! You'll see. My tía works magic. I won't have to use this old cowhide. (*He picks up the cowhide.*) When I was a kid I used to follow the dance down the street. I saw how people treated the Toro. They made fun of him, used him to frighten kids. But if I have a real costume, I'll put fear in their hearts.

RITA: Is that what you want? What about San Lorenzo?

ANDRES: Ah, people act so damned holy! They're hypocrites! They drink, sleep around, beat their kids, then they make promesas they don't keep. I'll keep mine.

The Priest enters at the gate, clears his throat.

RITA: Father. Come in.

PRIEST: Hello Rita . . . Andres. I was on my way to church. I stopped to see the danzantes.

RITA: They're not here yet.

PRIEST: (*looks at the Toro costume*) The Toro, huh?

ANDRES: Yeah, the bad, bad Toro. I'll see you later, Rita. Don't forget, tonight.

Andres exits.

RITA: Yes . . .

PRIEST: Ah, it's cool here in the patio. May I sit?

RITA: Papá's inside. Would you like to go in?

PRIEST: No, no, I'll sit out here, if it's all right? I'm on my way to rosary. It's hot . . . But you look as lovely as ever.

RITA: Thank you, Father. (*She lights a cigarette.*)

PRIEST: I was passing by. I heard your voice and stopped to say hello. How have you been?

RITA: Busy working.

PRIEST: But you haven't been at mass recently.

RITA: I stopped going. . . . Do you *really* think the saints answer our prayers?

PRIEST: What did you ask for?

RITA: Something I can't have. (*She studies the Priest intently.*) You wouldn't understand.

PRIEST: Perhaps I would, if you want to tell me, if you want to talk. That's what I'm there for. (*He goes to her, reaches to take her hand.*)

RITA: (*turns away*) Confession? Tell you all my secrets? I'm afraid my penance would be very long.

PRIEST: (*laughs*) I promise not to give you more than five Hail Marys. Besides, you're too beautiful to have many sins. You haven't murdered anyone, have you? (*He smiles.*)

RITA: It's not that easy, Father.

PRIEST: It can be if you talk about it.

RITA: Tell you my prayers haven't been answered?

PRIEST: What did you pray for?

RITA: Romance—no, love. A love so strong it's all I can think about. (*She pauses.*)

PRIEST: Love of a man?

RITA: Yes.

PRIEST: I understand. . . . Sometimes an attraction can be overwhelming . . . We're all human, we all have temptations. Only by turning to God can we put away . . .

(*She stubs out the cigarettes.*)

PRIEST: It's so warm.

RITA: Yes . . . even the nights don't cool off. (*She pours him a drink of water.*)

PRIEST: Yes. It's so hot. Where I'm from we don't have this intense heat. Ah, water. It quenches the thirst.

RITA: (*softly*) But not the desire . . .

PRIEST: Yes. Well, thank you. I must go. Are you coming to rosary tonight?

RITA: I can't.

PRIEST: I understand. You're getting ready for the Matachines. This is the first time I'll see the dance. And your sister is Malinche. That's a great honor.

RITA: Yes.

PRIEST: Were you ever Malinche?

RITA: No, Father.

PRIEST: Well, you would have made a lovely one.

RITA: Thank you, Father.

PRIEST: Well, I'd better be on my way. If you need to talk, please come and see me. That's what I'm there for.

The Priest smiles and starts out. At the gate he meets Andres, Juan, and Zonzo. They greet the Priest. Zonzo carries the box with the Matachines' costumes.

JUAN: Hello, Father. ¿Cómo está?

ZONZO: Bendicíon, Father, for I have sinned.

JUAN: Cállate, Zonzo.

PRIEST: A blessing to all of you. And don't forget rosary.

ZONZO: I already prayed at home, Father.

Priest shakes his head and leaves.

ANDRES: Á Zonzo le faltan tuercas.

JUAN: Leave him alone. He doesn't bother you.

ANDRES: (*to Rita*) What did the padrecito want?

RITA: To help . . .

ANDRES: I think he just wants to get you in the confessional where it's dark—

JUAN: ¡Ten respeto, Andres!

ANDRES: ¿Respeto? Hey, even the padrecito gets lonely. (*He slides his hand along Rita's back.*) And he has good taste.

ZONZO: Good taste. ¡Hijola!

JUAN: Calla, Zonzo. Where's Lore?

RITA: Inside.

JUAN: Did he get the job?

RITA: Yes.

JUAN: Hey, my bro's one lucky dude! (*gives Zonzo a high five*)

ZONZO: Yeah, a lucky dude!

JUAN: And the rest of us have no job, no money.

ZONZO: Lorenzo's lucky.

JUAN: Yeah, he gets Cristina, and the jale at the plant. (*He takes the cowhide from Andres.*) Is this the Toro outfit?

ANDRES: It's what they want me to wear, but I have other plans.

JUAN: Like what?

ANDRES: Like getting something nice, so the Toro can dance for Malinche.

JUAN: What do you mean?

ANDRES: The Toro and the Monarca should have a contest. The best dancer gets Malinche.

JUAN: That's crazy. There's no contest in the Matachines.

ANDRES: Yeah, we do the same old thing. Malinche waves the palma over the Toro and he's supposed to behave. That's too easy. Why not let the Toro shine? Let him dance!

JUAN: So you think you're a better dancer than Lorenzo?

Don Patricio, Cristina, and Lorenzo enter from the house.

DON PATRICIO: Buenas tardes, muchachos.

ALL RESPOND: Buenas tardes, Don Patricio. Buenas tardes.

DON PATRICIO: You ready to practice?

ALL RESPOND: Yes, sir, we're ready. Sí, señor.

ZONZO: *(salutes)* A sus ordenes, Don Patricio.

CRISTINA: You guys are late. I thought we were going to try on our costumes?

JUAN: We got 'em.

Zonzo gives her the box.

JUAN: Andres thinks there should be a dance contest between him and Lore.

CRISTINA: What kind of contest?

ANDRES: Let the Toro dance. If he's a better dancer than the Monarca, then he gets Malinche.

DON PATRICIO: That's crazy, Andres. The Toro doesn't dance. He has a very small role in the Matachines. Malinche, who is the Virgin Mary, dances around the Toro to control him. Then the abuelos put the rope around him, take him out, and castrate him.

LORENZO: That's what the sword is for.

ZONZO: Ouch!

DON PATRICIO: It's not real, Zonzo. It's just the idea. To take the power from the Toro you cut off—you know. (*He goes to his tomato plants.*)

ANDRES: But I'm a good dancer! Let me show my stuff! (*turns to Lorenzo*) I challenge you to a contest.

LORENZO: What do you think, Cristina?

CRISTINA: If Papá says that's not part of the Matachines—

ANDRES: Hey, you're adding the sword—why not try a new dance?

ZONZO: Bad, bad Toro.

CRISTINA: You're right . . .

ANDRES: Come on, at least try it.

CRISTINA: You're serious.

ANDRES: Yes.

JUAN: Why change the dance, ese?

ANDRES: Because the Toro deserves a chance.

CRISTINA: You really mean it? (*She circles Andres, intrigued.*)

ANDRES: Yes. (*to Lorenzo*) Unless you're afraid?

LORENZO: Of you? No way!

ANDRES: So, let's do it.

JUAN: Go on, bro, take him on!

LORENZO: Cristina?

CRISTINA: I like the idea . . .

JUAN: Ándale, Lore. Put him in his place.

ZONZO: The Devil will get you.

CRISTINA: Maybe you don't think I'm worth it?

LORENZO: Okay, you're on!

JUAN: All right!

Juan gives Zonzo a high five. Lorenzo and Andres shake hands.

CRISTINA: And if you win, do I belong to you?

ANDRES: Yes, you're the prize.

LORENZO: Wait a minute!

CRISTINA: What are you going to do, carry me away to your little house in Algodones?

ANDRES: I'll give you the world.

CRISTINA: I like that.

Don Cornelio, his wife, Doña Francisca, the guitarist, the violinist, and other danzantes enter with great clatter and joviality.

DON PATRICIO: Don Cornelio, Doña Francisca. Buenas tardes.

DOÑA FRANCISCA: Buenas tardes a todos.

MÚSICOS: Buenas tardes.

DON CORNELIO: ¡Ay, que calor! Come dice Don Cacahuate, is hot like Doña Cebolla's fundillo—

DOÑA FRANCISCA: ¿Qué sabes tú de Doña Cebolla?

DON CORNELIO: Sé que me hace llorar.

Everyone laughs.

DON PATRICIO: We can start practice.

ZONZO: Oh, goody! Los abuelos!

DOÑA FRANCISCA: Spanish cowboys. ¡Mascando chiquete y hablando en ingles!

ZONZO: Tell another joke about Don Cacahuate.

Don Cornelio and Doña Francisca affect an English accent.

DOÑA FRANCISCA: I no gonna bake you no more tortillas, Don Cacahuate.

DON CORNELIO: Okay, I go to Safeway and buy some, Doña Cebolla.

DOÑA FRANCISCA: Safeway tortillas get hard.

DON CORNELIO: No problem, I justa put 'em in your cooler.

DOÑA FRANCISCA: ¡En el tuyo!

There is laughter.

DON PATRICIO: Enough chistes! Vamo' a comenzar. Everybody ready. Line up, danzantes!

The dancers line up. Juan and Zonzo pass out palmas and gourds. The abuelos clown around. The músicos begin to tune up.

DON CORNELIO: Primero, la Marcha . . .

DOÑA FRANCISCA: ¡Los Matachines de San Lorenzo!

DON CORNELIO: ¡Una promesa a San Lorenzo! ¡Todos bailemos al santo!

ANDRES: (takes Cristina's arm) Come on. Dance with me.

DON CORNELIO: Hey, crazy Toro! Get back! Not your turn.

ZONZO: Crazy Toro!

JUAN: Anda, Toro. Let's see what you can do.

ANDRES: Dance with me.

RITA: (to Cristina) Go on, dance with him. (Rita holds Lorenzo back.)

CRISTINA: All right, Toro, show your stuff.

Andres dances around her. Cristina responds and is drawn toward Andres. She laughs, enjoying the dance and flirting with Andres.)

DON PATRICIO: ¡Paren! ¡Paren!

The music stops sharply. Andres and Cristina remain facing each other, panting for breath.

DON PATRICIO: ¡Esto es una locura!

ANDRES: Nice, huh?

CRISTINA: Yeah, I liked it. You're a good dancer.

ANDRES: You see. You have to give the Toro a chance to dance.

DON PATRICIO: No! You don't know anything about the Matachines!

ANDRES: I know what I want!

ZONZO: Malinche . . .

DON PATRICIO: Andres, I want to help you, but not this way.

ANDRES: You're all afraid to give the Toro a chance!

LORENZO: You're taking this too serious, bro. The idea is crazy. . . . It's all off.

ANDRES: You sound like Don Patricio. (He turns to Cristina.) What about you?

CRISTINA: It's different. (turns to her father) Maybe the people will like it.

DON PATRICIO: No, mi'ja. We cannot let the Toro dance.

ANDRES: (grinds his teeth in anger) You're afraid of me. All of you. Including you, Lore!

LORENZO: I'm not afraid!

ANDRES: I'll show you! (*Andres rushes out the gate.*)

DON PATRICIO: Andres!

DOÑA FRANCISCA: Déjalo, compadre.

DON CORNELIO: Está poco loco en la cabeza.

RITA: (*goes to Cristina*) You looked good with Andres.

CRISTINA: He's a good dancer. I think the Toro dancing with Malinche would add excitement to the dance.

LORENZO: You heard your dad. It's no go.

RITA: Are you afraid you'll lose her, Lore? Let them dance . . . I'll dance with you. (*She flirts with him.*)

CRISTINA: Two men, dancing for me! I like it.

DON PATRICIO: It's a crazy idea.

CRISTINA: He didn't mean any harm, Papá. We could add a part for Andres. You saw how good he is.

LORENZO: Good? He's just a show-off.

CRISTINA: Why can't the dance change, Papá?

DON PATRICIO: Hija, if we let the Toro dance— (*He turns to Doña Francisca.*) Anda, comadre. You explain.

DOÑA FRANCISCA: You see, mi'ja, the Toro is something evil. We use him to frighten the children, and we laugh at him, but deep in our corazón we're afraid of him. Malinche, who is the Virgin Mary, must control the Toro. The abuelos help. We rope him and take him away . . .

Don Patricio and Don Cornelio nod.

LORENZO: So the contest is out!

DON PATRICIO: Yes. Now let's get back to the practice! ¡Músicos!

The músicos play the traditional music for the Matachines and the dancers dance as the lights dim slowly on the stage. The dancers exit, and the stage is bare for a moment. The Bruja enters, carrying a lantern and the black hide of a bull.

Scene Two

ANDRES: (calling from backstage) Tía!

BRUJA: ¿Quién es?

ANDRES: Yo.

Andres and Rita move into the light.

BRUJA: Andres, diablo. ¿Y la muchacha?

ANDRES: Rita.

BRUJA: La hija de Don Patricio . . .

ANDRES: Sí.

RITA: Andres, let's go back.

ANDRES: You said you wanted to come—now you're here!

BRUJA: Does she need a potion for her lover?

ANDRES: Yes.

BRUJA: I have something for all lovers . . . Mira. (She holds up the hide.)

ANDRES: The Toro!

BRUJA: (caressing the hide) Sí. To please the Devil we killed el Toro de la luna oscura, el Toro de la noche. We offered his blood to the Lord of Night. Here! Take it!

Andres takes the hide.

BRUJA: Put on the hide and pray to the Toro. Anda, no tengas miedo.
(praying) Sangre negra, sangre del Toro . . . enter the soul of Andres. Give him your strength.

ANDRES: I want to be the Toro!

BRUJA: And you want revenge—

ANDRES: I will make them pay for killing my father!

BRUJA: You will be the Toro! I will make the mask of the Toro. You will dance for Malinche, and she will be yours!

ANDRES: I want her, Tía!

BRUJA: Will you pay the price, hijo?

ANDRES: Yes!

BRUJA: Give your soul to the Lord of Night. Ask him to make you the Toro.

ANDRES: (*holds the hide above his head and shouts*) Make me the Toro! Give me Cristina's love and you can have my soul!

BRUJA: A bargain! You have made a bargain with the Devil! (*She takes the hide and turns to Rita.*) And you? What do you desire?

ANDRES: She wants Lorenzo.

BRUJA: Lorenzo? ¿El novio de tu hermana?

RITA: She doesn't deserve him!

BRUJA: Do you desire him with all your heart?

RITA: (*softly*) Yes.

BRUJA: Then you will have him. Give your soul to our Lord of Night.

RITA: (*anguished*) I can't . . . I can't. (*She turns to Andres.*)

ANDRES: If you really want Lorenzo, do it!

RITA: I'm afraid.

BRUJA: Tell me you want him!

RITA: (*cries*) I love him . . . I want him.

BRUJA: Do you dream of Lorenzo? Do you hold him in your dreams?

RITA: Yes!

BRUJA: You want him to love you?

RITA: He loves Cristina . . .

BRUJA: I can make him love you.

RITA: How?

BRUJA: I place the hairs of the bull in a locket. You give it to him to wear, and he becomes yours.

RITA: Is that all?

BRUJA: ¡Sí, sí! It's easy to turn a man's love. If you pay the price.

ANDRES: Do it, Rita!

Rita nods.

BRUJA: Come, give your soul to the Lord of Night.

RITA: And I get Lorenzo?

BRUJA: Yes. This medicine is very strong. Lorenzo will be yours. Kneel and pray to the Toro. Toro de la luna oscura.

Rita kneels. Bruja places the hide around Rita's shoulders.

RITA: Take my soul! Give me Lorenzo's love! (*She falls to the ground.*)

BRUJA: It's done! (*Bruja turns to Andres.*)

BRUJA: You will be the Toro, mi'jo, and dance for the people of Plaza Vieja. They will pay for killing your father.

Andres kneels beside Rita. The Bruja chants.

BRUJA: Deseos de amantes . . . Deseos de la luna oscura . . . Con estas promesas levantamos el Monarca de la Noche . . .

Bruja picks up the lantern and walks off. Andres helps Rita up and follows.

Scene Three

A week later; afternoon in Don Patricio's patio.

Don Patricio, Cristina, and Lorenzo enter.

DON PATRICIO: (*coughs*) So the job is going well . . .

LORENZO: Yeah. It's kind of boring. I sit in an office, every hour I make the rounds. I have a lot of time to read.

DON PATRICIO: Hay viene el fresco de la tarde . . .

LORENZO: Hope it cools off Andres.

CRISTINA: He keeps insisting I should dance with him.

LORENZO: Just stay away from him. He's crazy.

DON PATRICIO: He's had a hard life. But right now, I'm more worried about Rita.

LORENZO: ¿Por que?

CRISTINA: She doesn't sleep. Walks around the house all night.

LORENZO: Maybe she's in love.

DON PATRICIO: It started a week ago. I found her en la cocina early in the morning, washing her muddy clothes. Something's not right. Maybe you and Lorenzo can help.

CRISTINA: We will, Papá.

LORENZO: Sure.

DON PATRICIO: Ah, if your mother were only alive. I feel tired.

CRISTINA: You need to rest.

DON PATRICIO: (coughs) Yes, time for my nap. Estoy cansado. (A troubled Don Patricio goes into the house.)

CRISTINA: Will you talk to Rita?

LORENZO: Why me?

CRISTINA: She likes you. I think she loves you.

LORENZO: No chance.

CRISTINA: She looks at you like a woman in love.

LORENZO: You're kidding, aren't you?

CRISTINA: No.

LORENZO: Hey, I never gave her any reason to—

CRISTINA: I know. But she's always liked you. It's like an obsession.

LORENZO: That's what I have for you. If you'd only let me—

CRISTINA: I'm not talking about sex, I mean something deeper.

LORENZO: Hey, sex is a good start. But you keep putting me off.

CRISTINA: (shakes her head) You don't understand . . .

LORENZO: (angrily) And Andres does, huh? Maybe you should dance with him!

CRISTINA: Don't be jealous. I'm trying to explain—

LORENZO: You like that crazy dance of the Toro he's doing, and I shouldn't be jealous? Hey, I'm the one you're going to marry.

CRISTINA: Don't be angry.

LORENZO: I'm not, but we never do anything! I try to understand you.

CRISTINA: My sweet Lorenzo . . .

LORENZO: I don't want to be sweet! I'm a man. Like Andres.

CRISTINA: I know—

LORENZO: Maybe I should be the Toro.

CRISTINA: No, amor, you're the Monarca. Help Rita.

LORENZO: So what's bothering her?

CRISTINA: I don't know. Talk to her, find out. Please.

LORENZO: All right, I'll do it, if you promise not to dance with Andres.

CRISTINA: That's not fair.

LORENZO: Okay, then I'll find a way to keep him away from you.

CRISTINA: Don't make him mad. Let him do his dance—it doesn't hurt anyone. It's Rita we have to help. Will you talk to her?

LORENZO: I said okay.

CRISTINA: I love you.

She holds him. They kiss.

LORENZO: Umm, you make me wild.

CRISTINA: (*holding him at arm's length*) My sweet Lorenzo. Here, wear my scapular. (*She removes her scapular and puts it around his neck.*)

LORENZO: Why?

CRISTINA: To keep you safe.

LORENZO: Hey, Plaza Vieja is the safest place in the world.

CRISTINA: I know—wear it anyway.

Lorenzo laughs. Rita appears at the gate.

LORENZO: With this I'll really be a santo.

CRISTINA: Shh. There's Rita. (*Cristina moves toward the house.*)

LORENZO: Hey!

CRISTINA: You need to be alone. (*Cristina goes into the house.*)

LORENZO: Hi!

RITA: Where's my dear sister off to?

LORENZO: I don't know. . . . Listen, I've gotta get to the jale.

RITA: I need to talk to you.

LORENZO: Yeah, Cristina wants me to talk to you.

RITA: My kind sister is worried?

LORENZO: What can I do?

RITA: (*seductively*) I need to know how you feel about me.

Rita sees the scapular, fingers the locket around her neck. The Bruja appears at the gate and moves away.

LORENZO: I like you, Rita, you know that.

RITA: You dated me before you dated Cristina.

RITA: Dated? We went to the movies—once.

RITA: You held my hand. All through the show you held my hand. I felt your touch for weeks. I began to dream about you.

LORENZO: That was a long time ago.

RITA: The dreams haven't gone away. They've gotten stronger. I love you, Lore.

She presses against Lorenzo. He holds her at arm's length.

LORENZO: You like me, Rita. There's a difference. I only want to help you.

RITA: Help me? I don't need help. I need to know how you feel about me.

LORENZO: I told you—

RITA: Okay, then do something for me. Wear my locket. (*She takes the locket from around her neck.*)

LORENZO: I don't know . . .

The sun sets, the light grows dim, orange.

RITA: Wear it if you really want to help me. (*She presses close to him.*)

LORENZO: Okay, if it helps.

RITA: A token of love . . . (*She puts the locket around Lorenzo's neck. At the same time she removes the scapular.*)

LORENZO: Hey, that's Cristina's!

RITA: You said you wanted to help. You must wear the locket.

LORENZO: All right. Just tonight.

Rita embraces him and kisses him. Lorenzo pulls away.

LORENZO: Cool it, Rita. I'll wear this, but that doesn't mean getting involved.

RITA: Don't you feel anything?

LORENZO: Hey, you're going to be my sister-in-law. I respect you. That's it.

RITA: (*disappointed*) It doesn't work.

LORENZO: What?

RITA: (*confused*) The bargain I made . . .

LORENZO: I don't know what you're talking about. I've got to go.

RITA: (*clutching at him*) No, don't go! Tell me what you feel!

LORENZO: (*tears away from her*) I gotta go, Rita.

RITA: I love you, Lorenzo! I love you!

LORENZO: Look, Rita. You're confused. I love Cristina. Nothing's going to change that.

RITA: The locket . . . Don't you feel—

LORENZO: I don't know what you're talking about. I gotta go. (*Lorenzo shakes his head, goes out.*)

RITA: Lore, oh Lore.

Teresa comes in through the gate.

TERESA: Boy, he's in a hurry.

Rita nods.

TERESA: What's the matter? You look pale.

RITA: He's supposed to love me . . .

TERESA: He loves Cristina.

RITA: Oh, God, I've made a terrible mistake.

TERESA: What mistake?

RITA: I sold my soul for his love . . .

TERESA: What are you saying?

RITA: Do something for me.

TERESA: What?

RITA: Go and find Andres. Don't let anyone see you, but tell him I need to talk to him.

TERESA: I don't like Andres.

RITA: (anguished) Please . . . please . . .

TERESA: What's the matter with you? You act like it's the end of the world.

RITA: Yes, the end of my world! Oh God, what have I done? Andres, go find Andres. Please!

TERESA: Okay, okay. I'll go. (to herself) Gee, weird.

Teresa races out the gate. Rita's shoulders slump.

RITA: I'm lost . . . I'm lost.

Cristina appears at the door, steps into the patio.

CRISTINA: Is Lorenzo gone?

Rita nods.

CRISTINA: Did you talk?

RITA: Yes.

CRISTINA: Lore is a saint.

RITA: A saint? Is that why my magic failed?

CRISTINA: What magic?

RITA: Love. Do you know what love is? (She goes to the table and takes a cigarette.)

CRISTINA: I thought I knew. . . . All summer I've had this feeling . . . it's frustrating. I wake up at night, trembling . . .

RITA: You feel like you're burning up?

CRISTINA: Yes.

RITA: For Lorenzo?

CRISTINA: I thought it was for him.

RITA: You're not sure?

CRISTINA: I'm not sure of my feelings. I don't know what I want. Do you understand?

RITA: I know what I want. (*She crumples the cigarette pack.*)

CRISTINA: You're lucky, Rita. I wish I was so sure. I'm supposed to love Lorenzo, but I'm not sure.

RITA: Have you tested your love?

CRISTINA: How?

RITA: By dancing with Andres.

CRISTINA: It's not right to test one's love.

RITA: If you don't dance with Andres you'll never know.

CRISTINA: You're right.

DON PATRICIO: (*from the house*) Time for supper.

Cristina goes into the house.

RITA: His favorite daughter!

There is a whistle behind the fence.

RITA: ¿Quién es?

ANDRES: El diablo.

RITA: Andres?

Andres enters, dressed in the Toro hide and carrying a bottle in a sack.

ANDRES: At your service.

RITA: You're drunk.

ANDRES: Celebrating!

RITA: What?

ANDRES: My love! My desire! I walk the streets of Plaza Vieja and frighten the children. "¡El Diablo!" they cry.

RITA: You were hiding.

ANDRES: I gotta watch my women.

RITA: You mean Cristina.

ANDRES: And you. We have a bargain.

RITA: Not anymore. I'm going to the priest . . .

ANDRES: For comfort?

RITA: You sonofabitch! (*She strikes at him.*)

ANDRES: Oh, there's fire in the woman! I like that.

RITA: I want to confess.

ANDRES: All right. If you believe in the padrecito, go.

RITA: I'm going to tell him everything.

ANDRES: Go ahead, I don't care. He can't tell anyone what you confess. Let him get his jollies having you in the confessional. Let him know everything! There's not a damn thing he can do!

RITA: You make everything sound evil.

ANDRES: It's there, mi'jita. Deep in the corazon. Call it love or lust, the padre and I know it's all the same. What people call brujería is desire. Desire for something that makes you hurt so much, you finally go to my tía. She can make it happen. A locket for Lorenzo, and he comes begging.

RITA: It didn't work.

ANDRES: What?

RITA: I put the locket around his neck and took Cristina's scapular— (*Rita hands him the scapular.*)

ANDRES: ¡Que suave! (*He throws the scapular down and grinds it into the earth.*)

RITA: He didn't kiss me.

ANDRES: It takes time, it takes time. He's going to love you.

RITA: And Cristina?

ANDRES: She's going to be mine. As long as I can remember I've wanted her. But I was a nobody. Now this nobody's going to make Plaza Vieja pay.

RITA: It's revenge you want, isn't it?

ANDRES: I'll show those holy rollers something they've never seen. My tía knows. Make Malinche yours, she said, and the people will pay for killing my father!

RITA: Your father killed a man!

ANDRES: Lies!

Teresa appears at the gate with Lorenzo.

ANDRES: What's he doing here?

RITA: I told her to get you—she brought Lore.

TERESA: Aquí 'sta.

LORENZO: You want me?

RITA: Yes.

ANDRES: We don't need you, bro. Little sister's playing games. (*Andres grabs Teresa.*)

TERESA: Get away!

LORENZO: Back off, Andres.

ANDRES: Be careful of dark alleys, little girl. I'll be there.

TERESA: I'm not afraid of you! Lore's here.

LORENZO: What the hell's going on?

ANDRES: Take her inside.

RITA: No.

ANDRES: I said take her inside!

LORENZO: Go on, Rita.

Rita pulls Teresa into the house.

LORENZO: I've been looking for you.

ANDRES: And I've been looking for you, carnal.

LORENZO: Stay away from Cristina!

ANDRES: What's the matter, can't you take a little competition? Is the Toro too good? Make you jealous?

They circle each other.

LORENZO: ¡'Stás loco!

ANDRES: I'm going to make her mine!

LORENZO: She's in love with me.

ANDRES: She belongs to the man who takes her!

LORENZO: You sonofabitch!

ANDRES: (*taunting*) She danced with the Toro and got a taste of a real man!

LORENZO: ¡Anda, cabrón! Let's settle this!

ANDRES: After you.

Lorenzo starts out, Andres follows, draws his knife, jumps Lorenzo, and stabs him just outside the gate.

LORENZO: Oh, God!

Teresa appears in time to see the murder. She screams. Andres rushes to her and threatens her with the knife.

ANDRES: If you talk, I'll cut your tongue out!

Teresa tries to scream, chokes, and falls to her knees sobbing. Andres drags out Lorenzo's body.

END ACT ONE

ACT TWO

The patio of Don Patricio's home on the feast day of San Lorenzo, a week after Lorenzo's murder.

A fearful and huddled Teresa sits with a shawl around her shoulder, staring into space. Andres appears at the gate and enters.

ANDRES: Ah, mi palomita, you're all alone. The good Don Patricio and your sisters are at church.

(Teresa shrinks from him.)

ANDRES: What's the matter, cat got your tongue? Or the Devil? (*He laughs.*) ¡Ave María Purisima, que susto! She saw the diablo! What did the Devil do? Tell me, what did you see? (*He pauses.*)

Pobrecita. You can't talk. They say you lost your marbles, and you're going to sit there slobbering the rest of your life. That's the price you pay for sticking your nose into other people's business, mi'jita. Today I make Plaza Vieja pay!

TERESA: (*struggling to talk*) Zon . . . zo . . .

ANDRES: Zonzo? What did you tell him?

TERESA: (*frightened*) Zon . . .

ANDRES: (*shouting*) What did you tell Zonzo? . . . No, you didn't tell him anything. You can't talk. You saw the Devil and you can't talk.

Teresa cringes in fear.

ANDRES: You're afraid? El susto del diablo. Que bueno . . .

There is noise in the street. Andres goes to the gate and ducks out. In a few moments Don Patricio, Rita, and Cristina enter. All are dressed in black.

RITA: Was that Andres?

CRISTINA: (*to Teresa*) Was Andres here? You're shivering.

DON PATRICIO: She's tired. Come inside, mi'jita—it's time to fix breakfast for the dancers.

TERESA: Zon . . . zon . . .

CRISTINA: Zonzo? What about Zonzo? (kneels before Teresa) Hermanita. If you could only tell us what happened. If we only knew what caused your susto.

DON PATRICIO: Anda, mi'jita, no llores. The doctor said she'll get well. With time.

CRISTINA: I can't help it, Papá. I can't believe Lorenzo's dead, and when I see Teresa . . .

Teresa struggles to speak.

CRISTINA: She knows something, Papá, she knows!

RITA: (to Teresa) Do you know who killed Lorenzo?

TERESA: Di-ab . . . Di-ab-lo . . .

CRISTINA: What's she saying?

RITA: Were you at the ditch where Lorenzo was killed?

Teresa cringes with fear.

RITA: Did you see Andres?

CRISTINA: Rita, that's not fair!

RITA: I don't care about fair! I want to know who killed Lorenzo!

DON PATRICIO: ¡Mi'ja! It's not right to accuse Andres. Let the Sheriff handle the matter. We have to take care of Teresa. Only time can cure her susto. Anda, mi'jita, ven— (He helps Teresa up.) You decorate the sword while I cook breakfast. Ay, Dios mío, who would have thought that today we would be dancing in memory of Lorenzo. (He helps Teresa into the house.)

CRISTINA: Do you really think Andres had something to do with Lorenzo's death?

RITA: I know what he's capable of doing. . . . Did you love Lorenzo?

CRISTINA: Yes.

RITA: Did you give yourself to him?

CRISTINA: No.

RITA: And now you have nothing, and I have nothing.

CRISTINA: (sighs deeply) I know you loved him—

RITA: Loved him? I worshipped the ground he walked on.

CRISTINA: He was wearing a locket when they found him. Was it yours?

RITA: Yes.

Cristina reaches out to touch her sister.

RITA: A bargain for his love . . .

CRISTINA: I didn't know you felt so strong—

RITA: I died with him.

CRISTINA: Don't say that. You have your future. The priest said it's all right to grieve, but it passes.

RITA: I don't feel grief, I feel guilt.

CRISTINA: Guilt?

RITA: I won't rest until I know who killed him.

CRISTINA: I'm sure Teresa knows. "The Devil killed Lorenzo!" she kept repeating when we found her in the patio. She was covered with blood. . . . Oh, God, whatever she saw was horrible.

RITA: It's the work of the Devil. Yes, we set the Devil loose, and now— We have to stop him!

CRISTINA: I don't understand.

RITA: Don't dance with Andres! Ask Father to cancel the dance!

CRISTINA: Why?

RITA: That's the only way to stop Andres!

CRISTINA: You know Papá would never cancel the dance. Besides, the dance is not about Andres.

RITA: You've seen him do the dance of the Toro! Don't you know what that means?

CRISTINA: It's just a crazy obsession—

RITA: He's become the Toro of la luna oscura.

CRISTINA: ¿Luna oscura?

RITA: When he puts on the costume, he thinks he really is the Toro. He wants you, Malinche!

CRISTINA: I know. He asked me to marry him.

RITA: What?

CRISTINA: Last night, after our last practice. He asked me to marry him.

RITA: What did you say?

CRISTINA: I said no. Lorenzo's only been dead a week. But I can't seem to resist him. It's as if he has me under a spell—

RITA: Yes, the spell of the Toro. The magic is working for him . . . His revenge—

CRISTINA: (doesn't understand) He's so forceful, so sure of himself. I can barely resist him.

RITA: The only way is to stop his dance!

Andres appears at the gate.

RITA: El diablo . . .

Andres enters, carrying his costume. He is arrogant, imposing.

ANDRES: Buenos días, mi'jitas. Ready for the dance? (To Cristina) You look beautiful . . .

He kisses Cristina. She doesn't respond.

ANDRES: Is that any way to greet the man who loves you? Oh, grief for Lorenzo? You'll get over that. Ya lo que pasó, pasó. Think of the future.

RITA: Your future.

ANDRES: You got it.

RITA: (to Cristina) Don't dance today! Please.

ANDRES: Hey! What do you mean, "Don't dance"? Today's the day. My day.

CRISTINA: We have to.

RITA: But it's become his dance!

ANDRES: You're right, amor. Today the Toro wins Malinche. So stay out of the way! You talk too much, and we might have to tell your sister our secret.

CRISTINA: What secret?

RITA: No! (She backs away, reaches for her cigarettes.)

ANDRES: That's better. A woman should know her place. This is between Cristina and me. Between the Toro and Malinche. (He turns to Cristina.) Right, mi'jita? Anda, let's dance!

CRISTINA: Not now—

ANDRES: Yes, now!

Cristina acquiesces, nods. Andres is in control.

ANDRES: The Monarca is dead. Now is the time of the Toro. (*He dances around Cristina.*) Malinche belongs to the Toro!

Juan and Zonzo, dressed in Matachines costumes but carrying their hats, enter at the gate.

JUAN: Hey, Andres, still showing off?

ANDRES: Why not? Today's my day.

JUAN: Today's the day of the Monarca.

ANDRES: You forget, the Monarca's dead.

JUAN: (*to Cristina*) Your dad gave me permission—

CRISTINA: You're going to be the Monarca?

JUAN: Yes.

CRISTINA: Thank God.

JUAN: It was either me or old Don Eliseo. He's got arthritis in the knees.

ZONZO: Long live el Monarca! Bad Toro!

ANDRES: You're not a very good dancer, Juan.

ZONZO: Yeah, he is! Great!

ANDRES: I watched you practice. When the abuelo pulls you by the foot, you keep falling. The Toro's going to run over you.

RITA: Don't do it, Juan.

JUAN: Hey, I thought you were on our side.

ANDRES: Don't listen to her.

RITA: We have to cancel the dance!

JUAN: Why?

ANDRES: Back off, Rita!

Rita starts to speak, then backs down.

ANDRES: All right. Go ahead and dance. It's me against you!

JUAN: No, no contest, Andres.

ANDRES: You're afraid.

JUAN: Of you? No way.

ANDRES: (taunting) ¡Tienes miedo! Just like your brother!

Juan charges Andres. Zonzo holds him back.

ANDRES: Come on, Juanito! Come and get it!

CRISTINA: Stop it! Both of you! This is no time to fight.

JUAN: Yeah, we didn't come to fight—we came to dance. For la gente.

ZONZO: ¡La gente!

Don Patricio calls from the house.

RITA: He's serving breakfast—

ZONZO: Oh boy! Huevos con chorizo, café con leche. Yummy.

JUAN: Okay, Zonzo, let's get some munchies.

ZONZO: Tortillas con mantequilla. Yummy.

Juan and Zonzo enter the house. Andres holds Cristina back.

ANDRES: Go on, Rita. I have to talk to Cristina.

RITA: About me?

ANDRES: (smiling) No, your secret is safe. We have to discuss our future.

Rita goes into the house. Andres makes sure they're alone.

CRISTINA: This isn't the time to talk.

ANDRES: It's not about us, it's about Rita.

CRISTINA: What about her?

ANDRES: She was in love with Lorenzo.

CRISTINA: I know.

ANDRES: She made a play for Lorenzo the night he was killed. He refused her. She kind of went crazy.

CRISTINA: What are you saying?

ANDRES: I'm telling you, she was crazy. Really crazy. She could've done anything.

CRISTINA: You're not suggesting—

ANDRES: I'm only saying she might tell you stories about me. Don't believe her! You have to trust me. I want you, Cristina. I've always wanted you. Lorenzo's dead—now there's only us!

CRISTINA: No. I feel Lorenzo's here—

ANDRES: He's dead!

CRISTINA: You saw him the night he was killed?

ANDRES: No! I left, and he said he had to see Rita. She had a locket to give him. It was supposed to make him love her.

CRISTINA: The locket he was wearing . . .

ANDRES: I'm telling you, she was acting crazy.

Cristina shakes her head. Andres grabs her shoulders.

ANDRES: Rita wanted Lorenzo. She told me if she couldn't have him, nobody could! Now it's just you and me.

DON PATRICIO: (*entering from the house*) ¡Mi'ja!

ANDRES: Buenos días, Don Patricio.

DON PATRICIO: Come and eat, mi'ja. Today is a long day.

ANDRES: Yes, Don Patricio, an important day. Today Plaza Vieja will see the dance of the Toro.

DON PATRICIO: I won't permit it, Andres.

ANDRES: You don't make the rules anymore, Don Patricio. The old dance is dead.

DON PATRICIO: (*putting his arm around Cristina*) The people won't let you.

ANDRES: (*laughs*) The people don't care if the Matachines dance or not. They're in the cantina having a good time! Their kids are on dope! Your world is gone, Don Patricio. Now is the time of the Toro!

The Priest enters at the gate.

DON PATRICIO: Padre.

PRIEST: Don Patricio. ¿Qué pasa?

DON PATRICIO: Ah, the same argument . . .

PRIEST: What are you going to do?

ANDRES: We're going to dance, Padre. Cristina and me are novios.

DON PATRICIO: Is this true?

CRISTINA: No. Andres thinks just because we danced together that makes us novios.

ANDRES: We will be after today. That's what the dance is for, to bring Malinche to the Toro. The Toro and Malinche belong together.

DON PATRICIO: Not as long as I'm in charge— (*He coughs and clutches at his chest.*)

CRISTINA: ¡Papá!

PRIEST: Don Patricio!

CRISTINA: You need your oxygen. Come inside.

DON PATRICIO: No. I'm all right. Let me sit awhile.

PRIEST: (*helping Don Patricio*) Here.

CRISTINA: You need to rest.

DON PATRICIO: I'll rest here. Go on, get ready . . .

CRISTINA: Are you sure?

DON PATRICIO: Estoy bien . . .

Andres takes Cristina's arm.

DON PATRICIO: Go, mi'ja. I'll be all right.

ANDRES: Yes, Don Patricio, you're tired. Sit in the shade and rest. Leave the dance to me.

Cristina looks at her father, then enters the house with a triumphant Andres.

PRIEST: He's so arrogant. He watches Cristina like a hawk. It's not natural, Don Patricio.

DON PATRICIO: I know, but our world is no longer natural. Men are driven by false desires—

PRIEST: Yes. They are. Each one of us. How can we judge evil if it's here— (*sits by Don Patricio*)

DON PATRICIO: Evil has always been in the world, Padre.

PRIEST: It's here, in the heart, in my heart.

DON PATRICIO: Not in your heart, Padre. You do good. You take care of the people—

PRIEST: But even the shepherd has desires . . .

DON PATRICIO: Yes, you're right. Sometimes we want too much. . . . We thought the new factory would solve all our needs. All it does is pollute our valley with bad chemicals. Where did I go wrong, Padre?

PRIEST: You didn't, Don Patricio. You only wanted what was good for your community.

DON PATRICIO: Yes, but I feel I'm the one that helped to kill Lorenzo.

PRIEST: You had nothing to do with his death.

DON PATRICIO: You're new here, Padre. You don't know the story. Years ago, when Andres was a child, his father wanted to do this dance of the Toro. He was training Andres to dance. He wanted to make a new dance for the Toro.

PRIEST: So that's where Andres got the idea.

DON PATRICIO: Andres's father had a very bad temper. When we wouldn't let him have his way, he attacked the mayordomo. He killed Luis Sandoval.

PRIEST: No!

DON PATRICIO: The Sheriff chased him down to the river, but before they caught him he hanged himself.

PRIEST: And Andres blames you.

DON PATRICIO: I did nothing. Perhaps I was jealous . . .

PRIEST: I don't understand.

DON PATRICIO: Andres's father was in love with my wife.

PRIEST: (shocked) Ay, Dios . . . But it wasn't your fault.

DON PATRICIO: I was a coward! I could have saved him!

PRIEST: All those years you've felt . . .

DON PATRICIO: Guilty? Yes.

PRIEST: That's why you put up with him.

DON PATRICIO: There's some good in every person.

PRIEST: Yes, and the sins of the father aren't the fault of the son. But Andres is different. I feel a chill when he's around.

The Sheriff enters at the gate.

SHERIFF: Don Patricio. Padre. Buenos días.

DON PATRICIO: (*stands*) Sheriff Montoya. Come in, come in. Can I get you some coffee?

SHERIFF: No, gracias. Just stopped by to check on you. There's a large crowd lining the street.

DON PATRICIO: Good, good. The dance will continue, as always.

PRIEST: So many people came to mass for Lorenzo. Is there any news?

SHERIFF: I'm sorry, but I've got no leads. I believe Lorenzo's body was dragged over to the irrigation ditch, but whoever did it covered his tracks. One stab wound and the boy was dead. Pierced the heart.

PRIEST: Have you found a weapon?

SHERIFF: (*shakes his head*) It's a blind alley. Lorenzo didn't have enemies. There's a couple of transients I'm checking out. Right now I figure it was just a robbery. Lorenzo was on his way to work . . . at the wrong place, wrong time.

PRIEST: Have you talked to Andres?

SHERIFF: Yeah, there's a lot of gossip about Andres. He left here and went to his tía's house. She vouches for him. So I'm where I started. No leads. (*takes off his hat and scratches his head*) Well, gotta go. Have a good day.

PRIEST: Thank you, Sheriff.

DON PATRICIO: Sí, sí, gracias.

As the Sheriff exits, he pauses to look at the ground where Lorenzo was killed.

PRIEST: Now what?

DON PATRICIO: What? Now we dance. We have to keep our promesa. Listen, here come the músicos! (*He goes to the gate.*) The abuelos are coming. Don Cornelio! Doña Francisca! ¡Buenos días de San Lorenzo!

Don Cornelio and Doña Francisca enter, dressed in their costumes. The músicos and dancers accompany them, carrying a litter with the statue of San Lorenzo, which they set to the side.

DON CORNELIO: Buenos días, Don Patricio. Padre.

DOÑA FRANCISCA: Buenos días le de Dios.

DON PATRICIO: ¿Por qué tan tristes? Sad abuelos don't make children laugh.

DOÑA FRANCISCA: Easy for you to say.

DON CORNELIO: You don't have to rope el Toro. Estoy viejo. Ya no puedo.

DOÑA FRANCISCA: Andres is crazy. We're afraid, compadre . . .

DON CORNELIO: That's not the way it should be. El Toro is the Evil One. He is to frighten the children, but we can't control him.

PRIEST: He has his rope around us.

DON CORNELIO: Call if off, compadre.

DON PATRICIO: No! I have never cancelled a dance. If we don't do it, who will dance for our santo? No, compadres, the dance is our salvation. It must go on.

PRIEST: But Andres has turned the dance to suit his purpose.

Cristina enters from the house. She is dressed as Malinche, in white lace and silk.

DON PATRICIO: Ah, mi'jita. How can we cancel the dance and not give this beauty to the people?

DOÑA FRANCISCA: Que bonita.

DON PATRICIO: Are you ready, mi'ja?

CRISTINA: Sí, Papá.

DOÑA FRANCISCA: You must be strong.

DON CORNELIO: Stronger than the Toro.

PRIEST: Where's the sword?

CRISTINA: Teresa has it. I tried to take it from her, but she wouldn't let me have it. She's staring at it as if she's praying.

DON CORNELIO: La cruz de Cristo . . .

DOÑA FRANCISCA: The cross de Quetzalcóatl, el dios de los Aztecas.

PRIEST: What do you mean, "the cross of Quetzalcóatl"?

DOÑA FRANCISCA: You don't know, Padre—you're too young.

DON CORNELIO: Too green behind the ears.

DOÑA FRANCISCA: The Aztecs say the sign of Quetzalcoatl was the cross. So the Spanish friars used the Christian cross to convert them.

DON CORNELIO: Just like they used the dance of the Matachines.

PRIEST: Yes, I know. Malinche is the Virgin Mary, who converts Moctezuma.

DOÑA FRANCISCA: Or maybe she is a diosa who takes the palma and the gourd to Moctezuma.

DON CORNELIO: You see, the españoles killed him.

DOÑA FRANCISCA: But she wakes him from death.

PRIEST: (confused) A resurrection?

DON CORNELIO: Sí, Padre, she brings him from the grave to help his people, the twelve tribes.

PRIEST: (still confused) But I thought the dance had to do with converting the Indians into the church?

DON CORNELIO: Pues, maybe yes, maybe no. Maybe the dance was the Aztec way of honoring Moctezuma, their Monarca.

PRIEST: (shakes his head) Do you mean it's a pagan dance?

DON CORNELIO: (shrugs) Pues, maybe yes, maybe no.

PRIEST: I see I have a lot to learn.

DOÑA FRANCISCA: Yes, Padre.

CRISTINA: I'm ready.

DOÑA FRANCISCA: ¡Bueno! ¡Que comience el baile de los Matachines!

DON PATRICIO: (calls) ¡Músicos! ¡Danzantes! ¡Todos listos!

The músicos strike up the music. From the house, Juan and Zonzo enter in full costume. Rita follows.

PRIEST: Are you well, Don Patricio?

DON PATRICIO: Yes, yes . . .

The Sheriff appears at the gate.

DON PATRICIO: Padre, la bendición.

DOÑA FRANCISCA: Ándale, padrecito, we're waiting.

PRIEST: (looking at Rita) Today we honor San Lorenzo. We ask forgiveness for our sins, and we promise . . . we promise to put away all false desire. We ask that God forgive our sins. . . . Bless the danzantes . . . bless San Lorenzo, who was burned alive by his tormentors. Help us cast out false desires . . .

DOÑA FRANCISCA: He's mumbling.

DON CORNELIO: Come on, Padre, make it short.

PRIEST: Yes . . . a blessing. Bless the dancers, in the name of the Father, the Son, the Holy Ghost—

DOÑA FRANCISCA: Amen!

DON CORNELIO: (pops his whip) ¡Los Matachines de Plaza Vieja! ¡La marcha!

The Matachines begin the dance. Don Cornelio calls out the first part of the dance. The dancers, who act as town's chorus, call for the Toro.

DANCERS: Where's the Toro? Abuelos, bring the Toro! . . . Toro! Toro! Toro!

Andres enters from the house, now wearing the full costume, mask and cape, of the Toro. He looks handsome and powerful. His muscles shine.

PRIEST: God help us.

Andres's eyes are fixed on Cristina as he dances toward her, a sensuous dance of the Toro.

ANDRES: The Toro has come to claim Malinche.

JUAN: (dressed as the Monarca) The Toro can't have Malinche.

ANDRES: Get out of my way!

JUAN: Or what? You push your weight around with old men, Andres! Now try it with me!

Zonzo, convinced the Toro is the Devil, makes the sign of the cross.

ZONZO: El diablo . . .

RITA: ¡Mira!

She points to the gate, where the Bruja appears and enters. The crowd grows silent.

ANDRES: ¡Tía!

BRUJA: This is what you've waited for! Take the girl! She belongs to you!

ANDRES: Yes! Dance with me, Malinche!

Andres and Juan dance around Cristina. The two compete until Juan shuts out Andres.

ANDRES: She's mine!

JUAN: Not as long as I'm around!

DANCERS: He wants Malinche! ¡Está loco! Something's not right!

ANDRES: (*grabs Cristina*) Come with me!

CRISTINA: Andres! No!

JUAN: Let her go!

Juan pulls Cristina away. Andres punches Juan and knocks him down. Don Patricio jumps up.

DON PATRICIO: Stop, Andres! What's gotten into you?

ANDRES: You killed my father!

BRUJA: Now revenge is ours!

DON PATRICIO: It was a mistake, Andres.

BRUJA: Don't listen to him! Take Malinche!

Teresa appears at the door, holding the sword.

TERESA: (*calling*) ¡Papá!

PRIEST: (*pointing to Teresa*) Don Patricio!

DON PATRICIO: ¡Mi'jita! (*He turns to her.*)

TERESA: Papá . . .

All are astounded she's talking.

TERESA: I saw Lorenzo . . . Just now, I saw Lorenzo . . . Andres stabbed him.

CRISTINA: Oh, dear God . . .

RITA: I knew . . . I knew . . .

TERESA: He killed Lorenzo.

ANDRES: She's crazy!

CRISTINA: What are you saying? What did you see?

TERESA: He killed Lore . . . there by the gate.

All are stunned.

DANCERS: (*all speaking at once*) ¿Qué dijo? // Andres killed Lorenzo! // ¡Válgame Dios! // Lo creo. // Le tenía envidia.

TERESA: I saw him stab Lorenzo.

DANCERS: ¡Esque mató a Lorenzo! // ¡Dice que lo mató!

ANDRES: She's lying!

Don Patricio holds Teresa; Zonzo takes the sword.

DON PATRICIO: Are you sure, hija?

TERESA: I saw him, Papá. He killed Lorenzo.

RITA: Damn you, Andres!

CRISTINA: Why, Andres? Why?

ANDRES: For you.

CRISTINA: You thought if you killed Lorenzo—

ANDRES: I've always loved you.

CRISTINA: Oh no, Andres, no . . .

ANDRES: If I can't have you, no one can!

SHERIFF: (*steps forward*) I've heard enough. You better come with me—

BRUJA: Take her, Andres!

ANDRES: (*brandishes a knife and grabs Teresa*) Stay back!

CRISTINA: Don't hurt her!

ANDRES: Come with me, Cristina!

SHERIFF: (*pulls his pistol*) Put the knife down, Andres! Let her go!

CRISTINA: Do what he says, Andres. Don't make it worse!

ANDRES: You love me, Cristina! Say you love me!

CRISTINA: (*sobs*) I loved Lorenzo!

ANDRES: No! You love me!

CRISTINA: I loved him . . . I know now how much I loved him . . .

A confused Andres turns to the Bruja.

ANDRES: It didn't work.

BRUJA: Don't listen to her! Avenge your father!

The Sheriff advances, but Andres holds him at bay by pointing the knife.

SHERIFF: Put the knife down!

TERESA: Diablo! You killed Lore!

ANDRES: Cristina!

ZONZO: Diablo!

Zonzo rushes Andres with the sword and stabs him. Andres falls, clutching at the sword. Juan goes to Cristina; Teresa runs to her father.

DANCERS: ¡Dios mío!

ZONZO: I killed the diablo . . .

The Priest rushes to kneel by Andres.

ANDRES: Cristina . . .

Cristina goes to him.

ANDRES: I love you . . .

CRISTINA: Oh God! Somebody call an ambulance!

ANDRES: I gave my soul for you . . .

CRISTINA: Shh, don't talk.

The Priest begins a prayer. Andres looks at the Bruja.

ANDRES: I was wrong— Oh, God, what I did was wrong . . .

CRISTINA: Lie still. We're getting an ambulance.

PRIEST: It's too late. He's dead.

The dancers whisper, grow subdued.

DON PATRICIO: Ven, mi hija. (*He pulls Cristina away.*) Ay, Dios mío. . . . ¿Por qué? ¿Por qué?

PRIEST: He wanted what he couldn't have.

RITA: We both wanted what we couldn't have.

DON PATRICIO: (*angry*) Yes, sometimes we want too much. We wanted that damned factory, and what did we get in return? Poisoned air! Poisoned water! (*He coughs and picks up the Toro mask.*) Andres wanted the mask of the Toro. Did he really think it would bring him love? (*He turns to the Bruja.*) You put the evil thoughts in his mind. You're to blame for his death!

BRUJA: He made a bargain—

DON PATRICIO: Yes, a bargain with evil. This mask of the Toro is evil. (*He throws the mask on the ground.*) Get rid of it! Burn it!

BRUJA: No! It's mine! (*She picks up the mask.*) The evil is not in the máscara. . . . It's in the heart. He wanted the girl, and for her he sold his soul. (*She looks around and points a finger to all of them.*) Each one of you has desire burning in your heart. Sooner or later you come to me, begging for help. I will save the mask of the Toro for you. When you're ready . . . you will come.

The dancers part as she exits.

ZONZO: (*dazed*) I killed el diablo.
    (*Teresa and Cristina go to Zonzo.*)

TERESA: You saved me.

CRISTINA: (*looking at the Sheriff*) What's going to happen?

SHERIFF: He wouldn't drop the knife. He could have killed Teresa. Zonzo saved her. . . . That's what I'll report.

The Priest takes a sarape from a bench and covers Andres's body.

PRIEST: May he rest in peace.

DON PATRICIO: Sí, que descanse en paz.

JUAN: What do we do now, Don Patricio?

Don Patricio shakes his head. He looks at the dancers.

DON PATRICIO: Take the statue of San Lorenzo to the church. Let the Matachines dance down the street. . . . The people are waiting.

The abuelos lift the litter with the statue. The dancers form two lines.

PRIEST: (*to Rita*) Are you coming?

RITA: I don't belong in church—

PRIEST: Yes, you do. There's forgiveness there . . . for all of us. (*He hands her his rosary.*)

DON PATRICIO: Go with them, mi'ja. The Padre is right. Whatever happened in the past is done. Now we have to look to the future.

Cristina and Teresa hold out their hands, and Rita joins them.

DON PATRICIO: Matachines, lead the way.

The dancers exit, dancing the dance of los Matachines. All follow, leaving the body of Andres on stage. The light dims, and thunder sounds in the distance.

END

Ay, Compadre!

CHARACTERS

LINDA
IGGY
DANIEL, Linda's husband
HELEN, Iggy's wife
STEVE, Daniel and Linda's son
ASHLEY, Steve's girlfriend

ACT ONE

A summer evening in the kitchen of the home of Daniel and Linda, who are entertaining their compadres, Iggy and Helen. The home is located in a new, middle-class suburb. One kitchen door leads to the patio, one to the dining room. Wine bottle, magazine, deck of cards, and tape player sit on the kitchen table.

Linda, dressed in shorts and a blouse, is at the kitchen counter finishing the guacamole. She is humming. Linda has put on weight, but overall she has kept her figure. She doesn't see herself as attractive. She may sip at wine, but she doesn't drink much. She puts aside the guacamole, waters the cactus, and sings a love song.

LINDA: "Cuando me vas a dar una flor . . ."

Iggy comes through the patio door, glances around, goes to Linda, and puts his arms around her waist. She enjoys it for a split second, then turns and pushes him away.

LINDA: ¡Compadre!

IGGY: Comadre.

LINDA: Behave yourself!

IGGY: ¿Por qué?

He starts for her again, but she hands him the bowl of guacamole.

LINDA: Here!

IGGY: I don't want guacamole.

LINDA: What do you want?

IGGY: (*grins*) A sweet empanada.

LINDA: It's not Christmas, but you can have corn chips. (*She holds out a bowl of corn chips.*)

IGGY: Ay, a man wants meat and they give him corn chips. Que tristeza. (*Iggy takes a corn chip and dips guacamole.*) Humm, I like your guacamole.

LINDA: Gracias.

IGGY: You're looking good, comadre.

LINDA: Estás loco.

179

IGGY: No, I mean it. Why can't a compadre admire his comadre?

LINDA: Because it might lead to, well, you know . . .

IGGY: I never played by the rules.

LINDA: And I bet you got burned a few times.

IGGY: Ah, it's worth it. Especially for a woman like you.

LINDA: After what happened . . . I thought we agreed not to talk about it.

IGGY: Okay, okay, I'm a man of my word. But you are looking good.

LINDA: Think of Helen—

IGGY: Helen's got her own life, her beauty shop.

LINDA: So you're lonely. Pobrecito.

She pinches his cheek, sets the bowls on the table. Iggy follows her.

IGGY: She doesn't understand how I feel.

LINDA: And you want me to understand.

IGGY: I could always talk to you.

LINDA: You tried, compadre. It didn't work.

IGGY: (*helping her set napkins, plates, etc.*) Ah, maybe it's me. I'm not getting any younger, but I still want to conquer the world!

LINDA: Does that include your comadre?

IGGY: I've always admired you. You know that! I like the way you talk, the way you walk, that inner beauty—drives me wild.

LINDA: Ay, Ignacio, and I thought it was Daniel who's the poet. Listen to you. You have a way with words, but—

IGGY: ¿Qué?

LINDA: Don't you see what you're going through?

IGGY: Midlife? Don't say it, comadre! I hate that word! I feel great! Never felt better! I'm selling a lot of insurance, and I've got plans to build a restaurant— The plans! I left them in the car. I want to show them to you and Daniel. (*He puts his arms around her waist.*) You wait, comadre. What I've got in mind will impress you!

LINDA: I'll be impressed if you two can cook the hamburgers. Is the grill ready?

IGGY: Daniel can't start the charcoal. ¡No tiene chispa!

LINDA: Shhh!

IGGY: Oh, he's sensitive?

LINDA: ¡Anda! Go help. And take these. (*She hands him the bowls of guacamole and chips.*)

IGGY: Only for you, comadre, and your guacamole! (*He laughs, goes out the patio door with the guacamole and chips, singing.*)
> La movida chueca, ya no quiere caminar,
> Porque le falta, porque no tiene,
> ¡Marijuana que famar!

LINDA: (*goes to the sink, looks at her cactus*) Don't you dare tell . . .

Daniel appears at the door, dressed in jeans and T-shirt. He is handsome, with graying, curly hair.

DANIEL: Ay que Ignacio, always happy.

LINDA: My guacamole turns him on.

DANIEL: (*goes to Linda, puts his arms around her*) Hey, you're looking good, vieja . . .

LINDA: Que milagro, you noticed.

DANIEL: I always notice.

LINDA: You never say anything.

DANIEL: Hey, I just gave you a compliment . . . some appreciation?

He goes to the fridge for a beer. Linda reaches for him.

LINDA: Are the coals ready?

DANIEL: I can't start the pinche charcoal. It's wet.

LINDA: I can cook them in the stove.

DANIEL: No, I'm going to use the new grill if it kills me.

LINDA: (*turns and looks out the kitchen window*) The sun is setting . . .

DANIEL: It's been a hot day.

LINDA: There go the vecinos for their walk.

DANIEL: The Smiths? They never say hello.

LINDA: They haven't been too friendly.

DANIEL: Mitoteros. Always looking out their window to see what we're up to. I miss our old vecinos. Don Arturo and his wife. Right now I bet he's watering his tomatoes. We should never have left the barrio. (*He sits at the table.*)

LINDA: The high school here was better for Steve.

DANIEL: Yeah, college prep classes, and in the barrio, nada.

LINDA: Anyway, it worked. Now he's finished the computer program. I'm proud of him. (*She starts making the hamburger patties.*)

DANIEL: Took him long enough. When I was thirty, I already had—

LINDA: I'm proud of him. Aren't you?

DANIEL: Seguro que sí. But it hasn't been easy. He's been bouncing from one job to the other, and the drugs—

LINDA: That's in the past. He's found himself.

DANIEL: By dating a gringa?

LINDA: A lot of Chicanos are dating gringas. Let's not get into that again!

DANIEL: Okay, okay, but if we had stayed in the barrio maybe he'd be dating a Chicanita. Hey, why don't we move back?

LINDA: Move back?

DANIEL: Why not? We have no friends here. They're all from California. . . . They're in their world, I'm in mine.

LINDA: You can say that again.

DANIEL: What do you mean?

LINDA: Nada.

DANIEL: Come on, what do you mean?

LINDA: Do you really think you'd be happier if we were back in the barrio, or is it just you?

DANIEL: Oh, now it's me?

LINDA: You know what I mean.

DANIEL: You like it here, don't you?

LINDA: Yes. For one thing, we have more room to entertain. Our casita in the barrio was the size of our living room!

DANIEL: You never complained.

LINDA: I'm not complaining. Steve needed a nice home to bring his friends.

DANIEL: Kids. You spend the best years of your life raising them, then they leave.

LINDA: Did Steve say something?

DANIEL: Yeah, he's going to take the offer in Frisco.

LINDA: That's great . . . (looks at Daniel more closely) ¿Qué pasa?

DANIEL: I guess I wanted him to be a plumber, someday go into business with me, be our own bosses.

LINDA: He likes computers, not fixing toilets.

DANIEL: And every company wants their token Chicano.

LINDA: He's not token, he's smart.

DANIEL: I know, I know. I'm going to miss him. . . . Son los años. I feel old.

LINDA: You're not old. You're just—

DANIEL: What?

LINDA: You're in the prime of life. (She goes to him and rubs his shoulders.)

DANIEL: Yeah, sure, the prime of life. And I have to get up at night to go pee. (He shakes his head sadly.) I never used to have to get up.

LINDA: You should go see Dr. Chávez.

DANIEL: I did. He put his finger up my— He has the fingers of a Dallas Cowboy fullback!

LINDA: Did you read the article on the prostate?

DANIEL: It's not my prostate! I'm okay . . . I just feel, I don't know.

LINDA: Like you're drifting . . . alone.

DANIEL: Yeah. It's a good thing I have my compadre. What would I do without him?

LINDA: Yes, what would we do without Iggy.

DANIEL: He's always around to help . . .

LINDA: He didn't help with the patio.

DANIEL: Iggy's never worked with his hands. For him it's all business. He really gets involved with his clients.

LINDA: But he can't build a patio. You did a great job. (*She kisses his ear, his cheek.*)

DANIEL: But I can't start a fire . . .

Helen enters from the patio. She is dressed in bright, tight stretch pants, a blouse that shows off her breasts, high heels, and lots of makeup. She is attractive, flashy. She is drinking wine.

HELEN: Ay, que calor— My, my, did I interrupt something?

LINDA: I was just telling Daniel what a good job he did with the patio.

HELEN: It's great, Danny—now if you could just cook the pinche hamburgers. The guacamole's great, but I need meat.

She puts out her glass and Daniel fills it.

LINDA: I'll cook them inside.

DANIEL: No! I'll pour gas on the charcoal!

LINDA: Isn't that dangerous?

HELEN: Iggy would just call for a pizza. I swear, he's so lazy he doesn't even cut our lawn.

DANIEL: In the barrio we didn't have lawns. I hate this keeping up with the Joneses.

HELEN: Ay, pobrecito. You sound like some sad homeboy.

She kisses Daniel on the cheek as Iggy enters. He is carrying a model of a restaurant, which he places on the table.

IGGY: Who's pobrecito?

HELEN: Daniel doesn't like to keep up with his neighbors.

IGGY: What's wrong with keeping up with the Cohens?

LINDA: You mean Joneses.

IGGY: Whatever.

DANIEL: Why should I?

IGGY: It's the American way, compadre. They buy a Chevy, you get a BMW. And I insure them both!

LINDA: Danny misses the barrio.

IGGY: In the barrio nobody buys insurance. (*He pours himself a glass of wine.*) You ought to start buying French wine, compadre—

DANIEL: French wine?

IGGY: Yeah, this stuff is awful.

DANIEL: Since when are we getting so facetas!

HELEN: Iggy's into French wine. For Christmas I gave a party at the beauty parlor, and Iggy brought French champagne. I got so mellow I burned a woman's hair.

IGGY: Mira, Danny, if you're going to entertain business associates, you need a little class.

DANIEL: Qué business associates?

IGGY: I thought we were gonna talk?

DANIEL: Let's just enjoy ourselves. No business.

IGGY: Mira. I had a friend make this model. (*He pulls Daniel to the model. All gather around it.*) There it is! Our dream!

DANIEL: Our dream?

LINDA: What is it?

IGGY: (*proudly*) It's a model of the restaurant we're going to build. Tio Taco!

DANIEL: Tio Taco?

IGGY: Yeah. We give Taco Bell a little competition.

DANIEL: (*pointing at the model*) What's this?

IGGY: Two arches, compadre. Like McDonald's. They look like two well-developed melones! (*He holds his hands to indicate breasts.*)

HELEN: Iggy!

IGGY: Advertising, advertising. The vatos go to McDonald's 'cause they see those two gold melones. It's, it's—

HELEN: Freudian.

IGGY: Simón, Freudian!

Iggy gives Helen a high five.

DANIEL: You can't just steal the McDonald's arches.

IGGY: Not steal, compadre, borrow. It's business. Look, AT&T announces a new telephone plan one day, and the next day MCI *borrows* it. Right? It's the American way, compadre. (*He puts his arms around Daniel.*) What do you say, Danny? You can't be a plomero all your life. Fixing people's toilets. Dirty sinks. That's the pits.

DANIEL: Hey! It's honest work!

IGGY: Okay, okay, it's honest work. But this place is ripe for a Mexican restaurant.

DANIEL: Here? In Enchanted Acres? There's nothing here but gringos!

IGGY: That's it! Why should they have to go all the way downtown for tacos? We build Tio Taco here and we'll make a killing. I promise, a killing!

DANIEL: I don't want to make a killing!

IGGY: What *do* you want, Danny boy? What?

DANIEL: (*shakes his head thoughtfully*) I don't know—

IGGY: That's your problem—you don't know. Leave it to me, compadre. I know what people need. We can make a fortune. (*turns to Linda*) What do you say, comadre?

LINDA: It sounds like a great idea.

DANIEL: Let's not talk business, okay? I'll go check the charcoal. (*He stalks out.*)

IGGY: Nervous, nervous.

LINDA: He's been working too hard . . . (*She turns to finish the patties.*)

IGGY: Working hard? Plumbers don't work hard. He rides around the neighborhood, the ladies invite him in for coffee, he's got it made. I admit, he did a great job with our new spa. (*He looks at Helen.*) He was there every afternoon for a month.

LINDA: He wanted to please you.

IGGY: Please me?

HELEN: I'll go help him—

IGGY: (*grabs Helen's wrist*) It took a month to finish.

They glare at each other.

HELEN: So, maybe we tested the spa when you were out selling insurance!

She jerks her arm free. Iggy glares at her.

IGGY: One of these days, vieja!

HELEN: What?

IGGY: (*raises his hand in a semi-threat*) I'm going to spank you!

HELEN: Oh, spank me, spank me!

IGGY: (*turns to Linda*) Hear that, comadre? Helen's acting naughty.

HELEN: All I get is promises . . .

LINDA: Daniel always tests what he puts in.

IGGY: Does that mean if he puts in a toilet he has to crap in it?

LINDA: He always does a good job.

HELEN: He's *good* with his hands.

IGGY: Yeah, how good?

HELEN: When he cleans out a line, he goes *all* the way.

IGGY: (*grins*) ¡No seas tan cabrona!

LINDA: Danny takes pride in his work.

IGGY: Ah, he's got it made. In plumbing the client calls you. Me? I gotta convince the suckers they need insurance.

HELEN: Yeah, to collect from you we have to die!

LINDA: Let's change the subject. How's Andy? Is he coming tonight?

HELEN: I asked him, but he's too busy with his friends. Come on, let's play cards.

IGGY: Helen doesn't want to talk about Andy, comadre.

LINDA: Why?

IGGY: Oh, pues, he's still making music with his *friends*—

HELEN: Knock it off, Ignacio!

IGGY: Okay, okay . . . We won't talk about my son, the musician. Like I was saying, plumbers have it made.

LINDA: (*sadly*) It's not easy for Daniel.

IGGY: He's got the blues.

LINDA: It's this place. He's never liked it here.

IGGY: Doesn't like Enchanted Acres? ¿Por qué?

LINDA: He misses the barrio, our friends—

IGGY: Misses the barrio? Holy shit. I can't sell insurance in the barrio! Everybody there is broke. Danny boy is old-fashioned. He needs to be in the barrio to be happy. Walk down the street, know everyone— thinks that's culture. I say screw it! Let's join the bandwagon! Chicanos are always ten years behind the gringos! They're into greed, and we're into cultura! Well, our cultura doesn't feed us! It's our turn for a little greed! (*He shouts toward the patio door.*) You hear that, Danny! Time for a little greed! Time for greedy Chicanos! A little greed will cure the blues!

LINDA: You don't mean that.

IGGY: You bet your sweet ass I do! Greed! Greed! Greed! Like the guy in the movie! Go get yours, raza, y chinga tu madre!

HELEN: Leave our mothers out of this. (*She downs her wine and serves again.*)

IGGY: Why so nervous?

HELEN: You haven't noticed? I take cold showers!

IGGY: Funny, funny.

LINDA: Daniel's not greedy. He's—

HELEN: Sensitive.

LINDA: Yes.

IGGY: No, he's crazy. The great American dream is to move to the suburbs, a two-car garage, send your kid to college! Now he's got it and he misses the barrio! Ah! Let's play cards.

HELEN: But we haven't eaten—

IGGY: We haven't eaten because my compadre can't light the fire! ¡Anda! Let's play! (*He pushes her to the chair.*)

HELEN: All right, all right, let's play. Don't be so pushy.

IGGY: Yeah, that's better. Nice and calm. Let's act like regular people. Don't want Linda's neighbors to say the Mexicans are arguing again. How about a little strip poker?

HELEN: Anda, deal them!

IGGY: (*shouts toward the patio*) Hey, compadre! We're going to play strip poker! Helen feels like taking it off! You've never seen Helen take it off, have you?

Helen slaps Iggy. He grabs her wrist.

HELEN: ¡Cabrón!

IGGY: Or, maybe he has.

HELEN: You're disgusting!

IGGY: Mi'jita, I'm just asking a simple question.

Helen frees her arm, jumps up, and turns to Linda.

HELEN: What the hell's the matter with you?

LINDA: Me?

HELEN: Yes, you! Why don't you stand up for your man!

IGGY: It's not her, it's Danny. He's got a little problem. Está nervioso. (*He looks at Linda.*) Right, comadre?

LINDA: He's just tired—

HELEN: Yes, tired. So mind your own business, Iggy.

IGGY: Mi compadre is my business!

LINDA: He's changing, but he doesn't want to talk about it.

HELEN: Of course he's changing—he's getting more handsome. (*She looks at Iggy.*)

LINDA: It's like I don't know him. We hardly talk to each other. He spends so much time alone, and Steve's leaving. . . . Let's talk about something else. (*In frustration she spills her wine.*)

IGGY: Pobrecita mi comadre . . . (*takes a napkin, kneels, wipes Linda's leg*)

LINDA: I'm okay. It's been a hot day . . .

IGGY: The weather's hot, and my comadre's hot, but my compadre's cold—ahí 'sta la problema.

HELEN: Drop it, Ig.

IGGY: I'm only trying to help. What's a compadre for? ¿Qué no, comadre?

Daniel enters.

DANIEL: ¿Qué pasó?

LINDA: Nada. I spilled some wine.

IGGY: She says she's hot.

Linda turns and goes to the sink.

HELEN: Too many copitas.

IGGY: Me? I can handle my copas. ¿Verdad, compadre? (*He embraces Daniel.*) Ah, que mi compadre. How long have we been compadres, huh?

DANIEL: You baptized Steve.

IGGY: And all that time you've been like a brother to me. No, more than a brother, like—

HELEN: A punching bag.

IGGY: A punching bag? Que tontería. I love my compadre. (*He holds Daniel tight, kisses his cheek.*) I love you more than anything in this world. Come on, compadre, let's build Tio Taco! The whole world will come to eat under our gold melones!

HELEN: He's been drinking.

IGGY: Hey, bruja, I can handle my vino. Where is Stevie?

LINDA: He has a date. He's going to bring her to eat.

IGGY: To eat her? Ay que plebe.

LINDA: No, to eat *here.*

IGGY: Good, good. I want to see my ahijado.

DANIEL: And your kids? We haven't seen them in months.

HELEN: Don't ask. Laurie's dating her boss. He's fifty! Ay que mi hija, she has no sense!

IGGY: Takes after her mother—

HELEN: I tried to get her to work at the beauty shop with me. With her looks she could do really well.

LINDA: She's so good looking . . .

IGGY: Chula como su mamá.

HELEN: Glad you noticed, *viejo*. Anyway, we don't see her. She works all week and parties all weekend.

DANIEL: And Andy?

Helen looks at Iggy.

LINDA: Andrew is so talented.

DANIEL: Yeah. I wish I could play la lira like Andy.

HELEN: When he plays, it's like he's making love to his guitar—

IGGY: (*glares at Helen*) I wish he'd pick a woman. Come on, let's play. How's the charcoal doing?

DANIEL: The charcoal's wet. No quiere.

IGGY: Ay, compadre, you let your gunpowder get wet.

DANIEL: What?

IGGY: Wet powder, no bang! (*He laughs.*) Que importa. We can eat guacamole. Like Maximilian said when the Mexicanos were starving: Let them eat guacamole!

They laugh and sit. Iggy shuffles.

IGGY: The salsa?

LINDA: (*serves the dish from the counter*) Aquí 'stá. Special from the deli.

IGGY: From the deli! First they start buying tortillas, now salsa. Next they're going to want to be liberated, just like the gringas.

HELEN: You said it.

LINDA: I ran out of chile colorado.

IGGY: Hear that, compadre? She's got no chile! Can't keep a woman without hot chile!

HELEN: Just deal, Iggy.

DANIEL: I need a beer.

IGGY: Linda needs hot chile . . .

HELEN: I'll get it. (*She jumps to the refrigerator.*)

LINDA: No, let me.

IGGY: Hey! Let him get his own! Pero que chingao, two women dying to serve the man. What's he got?

HELEN: He's sensitive.

IGGY: Sensitive? Oh, *ess-coo-se moi!* You hear that, compadre. You're sensitive. ¡Que chulo! (*He pinches Daniel's cheek.*)

DANIEL: Knock it off, Iggy!

IGGY: Sensitive, like Andy—

HELEN: ¡Calláte! Deal!

DANIEL: Andy's sensitive? Spends all his time with his friends? What are you getting at?

IGGY: ¡Chingao! Why so many questions! (*He slams the cards on the table, grabs his glass.*) I thought we were here to have fun! I could be watching the game! I'll light the charcoal! (*He goes out.*)

DANIEL: ¿Qué dije?

LINDA: He's upset . . .

HELEN: Everybody's upset. I'll go talk to him.

She goes out. Linda gathers the cards.

DANIEL: I should keep my mouth shut.

LINDA: Fifty-two pickup.

He helps pick up the cards, brushes against her.

DANIEL: ¿Qué?

LINDA: Remember? On our honeymoon we played fifty-two pickup?

DANIEL: Yeah, to see how the kings and queens landed. I was the king . . .

LINDA: I was your queen . . .

DANIEL: We made love . . .

They stand and look at each other tenderly.

DANIEL: Seems like a hundred years ago.

LINDA: I haven't forgotten.

DANIEL: Memorias . . .

LINDA: They're good memories.

DANIEL: But a man can't live with only memories.

LINDA: We have each other.

DANIEL: Yeah. In this crowd you're the only one not crazy. (*He puts his hands on her hips and kisses her lightly. She closes her eyes.*)

LINDA: You're still my king.

He turns to pick up cards. She opens her eyes.

LINDA: ¿Es todo?

DANIEL: ¿Qué?

LINDA: Just one kiss?

DANIEL: Hey, we're having a party! Don't start on me!

LINDA: I'm not. I just want to know—

DANIEL: What?

LINDA: Sometimes I feel like the nopal . . .

DANIEL: The nopal?

LINDA: Waiting to be watered.

DANIEL: Watered? What the hell are you talking about?

LINDA: I understand—really, viejo, I do.

DANIEL: No, you don't.

LINDA: I do! I know about change! I went through it, and you—

DANIEL: What?

LINDA: You didn't even know.

DANIEL: Ay, vieja, what could I do? I was working hard, worrying about Steve . . . What could I do?

LINDA: Nada. There was nothing you could do.

DANIEL: (*He goes to her, holds her.*) It seems I don't understand anything lately.

LINDA: Everybody changes—it's not the end of the world.

DANIEL: It's just the work. I took on that apartment complex, and I can't get good help. Soon as it's done I'll take a break.

LINDA: (*sadly*) Yes, it's the work.

DANIEL: I'm ready to retire.

LINDA: Why don't you? We could travel, go on cruises—

DANIEL: I feel the change . . . I just can't accept it.

LINDA: I've been reading—

He turns away from her.

DANIEL: (*sarcastically*) In your "women" magazines?

LINDA: (*picks up a magazine from the table and hands it to him*) Here's the article I want you to read.

DANIEL: (*taking it*) "New Woman"! What do they know! They don't even know Chicanos exist! Get one by a Chicano!

LINDA: I tried, but there aren't any! Nobody's writing about us. Mira, change happens to all men. . . . If you would only talk to someone.

DANIEL: It's not easy—

LINDA: Talk to Dr. Chávez. He said your glucose level is high—

DANIEL: I'm okay. I tried the Viagra. All it did was give me headaches. You know Mori down at the barbershop? They say he took Viagra and he got an erection that wouldn't go down. They had to take him to the hospital. (*He takes the magazine, thumbs through it.*) And all I got was headaches. So what does it say? More tofu?

LINDA: (*laughs*) Well, we tried.

DANIEL: If Iggy knew you've been feeding me tofu morning, noon, and night, I'd never hear the end. Next, rhinoceros horn powder mixed with tiger milk— (*He shakes his head.*)

LINDA: It was just an idea.

DANIEL: Maybe I should get an implant? Puff, puff, a little pump, and whamo!

LINDA: What you're going through is normal.

DANIEL: (*scoffs*) Normal! I hate that word! I know it's normal, but I don't like it! I want to be like I used to be! (*He grabs her.*) I'm healthy! I feel good! I've got these ganas burning me up.

LINDA: I've got ganas too!

DANIEL: You?

LINDA: Yes!

DANIEL: So what the hell do we do? (*He shakes her.*)

LINDA: I don't know, viejo! I don't know!

DANIEL: So much for free advice! (*He flings the magazine aside.*) Nobody knows! Nobody knows a damn thing!

LINDA: Together, we can—

DANIEL: I don't blame you, vieja. I blame myself.

LINDA: There's no one to blame! Things change! We all change!

DANIEL: What can we do?

LINDA: It's not the end of the world.

DANIEL: (*surprised*) Not the end of the world? I'm on fire and I can't— Ah, I can't explain it!

LINDA: Maybe a change would help.

DANIEL: What kind?

LINDA: Something interesting.

DANIEL: A vacation?

LINDA: We could go to Las Vegas with our compadres.

DANIEL: Iggy and Helen? We've been going to Las Vegas with them for the past thirty years. I'm sick and tired of it. Let's go to Mexico. Climb the pyramids! Do something really different.

LINDA: Do you really want to?

DANIEL: Why not? You said we should travel!

LINDA: Then let's go!

They hold hands.

DANIEL: Let's do it!

LINDA: ¡Con ganas! (*She pauses.*) Helen and Iggy . . .

DANIEL: Let them do their thing!

LINDA: They always go with us.

DANIEL: The hell with them! Iggy drinks all the time, and Helen parades around like a twenty-year-old. Familia's familia, but we need a break.

LINDA: Would that solve our problem?

DANIEL: (shrugs) No, I guess not . . .

LINDA: You're tired of them . . .

He nods.

LINDA: And you're bored with me . . .

DANIEL: That's not true, vieja.

LINDA: It's normal—

DANIEL: (shouting) Normal! Don't say that word!

LINDA: Maybe another woman—

DANIEL: (He looks surprised.) I'm not seeing another woman!

LINDA: What if you were?

DANIEL: What?

LINDA: I just thought—

DANIEL: (laughs) Young women aren't attracted to viejos. If they are, it's for money.

LINDA: Helen likes you.

DANIEL: ¿Mi comadre? Why bring her up?

Daniel picks up the magazine on the floor and throws it in the basket.

LINDA: I was just thinking. When I went through menopause I felt really low. Remember how I used to drag around? The doctor pumped me full of hormones, but I bloated up. Nothing helped, because inside I had changed. In a way it was a relief, not having to worry about getting pregnant. But I felt I wasn't a woman anymore!

DANIEL: (going to Linda) You are, vieja. The best woman I ever knew.

LINDA: Then the hot flashes—

DANIEL: I know it was hard on you.

LINDA: Nature plays tricks with us. A woman understands that.

DANIEL: Maybe I should take some of those hormone shots.

LINDA: Testosterone?

DANIEL: Yeah, why not?

LINDA: If you think you need them—

DANIEL: I need to try something. (*He shouts.*) ¡Testoroni con baloney! ¡Ajúa!

LINDA: I'll take you as you are. (*She reaches out, holds his hand.*)

DANIEL: So how about Mexico?

LINDA: ¡Vamos!

DANIEL: I'll finish the apartments! Then we take off! Climb the Pyramid of the Sun! Write poetry!

They are about to kiss when Iggy and Helen enter from the patio.

IGGY: Ah, our love birds. We're gone two minutes and my compadre gets horny. Hey, you got company, remember.

DANIEL: (*groans*) How could I forget.

IGGY: I poured lighter fluid on the charcoal.

DANIEL: Did it start?

IGGY: No matches.

DANIEL: No chispa, eh compadre? (*tosses a book of matches from his pocket to Helen*)

IGGY: Hey, I've got plenty of chispa—it's your charcoal that's wet. (*goes to the model at the table*) Mira, compadre, this gold arch we mark Enter, this one Exit. In between we serve the best tacos this side of the border. I know some Mexicanas who will work cheap.

DANIEL: (*shakes his head*) Hire them cheap, huh.

IGGY: Sure, compadre. Every dog has its day. Besides, only a real Mexicana can make good tacos.

DANIEL: Don't be racist, compadre.

IGGY: Hey, it's just business.

HELEN: Forget business. I'm hungry.

IGGY: You're always hungry . . .

HELEN: ¡Embustero! Not always. It comes in cycles. Sometimes I can't stop eating—but I hate to get fat.

LINDA: It's in the genes—

HELEN: No, it's in the tortillas.

IGGY: It's your destino, honey. Mexicanas have a baby and they start getting round. Big fat mommas. Nothing you can do about it.

HELEN: I'm not fat . . .

IGGY: Hey, I like it, vieja. There's more of you.

DANIEL: More to grab.

IGGY: (turns to Daniel) Hey, you been grabbing my vieja?

HELEN: I wish.

IGGY: One of these days, vieja—

HELEN: I know, you're going to spank me.

IGGY: (grins) Empanadas.

HELEN: I tried the gym . . . but I felt out of place. The girls are . . . you know.

IGGY: She goes on binges. One week it's diet, the next she's eating.

HELEN: Sometimes I feel I can't get enough.

LINDA: Enough de qué?

HELEN: De todo.

DANIEL: Yeah, I feel that way.

IGGY: How?

DANIEL: Con hambre. Inside. Con ganas—

HELEN: (studies Daniel closely) Ganas. I like that! Tengo ganas. I'm hungry . . .

Daniel nods in agreement. Iggy turns to Daniel.

IGGY: A man con ganas makes a good businessman. You gotta be hungry! Let's open Tio Taco, con ganas! And I guarantee in five years we'll be rolling in lana! ¿Qué dices?

He slaps Daniel on the arm. Daniel looks at Helen.

DANIEL: I don't want to get tied up in a restaurant.

IGGY: We're not getting any younger, compadre. Think of it as a nest egg. For retirement!

DANIEL: Retirement?

IGGY: Hey, you don't live forever. Five years and we turn around and sell the place, then we golf forever.

DANIEL: Golf?

IGGY: Simón, ese. The great American pastime.

HELEN: I could retire. I'm sick of all the old viejas who think a perm or a color job is going to perform miracles!

IGGY: Don't let Helen fool you. She knows you gotta make your clients feel good about themselves. She's become a great golfer.

HELEN: It kills time on weekends.

DANIEL: I don't have time to kill.

IGGY: Sure you do. Relax, hombre, or you'll have a heart attack. Let's play a little game before the chef's hamburgers? (*He pours a glass, sits, and takes up the cards.*)

LINDA: Yes, let's play. Daniel?

DANIEL: Por qué no . . . (*He joins them at the table.*)

HELEN: What are you doing with your time, Linda?

LINDA: I'm still volunteering at the library.

IGGY: And Danny boy?

LINDA: He's always busy.

DANIEL: Soon as I finish this big job I took on, I'm cutting back.

LINDA: Danny reads a lot.

HELEN: Iggy falls asleep reading the paper—ronca y ronca.

IGGY: Hey, hey, we're talking about mi compadre, not me. What do you read, compadre?

DANIEL: Everything.

LINDA: He writes poetry.

IGGY: Poetry? ¡Ya no la chingas! Compadre, real men don't write poetry! That stuff can ruin you!

HELEN: So, what's wrong with poetry?

DANIEL: Hey, our poets have a lot to tell us. It's part of our cultura.

LINDA: He's written some beautiful poems.

IGGY: Poetry is for women!

DANIEL: That's crazy!

IGGY: Andy used to read a lot of poetry—

DANIEL: So?

IGGY: Ruined him . . .

DANIEL: What the hell do you mean?

IGGY: ¡Nada! ¡Nada! Let's change the subject.

HELEN: Let's eat!

IGGY: She's got the hungries, compadre!

LINDA: Danny jogs every morning.

HELEN: Iggy can't jog—it's his knees.

IGGY: Hey, nothing wrong with my knees!

HELEN: You're always complaining!

IGGY: A little arthritis, es todo.

HELEN: You know what they say, first the knees go, then the chile.

IGGY: ¡Calláte!

DANIEL: Oh, que sensitive.

IGGY: Hey, I've got enough chispa to take care of ten women!

HELEN: That's what the viejos call Viagra. Chispa.

DANIEL: You mean you—

IGGY: Don't listen to her, compadre. That's stuff's for sissies. A real Mexican macho is built to last. So we get a little tired at the end of the day . . .

DANIEL: I know . . .

IGGY: Maybe you need vitamins.

DANIEL: I need a break.

IGGY: Like what?

DANIEL: I don't know . . . I want to travel, maybe go to Mexico. Write poetry—

IGGY: Damn. All these years and he's a closet poet. That's why I like you, compadre, you're a poet. (*He reaches across, embraces Daniel, kisses his cheek, spills the cards.*)

HELEN: Iggy!

DANIEL: When I was young I used to play the guitar, compose songs.

HELEN: You have a way with words.

IGGY: You say he has good hands and a way with words. Has he been whispering poetry in your ear—

HELEN: (*grabs Iggy by the collar*) Don't be a cabrón!

IGGY: Hey, just kidding! Just kidding! (*He sings.*) "Borracho perdido, por una mujer . . ."

HELEN: I'm going to get drunk! (*She pours a glass.*)

LINDA: Helen, you know it makes you sick. Danny, do something about the charcoal. We're all hungry.

HELEN: Goddammit, Linda! Don't you know there's more than hunger for food!

LINDA: (*looks at Daniel*) Yes, but—

IGGY: We got hungry women, compadre.

DANIEL: What the hell's gotten into everyone?

IGGY: Ganas! The hungries! Our viejas have the munchies!

HELEN: Yes, we need to be fed!

IGGY: I know all about las ganas— When I was a kid we had a mean dog we tied to a tree. A bitch in heat went by. Our macho nearly went crazy trying to get to her. Broke the chain. A chain, compadre, and he broke it to get the perra.

HELEN: So?

IGGY: That was my first lesson—

HELEN: Learn from a dog, act like a dog!

IGGY: For my perro it was la perra, for us it's la mujer! Mother Nature es una puta! Makes us act like dogs!

HELEN: Hey! We're not perras!

IGGY: Look at my compadre! Chained like the perro!

DANIEL: Yeah, I need to break out!

HELEN: Freud says you need to express what you feel inside.

IGGY: (surprised) What the hell do you know about Freud?

HELEN: I read! I've got magazines at the shop! I'm not stupid!

LINDA: He doesn't need Freud. (She turns to Daniel.) You just need to realize it's a phase—

DANIEL: It's normal, huh?

LINDA: Yes.

HELEN: No, you have to tell us how you feel.

DANIEL: What do you mean?

HELEN: It's like confession. Let it all hang out!

LINDA: (to Daniel) Maybe she's right—

IGGY: Don't do it, compadre! Don't confess! You confess y te chingan!

HELEN: What is it, Danny? You can tell us. We love you!

IGGY: ¡No te creas, compadre! Mujeres have a way of getting it out of you! Don't talk!

DANIEL: I've got nothing to hide!

HELEN: Yes, you do! Tell us!

Daniel stands up, knocks over his chair. Looks at Iggy.

DANIEL: You tell them!

IGGY: I'm not saying anything!

DANIEL: ¡Cobarde!

HELEN: Yeah! You tell us, Ig!

IGGY: I'm as good as I ever was!

HELEN: Talk is cheap, honey!

She pushes Iggy. He pushes her back and she falls.

IGGY: Mi'jita . . . I'm sorry. (*He reaches for her.*)

HELEN: Don't "mi'jita" me! You hit me!

She is mad, but it's a game they've played before.

IGGY: I'm sorry . . . Helen . . .

HELEN: Don't touch me . . .

IGGY: I didn't mean to—

HELEN: (*sobs*) ¡Grocero! ¡Condenado! ¡Sinvergüenza!

IGGY: ¡Soy bien desgraciado! Forgive me!

HELEN: (*turns to Linda*) My father used to get drunk . . . come home and beat my mother. God, I swore if a man ever touched me I'd cut his balls off!

IGGY: I had too much to drink—

HELEN: That's no excuse!

IGGY: ¡Pégame! ¡Pégame! I deserve it!

HELEN: If I really told the truth about you—

IGGY: No, Helen! Don't! No fair telling family secrets!

DANIEL: I thought familia was supposed to share everything, Ig.

IGGY: Shut up, Danny! She hit me first.

HELEN: (*nods, then smiles*) Yes . . . I did hit you first. I'm sorry, viejo.

IGGY: I'm sorry, too, mi'jita. We're even.

HELEN: Yes, we're even . . .

IGGY: (*holds Helen, pats her behind*) Se me va secar la mano . . .

HELEN: Se te va secar el weenie . . .

They laugh.

DANIEL: Holy caca, if the neighbors were looking in the window, they'd think we're bananas!

IGGY: (turns to Daniel) You forget, compadre, we got no bananas today. (He starts swaying, singing.) "Hey, Mr. Talley Man! Pela mi banana! Day-O! Day-O! Daylight come and we wanna go screw!" (He grabs Helen and they do a sexy dance.) "Hey, Mr. Talley Man—"

HELEN: (singing) ¡Dame tu banana!

DANIEL: ¡Están locos!

Helen places her hands on Iggy's hips and follows him around the kitchen.

IGGY: (singing) Oh, we got no bananas today!

HELEN: We got melones! And we got sandías! (She shakes her behind.)

IGGY: But we got no bananas today! Come on, compadre! ¡Comadre!

Linda jumps behind Helen, Daniel joins and places his hands on Linda's hips, and they all snake-conga dance around the kitchen.

IGGY: ¡Eso es!

LINDA: If you can't beat them! Join them!

DANIEL: Let it all hang out! ¡Ajúa!

LINDA: We got melones! (She holds her breasts.)

HELEN: And we got sandías!

IGGY: But we got no bananas today!

HELEN: ¡Ándele, viejo, una conga!

IGGY: (leads them, singing) One, two, three la conga! ¡Como me resonga! ¡Esa vieja bomba!

LINDA: One, two, three la conga! ¡Como me resonga! ¡ESE VIEJO BOMBO!

They laugh. Steve peers in from the dining room door.

IGGY: Tomorrow we got bananas!

DANIEL: Mañana bananas!

They snake conga out into the patio.

HELEN: Hey, Mr. Tally Man—

DANIEL: ¡Pela mi banana!

IGGY: Tomorrow banana day, mujeres!

LINDA: Promises! Promises!

There is laughter in the patio. Steve and Ashley enter the kitchen. He is tall and muscular; she is blonde, very attractive, dressed in a very skimpy halter and shorts.

STEVE: Talk about letting your hair down. Wow.

ASHLEY: Sounds like they're having a great time.

STEVE: When they party, they get weird.

ASHLEY: Cool. Where's the food?

STEVE: There's guacamole—

ASHLEY: Is that all?

STEVE: Hamburgers?

ASHLEY: Whatever. (*She puts her arms around him.*)

STEVE: Would you rather go out and eat?

ASHLEY: Yes.

STEVE: Still worried about meeting my parents?

ASHLEY: I don't want to bust in.

STEVE: Hey, you were invited. In no time they'll be going out for menudo.

ASHLEY: Menudo?

STEVE: It's kind of a soul food for Mexicans. My uncle Ig calls it the aphrodisiac of Chicanos.

ASHLEY: (*playing with his hair and teasing*) You certainly don't need it.

STEVE: I hate menudo, but let me show you my bedroom anyway.

ASHLEY: No way, Ho-say!

STEVE: All right, I'll feed you first. Let's grab some munchies.

They dip into the guacamole. He takes two beers from the fridge.

ASHLEY: Are you sure it's okay for me to show up?

STEVE: I told you, you were invited.

ASHLEY: It's the first time—

STEVE: What?

ASHLEY: You know.

STEVE: You ever dated a Mexican? Gee, I wish I could say it was my first time
with a gringa.

ASHLEY: You're awful!

STEVE: Sorry, bad joke. Look, we're just like everybody else. We're normal—

From the patio a loud Iggy sings, "Hey, Mr. Talley Man, pela mi banana!"

STEVE: Well, except my padrino . . .

ASHLEY: Who?

STEVE: Mr. Iggy. He's a midlife party animal! Great guy.

ASHLEY: You mention him more than your father.

STEVE: Dad's great, but too serious. My padrino knows how to have fun.

ASHLEY: A Latin lover, huh?

STEVE: Please, no stereotypes.

ASHLEY: Sorry. The past couple of months have been good—not just the sex.

STEVE: Hey, that's fantastic!

ASHLEY: So are the emotions.

STEVE: It doesn't have to end.

ASHLEY: Café con leche . . .

STEVE: Makes a nice mixture.

ASHLEY: But my parents . . .

STEVE: Yeah, conservatives—

ASHLEY: I'm not like them.

They kiss.

ASHLEY: Let's not interrupt their fun. Let's eat out.

STEVE: ¡Vamos! I'll grab a shirt and we'll go to Panchitas.

*They go out. Daniel and Helen enter, laughing, with tears in their eyes. She fills a bowl
with guacamole. He has brought in empty beer bottles.*

HELEN: That was fun.

DANIEL: Iggy knows how to have fun.

HELEN: And you?

DANIEL: Ah, I'm too serious. Linda says it's gotten worse—

HELEN: You're a poet, Daniel. You're sensitive. Being serious is part of you.

DANIEL: Maybe I'm too serious, but I've been thinking about life. There are things I'd like to do. I just feel like breaking out.

HELEN: Me, too.

DANIEL: I don't want to fix toilets the rest of my life.

HELEN: And I don't want to give perms to little old ladies the rest of mine. We're in the same boat, Danny. (She holds his hands.)

DANIEL: Iggy's right, you know. A person gets chained to something, and life passes him by. I don't want to be sorry at the end. I want to be able to say I lived.

HELEN: You have, Danny. It's in your poems. God, you're so lucky to be able to express yourself. The rest of us—

DANIEL: What?

HELEN: The rest of us are phony. We cover up. I dress loud, I talk loud, but inside I'm like you. I want to climb a mountain and listen to the silence. Listen to my heart beat.

DANIEL: Climb a pyramid . . .

HELEN: (draws closer to Daniel, puts her arms around him)Yes, climb a pyramid. Make love . . .

DANIEL: Now who's the poet?

HELEN: I want to hear you read your poems . . . Us, alone . . .

She starts to kiss him. He backs away.

DANIEL: It won't work, Helen.

HELEN: It won't if we don't give it a chance. I admire you, Danny. Why can't we—

DANIEL: Be more than compadre y comadre? Just won't work.

HELEN: You sure?

DANIEL: Do you know what you really want?

HELEN: Excitement . . . something new . . . Love? No, I don't know what I want. I feel I'm burning up.

DANIEL: We're all in the same boat.

HELEN: So why complicate things? Sometimes I think we're all just bored, so we run around looking for a little excitement. And that's not fair to the others.

DANIEL: Maybe it's not too late—

Linda and Iggy enter from the patio.

LINDA: Ay Dios, we haven't done anything this crazy since—

DANIEL: The night Iggy went skinny dipping at Caesar's Palace!

IGGY: You dared me.

HELEN: You were drunk!

IGGY: I was drunk? We were *all* drunk!

LINDA: That was a great trip.

IGGY: (*sitting*) Ah, we used to be able to drink, dance, gamble all night, and still—

HELEN: Do it.

DANIEL: (*looks at Linda*) Yeah.

IGGY: The good old days.

HELEN: (*picks up a towel and dances*) We can still do it! (*She twists.*) Come on, baby, let's do that twist! (*She tries to pull Iggy out to dance.*)

IGGY: Ya no puedo.

HELEN: Come on, Iggy, let's twist!

IGGY: Que twist ni que twist . . . ¡Mis rodillas!

HELEN: Pobrecito. ¡Ya no puede twist!

IGGY: As my grandpa used to say, todo se acaba.

DANIEL: I remember my jefito saying that.

LINDA: Why?

DANIEL: Why what?

LINDA: Why does it have to end?

DANIEL: It's normal, remember?

IGGY: Banana wilt.

LINDA: So it ends. There's something else.

IGGY: ¿Qué?

HELEN: There's cariño . . .

LINDA: Yes.

DANIEL: ¿Cariño?

HELEN: Have you pendejos forgotten what cariño is?

IGGY: Ah, women. If I live to be five hundred, I'll never understand them.

HELEN: What's there to understand?

IGGY: Amorcitos, cariño, coo-chee-coos, honey this and honey that . . . that's for women. Right, compadre?

DANIEL: The man needs . . .

IGGY: A stiff banana. Without it, you're nothing!

HELEN: You guys don't know shit!

IGGY: Hey, why so mad, mi'jita?

HELEN: Tell them!

LINDA: Me?

HELEN: Yes, you! Who do you think I mean?

LINDA: Women need—

DANIEL: There she goes with all the "New Woman" free advice.

HELEN: Let her finish!

LINDA: We need—

DANIEL: What?

LINDA: We don't need what you think we need!

IGGY: You don't need it hot?

LINDA: No!

IGGY: Bullshit! (*He looks at Helen.*) You need it every night, don't you?

HELEN: Yes! Yes! Yes!

IGGY: Just like the man!

HELEN: If it's good for men, it's good for us!

DANIEL: Wait! (*to Linda*) Go on.

LINDA: For us, menopause—

IGGY: Oh, dirty word, comadre, dirty word! Helen won't listen. Don't listen, Helen!

HELEN: I'm not in menopause!

IGGY: She denies it!

HELEN: (*turns on Iggy*) You sonofabitch! You told?

IGGY: I swear on my mother's grave I didn't tell!

HELEN: Don't you know—it was difficult!

LINDA: (*comforts her*) That's all right, Helen, it's all right.

HELEN: No, it's not all right! What do men know? Nothing!

IGGY: What we don't know won't hurt us, is that it?

HELEN: They don't know what it's like . . .

DANIEL: (*looks at Linda*) Linda went through it.

LINDA: It wasn't so bad. I learned to look at myself, and—

They all wait breathlessly.

LINDA: I found out that I, I . . .

DANIEL: What?

LINDA: I still felt sexy!

HELEN: Good for you!

LINDA: I felt sexy and I wanted—

IGGY: Hot chile?

LINDA: I just wanted to be loved, to be touched . . .

HELEN: Being sexy doesn't stop at meno—

IGGY: Don't say it!

DANIEL: I didn't know—

LINDA: It was like freedom. But I still had—

HELEN: Ganas!

LINDA: Yeah! I had ganas, all over!

DANIEL: All these years? And I didn't know . . .

LINDA: You never wanted to talk about it, viejo.

IGGY: You can talk till you're blue in the nalgas, but if a man can't perform—

HELEN: Perform? That's what you think sex is? Performance? If that's what we wanted, we'd go to the movies!

DANIEL: Maybe Iggy's right. If a man can't do it—

IGGY: To be is to screw. (*He laughs.*) Is that poetry, compadre?

LINDA: (*reaches for Daniel, pleads*) There's still time.

DANIEL: ¿México? The pyramids?

LINDA: Yes!

He reaches for her but Iggy interrupts.

IGGY: Come on, let's drop this bullshit and eat. ¡Tengo hambre!

HELEN: Now who's hungry?

IGGY: Let's play cards!

HELEN: I don't want to play. Too hot. Is the air on?

LINDA: It is hot . . . the dancing.

IGGY: Helen's always hot.

HELEN: (*fills her glass of wine*) We eat too much when we aren't getting any—

IGGY: Don't blame being gorda on somebody else! You can't run a business by blaming others! It's all in your attitude!

HELEN: I'm not blaming anyone! I just want to eat! ¡Quiero comer! ¡Tengo hambre! I'm starving!

IGGY: ¡Ay, Dios mío! Starving women!

LINDA: I'll check the charcoal . . . (*She takes the hamburger patty plate out onto the patio.*)

HELEN: I need fresh air. (*follows Linda*)

IGGY: She gets hot flashes.

DANIEL: Linda used to.

IGGY: Chinga, chinga, chinga . . .

DANIEL: ¿Qué?

IGGY: Las mujeres.

DANIEL: We can't live with them, we can't live without—

IGGY: We're hooked.

DANIEL: It's an addiction. . . . Where did it start?

IGGY: When Eva gave Ádan a little panocha. He got used to it, and he passed the virus to us.

DANIEL: And we love it!

They laugh and give each other a high five.

IGGY: Simón que we love it. We can't do without it!

DANIEL: ¿Y ahora?

IGGY: ¿Qué?

DANIEL: What do we do with las ganas?

IGGY: Compadre, you're worrying too much. Stress isn't good for you. ¿Sabes?

DANIEL: Mother Nature . . .

IGGY: Mother Nature es una puta! She loves to whore, but she gives it to the young. Young boys and girls, young rabbits, pigs, even the piojos in your hair! When you're young it's puro bang, bang, bang! But you hit the sixties, y adiós, chango, you had your time.

DANIEL: And not a damn thing one can do. Except maybe one of those implants . . .

IGGY: You're not thinking—

DANIEL: I'll go crazy if I can't bust out!

IGGY: There's other ways.

Daniel looks at him. Iggy checks the patio, then speaks confidentially to Daniel.

DANIEL: ¿Como que?

IGGY: Viejo el viento, pero todavía sopla.

DANIEL: What do you mean?

IGGY: Mira, compadre, you need a woman.

DANIEL: I've got a woman.

IGGY: Not a wife, a woman.

DANIEL: Mess around?

IGGY: Hey, you're a plumber. You show up in the morning when the vieja's home. She takes off her curlers, pours you a little coffee, tells you how lonely she is—you know. Don't tell me you haven't made a movida?

DANIEL: No.

IGGY: You haven't? The whole world's on la movida chueca. In China, Russia, France—even in Peru . . .

DANIEL: Peru?

IGGY: Pues, it gets lonely in the Andes.

DANIEL: And you?

IGGY: How do you think I keep, como dicen—*virile*?

DANIEL: You never told me.

IGGY: You never asked.

DANIEL: Damn, Ignacio, you mean to say—

IGGY: Hey, my business is mine, yours is yours. I'm just trying to help. Look, ninety percent of it is attitude. You gotta have a positive attitude. Like selling an insurance policy. You got a poor attitude, and the client does not buy.

DANIEL: Attitude?

IGGY: Simón. Look at me. I dress right, I present a good image, I meet a lonely vieja, y vamos! With my attitude I can do anything! Look at you. Look at the way you dress. Sloppy, compadre, sloppy. You think sloppy, and you perform sloppy.

DANIEL: Aw, fuck off! Dressing in a suit and dying my hair isn't going to fix anything!

IGGY: Hey, who said I dye my hair? I touch it up a little, that's all. Image, compadre, it's all in the image. (*He whispers.*) You'd be surprised, compadre—some of the lady clients I take out are starved for a little attention. A bottle of wine, roses, soft music, y vamos a echar un cohete!

DANIEL: It works?

IGGY: Hey, I'm scoring every time.

DANIEL: You don't even jog—

IGGY: It's all attitude.

DANIEL: How in the hell do you know so much?

IGGY: El diablo es diablo por ser viejo.

DANIEL: You got a movida on the side?

IGGY: Pues.

DANIEL: Who?

IGGY: If I told you you'd kill me— (*Realizes his slip and looks surprised.*)

DANIEL: Why the hell should I care who you're screwing—

Daniel looks puzzled, then realizes something and shakes his head.

DANIEL: No—

IGGY: Look, compadre—

DANIEL: Not Linda?

IGGY: I was explaining an insurance policy, that's all—

DANIEL: And you? And she?

IGGY: It's not what you think.

DANIEL: You did it?

IGGY: I got a little carried away—

DANIEL: You screwed my wife?

IGGY: No, it was just an innocent—

DANIEL: (*jumps forward*) What do you mean, "innocent"?

IGGY: Shhh! Not so loud.

DANIEL: You're having an affair with Linda!

IGGY: I was doing you a favor, compadre.

DANIEL: A favor?

IGGY: If it wasn't me, it would've been somebody else.

DANIEL: My wife's not a whore!

Daniel attacks Iggy and wrestles him to the floor. They roll around until Daniel grabs Iggy by the throat.

IGGY: It was innocent!

DANIEL: I'll kill you!

IGGY: I was doing you a favor!

DANIEL: ¡Cabrón! *(Daniel straddles Iggy and chokes him.)*

IGGY: ¡Compadre! ¡Por el amor de Dios!

Steve and Ashley appear at the door.

STEVE: Dad?

DANIEL: *(turns)* What?

STEVE: What are you doing?

DANIEL: I'm killing your padrino!

STEVE: Why?

DANIEL: Never mind. Go away!

STEVE: Are we going to eat?

DANIEL: No!

STEVE: I'm out of gas—can I borrow your car?

Daniel stops choking Iggy and reaches in his pocket for keys. Iggy sits up and looks at Steve and Ashley.

IGGY: Hi, Stevie.

STEVE: Hi, Padrino. Ah, this is my friend. Ashley, this is my padrino.

ASHLEY: Hi, Pad-reen-o.

IGGY: Hi, Ashley. Ay, compadre, que cosas hace Dios.

There's an explosion in the patio.

STEVE: (shouts) What was that?

Helen and Linda appear at the patio door, faces black with soot.

HELEN: The pinche grill exploded!

END ACT ONE

ACT TWO

In the kitchen, an hour later.

Linda and Helen sit at the kitchen table looking at a high school yearbook. Linda is dressed in a summer dress. Helen is applying fresh makeup, teasing her hair.

HELEN: That pinche fire singed my eyelashes!

LINDA: Here we are at the junior prom. Cindy, the editor of the yearbook, was secretly in love with Daniel.

HELEN: You can't trust those gringitas. . . . Que guapo.

LINDA: He still is.

HELEN: He looks like a movie star—like Jimmy Smits. Sometimes I dream I'm making it with Jimmy. He is *so* sexy.

LINDA: I liked Anthony Quinn. But he died.

HELEN: He had a kid at seventy-eight. Wish our viejos were that good!

LINDA: Helen!

HELEN: It's true. Like Iggy says, Mother Nature es una puta. Some guys keep going till they drop dead. But ours are flojos.

LINDA: It's not just laziness . . .

HELEN: Midlife crisis? Puro pedo. They just hate to admit que ya no pueden. They peter off. . . . Get it? Peter off!

Linda nods, but then turns serious.

LINDA: I was thinking—

HELEN: ¿Qué?

LINDA: Nada. It's the wine.

HELEN: One glass? I can drink this stuff all night and barely get a buzz. I liked it better when we used to smoke grass. (*She pours a fresh glass.*)

LINDA: You smoked?

HELEN: Listen, comadre, what I've done you don't want to know. Andaba con las pachucas when I was young. See, I've got the tattoo of my old gang. (*She holds out her hand and shows Linda the tattoo.*)

LINDA: I guess there are things I don't know about you.

Helen winks at Linda, pats her knee.

HELEN: And a little I don't know about you. Sometimes it's better to keep secrets. . . . Anda, flip the page.

LINDA: Here's Steve's baptism—you and my compadre.

HELEN: Hey, I look poor-tee good, eh?

LINDA: You look beautiful. You always knew how to dress.

HELEN: Ah, we were young. Now I could come to breakfast in a bikini and Iggy would tell me to put on a coat so I don't catch cold. Pinche viejos, they lose interest.

LINDA: It's just more difficult for them.

HELEN: Yeah, it's their identity. Me? I still feel sexy.

LINDA: You *are* sexy.

HELEN: We're *both* sexy! Our viejos think they got all the ganas! ¡Cabrones! We've got ganas too!

LINDA: Yes, they take us for granted.

HELEN: We get up in the morning, and Iggy rushes for his coffee and the newspaper. He wants to know what's going on in City Hall. Sometimes I get up real early and gargle with Scope, put on a little cologne, but he's watching the *Today Show.*

LINDA: And Daniel goes jogging . . .

HELEN: Iggy reads the paper in bed. The other night I put on my sexy gown, but when I came out of the bathroom, ya 'staba roncando! ¡Y unos pedos! ¡Dios mío!

LINDA: It's not that bad.

HELEN: Yes, it is, but we put up with it. You know why? Because a new husband would be too much work to train. Besides, I'm not a young chick anymore. I've got him insured—and the Social Security. No señora, I'm not giving up what I've earned!

LINDA: Earned?

HELEN: You goddamn right I earned it! All those years of putting up with his cohetes.

LINDA: Cohete? Like a firecracker?

HELEN: Like a shotgun. "Oye, vieja, vamos a echar un cohete." Like he's going hunting. But he's pointing it at me!

LINDA: (laughs) Ay, comadre.

HELEN: You know, they like to name their cosita. Iggy calls it "El Shotgun." He says, "Come on, mama, vamos echar un cohete!" And I know it's shotgun time.

LINDA: (laughing) Stop, comadre.

HELEN: Then the gunpowder gets wet. All their lives they're used to getting it up, and suddenly gravity's too strong. One day it just doesn't stay up. They look lost. Like one of those sad Bassett hounds.

LINDA: Why is it so important to them?

HELEN: It's their identity.

LINDA: Pobrecitos.

HELEN: ¡Que pobrecitos! ¡Son bien cabrones! But Sunday at church, they act like santitos.

LINDA: You said it.

HELEN: Es como dicen: Life's a bitch, then there's menopause. You know, I have this dream . . .

LINDA: Yes . . .

HELEN: (lights a cigarette) Once a month, on the dot. I think it comes instead of my period. I'm on an island . . . like Hawaii. Alone. No Iggy. And I'm surrounded by these dancing men. Big, brown, sexy machos. ¡Bien cuerotes! Dozens of them. And I'm in a bikini— Imagine me, in a bikini! But I look good, in my dream I look good! Then one by one they start to—

LINDA: No!

HELEN: Yup. It's the best orgasm I ever had.

LINDA: ¿De veras?

HELEN: In the morning I wake up with a smile. Iggy me pregunta, "Good dreams, honey?" And I say, "*Oh yes, baby.*"

LINDA: It sounds so real—

HELEN: It's real to me. Every woman needs a dream. And you?

LINDA: I dream about Daniel.

HELEN: You're a romantic.

LINDA: Maybe. Sometimes I can't sleep. I keep wishing he would just talk to me, hold me like he used to . . .

HELEN: They like to be the strong, silent type. Remember Eddie Olmos in *Miami Vice*? I swear, that guy never said two words! Son bien pendejos. Speaking of pendejos, where are they?

LINDA: They went for menudo. . . . Here's Daniel at our homecoming picnic. That's when we first—

HELEN: Did it?

LINDA: Yes.

HELEN: Que bonito. The first time's always for love. After that it's puro "Vamos a 'char un cohete." . . . Tell me! ¿Qué pasó?

LINDA: We stayed late. I was so in love—

HELEN: He came on strong?

LINDA: I encouraged him—

HELEN: Atta girl! Sometimes you have to put the movida on them. In the back seat?

LINDA: Sí.

HELEN: That's where I got mine.

LINDA: With Iggy?

HELEN: No, that was long before Iggy! How was it?

LINDA: I closed my eyes.

HELEN: I didn't ask you what you saw! How was it?

LINDA: Like dying and going to heaven.

HELEN: All right! (*gives Linda a high five*) It's like my father used to say, the picky nickies become picky fookies. He never let us go on picnics.

LINDA: My parents were strict. In a way, Daniel's a lot like my father.

HELEN: Old-fashioned.

LINDA: He never wanted me to work. The man takes care of his familia, he said.

HELEN: Te digo, son bien tercos.

LINDA: I know you'll hate me for this, Helen, but I haven't minded it.

HELEN: You haven't?

LINDA: I liked raising Steve, and helping Daniel in his business. Now I volunteer at the library. It's only recently . . .

HELEN: That the romance has gone out of life?

LINDA: We can put it back. Daniel wants to travel—

HELEN: A trip! I love a trip!

LINDA: To Mexico City.

HELEN: Why not Las Vegas?

LINDA: Adventure, comadre—we need something different in our life.

HELEN: Iggy would never go to Mexico.

LINDA: Why not?

HELEN: He's afraid of the water.

LINDA: There's nothing wrong with the water—

HELEN: It's an excuse. All he thinks about is business. I feel stuck. We got married, had the kids, went to work, bought a house . . . all those years of los cohetes. Damn, where in the hell did romance go?

LINDA: I'm going to find it . . .

HELEN: Mexico . . . Climb the Pyramid of the Sun with Danny . . . That's about the most romantic thing . . . (She clears her throat.) Ah, you've got me crying in my wine.

Linda hugs Helen.

LINDA: And you're supposed to be the liberated one.

HELEN: It's all a show, comadre. I know how you feel. I lied to myself when I went through menopause. "I won't let it get me down," I kept telling myself!

"I look good! I feel good!" Maybe a woman can just hide it better. For a man, if the cosita don't get hard, pues—

LINDA: But life isn't just all sex.

HELEN: No, just ninety-nine percent.

LINDA: I think romance takes work. We've tried a few things.

HELEN: Like what?

LINDA: We tried tofu.

HELEN: Tofu? Why not Viagra?

LINDA: It gave him headaches.

HELEN: And the tofu?

LINDA: He ate it with hot salsa.

HELEN: Did it work?

LINDA: (*shakes her head sadly*) It gave him indigestion.

HELEN: What about love medicine—a little marijuana or brujería!

LINDA: Daniel never smoked pot. But we did go to Chimayó.

HELEN: You went all the way to Chimayó to screw?

LINDA: No! We went to pray to the Santo Niño.

HELEN: Do you think the Santo Niño cares if you're doing it or not?

LINDA: No, silly. They have the holy earth there. Like if you have arthritis, you rub the dirt on your body—

HELEN: Yeah, soooo?

LINDA: We tried it.

HELEN: Rubbed it on his . . . (*gasps*) No!

LINDA: It was worth a try!

HELEN: Dios mío, I can't believe it! Did it work?

LINDA: No.

HELEN: Pues cuando se acaba, not even the santos can help.

LINDA: For a while we felt close, like we used to. Then Daniel got nervous again.

HELEN: You have to get down—

LINDA: What do you mean?

Helen whispers in her ear.

LINDA: No!

HELEN: Yes.

LINDA: Isn't it against the law?

HELEN: No! And it keeps them happy.

LINDA: But the church?

HELEN: For crying out loud, comadre. There's a sexual revolution going on! Jennifer Lopez! Frida Kahlo! Esa tontita, Britney Spears! And here we are, still living in the dark ages! If our daughters are liberated, why can't we? Let's start a club—Liberated Comadres! Catch up before it's too late! Like Iggy says, we gotta practice a little greed. Greedy comadres!

LINDA: Maybe I'm too old-fashioned.

HELEN: Afraid to let your hair down?

LINDA: I'm not like you, Helen.

HELEN: Ah, you're right. I talk tough, but deep inside I'm—

There is a clamor in the patio. Daniel and Iggy enter with packages of menudo, tortillas, chile. Daniel has changed into a summer shirt, dress pants.

IGGY: Oye, vieja, here comes your lover man!

HELEN: (*groans*) Ay, viejo, I missed you . . .

Helen kisses Iggy. Linda takes the packages.

IGGY: See, Danny, she can't be without her lover for an hour. Hey, you won't believe who we saw at the café.

HELEN: ¿Quién?

IGGY: Remember Carmen, la feminista?

HELEN: Yeah.

IGGY: She was with this big panzón—I mean three hundred pounds.

DANIEL: And ugly.

IGGY: He looks like King Kong.

DANIEL: And she was hanging on to him like he was the last man on earth.

IGGY: Bien prendida.

HELEN: There goes our hope for Liberated Comadres.

DANIEL: Liberated comadres?

IGGY: She's always giving me the chingas. Calling me a male chauvinist pig. Now she's in love! ¡Qué loco!

LINDA: She can be a feminista and still like a little company.

All look at her.

HELEN: You're right. So she trains one pendejo at a time. Maybe that's the only way to get it done.

IGGY: (*ignoring her*) Look what we brought you morenitas! Menudo, red chile, tortillitas calientes. Gracias a los Aztecas for inventing menudo!

DANIEL: What'd you do with the hamburgers?

LINDA: Steve and his girlfriend ate them.

DANIEL: They were fried to a crisp!

IGGY: La plebe, compadre. They have no taste. The McDonald's generation— fast food, fast cars, fast sex.

DANIEL: Hey! Quickie time!

IGGY: All the time!

The men laugh, exchange high fives, low fives. Iggy pours himself a wine, Daniel grabs a beer.

HELEN: Fantasy time . . .

IGGY: Hey! My compadre and me are as good as ever, eh, compadre?

HELEN: Except when the gunpowder gets wet.

DANIEL: Gunpowder?

IGGY: Bang, bang, compadre. Like in the old West—keep your gunpowder dry, partner. Don't fire till the biscocho's hot!

DANIEL: 'Stas loco.

LINDA: Siéntense, cowboys. Food's ready.

IGGY: All right! Tonight we dance!

Daniel looks at Helen.

LINDA: We haven't been dancing since Lupe's wedding.

DANIEL: It just doesn't turn me on anymore.

IGGY: ¿Por qué?

DANIEL: I'd rather stay at home and read.

IGGY: You gotta stop reading that poetry, compadre! Snapea! Drop that todo se acaba crap! (*Iggy intones a prayer over a glass of wine.*) Todo se acaba . . . Dominus obiscum, tú te enpinas y yo te peliscum! En este mundo, todo se acaba. Se acaban las ganas, se apaga la chispa, goodbye rendija, dominus obiscum! (*He looks at the others.*) Bullshit. I don't go for that todo se acaba! I still have ganas! I can strap on the world! Come on, world! Line up!

HELEN: I'll go first. When I'm done with you, no more ganas.

IGGY: Ay, vieja, don't be cruel.

HELEN: Pues, put up or shut up.

IGGY: I'm too sore from Danny's beating.

LINDA: You play too rough, Daniel.

IGGY: He got pissed off. I told him my best-kept secret.

LINDA: You told? (*looks at Daniel*)

HELEN: ¿Qué secreto?

IGGY: I told him a steady diet of menudo will take care of the blues. A little cebollita, oregano, hot chile, y dale gas!

LINDA: He has to watch his cholesterol.

IGGY: You got high cholesterol, compadre?

Daniel nods.

IGGY: You keep in shape, you jog, and you still got high— Que chinga. Look at me, I eat what I want and I have no problems—

Helen chokes on her menudo, clears her throat.

HELEN: Let's not fantasize—

IGGY: Fantasy? Hijita, I'm in A-one shape.

HELEN: First his knees went out, then—

IGGY: ¡Cállate! En boca abierta entran moscas.

HELEN: Then the hair—

IGGY: Okay, okay. So I touch it up. So what? Makes me feel younger.

HELEN: What about the other stuff in the medicine cabinet?

IGGY: ¡Cállate, bruja! No fair telling family secrets.

HELEN: And they say women are vain. Watch out when the viejo colors his hair!

IGGY: Wait till we get home! Grrr!

HELEN: Ooo, the perro is coming alive.

Iggy reaches across and kisses her arm. Barks.

HELEN: Bite me! Bite me!

IGGY: You love your perro, don't you, vieja?

HELEN: All bark and no bite.

IGGY: Ay, vieja, you really know how to hurt a homeboy. (*turns to Daniel*) How about you, Danny, you touch up your hair?

Helen walks behind Daniel, fondles his hair.

HELEN: I bet women love to run their fingers through your hair.

IGGY: How would you know?

HELEN: Thick hair means a great lover.

IGGY: Maybe he gets implants?

DANIEL: You thinking about an implant, Ig?

IGGY: Hell no, I don't need one. I'm puro macho!

LINDA: Can I serve anyone?

IGGY: Muchas gracias. That's what I like, old-fashioned women. My mother used to serve my father—

HELEN: Don't start on that old-fashioned crap, Iggy.

DANIEL: Things were simple then.

LINDA: We're thinking of moving back to the barrio.

Daniel looks at her, surprised, then nods.

IGGY: Back to the barrio! You gotta be kidding!

DANIEL: Why not?

IGGY: You're still into the culture trip, aren't you? Viva la Raza and all that. Forget it, ese! Money is the grease. You got it or you don't! It buys self-respect.

DANIEL: I don't believe that!

IGGY: Believe what you want! Out there if you ain't making money, you ain't nothing! Screw cultura! Mariachis, I like, but forget the rest. Let's get on the bandwagon!

DANIEL: There's more to our cultura than mariachis.

IGGY: Like Cinco de Mayo? Yippee! Look, we worked like hell to get out of the barrio, and you want to go back! Do you think Steve wants to live in the barrio?

DANIEL: No . . .

IGGY: You damn right! He landed a good job in Frisco. He's going to go up there and make a million. It's the American way, compadre! Tell me, does he eat menudo?

DANIEL: He hates it!

IGGY: ¡Ahí 'stá! Times have changed, compadre. The kids are changing. Video games! Rap music! Adiós to the barrio and pobreza. Good morning, America!

HELEN: That's not Danny!

IGGY: And if Steve marries that blonde amazon, all your nietos are going to be gueros. You think they want to live in the barrio?

DANIEL: No.

IGGY: So let's get with it!

LINDA: Life isn't about money, it's about happiness.

Daniel looks at her.

IGGY: As the old pachuco said, give me the money and I'll buy my own happiness.

Helen rubs Daniel's hair, massages his shoulders.

HELEN: What will make you happy, Danny?

IGGY: He needs something different.

HELEN: That's exactly what he needs. (*whispers into Daniel's ear*)

DANIEL: ¡Comadre!

HELEN: Why not?

IGGY: No fair whispering!

LINDA: What did she say?

HELEN: You know, what we were talking about—

LINDA: You didn't?

HELEN: I told him he needs a good vacation!

IGGY: Hey, it's Vegas time!

DANIEL: No! Not Vegas!

IGGY: What's wrong with Vegas? We always go to Vegas.

DANIEL: We want to go to Mexico.

IGGY: Okay, México. ¡Ajúa!

DANIEL: Just me and Linda.

IGGY: (*frowns*) You and Linda, alone? . . . Hey, I know when I'm not wanted. (*to Helen*) Anda, vieja, vamonos.

DANIEL: Buenas noches.

LINDA: (*jumps up*) He's joking. It's just that we haven't been on a vacation alone in—

HELEN: Thirty years.

LINDA: It'll do us good.

HELEN: I agree.

IGGY: What's a vacation without your compadres? Aren't we familia?

DANIEL: Familia doesn't give the jodas.

IGGY: Jodas? I love you like a brother. (*He leans across and hugs Daniel, kisses his cheek.*)

DANIEL: I want to climb the pyramids.

IGGY: I can climb with you.

LINDA: We need to be alone.

IGGY: Alone? You're alone all the time.

HELEN: (*to Daniel*) Don't forget what I told you.

IGGY: (*grabs Helen's wrist*) What?

HELEN: (*jerks away*) ¡Nada!

IGGY: They plot against us, compadre. Sooner or later the women are like black widow spiders. They eat the man.

HELEN: (*laughs*) And you like it!

IGGY: I like it! I like it! (*He pants like a dog, barks.*) Remember my perro trying to get to the perra! They got us trained, compadre!

HELEN: You love it! (*She swishes her behind in front of Iggy, and he barks.*)

IGGY: Love it! (*He grabs her.*) Put on the music! Let's dance!

Linda turns on the tape player. Iggy and Helen dance around the kitchen. They are very good, sensuous.

IGGY: Let's go dancing!

Linda looks at Daniel.

DANIEL: I don't feel like dancing . . .

Linda turns off the tape.

IGGY: What do you feel like doing?

DANIEL: Nada.

Iggy sings, imitating a Bing Crosby croon.

IGGY: Do na-da . . . to you na-da . . . en la al-ma-da . . .

Daniel takes a swipe at Iggy.

DANIEL: ¡Cabrón!

IGGY: ¡Órale!

They jab at each other, having fun.

IGGGY: ¡Dame tu vobiscum!

DANIEL: Tu te'empinas—

IGGY: ¡Y yo te peliscum!

HELEN: 'Stán locos.

LINDA: I'll clear the table.

IGGY: May I have this dance, señorita?

Iggy sweeps Helen out into the patio.

HELEN: Ay, Rudolph Valentino . . .

Daniel helps Linda clear the table.

DANIEL: Sometimes I get tired of my compadre.

LINDA: He's just having fun—

DANIEL: Fun? He's fun, huh!

LINDA: What did he tell you?

DANIEL: Let's not talk about—

LINDA: (*grabs Daniel*) You brought it up! Tell me!

DANIEL: He told me he was having an affair with you!

Linda slaps him.

DANIEL: Great! You're screwing my compadre and I'm the one that gets slapped!

LINDA: I'm not screwing him!

DANIEL: You deny it?

LINDA: Yes!

DANIEL: He told me! Do you deny it?

LINDA: It's not what you think!

DANIEL: What do I think?

LINDA: He paid attention to me!

DANIEL: Oh! And I don't!

LINDA: No, you don't!

DANIEL: Is that it? You jumped in bed with my compadre because I don't pay attention to you!

LINDA: We weren't in bed!

DANIEL: So where?

LINDA: In his car!

DANIEL: You screwed in his car!

LINDA: No! We talked. . . . He came on strong!

DANIEL: One of these days I'm going to kill that cabrón!

LINDA: Nothing happened!

DANIEL: What do you mean?

LINDA: Nothing, I told you, nothing— (She is about to cry.)

DANIEL: Why did you go with him?

LINDA: He gave me a ride from the library!

DANIEL: And he tried to—

LINDA: It wasn't just his fault!

DANIEL: You led him on?

LINDA: You made me do it!

DANIEL: Me? I made—? What the hell do you mean?

LINDA: You don't touch me, you don't hold me! You never say anything.

DANIEL: I've been busy—

LINDA: And I've been lonely! I thought I wasn't attractive anymore! Iggy came to the library. Remember, we talked about getting an insurance policy—

DANIEL: I'm not buying insurance from that pinche!

LINDA: He complimented me. Do you know how long it's been since you complimented me?

DANIEL: Just a while ago!

LINDA: Yes, then you turn away! You don't touch me.

DANIEL: Oh, so he touched you!

LINDA: No! It didn't go that far! But I wish it had!

DANIEL: You wish it had!

LINDA: Yes!

DANIEL: Great! How far did it go?

LINDA: It didn't. We just sat there.

DANIEL: Did he try anything?

LINDA: He couldn't.

DANIEL: What do you mean, he couldn't?

LINDA: Don't you get it? A woman knows when a man can't . . . we know when a man's bragging.

DANIEL: And Iggy can't?

LINDA: He talks a lot, but—

Daniel laughs, slowly at first, then slaps his thigh, laughs loudly.

DANIEL: But he can't deliver! The sonofabitch! He goes around bragging that he's numero uno macho, y no tienas gas! ¡Pero que cabrón!

LINDA: No te rías. I feel guilty.

DANIEL: So what did you do?

LINDA: Well, he talked. He told me about how good he used to be—

DANIEL: Used to be! (*Laughs anew.*) I can't believe it! (*He stops, looks softly at her.*) I guess I just didn't realize . . . how you felt.

LINDA: You haven't paid attention.

DANIEL: I . . . I'm sorry.

LINDA: I don't want you feeling sorry! You men are just too spoiled! When you're babies your mamá gives you chichi, takes care of your cosita, makes you feel like a king. Then you expect your wife to be like your mamá!

DANIEL: But—

LINDA: Shut up! Listen! When my dad got the stroke, it was like taking care of a baby! We take care of you when you're babies, and we take care of you when you're old! You know what I learned! A prick is a prick! There! I've said it!

DANIEL: (*surprised*) You never talked like that before.

LINDA: It's about time! Don't you see? I have to. I don't want to go around feeling sorry!

DANIEL: (*shakes his head*) Is that why you . . . and Iggy . . .

LINDA: You haven't heard a word I've said! Don't you know why I talked to him?

DANIEL: Why?

LINDA: I wanted to know if I'm still— (*Tears come to her eyes.*)

DANIEL: (*softly*) What?

LINDA: Still sexy . . . (*She cries softly.*)

DANIEL: Is that why—

Linda nods.

DANIEL: Ah, mi'jita—

LINDA: Don't call me "mi'jita"!

DANIEL: I've always called you "mi'jita"!

LINDA: I'm not your hijita! I'm your wife! I'm a woman!

Daniel, shocked, reaches out for her, holds her.

DANIEL: A woman . . .

Iggy and Helen enter from the patio.

IGGY: Compaaaaaadre!

DANIEL: Oh, no . . .

IGGY: Look at the lovebirds. One minute alone and they're coo-chee-coo.

HELEN: Wish I could get a little.

IGGY: Very cute . . . I need a drink. (*He pours a glass of wine.*)

HELEN: So, are we going dancing?

LINDA: We're not in the mood.

IGGY: Mood? Oh, dirty word, dirty word. Anda, compadre, dancing cures the blues.

HELEN: (*goes to Daniel*) It'll do you good, morenito. Come on.

IGGY: She's after you, compadre. She wants you in a slow waltz. (*He waltzes around alone, humming.*)

HELEN: I can fix him up.

IGGY: Not what he's got.

HELEN: Wanna bet?

IGGY: A dollar ninety-nine.

Helen tousles Daniel's hair, curls around him.

HELEN: All he needs is a real woman.

LINDA: Helen! (*She glares at Helen and dashes out the living room door.*)

HELEN: Oh shit!

IGGY: Foot in mouth!

Helen dashes after her.

DANIEL: Linda!

IGGY: Let them go. You know women.

DANIEL: I guess I don't.

IGGY: Pues, let me tell you.

DANIEL: You, the expert?

IGGY: I don't want to brag, but—

DANIEL: Linda told me.

IGGY: What?

DANIEL: What you did.

IGGY: Hey, I thought we agreed to forget it.

Daniel smiles, walks around Iggy.

DANIEL: Okay, okay. I agree. We've been compadres a long time.

IGGY: Since Stevie was born.

DANIEL: And what's a compadre for?

IGGY: ¡Pura familia! Tighter than brothers! ¡Sangre! (*He embraces Daniel.*) As long as we have compadres, we have cultura.

DANIEL: I thought you weren't into cultura.

IGGY: Danny, I want to preserve the ways of my ancestors—

DANIEL: Does that include going to bed with your comadre?

IGGY: Danny, Danny, we agreed.

DANIEL: What suits you, eh, compadre?

IGGY: (*getting angry*) All right! You brought it up! (*He grabs Daniel by the collar.*) You shithead! Don't you know compadres and comadres have been doing hanky panky since Adam and Eve! What's a compadre for, uh! Your wife is unhappy! You want her to go out to the street like a puta!

Daniel laughs and pushes him away.

DANIEL: Maybe then she'll get a real screw!

IGGY: (*surprised*) ¿Qué dices?

DANIEL: You've been going around like you are a número uno gallo—

IGGY: So?

DANIEL: You have no problems?

IGGY: Problems? Me? Hey, it's bang, bang, every night! That's why I can't understand you!

DANIEL: Bang, bang, huh?

IGGY: (*strutting, self-confident*) Ask Helen. Un cohete, every night.

DANIEL: ¡Mientes!

IGGY: Compadre, I wouldn't lie to you.

DANIEL: Linda told me!

IGGY: What?

DANIEL: You couldn't— You spent your time bragging!

Iggy pulls back, stunned.

IGGY: She didn't . . .

DANIEL: You're all hot air! When it came right down to it, you couldn't!

IGGY: ¡Compadre! I was just trying to explain the insurance—

DANIEL: Your gunpowder's wet! No more cohetes! (*He laughs loudly.*)

IGGY: A woman's not supposed to tell.

DANIEL: Yeah, we go around bragging about the movidas chuecas, the women we conquer. But a woman's not supposed to talk. I'm going to enjoy telling this story at the coffee shop!

IGGY: No! You wouldn't!

DANIEL: I sure would!

IGGY: I've got a reputation!

DANIEL: Should of thought about it when you were getting calentito with my wife.

IGGY: You don't understand.

DANIEL: I don't understand? ¡Cabrón! I thought I was the only one with the problem!

IGGY: A man needs a little sympathy.

DANIEL: So you went to my Linda!

IGGY: I'm going through hard times, compadre.

DANIEL: Sure, tell me about it.

IGGY: Andy . . .

DANIEL: What about him?

IGGY: I'm afraid, compadre. I've never been afraid in my life, and now— (He shakes his head sadly.)

DANIEL: What the hell are you talking about?

IGGY: A man gets my age, and he wants nietos. Think of it, me, Ignacio Borrego, cruising with my grandchildren. A car full of Borregitos! That would make me happy.

DANIEL: So what's the problem?

IGGY: Andy.

DANIEL: What about him?

IGGY: He hangs out with other guys, you know . . .

DANIEL: You mean . . . Andy's gay?

IGGY: Don't say it, compadre. Don't say it.

DANIEL: I didn't know. All these years— (He puts his arm around Iggy.)

IGGY: It's sad, compadre . . .

DANIEL: But Laurie. She'll get married, you'll have grandchildren.

IGGY: It's not the same, compadre.

DANIEL: Not the same? She's your daughter!

IGGY: A man wants his son to produce a son. Keep the family name. Think of it, compadre, I'm the last Borrego on earth.

DANIEL: It's not that bad, Ig—

IGGY: Easy for you to say. You've got Steve! He and that amazon are going to make a dozen coyotitos! Me? Nada. (*He hangs his head.*)

DANIEL: Iggy, you've got two great kids. So one of them's a joto.

IGGY: Don't say that word, compadre! Please don't say it!

Helen appears at the door.

HELEN: Say what?

DANIEL: Iggy told me about Andy.

HELEN: Iggy worries too much.

IGGY: Do I? So why doesn't he bring over lady friends?

HELEN: He's different, okay? Let him be!

IGGY: I want nietos!

DANIEL: I'm sorry—

HELEN: (*angry*) Don't be! We don't need pity! So he's gay! He's still our son!

DANIEL: Yes, you're right. We have to accept—

IGGY: Accept?

DANIEL: Accept what comes our way.

Steve and Ashley enter.

IGGY: Steve! Señorita Ashley. Ah, it does me good to see you. (*He kisses Ashley's hand.*)

STEVE: Hi, Padrino.

ASHLEY: Hi, Pad-reeno. Hi, Mr. Martinez.

DANIEL: I thought you two went out?

STEVE: I was showing Ashley my bedroom.

IGGY: Ay, Dios mío.

STEVE: You feeling all right, Padrino?

IGGY: Fine as wine.

STEVE: Why was Mom crying?

HELEN: I put my foot in my mouth.

STEVE: But you do that all the time, Madrina.

HELEN: Thanks, Stevie. (*She pinches Steve's cheek as she goes out.*) I'll check on her.

DANIEL: Where are you manners?

IGGY: Leave him alone, compadre, he's right. Helen has foot in mouth disease.

DANIEL: Don't we all.

STEVE: Sorry I asked. Beer, Ash?

ASHLEY: I'd love one.

STEVE: Dad? (*Steve reaches in the refrigerator for beers.*) So where did you two skip to?

DANIEL: Down to the barrio to get menudo.

ASHLEY: Steve told me you think men-oo-do is an aphrodisiac?

IGGY: What else does he tell you?

ASHLEY: All sorts of things.

STEVE: I told her we need a Mexican restaurant here in Enchanted Acres.

IGGY: Tio Taco! I'll drink to that.

STEVE: Here's to your dream, Padrino. (*Steve raises his beer.*) Come on, Dad. Chug.

Daniel takes one drink, Steve chugs.

STEVE: Hey, Dad, remember when you could do that?

DANIEL: That's not good for you.

STEVE: I can handle it. Can't I Ashley?

ASHLEY: He can, Mr. Martinez. He can chug all day—

IGGY: What else can he do all day?

STEVE: Show them Ashley.

Steve puts the can aside and flexes his arm. Ashley feels his biceps.

ASHLEY: Oooh, pure muscle.

STEVE: A perfectly tuned machine. Feel that? (*He holds his arm out for Iggy.*) Puro Arnold Schwarzenegger, eh Padrino?

IGGY: (*lamely*) Nice . . .

STEVE: I've been working out at the gym. That's where I met Ashley.

ASHLEY: I teach aerobics.

IGGY: Where can I sign up?

STEVE: It's never too late, Padrino. You need to work on that panza.

DANIEL: Oye, sinvergüenza, leave your padrino's panza alone.

STEVE: You need to work on yours too, Dad.

IGGY: Let's do it, Danny.

STEVE: So how's Andy? Still playing music? (*He pats Ashley.*)

IGGY: Yeah, still playing . . .

STEVE: I'd like to see him before I head for Frisco.

ASHLEY: Maybe we can double date sometime?

STEVE: Knowing my padrino I bet Andy scores all the time! Just like me, I take after my dad. Two studs. Right, Dad? (*Steve puts his arm around Daniel.*)

DANIEL: Yeah, like father, like son.

IGGY: Full of ganas . . .

ASHLEY: (*turns to Steve*) What are ganas?

STEVE: It means you want something really bad.

ASHLEY: I like that.

IGGY: But sometimes you want it so bad you make a fool of yourself.

STEVE: You're no fool, Padrino. I told you, Ash, these two vatos are boys in the hood. (*He gives Iggy a high five.*) Show her how tough you are. Let's arm wrestle. (*Steve sits at the table and puts his arm on it.*)

IGGY: Nah, I don't want to hurt you.

STEVE: ¿Qué pasa, Padrino? ¿Ya no puedes?

Angry, Iggy sits down and puts his arm on the table.

IGGY: ¡Anda, baboso!

Daniel stops him.

DANIEL: No, compadre. Don't hurt your arm. You need it for lifting the wine glass.

IGGY: Right. And for pulling the one-armed bandits in Vegas. Next time, Stevie, next time.

DANIEL: Why don't you two get out of here? Weren't you going out?

ASHLEY: Steve's taking me for enchiladas.

DANIEL: I thought you ate the hamburgers?

STEVE: Just warming up, Dad. Aren't we Ashley?

ASHLEY: I'm starved. I have . . . ganas!

Iggy looks at her longingly.

IGGY: Me too.

DANIEL: So go on.

STEVE: Dad, I'm broke. Lend me twenty.

Daniel mutters, digs in his wallet.

DANIEL: You're always broke. You get up to San Pancho and who are you going to call when you're broke?

STEVE: I'll call you, Jefe. Who else?

Daniel hands him a twenty and embraces him.

DANIEL: I'm going to miss you, hijo.

STEVE: Hey, I'll miss you too, Dad. Sorry for what I said about your panza. Don't sweat it, you two look great. Don't they Ash?

ASHLEY: Muy guapos. If I weren't dating you, I might get interested.

IGGY: Let me give you my business card—

DANIEL: Iggy!

IGGY: For aerobics class, compadre, for class.

DANIEL: You two have fun.

ASHLEY: We will. It's so nice to meet you, Mr. Martinez. (*She turns to Iggy and shakes his hand.*) And so nice to meet you, Pad-reeno.

STEVE: She's got a lot to learn, but ain't she great?

IGGY: Fabulous, just fabulous. And Steve, don't worry about your dad having someone to bug him when you're gone. He's got me!

DANIEL: You're like Elmer's Glue, Ig.

ASHLEY: Well, adiós for now.

STEVE: We're going to Tomasita's.

ASHLEY: I love their hot chile!

STEVE: (*winks*) She likes it hot, Padrino. Come on Ashley, let's blow.

He winks again as they go out, Steve embracing Ashley.

STEVE: Good night, Dad. Buenas noches, Padrino.

IGGY: (*slumps*) Ay, que cosas hace Dios.

DANIEL: Times have changed, compadre.

IGGY: They're making them like amazons.

DANIEL: Yeah. Gets my spirit up.

IGGY: Is that all it gets up?

DANIEL: Todo se acaba. Gotta accept it.

IGGY: No!

DANIEL: There's nothing you can do about it.

IGGY: Hey, I'm going to be good till I'm a hundred and ten. It's all in the attitude. You watch.

DANIEL: Buena suerte, compadre. Me, I guess I'll listen to my vieja—I mean Linda.

IGGY: Traitor!

DANIEL: ¿Por qué?

IGGY: Porque it's us or them! If we don't stick together, they eat us up!

DANIEL: Compadre, it's not war. We need to be more accepting—

Helen and Linda enter, their makeup fresh.

HELEN: ¿Qué pasa?

IGGY: My compadre's gone soft!

DANIEL: (*goes to Linda, holds her*) You okay?

LINDA: (*nods, looks at him*) Danny always was soft, inside.

IGGY: A poet.

HELEN: Que romantic. (*She turns to Iggy.*) See, viejo, there's nothing wrong with a little cariño.

IGGY: Grrr!

HELEN: Don't bark. Please don't bark.

IGGY: Be a nice doggie, huh?

HELEN: Just tonight.

IGGY: (*laughs*) Okay, vieja, I'll be nice, just tonight. But I still think he's a traitor!

DANIEL: What the hell did I do?

IGGY: You're giving up!

DANIEL: I'm not giving up, I'm just accepting reality. Okay, I'm not as good as I used to be—

IGGY: Don't say it!

LINDA: You're better than ever, Danny.

HELEN: You admit it?

DANIEL: (*nods*) Yeah . . . I do.

HELEN: Freud says you have to face your deep-seated complex. It's no good unless you look in the mirror and say it.

LINDA: That's what I did when I went through menopause.

IGGY: Dirty word, compadre! Don't listen to them! Don't listen!

HELEN: Say it, Daniel.

DANIEL: (*anguishing*) I can't!

LINDA: Yes, you can. It's normal. Accept it.

IGGY: Don't do it, compadre! You'll be sorry!

DANIEL: Okay, I accept it! There, I said it!

HELEN: No, you have to say it!

LINDA: Go on. It won't hurt. I'm here. I love you the way you are.

DANIEL: (*muttering*) I—

IGGY: Don't say it, compadre! It's a woman's trick! They get you to say it, then they bite it off!

DANIEL: Midlife . . .

IGGY: (*shudders*) Ay Dios . . .

HELEN: Louder. Shout it to the world!

Daniel runs to the window and shouts.

DANIEL: I have trouble getting it up! Can you hear me! I'm not as good as I used to be! (*He turns to them.*) ¡Ahí 'stá! I said it!

Linda steps forward and holds him.

IGGY: (*moaning*) Oh, compadre, compadre . . .

LINDA: I love you.

DANIEL: And I love you.

LINDA: It didn't hurt, did it?

DANIEL: (*looks at her, then around*) No. It didn't hurt. I feel . . .

HELEN: Free.

DANIEL: Yes, free. Liberated . . .

LINDA: You had to say it for yourself.

DANIEL: And life doesn't end.

LINDA: No, it's just beginning.

IGGY: Bullshit. How can it be a beginning! He just drove a nail through his cosita!

Daniel and Linda turn to look at Iggy and start toward him.

IGGY: Why are you looking at me like that?

DANIEL: It's your turn, compadre.

IGGY: My turn? You're crazy!

DANIEL: Say it, compadre. It doesn't hurt. Look at me—it's over, I have nothing to hide.

IGGY: It's good for you, but I've got no problem. I'm as good as I ever was. (*He turns to Helen.*) Tell him, Helen!

HELEN: (*reaching out for Iggy*) Iggy. It's okay—

IGGY: Tell him! Tell him how good I am!

HELEN: (*embraces Iggy*) Mi hijito . . .

IGGY: Tell him . . .

HELEN: He's good, compadre. Every night, bang, bang . . .

IGGY: (*smiles*) See, I told you. It's all in the attitude, compadre. And it helps to have a sexy vieja.

Helen holds him in her arms like a child.

IGGY: God bless you, vieja.

HELEN: God bless you, viejo.

IGGY: (*loudly*) God bless my vieja, compadre! She knows me like a book.

HELEN: Now let's go dancing.

IGGY: Just like the good old days?

HELEN: ¿Por qué no?

IGGY: Are you pissed off?

HELEN: No, not pissed off.

IGGY: I've been good—

HELEN: When you're asleep.

IGGY: ¡Vieja!

HELEN: It's time for las comadres to be a little greedy!

IGGY: Women's liberation! I knew it! I knew it!

HELEN: Take it or leave it!

IGGY: Hijo, compadre, I feel like getting bien pedo.

DANIEL: Let's do it!

LINDA: ¿Qué dirán los vecinos?

DANIEL: Screw the vecinos! I don't want to be like the Smiths!

He grabs Linda and goes out to the patio.

DANIEL: (*shouting*) ADIÓS, MR. SMITH! ADIÓS, MRS. SMITH! I'M GOING BACK TO MY BARRIO!

HELEN: Great! He did it!

IGGY: Easy for him.

HELEN: Not easy for you?

Iggy shakes his head.

HELEN: Because of my comadre?

IGGY: (*shocked*) You knew?

HELEN: You can't hide things like that from your vieja.

IGGY: I really screwed up, no?

HELEN: (*shrugs*) Las ganas.

IGGY: ¡Sí! Las ganas! I want to make love to every woman I meet!

HELEN: You don't get it, do you, viejo?

IGGY: ¿Qué?

HELEN: It's okay to have ganas, but it's not like when you were young.

IGGY: What do you mean?

HELEN: It's like a desire for life. It's not just a screw, it's a desire for life.

IGGY: Ganas for life?

HELEN: For trees and flowers, our sons and daughters, a little cariño for everything . . .

IGGY: You know I never was into trees and flowers. You still want me around?

HELEN: Sí, viejo, I want you around. I'm used to you. Besides—

IGGY: ¿Qué?

HELEN: I've got you insured.

IGGY: ¡Ay, como eres cabrona!

They embrace.

HELEN: Y tú cabrón.

IGGY: You're right. Maybe you've always been right.

HELEN: So, listen to me.

IGGY: The way I've treated Andy . . . It's not right. He is my son.

HELEN: Our son.

IGGY: Maybe he'd like to take a trip with me. We could go fishing. He always liked fishing, then I got too busy. We need time to talk, get to know each other.

HELEN: (*lovingly*) Ay, viejo, beneath that personality of a pinche, there's a real heart of gold.

IGGY: Don't tell anyone. I have a reputation, you know.

HELEN: I know.

IGGY: I love you, vieja.

HELEN: And I love you, viejo.

Daniel and Linda return.

DANIEL: ¡Vamos!

IGGY: I warn you, I'm the best dancer in town. Drive women wild.

HELEN: I know, mi'jito, you're terrific.

IGGY: There's just one thing I want to know.

They pause.

HELEN: What?

IGGY: About the spa Danny boy put in. Why did it take him so long?

Daniel looks at Helen, then at Linda.

DANIEL: I guess I should tell—

HELEN: Don't tell him anything! Keep him guessing, it's good for him. Isn't it, viejo? (*She puts her arm around his.*)

IGGY: ¡Como eres mala!

HELEN: And you love it.

IGGY: (smiles) Love it, love it. . . . ¡Anda, vamos!

LINDA: Keep 'em guessing?

HELEN: It's the only way we can survive with them, comadre. ¡Viejos apachurados! It's good for them.

LINDA: Keep them thinking we're making love to Jimmy Smits.

Helen laughs, gives Linda a high five.

HELEN: Or Antonio Banderas.

Helen and Linda embrace. The men start out, but Iggy returns for the Tio Taco model.

IGGY: Hey, after we get back from Mexico we can start on Tio Taco!

DANIEL: You're going with us?

IGGY: Of course, compadre. You think I'd let you go down there alone? No way. What's a compadre for?

DANIEL: You'll never change, will you Ig.

IGGY: (grins and puts his arm around Daniel) Gracias a Dios.

They go out arm in arm, laughing. Helen and Linda stop at the door.

LINDA: Wait! (She goes back and puts a cupful of water in the cactus plant.) You never can tell when it will bloom . . . (She rejoins Helen.)

HELEN: Ay, comadre!

Arm in arm they go out. Linda flips the light off.

END

Billy the Kid

CHARACTERS

ASH UPSON

BILLY

ROSA

PAT GARRETT

DON PEDRO MAXWELL

JOSEFINA MAXWELL

PACO ANAYA

CATHERINE MCCARTY ANTRIM

WILLIAM ANTRIM

JOE MCCARTY

WINDY CAHILL

CAHILL'S FRIEND

SOMBRERO JACK

LILY

DON MANUELITO

JOHN TUNSTALL

ALEXANDER MCSWEEN

FRED WAITE

BILLY MORTON

JESSE EVANS

TOM HILL

SHERIFF BRADY

TOM O'FALLIARD

DON JESÚS

DOÑA ANA

SHERIFF DESI ROMERO

GOVERNOR LEW WALLACE

SQUIRE WILSON

PHOTOGRAPHER

JOE GRANT

OLINGER

BELL

DEPUTY POE

LA MUERTE

ACT ONE

July 14, 1881, the night Billy the Kid dies. It is just before midnight at the home of Pedro Maxwell in Fort Sumner, New Mexico. The stage is dark; the outlines of the room may be suggested by curtains.

Sitting on a stool fore and left of stage is Ash, observing the events while he writes in a notebook. Next to him rests a small pile of books.

Billy lies on a bed, reading a land contract, his boots on the floor nearby. Billy is twenty-one, curly-haired, and has a fine face with an always ready smile. The only light is a lantern near the dresser where Rosa is combing her hair. Rosa is eighteen, dark and lovely. She is dressed in a chemise, her long black hair flowing. She and Billy are sweethearts. He sees her whenever he visits Fort Sumner. Both are clearly happy.

BILLY: Time to settle down . . . give up being a vagamundo.

ROSA: Siempre lo prometes . . .

Billy rises, paper in hand, goes to Rosa, holds her.

BILLY: Esta vez lo voy hacer. Mira. A hundred acres, enough land to run a small herd. You should see it, Rosa. There's good grazing, plenty of water, and the beauty of the mountains. It's what I always wanted—

ROSA: Es un sueño, Billy.

BILLY: Tú eres mi sueño, amor . . .

They start to kiss, he turns away. Rosa reaches after him.

ROSA: Billy. (She holds him.)

BILLY: ¿Te vas conmigo?

ROSA: Mi padre no lo permite.

BILLY: Yo hablo con él. Vas a ver. Voy a cambiar . . .

He returns to the bed, lies down, studies the contract.

ROSA: ¿Por qué te gusta tanto ese maldado condado de Lincoln? Quédate aquí.

BILLY: Me gustan las montañas, y la gente.

ROSA: Pero los tejanos no te quieren.

BILLY: Qué importa. Anda, cásate conmigo. Quiero hijos . . .

ROSA: ¿Sería posible?

BILLY: Sí, es posible. Ven. (*He slaps the bed beside him.*) Imagina. El Bilito, con hijos. Let the papers write about that. Y después, I'll be a grandfather.

Billy laughs gaily. Rosa smiles and starts toward him when there is a knock at the door. She stops.

BILLY: ¿Quién es?

ROSA: ¿Será Don Pedro?

Billy rises, pulls a hunting knife from his belt, starts toward the door.

BILLY: ¿Quién es?

The door swings open and Pat Garrett rushes in, pistol in hand. He fires a shot, Billy falls back on the bed. Rosa screams, Garrett fires a second shot.

ROSA: Billy!

Rosa flings herself on Billy, protecting him, holding him in her arms. There is shouting offstage, people running to the scene. Don Pedro Maxwell and his daughter Josefina are among the first to enter, followed by Paco and other Nuevo Mexicanos who work for Don Pedro. Josefina pauses to look at Pat Garrett, who turns aside.

DON PEDRO: ¿Qué pasa?

ROSA: (cries) ¡Mató a Billy! ¡Mató a Billy!

PAT GARRETT: He was armed. I had no choice . . .

A visibly shaken Pat Garrett turns away. Paco picks up Billy's knife.

PACO: A hunting knife!

PAT GARRETT: I thought it was a pistol— (*He winces as if in pain.*)

PACO: ¡Cobarde! (*An angry Paco cocks his pistol and aims at Pat Garrett.*)

PAT GARRETT: It was him or me . . .

The men pull Paco away before he can shoot Garrett.

FIRST MAN: Vente, Paco. No lo vayas a matar.

SECOND MAN: No vale la bala . . .

PACO: ¡Cobarde! You're the sheriff, Mr. Garrett, but you're going to pay for this.

The men pull Paco away. They cover Billy with a sheet, then slowly raise the bed and carry it out as if carrying a coffin. Rosa follows, the other women comforting her. Paco remains. Ash rises from his stool and looks at the audience. The actors sing "El Corrido de Billy the Kid."

> Fue una noche oscura y triste
> en el pueblo de Fort Sumner,
> cuando el sheriff Pat Garrett
> a Billy the Kid mató,
> a Billy the Kid mató.
>
> Mil ochocientos ochenta y uno,
> presente lo tengo yo,
> cuando en la casa de Pedro Maxwell
> nomás dos tiros le dio,
> nomás dos tiros le dio.
>
> Vuela, vuela palomita,
> a los pueblos de Río Pecos,
> cuéntale a las morenitas
> que ya su Billy murió,
> que ya su Billy murió.
>
> Ay, qué tristeza me da
> ver a Rosita llorando,
> y el pobre Billy en sus brazos,
> con su sangre derramando,
> con su sangre derramando.
>
> Vuela, vuela palomita,
> a los pueblos de Río Pecos,
> cuéntale a las morenitas,
> que ya su Billy murió,
> que ya su Billy murió.

The corrido fades, and Billy is carried out. Paco remains, glaring at Ash. Ash turns to address the audience.

ASH: My, my, isn't that sweet. They even composed a corrido for him. Sure, he liked the Mexican señoritas, but he didn't die in the arms of Rosita. The way I heard it, Billy had just walked into Don Pedro's room, and Pat Garrett was waiting for him. Challenged him and shot him dead.

PACO: (*jumps forward to rebut Ash*) Billy wasn't armed!

ASH: Who the hell are you?

PACO: Paco Anaya. I was in Fort Sumner that night! Pat Garrett never gave Billy a chance.

ASH: How would you know?

PACO: I was there!

ASH: My, my, everybody's got a story to tell. Since that fateful night of July 14, 1881, I've heard the stories of a hundred men—each one claims he was there. That bedroom must have been a crowded place. (*He chuckles.*)

PACO: I was there, cabrón! I helped bury the Kid! I wrote it in my book! (*He pulls a crumpled book from his back pocket.*) ¡Mira! ¡Aquí 'sta! Billy's story! Just like he told me. And what I saw that night!

ASH: (*takes the book, looks at it, smirks*) A little vanity press publication. Don't you know there's been a hundred dime novels written about Billy's death, and each one claims to know the truth. (*He turns to the audience.*) This doesn't look like a very literary work.

PACO: I was there! You weren't!

ASH: True, I wasn't there. But I got the real story from Pat Garrett. I helped him write the true account; I was the "ghost writer." (*He reaches for his book.*) See here, *The Authentic Life of Billy the Kid*, as told to me by Pat Garrett.

PACO: ¡Mierda! That's what I call *your* truth! You didn't know the Kid the way *we* knew him.

ASH: You Mexicans. Yes, you had a soft spot in your heart for Billy. He spoke Spanish like a native . . .

PACO: He treated us como hombres! ¡Mexicano o gringo, todos eranos iguales!

ASH: ¿Iguales? Sure, if you carried a Colt and a Winchester you were iguales. That was the problem. Violence was a way of life! Live by the sword, die by the sword. As Billy lived, he died.

PACO: (*turns away, covers his face*) A good man died . . . just when he was ready to—

ASH: To settle down? With the señorita? No, Billy couldn't settle down. Don't you see, he had the seed of violence in him. (*Turns to audience*) You might say he was a product of his time. The New Mexico Territory after the Civil War was a violent place. Everyone was armed, and human life was cheap.

Southern soldiers whose own land had been devastated and Texans look-ing to make a quick buck rustling cattle were rushing into Lincoln County. The only law was the quick gun. Shoot first, ask questions later. That same violence was bred into Billy. I saw him turn from an innocent kid into a cold-blooded killer. You want to know the real story? I'll tell you.

PACO: The real story? You call what Pat Garrett told you la verdad? I should have shot that sanamabiche!

ASH: I'll tell the truth as I know it. . . . We newspapermen are trained to tell the truth—

PACO: Ha!

ASH: I have no reason to lie. I never took sides in the Lincoln County War. I just reported what happened. Told it like it is—

PACO: You believed Garrett!

ASH: Tell you what. I'll make a deal with you. I'll tell my story as I know it, you tell yours.

PACO: (suspicious at first) You promise to tell the truth?

ASH: As near as I know it.

Paco nods. He goes to the right and sits.

PACO: Okay. But tell the truth. (He pats his pistol.)

ASH: That's right, you just sit there. No need for violence. After all, this is just storytelling. . . . (He turns to audience.) Marshal Ashum Upson, at your ser-vice. You may be asking what qualifies me to tell the story of Billy the Kid. Well, friends, I helped Pat Garrett write the true life of Billy. You might say I got the story straight from the horse's mouth. (goes to his chair and picks up notebook) Now I'm writing a new book. I want to know more than the events—I want to know what made Billy tick. I want to know why this boy became a cold-blooded killer.

PACO: Because that sanamabiche Dolan gang killed Tunstall. That's why!

ASH: Well, you're partly right. Tunstall had become like a father to Billy. And Billy never knew his father . . .

Paco nods.

ASH: Where was I? Well, I arrived in New Mexico during the Civil War. Worked in newspapers from Albuquerque to Mesilla. I was postmaster in Roswell for a while, and a J.P. in Lincoln County. I met the Kid on various occa-sions. First time I met Billy was March 1, 1873, in Santa Fe. His mother,

Catherine McCarty, was marrying William Antrim. Marriage took place in the La Fonda Hotel. I hear the hotel's still there. Billy was fourteen. His older brother, Joe, was there. Joe didn't say a word that day, but keep this in mind, he's going to be important to the story.

Catherine McCarty, dressed in a white dress, and William Antrim enter to the tune of a wedding march. Catherine is thin and pale; she has tuberculosis. She turns aside to talk to Billy and Joe.

CATHERINE: William is a fine man.

Both boys nod.

CATHERINE: He wants to move to Silver City. Get away from the politics of Santa Fe, the violence. Make a fresh start.

JOE: Yes, ma'am.

CATHERINE: He'll make a fine father . . .

BILLY: Yes, ma'am.

CATHERINE: (*draws Billy to her and holds him*) Oh, Billy, I want you to be happy for me—

BILLY: I am happy, Mother.

CATHERINE: I do worry for you. Joe's older, he can take care of himself, but I do fear for you. My orphan son. It hasn't been easy growing up without a father. But it's going to change. We don't have to keep moving anymore. (*She coughs, lets go of Billy, and turns away.*)

BILLY: Mother.

CATHERINE: I'm better. Really, I am. (*She turns back to Billy.*) Billy, I'm afraid.

Billy embraces her, they hold onto each other.

BILLY: Don't be afraid, Mother. I'll take care of you.

CATHERINE: Oh, this world is too much with us. So much violence, the men drinking and fighting, and everyone carries a gun. Promise me, Billy, promise me you won't carry a gun.

BILLY: I promise . . .

CATHERINE: Promise me you'll never drink, Billy.

BILLY: I won't, Mother.

CATHERINE: Promise me you'll always be a gentleman.

BILLY: I promise . . .

CATHERINE: Men just don't know how much women suffer. Do you understand, Billy? Men don't know how much women suffer. . . . (*She coughs again, turns away.*) I'm afraid . . . afraid of the dark germs eating away at my lungs. I thought coming out here from New York would help. The desert air, the doctor said. But once the germs starts eating away . . . there's no cure, Billy, no cure . . .

BILLY: Silver City will be good, Ma—high mountain air, plenty of sunshine. You'll get better, you'll see.

CATHERINE: Oh, you're such a fine son. Yes, we'll move south. Clean mountain air and plenty of hot chile. I've heard the Mexicans say the chile burns away the germs.

She pauses, looks at Billy. Billy coughs.

CATHERINE: I'm afraid for you, Billy. Afraid of this curse I carry—

BILLY: I'm all right, Mother, I am. I'm strong, and I got Joe.

JOE: I'll take care of him, Ma—really I will.

CATHERINE: You're brave boys. Yes, Joe will watch over you. So let's be happy. This is my wedding day. Dance with me, Billy.

Billy and Catherine dance to "Turkey in the Straw," showing off Billy's skills as an excellent dancer. Lights dim as the scene fades. Ash turns to the audience.

ASH: She was consumptive, you know. TB. No cure. It was a slow and sure death in those days. That's why they left New York, wandering through the Midwest to Denver, Santa Fe, and finally Silver City, where she died just eighteen months after her wedding day.

Catherine pauses and coughs. She slumps in pain, then she looks up and raises her arms. A light shines on her.

CATHERINE: I see them coming, Billy.

BILLY: Who, Ma?

CATHERINE: A horde of angels, Billy. A horde of angels coming to take my soul to rest . . . (*She raises her arms in ecstasy, then looks at Billy.*) Be good, Billy. Be good. Oh, my orphan son. Now you are truly alone . . .

Catherine falls into Billy's arms. Six of the men on the dance floor reach for her, put her on a coffin-like litter, and carry her across the stage to where Billy's bed rests. The music turns to dirge. Billy follows and kneels before Catherine.

BILLY: I love you, Mother. I'll be good. I promise.

Billy rises, coughs. A chorus of "Amazing Grace" ends the scene. Light fades on the scene, rises on Ash and Paco.

ASH: Billy never married. Oh, he had a way with women. They flocked to him. He didn't drink or smoke, and he loved to sing and dance . . . but he never married.

Ash looks at Paco, who nods.

PACO: Estaba tísico. He had TB, just like his mother. Oh, he could hide it real good, but we knew. This old Mexican curandero he met in Sonora gave him a weed to chew for the cough.

ASH: Who was that old man?

PACO: Manuelito. Billy met him in Mexico right after he killed Cahill. The old man taught him Spanish, came back with him. He was always trying to help Billy.

ASH: So that's the old man always hovering around the Kid?

PACO: Billy would chew on that weed and never cough. But even the old curandero couldn't get rid of the TB. One night we were out at my campo where I took care of sheep. Billy told me. "It's a curse," he said, "and not even Don Manuelito can get rid of it."

ASH: And Rosita?

PACO: She loved him. She wasn't afraid.

ASH: So now Billy is an orphan. The mother had taught him song and dance, and for a while he joins a minstrel show. Think of it, folks, a cold-blooded killer who as a child loved to sing and dance. What if someone with compassion had taken him in? Encouraged his abilities. Instead he fell in with Sombrero Jack, took to reading the *Police Gazette*, and petty thievery . . .

PACO: But he wasn't a cold-blooded killer!

ASH: He killed Cahill.

PACO: Cahill had it coming.

ASH: Well, maybe Cahill was a bully. But dammit, Billy was hanging out with Sombrero Jack. They were up to no good.

PACO: That's not the way I see it. (*He opens his book.*) April 17, 1877. Billy was over in Arizona, hanging around the army camps . . .

Lights rise on scene of a bar, music, army soldiers, bar women. Windy Cahill stands at the bar with a friend. Billy, his friend Sombrero Jack, and Billy's brother Joe enter the bar. Jack and Joe order a drink. Lily, one of the young bar girls, goes to Billy and puts her arm through his. Two of the other girls gather; Billy is obviously a favorite.)

LILY: Come dance with me, Billy.

BILLY: Whoa, give me a chance to clear the dust from my throat.

CAHILL: That's right, bartender, give the squirt a glass of lemonade.

Cahill and friend laugh. Billy whirls but Lily pulls him away.

LILY: Pay no attention, Billy. Sing us a song.

BILLY: If the piano man can play a decent melody.

The piano man smiles and plays, Billy sings, the women gather around him.

BILLY

> (singing) When Irish eyes are crying
> And the boys are off to war
> Then I'll raise my cup in parting
> And kiss the tears away,
> Then I'll raise my cup in parting
> And kiss the tears away.

The women clap.

LILY: That's beautiful, Billy.

BILLY: My mother taught me the song. She was my bonny lass—

LILY: And you're our bonny boy, Billy.

BILLY: Hey, I like that. Bill Bonny.

CAHILL: My, my, isn't that sweet.

CAHILL'S FRIEND: Sweet as a pimp bird.

Billy whirls and faces Cahill. The bar goes silent.

BILLY: You have a loud mouth, Cahill. Put up or shut up!

CAHILL: (*reaches for his pistol, hesitates*) I got no quarrel with you, Billy boy. It's your brother who turned me in to the law.

Joe steps up next to Billy.

JOE: You deserved what you got, Cahill. So make something of it.

Cahill sees the odds, curses, turns back to the bar.

BILLY: Come on, Joe, the bully don't have it in him. (*He turns to Lily and the piano man.*)

BILLY: Play another tune, piano man.

CAHILL: (*glares at Joe, whispers through clenched teeth*) There's two of you little bastards, otherwise I'd whip your ass.

JOE: There's just one of me. Let's step outside and see whose ass gets whipped.

Joe starts toward the door. Cahill follows, then draws his pistol and shoots Joe in the back. Cahill turns and aims at Billy, but Billy is too quick. Billy fires and kills Cahill. Everyone takes cover as Billy rushes to Joe.

BILLY: Joe! Joe!

JOE: He got me, Billy. Oh, Lord, it burns . . .

BILLY: We'll get you to the doctor! Jack! Give me a hand!

JOE: No, Billy, don't move me. I'm dying . . .

BILLY: Jack! Get the doc!

Sombrero Jack rushes out.

JOE: Don't turn your back on any man. . . . Listen.

BILLY: What is it?

The strains of the old spiritual "I Looked Over Jordan" sound far away.

JOE: It's Mother. I see her . . .

Catherine appears in white.

CATHERINE: My son, my son, the violence has come to claim you.

BILLY: Where, Joe? Where? (*He looks around anxiously.*)

JOE: Mother . . . (*He reaches out.*) I'm dying, Billy. You gotta run. The sheriff is friend to Cahill! Run, Billy, run . . .

Joe coughs, dies. Billy holds him, rocks him and begins to cry.

BILLY: Don't die, Joe. You're all I got. You're all I got . . .

There is one chorus of "I Looked Over Jordan" as the light fades. Billy rises and goes out, moving to a new scene: a Mexican sheep camp, where Don Manuelito sits at the fire.

MANUELITO: ¿Cómo te llamas?

BILLY: Billy.

MANUELITO: Bilito, eh. Siéntate. Come . . . *(He offers Billy a plate of food, coffee.)* You run from the law?

Billy nods, coughs.

BILLY: Thanks for the food, Don . . .

MANUELITO: Manuelito.

BILLY: Gracias, Don Manuelito.

MANUELITO: How long do you have the tos?

BILLY: Cough? It's nothing.

MANUELITO: How long?

BILLY: 'Bout a year . . .

MANUELITO: Maybe your father or mother also had the tos?

BILLY: *(nods)* It killed my mother . . .

MANUELITO: Sí. It grows in the lungs, makes you spit blood, then it kills you. It is a germ that has no cure. I have some medicine, a plant we Indios use. It takes away the cough, but not the germ.

BILLY: Nothing I can do, huh?

MANUELITO: Stay in the desert, in the sun, in the air, eat the goat cheese, and you will live. Return to el norte, and you will die.

BILLY: *(laughs)* I'll stay with you, old man. You give me some of that medicine and you teach me Spanish, and I'll herd sheep for you.

They both laugh in agreement. Light fades on the scene, rises on Ash and Paco.

ASH: Is that what you think happened?

PACO: *(nods)* He stayed with the old man a year, and when he came north Don Manuelito came with him.

ASH: Nobody mentions the old man in their writings.

PACO: Why would they write about an old Mexican?

ASH: (*uncomfortable*) Ah-hem, you got a point there.

PACO: Don Manuelito could see Billy's destiny. He could see the soul. He knew the violence would kill the Kid.

ASH: Well, one more story to add to the myth of Billy the Kid.

PACO: El Bilito.

ASH: You really did have a soft place for him?

PACO: He was a boy. I was just a few years older, but I could tell, in his heart he was just a kid.

ASH: You're right. In a manner of speaking. At that point, he still could have been saved. If he shot Cahill in self-defense. But, Lord, the times were just too violent for a kid to make it on his own.

PACO: He needed a familia . . . that's what he was looking for. The Mexicanos always made a place at the table and accepted him as one of the familia. They understood the bad breaks he had with the law.

ASH: So Billy was looking for love, huh? He picked a strange place to find it. Lincoln County. Lord, if there was a lawless place in the New Mexico Territory, it was Lincoln County. The Texans were coming in and grabbing up the land, rustling. . . . There were fortunes to be made supplying the army with beef. So Billy came up from Mexico and began to call himself William Bonney. Took up with the Jesse Evans gang . . . met John Tunstall. . . . And thus began the last three violent years of his short life . . .

Scene shifts to John Tunstall's ranch. Alexander McSween, Tunstall's attorney, is there with Tunstall. Billy and Fred Waite enter.

TUNSTALL: Billy, good to see you. Howdy, Fred.

FRED: Mr. Tunstall.

Tunstall embraces Billy. Both are glad to see each other.

BILLY: Sorry we're late, Mr. Tunstall. Fred and me were over on the Peñasco—

TUNSTALL: What's this I hear 'bout you buying a place?

BILLY: Yeah. Fred and me, we figure we can run forty, maybe fifty head up there—

TUNSTALL: Billy, Billy. You know I need you here . . .

BILLY: Yes, sir.

TUNSTALL: (*turns to McSween*) Billy's the best vaquero I've had since I came here. He can ride, shoot, and he knows no fear.

MCSWEEN: And he's a good dancer. Sue says he's the only cowboy in Lincoln County who can carry a tune. So how you been, Billy?

BILLY: Been fine, thank you.

TUNSTALL: (puts his arm around Billy's shoulder) You know a small place ain't gonna make it, Billy. U.S. Army wants beef to feed the black soldiers at Fort Stanton. Fifty head is a drop in the bucket. You gotta think big, Billy.

MCSWEEN: They need the kind of Texas doggies John Chisum is rustling up.

McSween and Tunstall laugh.

TUNSTALL: Chisum's a good man. Sonofabitch I can't stand is James Dolan. You know what that cocksucker's gone and done?

BILLY: We heard. That's why we came right away.

TUNSTALL: Sonofabitch began by getting Sheriff Brady to confiscate Mac's office—now the sheriff's taken over my store! My store, Billy! My merchandise! Dolan wants to be número uno, and he's got that no-good sheriff doing his dirty work! I won't stand for it!

BILLY: Yes, sir.

TUNSTALL: What do you think about that, Billy?

BILLY: Well, sir . . .

TUNSTALL: You've been like a son to me, Billy. You're part of the family.

BILLY: Yes, sir. I appreciate everything you've done, sir. I—I never knew my father. I mean, it was just Mom and Joe . . .

TUNSTALL: And they're dead.

BILLY: Yes, sir.

TUNSTALL: It hasn't been easy for you, Billy. But you've found a home here.

BILLY: Yes, sir. I feel I belong.

MCSWEEN: But they've got a warrant out for you in Arizona. . . . They ain't never gonna let you forget the Cahill killing.

TUNSTALL: The law can be for you or against you, Billy. If the sheriff don't like you, he sure as hell is going to make it hard on you. Just like Dolan has Sheriff Brady on my back.

MCSWEEN: Dolan charged me with embezzling a life insurance policy, and he got one of the heirs of the policy to sue me! That no-good Judge Bristol over in Mesilla has attached my property! And John's too!

TUNSTALL: It's war! Dolan wants war, and I know I can depend on you. (*He puts his arm around Billy.*)

BILLY: I'll do what you need done, Mr. Tunstall.

TUNSTALL: You see, Mac. He's a good boy. I can depend on Billy. (*He slaps Billy on the back.*) We're gonna fight back! Show Dolan and Sheriff Brady we got the best vaqueros in Lincoln County. What do ya say, Fred?

FRED: I stick with Billy. Where he goes, I go.

TUNSTALL: You see, Billy, you've got friends here. You go up to the Peñasco on your own, and men like Dolan will burn your place down.

MCSWEEN: And use the law to cover their tracks.

TUNSTALL: The law's rotten in Lincoln County! It's law-abiding citizens like us who have to be the law! You understand?

BILLY: Yes, sir. I do.

TUNSTALL: I knew you would.

BILLY: Just tell me what you need done, I'll do it.

TUNSTALL: Dolan's got a posse. Forty-three men. They stole my cattle from the Rio Feliz Ranch. I say we start out at first light and teach them a lesson. Meet 'em head-on! Get my cattle back!

BILLY: We'll be ready.

TUNSTALL: Good. And remember, we're doing the right thing. We've got the law on our side.

BILLY: Yes, sir.

Billy and Fred start for the door.

TUNSTALL: Billy.

BILLY: Yes, sir.

TUNSTALL: Thanks for your loyalty. It's loyalty that makes a man. I know I can depend on you, son.

BILLY: You just stay close to me and Fred, Mr. Tunstall. We'll take care of you . . .

They go out, the light fades. Two opposing groups of cowboys enter the stage. The spotlights are on Tunstall facing Billy Morton, Jesse Evans, and Tom Hill.

MORTON: There's Tunstall, alone. If he resists, shoot 'im!

BILLY: (*offstage*) Mr. Tunstall? Where are you, Mr. Tunstall?

TUNSTALL: Over here, Billy! Over here!

MORTON: Hold up, John Tunstall! We've been deputized by Sheriff Brady to bring you in.

TUNSTALL: You're not deputies! You're crooks! (*He turns and shouts.*) Billy?

The three men open fire and Tunstall falls, mortally wounded. The three exit as Billy enters and finds Tunstall on the ground. Billy rushes forward and holds Tunstall in his arms.

BILLY: Mr. Tunstall . . . Oh, God . . .

McSween rushes in.

MCSWEEN: He's dead.

BILLY: I came too late. . . . We got separated in the thicket . . .

MCSWEEN: They murdered him, Billy.

BILLY: Oh, God, I promised him, I promised him . . .

MCSWEEN: Cold-blooded! They ambushed him in cold blood!

BILLY: I swear I'll get them, Mr. Tunstall, I swear . . .

Light fades, with Billy holding Tunstall in his arms. Lights rise on Ash and Paco.

ASH: The murder of John Tunstall was the spark that ignited the Lincoln County War. For Billy, the only man who ever treated him like a father had just been murdered. Think of it. Those he loved were now gone—his mother, his brother Joe, now Tunstall. Open warfare had come to Lincoln County. Vigilantes riding at night and firing on innocent people, one gang of cowboys against the other . . .

PACO: And we were in the middle—

ASH: The Mexicans? But you were armed, too.

PACO: We had to protect ourselves! We didn't make the war! We were herding sheep and raising beans and corn along the Río Pecos! There was enough land for everyone to make a living, but people like Dolan and the others wanted too much! The posses came and went! The innocent suffered!

ASH: Ain't that the way with war. Each side thinks it's in the right. Dolan's side had warrants to arrest McSween and his vaqueros, and McSween got the J.P. to issue warrants to arrest Sheriff Brady. So McSween, crazy as he was, sends Billy and Fred Waite to arrest Brady. He sends two young boys right into Dolan's store. Like sending lambs into the lion's cave.

Lights rise on Billy and Fred Waite as they enter the store. Sheriff Brady is backed by a posse.

BILLY: Sheriff Brady, we got a warrant for your arrest—

BRADY: (*laughs*) Sonofabitch if the kid don't have balls! Did I hear right? You're here to arrest me?

BILLY: We've got a warrant from Constable Martinez. States you committed larceny on the Tunstall store. And we got a warrant for members of your posse for the murder of John Tunstall—

BRADY: You little sonofabitch! You can't arrest me! I'm the sheriff!

Brady approaches Billy and Fred. His posse surrounds them.

BILLY: If you come peacefully, we assure you safe conduct—

The posse overpowers Billy and Fred, takes their pistols and holds them.

BRADY: That McSween must be loco if he thinks he can arrest me! (*He strikes Billy across the face.*) Next time you pull a pistol on me, kid, you better be prepared to use it!

Brady strikes Billy again. Billy struggles but the men hold him.

BRADY: You little squirt! Go back and tell McSween to send a man to do his dirty business! Not a kid!

Brady pushes Billy and Fred out the door. The men laugh.

FRED: Sonofabitch was waiting for us. You okay, Billy?

BILLY: Nobody pushes me . . .

McSween appears.

MCSWEEN: Did you get Brady?

BILLY: He's got too many men.

MCSWEEN: You let that stop you? I thought you were fast—

Billy draws his pistol and points at McSween.

BILLY: I am, Mac. But no sense in dying when you don't have to!

MCSWEEN: All right, Billy, all right. I've got another plan. Dolan's taken the law in his hands, so I'm going to form a posse. Call ourselves the Regulators . . .

FRED: What do you mean?

MCSWEEN: I mean we're the only law in Lincoln County! And the first sonofabitch we'll get is Brady. He's sitting on my property and acting like a king! I aim to put a reward on his head! Bring him in dead or alive!

McSween laughs crazily as he exits. Other cowboys come in to join Billy and Fred.

BILLY: Mac just put a bounty on Sheriff Brady.

FRED: We've got a warrant for his arrest. Nothing worse than a bully with a badge.

BILLY: He killed Tunstall . . . the only man who ever treated me like a son. Ain't it right for a son to want revenge on those who killed his father?

The other cowboys nod.

FRED: We're with you, Billy!

Don Manuelito has kept to the background but now steps forward.

MANUELITO: No, Billy! If you seek revenge, it never stops. You kill them, they come to kill you. Let the law take care of this.

BILLY: Brady is the law, and he's a cold-blooded murderer! I'm sorry, Don Manuelito, but I've got to settle this my way.

MANUELITO: Revenge will start a war you cannot end.

FRED: We are the law, Billy. We been deputized! We're the Regulators!

BILLY: And I say we get the sonofabitch! He didn't give Mr. Tunstall a chance. Gunned him down in cold blood. He deserves the same!

MANUELITO: No, Billy . . .

The cowboys shout their approval. Billy, Fred, and friends run to hide. Sheriff Brady and two deputies walk down the street. Billy and friends open fire. Brady goes down. Billy runs to him and takes the pistol from Brady's belt.

BILLY: An eye for an eye, Sheriff Brady! We're even!

Billy and friends exit. The frightened and subdued townspeople come out to stand over the sheriff's body. Lights fade, rise on Ash and Paco.

ASH: Now there was no turning back. . . . Governor Axtell had declared Sheriff Brady the law of Lincoln County, and now he'd been assassinated. On April 29 the Battle of Lincoln begins. Dolan's boys against McSween's Regulators. A warrant is served on Billy.

On July 14 there is an open battle on the streets of Lincoln. Colonel Dudley, who's in charge over at Fort Stanton, marches in with his black soldiers, but that only makes things worse. For five days the battle wages back and forth, until McSween's house is burned down and he's killed. Billy escapes. (*He looks at Paco.*)

PACO: Billy, his friend Tom O'Falliard, and Don Manuelito rode north on the Río Pecos. That's where I met him. I was just a boy, herding sheep. They showed up at my camp over by Ojo Hiedondo. I took them to my home in Fort Sumner.

Lights rise on Billy, Tom, and Don Manuelito entering Paco's home, where they meet Don Jesús and Doña Ana, Paco's father and mother, and his sister, Rosa.

PACO: Mamá, Papá. Estos son amigos . . .

DON JESÚS: Pasen, pasen.

BILLY: Muchas gracias, señor. (*He looks at Rosa. They smile at each other.*)

DON JESÚS: ¿Cómo te llamas?

BILLY: Billy Bonney, a sus ordenes.

PACO: Es el Billy the Kid.

DON JESÚS: Oh, el Bilito. Te anda buscando la ley.

BILLY: Allá en el condado de Lincoln no hay ley, señor. Solo la pistola es la ley. (*He pats his pistol.*)

DON JESÚS: Así es el tiempo, muy violento. Los sharifes son un bola de sinvergüenzas. Yo soy hombre de paz. No quiero violencia en mi casa.

Billy looks at Rosa, then unbuckles his pistol belt and hangs it on a hook on the door.

BILLY: En su casa, también yo soy hombre de paz.

DON JESÚS: Entonces, bienvenido. Siéntense. Oye, vieja, dales de comer a estos jovenes.

PACO: This is my sister, Rosa.

Ash looks surprised.

BILLY: A pleasure to meet you, señorita . . .

Billy holds her hand. They look at each other with deep attraction. Rosa blushes.

ROSA: So you're the famous Billy the Kid? You look like a plain and dusty vaquero.

BILLY: *(smiles, turns to Paco)* I am dusty. Been riding hard from Lincoln County. Where can I clean up?

PACO: There's a cajete outside. Ven.

ROSA: *(steps in front of Paco)* I'll show him. He needs lots of hot water and soap.

Paco looks at Billy and shrugs. Billy laughs.

BILLY: Gracias.

Rosa lifts a kettle of hot water from the stove and leads Billy outside. Don Manuelito follows silently. Rosa pours the water in the washtub, and he strips his shirt to wash.

BILLY: I hear there's a baile tonight.

ROSA: Yes. Don Pedro Maxwell is having a fiesta. You know Don Pedro?

BILLY: Yes, I know him. We brought some cattle to him a year ago. I only wish I had met you then.

ROSA: So, are you going to the baile?

BILLY: Only if the girl of my dreams will accompany me.

ROSA: She must be very brave.

BILLY: Why?

ROSA: Because you're a bandido.

Billy laughs, reaches for the towel she hands him.

BILLY: Bandido? I only draw my pistol when I have to protect myself.

ROSA: We hear about the killings.

BILLY: And about me?

ROSA: Yes. They say el Bilito killed Sheriff Brady.

BILLY: Brady killed John Tunstall. I was just settling the score.

ROSA: We don't want the violence of Lincoln to come here. We want to live in peace—

BILLY: Yeah, I can understand that. Live and let live . . . But down the Pecos the Dolan vaqueros don't think like that.

ROSA: And you?

BILLY: Some of those vaqueros want my hide . . . so I keep my pistol handy.

ROSA: A person can change.

BILLY: I've thought about that. Thought about getting myself a place, minding my business, running a few head of cattle. Pero no es posible.

ROSA: ¿Por qué?

BILLY: (shrugs) The territory changed after the war. All those Texans and southern soldiers returning home found nothing but ruin. They spent four years killing each other, living day to day with death. And when the war ended they found the South was in ruins. Devastation all around. They came West, and they were armed. So this has become the new battlefield, and the man who isn't armed gets pushed out.

ROSA: My father isn't armed.

BILLY: Yeah, but the Mexicans down in Lincoln County are armed. . . . Look, when it comes to war you need to protect your place. Protect your family. (He puts on his shirt.)

ROSA: You have a familia?

BILLY: No.

ROSA: No one?

BILLY: They killed my brother, and they killed the only man who ever treated me like a son. Now I trust only my pistola.

ROSA: That's sad.

BILLY: You said a person could change . . .

ROSA: Any man can change.

BILLY: (moves toward her) Become a sheepherder on the llano?

ROSA: We are happy, we are content. We have our families, the vecinos who help, the fiestas of the church . . .

BILLY: I'm afraid if I came here—

ROSA: What?

BILLY: The vaqueros would follow me. There's a U.S. warrant for my arrest. Somebody would come looking for me. One day I'd be standing behind a plow, and—

ROSA: Is your destino to live by the gun?

BILLY: (turns and looks at Don Manuelito) An old friend told me that revenge only makes for more killing, but every time I try to change, someone starts a new fight. (He stops, ties his bandana around his neck, smiles.) There. How do I look?

ROSA: Muy guapo.

BILLY: Now I'm going to ask the most beautiful señorita of Fort Sumner to the dance.

ROSA: Oh, and who is that?

BILLY: You.

ROSA: You are a flirt.

BILLY: I mean it.

ROSA: I will go with you, if my father permits it.

BILLY: Let's ask him.

Billy takes her hand and they walk into the house. The scene changes to the dance. A wild polka is playing; all, including Billy and Rosa, are dancing. Rosa's father and mother sit and watch. They nod approval.

DON JESÚS: Es buen muchacho. No toma como los otros.

DOÑA ANA: Tiene mucha cortesía. Y habla bien nuestro idioma.

DON JESÚS: Es simpático . . .

Don Pedro Maxwell enters with his daughter Josefina. Don Pedro is middle-aged, with silver hair, dressed in the fine suit of a rico. Josefina is tall and slender, her black hair tied back, and dressed in a very expensive gown for the period. The music stops and all, including Billy and Rosa, step forward to greet Don Pedro. Don Jesús and his wife stand to greet him.

DON JESÚS: Bienvenido, Don Pedro, Josefina . . .

DON PEDRO: Don Jesús, Doña Ana. Buenas noches. ¿Cómo 'stán?

DON JESÚS: Todo pacífico, gracias a Dios.

DON PEDRO: ¿Y estos jovenes?

DON JESÚS: El Bilito y su amigo—

DON PEDRO: ¿Bilito? ¿Pero que haces aquí? (*He warmly embraces Billy.*) Josefina, mira quien anda aquí. Billy.

BILLY: Buenas noches, Don Pedro, Josefina.

JOSEFINA: (*smiles, greets Billy warmly*) Billy, it's been a long time. Shame on you for not telling us you were here.

BILLY: I came in a hurry . . .

DON PEDRO: No excuse. Sabes que aquí tienes tu casa. ¿Cuánto hace?

JOSEFINA: It's been a year since he stayed with us. (*to Billy*) And you didn't write as you promised. I should be angry.

DON PEDRO: But you forgive him.

JOSEFINA: Yes, I forgive him, if he will dance with me.

Billy fidgets, introduces Rosa.

BILLY: This is Rosa . . . hija de Don Jesús.

DON PEDRO: Of course I know Rosa. Rosa is my god-child. ¿Como estás, Rosa? (*He embraces Rosa.*)

ROSA: Bien, Padrino.

JOSEFINA: How are you, Rosa?

ROSA: Bien, gracias. ¿Y tú, Josefina?

JOSEFINA: (*straightening Rosa's collar*) I am fine, but look at you. You're wearing the same gown you wore last year. Come by the house and I'll give you one of mine. It will fit perfectly.

Rosa lowers her head.

DON PEDRO: (*to Billy*) And you come home with us tonight. I want you to tell me what's happening in Lincoln County.

BILLY: (*looks at Rosa*) I—

JOSEFINA: No argument. The guest bedroom is always ready for you.

The music strikes up a waltz.

JOSEFINA: Now dance with me. I, too, want to hear of your adventures.

Billy looks at Rosa, who dashes out. He takes Josefina's hand and dances.

JOSEFINA: I should be angry with you.

BILLY: ¿Por qué?

JOSEFINA: Not coming to see me.

BILLY: I just rode in. Met Paco, and he—

JOSEFINA: Billy! You surprise me.

BILLY: ¿Por qué?

JOSEFINA: Being in the company of sheepherders? Tch, tch.

BILLY: Many a sheepherder has saved my life out in the llano. Son buena gente.

JOSEFINA: Pero no tiene mañas.

BILLY: Me gusta la gente humilde.

JOSEFINA: Y yo. ¿Ya no te gusto?

BILLY: Sabes que sí . . .

JOSEFINA: You promised to write, and you didn't.

BILLY: I've been too busy.

JOSEFINA: Did our night of love mean so little to you?

BILLY: Things changed when I got back to Lincoln.

JOSEFINA: And now the law has offered a reward for you. I worry for you.

BILLY: Why?

JOSEFINA: Because I care for you. And Papá cares. He can help you.

BILLY: ¿Cómo?

JOSEFINA: Come tonight and talk to Father. He knows the governor. A pardon? Maybe he can get you a pardon.

BILLY: A pardon? Me, a free man?

JOSEFINA: Yes, it's possible. Come and stay with us. We can help you. Unless you're still friendly with John Chisum's niece, Sallie? Is that why you didn't write?

BILLY: Oye, new travels fast on the Río Pecos.

JOSEFINA: There are no secrets. Father's sheepherders and vaqueros move up and down the river. They hear everything.

BILLY: My life is a book.

JOSEFINA: Yes, what you do is known to all. The Mexicanos think you're Robin Hood. They say you rob from the rich, give to the poor.

BILLY: The poor need help—

JOSEFINA: I am rich, Billy, and you robbed me.

BILLY: ¿Qué dices?

JOSEFINA: You stole my heart.

BILLY: What would your father say?

JOSEFINA: He likes you. He wants to help you.

Billy looks toward the door.

JOSEFINA: Come tonight. I've waited a year . . .

The waltz ends.

BILLY: I'll come. I promised Don Pedro.

Billy goes out the door, where Rosa stands alone. She has been crying. He goes to her.

BILLY: Rosa. ¿Qué pasa?

ROSA: Nada.

BILLY: Why did you leave?

ROSA: It's warm inside.

BILLY: Nice and cool out here. Stars look like the milk of heaven. Peaceful. A man could—

ROSA: Yes.

BILLY: Just meeting you makes me think there's a chance.

ROSA: A man has to decide, Billy.

BILLY: I know, and I've been thinking. There's a new governor in Santa Fe. Lew Wallace. He's granted a pardon to those who fought in Lincoln County. I won't surrender to Dolan's posse, but I might turn myself in to the army, or to the governor.

ROSA: The governor would protect you!

BILLY: Yes. If the pardon's good, I could leave Lincoln, come up here— (He pauses, holds her at arm's length.) Maybe I'm putting the wagon before the horse.

ROSA: What would it take to make you change your ways?

BILLY: If I knew the beautiful woman I've met tonight would wait for me while I go down to Lincoln and settle things.

ROSA: You mean Josefina?

Billy laughs, draws her into his arms.

BILLY: You know who I mean.

ROSA: Do you make these promises so easily?

BILLY: I never have, not to a single woman.

ROSA: (*cynically*) Can I believe your sweet words?

BILLY: I never felt like I feel toward you.

ROSA: (*turns serious*) ¿Qué sientes?

BILLY: Un amor . . . (*He holds her close.*)

ROSA: I was jealous when you danced with Josefina. I have never felt that before.

BILLY: I never said "I love you" to a woman till tonight . . .

They are about to kiss when Billy turns away.

ROSA: Billy? ¿Qué pasa? What did I say?

BILLY: It's not you.

ROSA: ¿Pero qué?

BILLY: I can't.

ROSA: Why, Billy?

BILLY: A curse, Rosa. A curse I carry . . .

ROSA: I don't understand.

BILLY: My mother's curse . . . (*He coughs.*)

ROSA: There is no curse between us. Not if we love—

BILLY: I do love you. (*He takes her hands in his.*)

ROSA: Do you want to kiss me?

BILLY: Yes. I want to kiss you, and hold you, and love you. But I can't!

Rosa holds him.

ROSA: Our love can be stronger than any curse.

Billy looks at her, believes.

BILLY: ¿Sería posible?

Billy gathers Rosa in his arms in a warm embrace as Tom comes running out the dance hall door.

TOM: Billy! It's a posse!

BILLY: Go inside, Rosa!

Billy pushes Rosa toward the door as a group of heavily armed men appear in the shadows. They are tall and stocky, armed to the teeth with belts of cartridges, pistols, Winchesters.

BILLY: Make a run, Tom!

TOM: I'm stickin' with you, Billy!

The man in charge of the posse is Sheriff Desidero Romero. He calls out.

ROMERO: Billy!

BILLY: ¿Quién es?

ROMERO: ¡Soy Desidero Romero, sharife del condado de San Miguel!

There is a tense moment at Billy and Tom get ready to draw their pistols.

BILLY: ¿Qué quieres?

ROMERO: Oímos que vas al rumbo de Las Vegas.

BILLY: It's a free country, Sheriff.

ROMERO: No queremos pleito en Las Vegas. Márchate pa' Lincoln.

BILLY: Me marcho a donde quiero. No sharife is going to tell me where to go!

ROMERO: I'm warning you, Bilito!

BILLY: Consider I've been warned.

TOM: Billy, there's too many of them . . .

There is a tense moment as the men place their hands on their pistols, ready to draw.

BILLY: (*whispers*) Yeah. Armed to the teeth . . . (*to the sheriff*) Come to think of it, Sheriff, we were really headed for Puerto de Luna.

ROMERO: We just don't want no trouble with you.

BILLY: I promised Don Jesús not to make trouble here. Why don't you and your boys come in and have a drink?

There's a break in the tension.

ROMERO: (*nods*) I sure could use one. We've been riding all day . . . (*He steps forward.*)

BILLY: Who told you I was headed for Las Vegas?

ROMERO: Some sheepherder.

BILLY: ¡Esos borregeros saben todo!

The posse laughs.

ROMERO: We got some good gambling in Las Vegas, and a few people thought you might be coming up.

BILLY: I earn my living at cards, Sheriff, and one of these days I'll come up north—

Romero frowns, places his hand on his pistol.

BILLY: But not tonight, Sheriff, not tonight!

They all laugh and go into the dance hall. The lights dim and come up on Ash and Paco.

ASH: All's well that ends well.

PACO: Not so well . . .

ASH: Why the reservation? Sheriff Romero and his Las Vegas posse had their drink and headed home. There was no shoot-out.

PACO: I wasn't thinking of Romero.

ASH: Ah, Josefina.

PACO: She lured him home that night. Promising her father could get a pardon from Governor Wallace. Hell, the warrant on Billy was a federal warrant! Nothing the governor could do!

ASH: She wanted him—

PACO: In her bed.

Ash turns to the audience.

ASH: Now I swear, folks, I don't know anything about this. I never got into Billy's love life. Oh, everyone knew the women loved him. He didn't drink, didn't smoke, could sing and dance. He was quite a ladies' man. But this thing with Josefina is part of the myth, part of the many stories people were to tell about the Kid. "Take it with a grain of salt" is all I've got to say.

PACO: Someone knows.

ASH: Who?

PACO: Rosa.

ASH: She found out?

PACO: A woman knows those things in her heart. Don Pedro's house was very near our house. A short walk. Billy spent some time talking to Don Pedro, then he was put in the guest bedroom.

ASH: The same room in which Pat Garrett later gets him?

PACO: (nods) The guest room is right next to Don Pedro's bedroom.

Lights up on Billy entering the dark room. A candle burns on the dresser. He takes off his shirt and lies down. Josefina appears at the door, dressed in a nightgown.

JOSEFINA: Billy?

BILLY: ¿Quién es?

Josefina enters, goes to him.

BILLY: You shouldn't be here.

JOSEFINA: The last time you were here you told me you loved me. (*She goes to his bed and sits by his side.*)

BILLY: Josefina. I was here a few days. I—

JOSEFINA: I've dreamed of you day and night. I want you. I want you more than anything.

BILLY: Your father—

JOSEFINA: Father knows how I feel. I love you, Billy . . .

Josefina lets the nightgown slip from her shoulders and reaches to snuff out the candle. The stage goes dark.

PACO: ¡Ay, qué mujer! She would do anything to get Billy!

ASH: An aggressive woman. And you think Rosa knew . . .

Paco nods.

ASH: Lord, ain't life complex. What dark webs we weave when first we practice to deceive . . . (*He turns to the audience.*) The plot begins to thicken, as the theatre people are wont to say. I suggest we take a short intermission. ¿Qué dices, Paco?

PACO: Bueno. I need a drink.

ASH: Yes, and I'm sure some of our friends want to wet their whiskers and stretch their legs while they try to sort out what's fact and what's fiction. This story ain't done yet. What I've learned so far makes me worry for Billy.

PACO: Now you know Billy wasn't all bad. He deserved a better life, he deserved to settle down in his ranchito with Rosa, but things worked against him.

ASH: They were star-crossed lovers?

PACO: Las estrellas, o el destino, ¿quién sabe? Some men have a destiny they can't fight. Billy tried, but he couldn't change his destino.

ASH: Is this destino some of that Mexican fatalism we hear about?

PACO: Ash, for an educated man you disappoint me. Destino is a way to explain life. Time repeats itself; life repeats itself . . .

ASH: You got a point. I've seen men, and women, so trapped by circumstances that they die. Just wither away, or die violently. So Billy was destined to be in that room when Pat Garrett shot him.

Paco shrugs. Ash turns to the audience.

ASH: That question has plagued me, and Pat Garrett never answered it for me. How did the sheriff know what room in Pedro Maxwell's house Billy was going to be in? No, it wasn't a one-room house, it was the big house of a rico. Richest man in Fort Sumner, to be exact.

PACO: I know.

ASH: You telling?

PACO: Read my book. (*He laughs.*)

ASH: Let's go get that drink.

Ash and Paco walk offstage.

END ACT ONE

ACT TWO

In a bedroom.

Billy lies asleep on a plain cot. On a nearby trastero a short candle burns next to a small, plain cross. There is small table nearby. There is a cough in the shadows. Billy awakens, sits up, and reaches for the pistol at his bedside.

BILLY: ¿Quién es?

Catherine, Billy's mother, appears from the shadows. She is ghost-like, dressed in her faded wedding dress.

CATHERINE: It's me, Billy—your mother.

BILLY: Mother?

CATHERINE: Did I disturb you?

BILLY: No, Mother. (*He puts aside the pistol.*)

CATHERINE: You have a gun? Oh, Billy, I warned you about guns.

BILLY: It's for self-defense, Ma. I need it.

CATHERINE: I don't care for guns. They frighten me. I was afraid that the "law of the West," as the men are apt to call it, would catch up with you. Get rid of it, Billy. Guns only bring trouble.

BILLY: I can't, Ma.

CATHERINE: You're disobeying me?

BILLY: I never disobeyed you, Ma.

CATHERINE: No, you didn't. But you know, he who lives by the sword will perish by the sword.

BILLY: Ma, if a man don't carry a pistol he's nobody. He gets stepped on.

CATHERINE: And if he carries one— You know what happened to Joe.

BILLY: (*nods*) Cahill shot him.

CATHERINE: Now I'm afraid for you.

BILLY: Cahill was a bully, Ma. But I got him!

CATHERINE: But the law, Billy—

BILLY: There is no law! Every man takes care of himself.

CATHERINE: And you had to avenge Joe's death?

BILLY: Yes.

CATHERINE: Vengeance is for the Lord, Billy, not for us mortals. Don't you see, once you take up arms and put the law aside, you might as well live in the jungle. There is no end to vengeance.

BILLY: (getting up) I tried, Ma, I tried! But everyone I ever loved was taken from me.

CATHERINE: (reaches for Billy but does not touch him) My son, my poor orphaned son . . .

BILLY: I ride with a few of the boys—

CATHERINE: But you are alone.

BILLY: Yeah. Most of the time. Out there the only mother I know is the llano, and the only father, the Pecos River. At night I sleep under the stars . . . I cover myself with that glittering blanket . . .

CATHERINE: Alone.

Billy nods.

CATHERINE: If you found a woman—

BILLY: There is one.

CATHERINE: A good woman can help a man. Who is she, son?

BILLY: Rosa. She's beautiful as her name. I've known a lot of women, but never one like Rosa. (He grows animated.) She lives up on the Pecos. She comes from a good family, Ma. And I love her. I know in my heart I love her!

CATHERINE: You don't know how happy that makes me. Go to her, Billy. Put away the gun and make a life with her. Make a life of peace, or the violence will consume you. (She coughs.)

BILLY: And take the curse to her?

CATHERINE: If she loves you, Billy, she'll understand.

BILLY: (shakes his head) I can't infect her with this germ I carry—this germ I have to hide from everyone. Don Manuelito has tried everything he knows, but there's no cure, Ma. There's no cure!

CATHERINE: (*yearningly reaches for Billy but does not touch him*) Her love, Billy! Her love will make you strong! Don't you see, we have lived with this scourge forever. And we have conquered it!

BILLY: (*surprised*) It killed you, Ma!

CATHERINE: Is that what you think? Oh no, Billy. The tuberculosis didn't kill me. . . . (*With great effort and love she finally can take Billy in her arms and embrace him like a child.*) I died of a broken heart, my son. I died because it hurt me to see the violent world you would inherit.

There was nothing I could do, Billy. Perhaps I was too meek, too sensitive—but you're strong! You and Rosa can be strong together! (*She pushes Billy away from her.*) Go to Rosa. Go to her, son! There is salvation in her love. I know that now! (*She turns and disappears into the shadows.*) Goodbye, Billy.

BILLY: Ma! Ma! Don't leave me, Ma! Don't leave me . . .

Billy follows his mother. The light fades. New light comes up on Ash and Paco, who appear from the left. They carry a bottle of whiskey, two tin cups. They have been drinking.

ASH: You got it wrong, Paco! It was February 18, 1879, when Billy and Dolan met to declare a truce.

PACO: You want every pinche date to be correct! What the hell are you, a historian?

ASH: Well, yes, in a manner of speaking—

PACO: What about the man? What about the espíritu inside? Don't that count?

ASH: Yeah, it counts. I guess it matters to Saint Peter. (*He laughs and fills their cups.*) Get it, "It matters to Saint Peter"! (*He laughs loudly.*) Saint Peter cares about your soul; in Lincoln County they cared how fast you could draw your pistol!

PACO: I think Lew Wallace was a no-good sanamabiche!

ASH: There you go again, demeaning the good governor. You just can't go around saying bad things about those you don't agree with.

PACO: He was only interested in writing that book—

ASH: Ben-Hur.

PACO: Yeah. He didn't give a plug of tobacco for Billy!

ASH: Governor Wallace was a righteous man. He gave Billy a chance.

PACO: But he wanted Billy to put the finger on Dolan!

ASH: No, not put the finger on Dolan, not snitch—testify! He wanted Billy to testify!

PACO: ¡Poner dedo! It's the worst thing a man can do.

ASH: How else you gonna put the crooks in jail?

Paco shrugs, both sit to enjoy a drink. Scene shifts to Governor Wallace and Squire Wilson, who enter and sit at the small table.

WALLACE: A cold night for March.

WILSON: These "northers" have no respect for spring. The land starts to warm up, lambs are born, and a storm can come down and freeze everything.

WALLACE: Yes. I find the New Mexico Territory to be the land of Canaan, but with spring winds and winter storms to match its beauty. There's a deep history here, but there's also violence in the land.

WILSON: Men make violence, Governor. The land abides, the land will nurture. It's men that make the violence.

WALLACE: It's gotten out of hand. The newspapers back east are calling us savages. We're not savages, we're Christians! By the will of God, I intend to bring a modicum of civilization to this land. (*He pauses.*)
  Do you think he'll come?

WILSON: If Billy gives his word, he keeps it.

WALLACE: You have faith in the Kid?

WILSON: Lots of people 'round here do. The Mexicans treat him like a hero. For them he's a Robin Hood. He watches out for them, and they watch for him.

WALLACE: They think we're too harsh, don't they?

WILSON: (*shrugs*) It's our destiny . . .

WALLACE: The white man's destiny? It is a heavy load. (*He stands and muses.*) I've been studying these people since I came to Santa Fe. They are good workers, no doubt. Consistent, except when one of their saints' fiestas comes along. Then they spend their time at church, hauling images of their saints back and forth. They seem to have a good time at their religion, dancing and drinking after the praying is done. Spending all day with their families . . .

WILSON: Sounds pretty civilized to me—

WALLACE: Humph. God knows we could never get along without the work they do. They build our houses, clean our streets, prepare our food, bring wood down from the mountain to heat our homes, and at end of day they leave. I often muse on where they go. What do they say about us in the privacy of their homes? I've been observing them, but it seems I don't know them. (*He straightens his shoulders, his voice rising.*) But they're God's children, and they are under the protection of the United States government. I was sent to institute law and order over them, and I intend to keep my pledge.

WILSON: Not so much them that need law and order.

WALLACE: Yes, you're quite right. In general, they are quiet, law-abiding citizens. I agree, it is our own kind that has created this mess in Lincoln County.

There is a knock at the door. Wilson looks at his watch.

WILSON: Right on time.

WALLACE: Enter!

Billy enters, pistol in one hand and Winchester in the other. He looks around, holsters his pistol, and steps forward.

BILLY: Governor Wallace?

WALLACE: Billy Bonney. Pleased to make your acquaintance.

They shake hands.

WALLACE: You know Squire Wilson.

BILLY: (*nods*) Howdy, Squire.

WALLACE: Please, sit.

Billy places his rifle on the table and sits.

WALLACE: I'm glad you came. I received your letter and I am very encouraged that you will testify in this matter. As you know, I am eager to put an end to this lawlessness which has gripped the territory.

BILLY: Whoa, Governor. Go slow. I already made a truce with Dolan's gang. I don't bother them, and they don't bother me.

WALLACE: A truce among gang members isn't worth the paper it's written on. I need convictions! I need to show them I mean business!

BILLY: What do you want me to do?

WALLACE: Testify! Come into the courtroom and testify against them!

BILLY: You mean snitch? Tell what I know about Dolan's gang?

WALLACE: In a courtroom. All nice and proper—

BILLY: If I testify, they'll kill me.

WALLACE: Thou shalt not testify against your fellow gang member, is that the code of the West?

BILLY: Something like that.

Wallace sits across the table from Billy and looks at him intently.

WALLACE: I can offer you protection.

BILLY: Protection? The law out there can't be trusted. Sheriff Peppin is a Dolan man. It was Peppin who attacked us for no good reason.

WALLACE: I will use the full extent of my office . . .

BILLY: (*studies Wallace closely*) Out here, a man's life depends on trust.

WALLACE: I understand that. I may be new to the New Mexico Territory, but I understand law and justice. I have read the law and the prophets, Billy, and we can trust in that.

BILLY: What's the prophets got to do with Dolan's boys?

WALLACE: I've studied the Bible, Billy. I know it inside out. This land looks exactly like the Israel of the prophets. Dry deserts and high mountains, the wind moaning across the landscape like the word of God. Jew and Muslim struggling to live side by side, to raise their sheep and crops! There is a seed of mistrust between the two. God has planted the seed of enmity!

BILLY: Am I the Jew or the Muslim, Governor?

WALLACE: You're a Christian, Billy. I've read a few of the dime novels written about you. Your mother brought you up a Christian. Don't you see, we Christians are the soldiers that strike away enmity! That is our role in these occupied territories! We have come to deliver the citizens of these harsh climates to a better future!

WILSON: The white man's destiny . . .

WALLACE: Yes! Let us recognize our role and be proud of it! It is our manifest destiny to Christianize these lands! Join me, Billy, and together we can bring forth a new millennium of peace!

BILLY: All I have to do is rat on Dolan.

WALLACE: Testify, Billy. Testify. We have to start somewhere.

Billy stands, looks hard at Wallace.

BILLY: I have no love for Dolan and his gang. And I'm not interested in Christianizing the folks here. Most of them do well by what they got. I have my own honor, and I'm going to tell you what I know because I trust you. And because I truly want this peace you promise.

WALLACE: You won't regret it, Billy. You name will be writ in history as a peacemaker. (*He puts his arms around Billy's shoulders.*)

BILLY: I hope so, Governor, 'cause what I'm doing ain't easy.

WALLACE: This is a historic moment! Squire? Call the photographer!

Wilson lets in the photographer with camera. He sets up.

BILLY: Photographer? (*He reaches for his Winchester.*)

WALLACE: I knew you would see things my way. I came prepared to record this moment. A photograph, Billy. An image I can send to Washington. I've brought peace to the territory, Billy! I want it recorded for posterity!

WALLACE: One of you and me, Billy. Shaking hands. I give you a warrant and you agree to testify against Dolan!

Billy reluctantly shakes hands with the governor. The flash explodes.

WALLACE: Excellent! Now one of Billy alone. For the newspapers! Without your guns, Billy. Without your guns!

BILLY: With all due respect, Governor, you can take my picture till hell freezes over, but you can't take my pistol or my rifle till Dolan signs the peace.

The flash explodes. The classic picture of Billy standing with his Winchester appears on the screen in the background.

WALLACE: Dolan will sign. The days of gang warfare in Lincoln County are over! Now sit here, Billy. The squire will take down all the names and events exactly as you state them. This is the beginning of a new time, Billy, and it's going to mean a pardon for you.

Billy and Wilson sit, and as Billy talks, Wilson writes. Wallace rubs his hands in accomplishment. Light fades on the scene, comes up on Ash and Paco.

ASH: A week later Billy was arrested in San Patricio.

PACO: And Governor Wallace was there to enjoy it.

ASH: I admit, he was a bit condescending—

PACO: Just like all the others. They come here from the East and look down their noses at the paisanos.

ASH: Not all of us—

PACO: You're no different!

ASH: I am! I've gotten to know your people. A lot of those prejudices I had early on—

PACO: Like Christianizing the territory—

ASH: All right, all right! So the governor was a sonofabitch! He really believed his mission was to Christianize the New Mexico Territory.

PACO: Not much has changed in a hundred years. Every time we get a new expert in here, he thinks he knows what's best for us.

ASH: Hey, amigo, give me some credit. I'm learning.

PACO: Mucha suerte. We might all be gone and forgotten by the time you finish your lesson. ¡Pasa la botella!

ASH: (*passes the bottle*) They jailed Billy in Juan Patrón's house—

PACO: And Governor Wallace was staying next door. That night he learned just how much la gente loved Billy. They came to the window and serenaded him.

Billy, behind bars, smiles at the group that has gathered to sing a quickly composed corrido to the tune of "Las Mañanitas."

CHORUS OF PEOPLE: (*one calls out*) Buenos días, Bilito. We came to sing you a song.

BILLY: (*laughs gaily and waves*) I hope you tell how the governor double-crossed me.

CHORUS

     (*singing*) Buenos días, Bilito Bonney,
     Hoy te vengo a celebrar.
     Hoy por ser día de tu santo,
     ¡Te venimos a cantar!

     La semana antepasada,
     Nos llegó el governador,

Hoy te encuentras en la carcel
Lamentando su traición!

El Wallace nos trae mas "taxes"
¡Y promesas de Santa Fe,
Y el pelado que no se cuida
Hasta la camisa va perder!

Despierta, Bilito Bonney,
Mira que ya amaneció,
Y tú como pajarillo cantas
¡En la jaula que's tu carcel!

The Chorus roars with laughter; Billy applauds.

ASH: There was a flurry of action after that.

PACO: Old Judge Bristol got busy.

ASH: Yeah. The grand jury over in Mesilla handed out two hundred indict-
ments. Billy testified and identified Dolan and Campbell as the men who
killed Chapman.

PACO: And not a man went to jail.

ASH: The law works in mysterious ways. . . . Any of that hootch left?

PACO: (*passes Ash the bottle*) So Billy kept his promise to Wallace, but got no
pardon. He went up to Fort Summer to see Rosita.

ASH: (*clears his throat*) And other women?

PACO: There were a lot of women in love with the Kid. But after he met Rosa
he was interested only in her.

ASH: He felt betrayed by Governor Wallace.

PACO: If the governor had kept his word, the Kid would've settled down. Instead he started rustling cattle to sell down at White Oaks and Tularose.

ASH: What could Wallace do? January 10, 1880, Billy kills Joe Grant in a Fort
Sumner saloon.

PACO: Joe Grant was a bully!

ASH: I know that, and you know that, but you can't kill people just 'cause
they're bullies!

PACO: Joe Grant drew on him!

ASH: And Billy was faster.

Lights come up on Bob Hargrove's saloon. Billy and Tom are at a monte table. Joe Grant is at the bar, drunk.

GRANT: I hear you're fast, Billy Bonney.

BILLY: (*stands, faces Joe Grant*) Fast enough to stay alive. But I'll tell you, I'd rather be smart than fast.

GRANT: Hear you got it in for John Chisum.

BILLY: Sonofabitch owes me some money.

GRANT: He's standing right there. If you're man enough, take your money now.

BILLY: That's not John. That's his brother Jim. I got no quarrel with him.

Billy turns to sit. Joe Grant draws his pistol.

GRANT: You're yellow, that's why!

Joe Grant shoots but his pistol misfires. Billy whirls and shoots him dead. As Billy holsters his pistol, Rosa rushes in.

ROSA: Billy!

BILLY: You shouldn't be here.

Billy takes her arm and walks her outside. Manuelito is standing in the background.

BILLY: The cantina's no place for a woman.

ROSA: You killed him!

BILLY: He fired first. I knew the hammer would fall on an empty cylinder.

ROSA: You knew?

BILLY: I placed it there earlier this evening. Like I told him, sometimes a man stays alive just being smart.

ROSA: And you shot him . . .

BILLY: It was him or me. Let me take you home—

ROSA: (*tears away*) No!

BILLY: This is no place for you!

ROSA: And it is for you?

BILLY: I can't help it.

ROSA: Why, Billy, why?

BILLY: It's the only thing I know.

ROSA: How can you promise me love?

BILLY: What I do for a living has nothing to do with us!

ROSA: Yes it does! That's what you can't see!

BILLY: I earn my living playing cards—

ROSA: And rustling cattle.

BILLY: Nothing wrong with that. You see a loose steer and you take it.

ROSA: Take what's not yours?

BILLY: Everybody rustles. Chisum, Dolan, the Santa Fe Ring at the capital. Everybody rustles!

ROSA: My father doesn't!

BILLY: He's the only honest man in the territory.

ROSA: No. There are many honest men.

BILLY: I guess I just haven't been riding with them.

ROSA: It's not too late to ride with honest men.

BILLY: What do you mean?

ROSA: My father is delivering sheep to Mexico. I'm going with him.

BILLY: I thought we—

ROSA: Come with us.

BILLY: Saddle up and leave?

ROSA: What do you have here?

BILLY: Only you.

ROSA: Then come with me. Leave this behind you.

Billy goes to her, embraces her. He looks at Manuelito.

BILLY: That's what my friend has been telling me—¿Qué dice, Don Manuelito? ¿Nos vamos a México?

MANUELITO: ¡Vámonos!

ROSA: We can start a new life. You can leave your gang. But you have to decide.

BILLY: I decided the day I met you. Wherever you go, I'll go.

Rosa and Billy embrace tightly.

ROSA: Oh Billy, you'll see, together we can make a new life!

BILLY: Forget the past . . .

ROSA: Make a new future. For our children.

BILLY: (*looks at Rosa*) It's what I wanted. Una familia, un ranchito . . . not the shootings . . .

ROSA: (*pulls Billy*) Let's tell Father.

BILLY: You go on. I'll be right there. There's a few accounts I have to settle.

ROSA: (*kisses him lightly*) Don't be long.

Rosa goes out. A smiling Billy looks after her. Josefina enters.

JOSEFINA: ¿Bilito?

BILLY: (*turns*) Josefina. ¿Cómo estas?

JOSEFINA: I've been looking for you. Was that Rosa?

BILLY: Yes.

JOSEFINA: You promised to come. Father is waiting.

BILLY: I was on my way—

JOSEFINA: Before you met Rosa.

BILLY: We're going to Mexico!

JOSEFINA: You and Rosa?

BILLY: I'm sorry, Josefina.

JOSEFINA: Sorry? Don't you dare feel sorry for me!

BILLY: I meant—

JOSEFINA: Tell me it's not true!

BILLY: It is true, Josefina. I'm going with Rosa.

JOSEFINA: You made love to me!

BILLY: I made no promises—

JOSEFINA: You used me!

BILLY: I never meant to hurt you.

JOSEFINA: (*clutches at him*) I won't let you go! I love you, Billy! Only you! (*She falls to her knees.*) Father is going to talk to the governor! You can stay here, Billy! Stay with me!

BILLY: It's no good—

JOSEFINA: You can't leave! I won't let you. I love you, Billy, I love you!

She sobs. Billy tears away.

BILLY: I'm sorry . . .

JOSEFINA: (*sobbing*) I won't let you go, Billy!

Billy goes out, Josefina rushes after him. Paco has been watching the action. Ash is scribbling in his notebook.

ASH: A tearful scene . . . but I don't like what you're getting at.

PACO: No, you don't like it, because you listened only to Pat Garrett! You wrote what he told you! You didn't know what was going on in Fort Sumner!

ASH: I never claimed to know a woman's heart. . . . I looked for facts. (*He reads from his notes.*) November 2, 1880, Pat Garrett is elected sheriff of Lincoln County.

PACO: There you go with all your pinche dates again!

ASH: Just trying to keep the record straight. I mean, it is Pat Garrett that's going to kill the Kid. You know, after Billy and his amigos shot Carlyle at Coyote Springs, he lost a lot of friends.

PACO: Not us.

ASH: No, not the Mexicans, but the ranchers and Governor Wallace turned against Billy. Wallace even put a five-hundred-dollar reward on the Kid's head. And the New York papers wrote him up. Called him the bandido número uno of the territory.

PACO: You can't believe the goddamn papers! (*He spits.*)

ASH: We tell the truth!

PACO: What is the truth? You made up half that book you wrote!

ASH: I embellished a little . . . but so did you.

PACO: (*jerks as if slapped*) I was an old man when I wrote my book. I had forgotten a few things—

ASH: So you stuck in this and that—

PACO: I told the truth!

ASH: It's mostly myth when it comes to Billy's story. People believe what they want.

PACO: So what are we doing here?

ASH: Well, amigo, we came to tell stories, and to have a drink.

Ash laughs, then Paco laughs.

PACO: ¿Por qué no? Let's have a drink!

ASH: ¿Solamente una copita?

PACO: ¡Una, nada más! We have nothing else to do. We're two writers out of work! Just making up stories!

They laugh loudly.

ASH: A couple of sinvergüenzas!

A roaring laughter.

ASH: Making up stories!

PACO: Making up the truth!

ASH: A little of this, a little of that!

PACO: (*gets serious and looks at the audience*) And them?

ASH: They're fools if they believe the musing of two drunks.

PACO: (*shouts at audience*) ¡Pendejos!

ASH: Leave them alone. They paid their money.

PACO: Well, maybe they're finding out what *really* happened to Billy the Kid.

ASH: At least your point of view. Now where were we?

PACO: (*sits, takes a drink*) Garrett killed Tom O'Folliard, then he followed Billy and his compañeros to the old Rock House near Fort Sumner. There he killed Bowdre and took Billy prisoner.

ASH: He took him to Las Vegas, where Billy met old Sheriff Romero again. Slept in his jail. Then down to Mesilla, where on April 13, 1881, Judge Bristol sentenced Billy to hang for the murder of Sheriff Brady.

PACO: And Governor Wallace washed his hands . . . like Pontius Pilate.

ASH: Except Billy was no Christ.

PACO: Billy was the scapegoat! Wallace wanted to show the New York papers that he had brought law and order to New Mexico. It was politics! They played politics with the Kid's life! Wallace left the state for a new appointment and left Billy to hang! What kind of justice is that?

Ash shrugs. Garrett enters, leading a shackled Billy. Two deputies, Bell and Olinger, follow with shotguns.

GARRETT: Well, Billy, this is your new home for a month.

Billy is cheerful. He looks around.

BILLY: Dolan's old store.

GARRETT: County can't afford a courthouse, so we're using this.

Garrett goes to the window, looks out. Sound of hammer banging on wood.

GARRETT: They're building the scaffold, Billy.

BILLY: (*sits at the table*) We covered our tracks when we headed up to the Rock House. How'd you find me?

GARRETT: Let's say I had a tip. (*Garrett sits, takes a pack of cards from his pocket and tosses it at Billy.*) Might as well make ourselves comfortable till hanging day . . .

BILLY: I ain't gonna hang.

GARRETT: Court said to hang you come May 13, and I intend to follow the orders of the court.

BILLY: And I got a trip to Mexico planned. Hey, I can play better if you take these bracelets off.

Billy holds up his hands and Bell starts forward with a key.

GARRETT: No! You give Billy Bonney a break and it'll cost you your life.

Billy smiles. The two deputies back off as Garrett and Billy play monte.

BILLY: Sure makes it hard to deal . . .

GARRETT: I'll deal.

BILLY: How long we known each other, Pat?

GARRETT: First met in the autumn of '78, up in Fort Sumner.

BILLY: You were rustling cattle.

GARRETT: (*looks uncomfortable and glances at the deputies*) Some things in a man's life he'd rather forget.

BILLY: And now you're sheriff of Lincoln County.

GARRETT: That's fate.

BILLY: The Mexicans call it el destino. Forces that shape our life—

GARRETT: You are what you do, Billy. Don't go blaming anything or anyone.

BILLY: Oh, I'm not blaming anyone. I just remember Don Manuelito telling me I was going to die at the hands of someone I helped. . . . My destiny was to be betrayed by a friend.

GARRETT: (*stares at Billy, again uncomfortable*) Our friendship was over long ago.

BILLY: Yeah, I guess. You know, I thought I was doing the right thing when I joined Tunstall and McSween.

GARRETT: Maybe so, but that gave you no right to shoot Sheriff Brady.

BILLY: I wasn't the only one who shot at Brady! Anyone of us could have killed him! Besides, he killed Tunstall!

GARRETT: Tunstall treated you right, did he?

BILLY: Closest thing to a father I ever had.

GARRETT: I see.

BILLY: Back in '78, when we first met, I admired you, Pat. I still do.

GARRETT: There were good times. I haven't forgotten you saved my ass.

BILLY: Salazar and his boys were going to shoot you for rustling their cattle.

GARRETT: I was just trying to set up a meat store.

They both laugh.

GARRETT: I needed a few sides of beef to start.

They laugh harder.

BILLY: You owe me one.

GARRETT: Yeah, I guess I do.

BILLY: (*leans across the table*) You know it ain't right I should be the only one to pay for a gang war I didn't start.

Garrett nods.

BILLY: Turn me loose, Pat. Let me walk out of here and I'll get my woman and head for Mexico. I swear you'll never see me again.

GARRETT: (*hesitates, then shakes his head*) I can't.

BILLY: I never begged, Pat. You know that. But you got me tied up like a monkey in cage. (*He holds up his shackle.*) This ain't right, Pat! I'm a man! If I ain't free I'll die.

GARRETT: (*stands*) You should've thought of that when you took up the gun! Took up with your gang!

BILLY: Dammit, Pat! Bowdre and Tom and me were only protecting ourselves! You know where the real gangs hang out—up in Santa Fe! The politicos of the Santa Fe Ring are the real gang! Thomas Catron and his business buddies make the money, and we small fry got caught! Turn me loose, Pat! I'm begging you . . . (*He pleads, looks up at Garrett.*)

GARRETT: I'm sorry, Billy . . .

BILLY: I'm not going to hang, Pat.

Garrett, shaken, turns to the two deputies.

GARRETT: I've got to ride up to White Oaks. You two watch Billy real close.

Olinger approaches with shotgun in hand.

OLINGER: Why don't we just shoot him right now? Shoot him cold, like he shot Beckwith! (*He strikes Billy with the rifle butt.*)

GARRETT: Back off, Bob! The Kid's a prisoner! He's in irons! (*He helps Billy to his feet.*)

BILLY: You like to hit unarmed men. I've met bullies like you . . . and they're dead.

Billy's glare frightens Olinger.

OLINGER: Let me kill 'im, Garrett! Kill 'im and be done!

GARRETT: The law will do that. You just watch him. (*He turns to Billy.*) Dammit, Billy! I wish there was something I could do.

Garrett turns quickly. As he goes out Olinger warns him.

OLINGER: Hurry back from White Oaks, Sheriff! You might not have a live prisoner when you return. (*He turns and points his shotgun at Billy.*) I'd just as soon shoot you!

BELL: Hold on, Bob! You got no call.

OLINGER: I'm gonna dance the day you hang, Billy.

BILLY: I made a promise, Bob. I ain't gonna hang.

OLINGER: (*laughs*) I'd like to hear those words when I put the noose around your neck.

BELL: Give the Kid a break.

OLINGER: Okay, okay. Let 'im think about the noose. Let 'im squirm a little. You watch 'im, I'm goin' for a drink. (*He places his shotgun by the door and goes out.*)

BILLY: Play a little monte?

BELL: (*nervous*) No.

Billy sits at the table, slips out of one handcuff.

BILLY: I just thought we'd pass the time.

BELL: I never played monte. I got my orders, I do 'em, and that's it.

BILLY: Then how about letting me go to the outhouse? It's been a long day.

Bell turns to open the door. Billy jumps up, strikes Bell over the head, and takes his gun in the scuffle.

BILLY: Don't make me kill you!

A frightened Bell turns and runs. Billy shoots him. Somebody shouts "He shot Bell! He shot Bell!" Billy reaches for Olinger's shotgun. Olinger rushes in.

BILLY: Greetings, Deputy.

OLINGER: (*draws his pistol but realizes he has no chance*) Oh, God, he's killed me, too.

BILLY: Rot in hell! (*He fires and kills Olinger, then goes to the window and spies the blacksmith.*) Gus! Bring up an axe and cut my irons! (*Billy turns and speaks to the audience.*) You folks out there know I won't hurt you. I'm sorry I had to kill Bell, but he ran. Olinger was a rattlesnake who deserved killing. I'm gonna ride out of Lincoln, and I ain't never coming back.

Sheriff Garrett wanted to hang Billy Bonney to teach you a lesson! You just remember, I didn't start the Lincoln County War! Big rancheros with a lot of greed in their hearts started the shooting. And they've got friends up in Santa Fe! That whole Santa Fe Ring wants to take your land and cattle and everything you got.

Dolan killed my friend Tunstall, and I evened the score. A hundred men took part in the fighting, and many a good one died. But it's not right only Billy Bonney be sentenced to death. Is it?

Someone shouts "Head for Mexico, Billy! They won't find you there!"

BILLY: Thanks for the advice.

Gus enters with axe and cuts Billy's leg irons and shackles. Billy shouts a cry of freedom and rushes out.

PACO: (*whispers*) Head for Mexico, Billy . . .

ASH: He didn't.

PACO: (*nods*) He went for Rosa . . .

ASH: Ah, I see what you mean about destino. Fate is about to catch up with Billy. Garrett recruits John Poe and Tip McKinney to go up to Fort Summer to arrest Billy. On the night of July 14, by sheer coincidence, Garrett enters the bedroom of Pedro Maxwell and is asking him if he's seen Billy, when Billy backs into the room—

PACO: You don't believe that, do you?

ASH: It's what Garrett told me.

PACO: He lied!

ASH: Pat Garrett was an honest man! There was no reason for him to lie!

PACO: Then you tell me! Why would Garrett go into Don Pedro's bedroom in the middle of the night?

ASH: I've thought of that . . .

PACO: And if Billy ran into Poe outside, why didn't Poe shoot? Why did Billy enter Don Pedro's bedroom right at that moment?

ASH: (*shakes his head*) I don't know.

PACO: I'll tell you why.

A single light comes up on Garrett, stage left, waiting in a dark room. At the right there is a bed with Don Pedro in it. A lantern appears.

GARRETT: ¿Quién es?

JOSEFINA: Yo.

GARRETT: Josefina?

JOSEFINA: Buenas noches, Sheriff Garrett.

GARRETT: Buenas noches. You're up late.

JOSEFINA: I can't sleep, Sheriff. I walk the lonely streets at night . . . the people call me la Llorona. In my heart I am crying.

GARRETT: I'm looking for Billy.

JOSEFINA: (*bitterly*) He's here. Walking the streets of Fort Sumner like a free man.

GARRETT: Where is he now?

JOSEFINA: With his querida.

GARRETT: I've got a warrant for his arrest. If you help me—

JOSEFINA: Billy won't be taken alive.

GARRETT: I've got two deputies with me. I aim to take him, dead or alive.

JOSEFINA: (*shudders, moans softly*) If I cannot have him . . .

GARRETT: Do you know where he is?

JOSEFINA: Yes. Go to my father's bedroom. Wait there. Billy will come to you.

Josefina goes out. Garrett moves across the stage to the bed of Don Pedro Maxwell.

GARRETT: Don Pedro?

DON PEDRO: ¿Quién es?

GARRETT: Sheriff Garrett.

DON PEDRO: Sit down, Pat. Don't make any noise.

A light shines, Billy and Rosa enter. He holds her.

BILLY: Espera aquí.

ROSA: No. Voy contigo.

BILLY: (*laughs*) We have plenty of time to be together, querida. Tomorrow we leave for Mexico.

ROSA: A new life . . .

BILLY: Don Pedro wants to see me.

ROSA: Why so late?

BILLY: He owes me some money. Josefina said he's ready to pay.

ROSA: Josefina? No, Billy, don't go!

BILLY: Why are you trembling?

ROSA: There's no light in his room . . .

BILLY: The old cheapskate doesn't like to burn his oil. Wait.

ROSA: Billy.

BILLY: ¿Qué?

ROSA: I love you.

BILLY: Y yo te amo a ti.

They embrace warmly. Deputy Poe appears.

ROSA: ¿Quién es?

Billy pulls out his knife. Poe backs away.

BILLY: (*whispers*) Just one of Don Pedro's vaqueros. Espera aquí. (*He leaves Rosa and quietly enters Don Pedro's bedroom.*)

BILLY: Don Pedro. Who is the man outside—

Garrett stands. Billy faces him.

BILLY: ¿Quién es? ¿Quién es?

DON PEDRO: That's him!

BILLY: Garrett?

GARRETT: It's me, Billy!

Garrett fires once. Billy grabs at his gut in pain, steps forward, reaching for Garrett. The figure of death, La Muerte, appears. Catherine also appears, but La Muerte pushes her aside and goes to stand by Billy.

BILLY: Pat . . . You got me cold-blooded, Pat . . .

Garrett fires again. Billy winces, stumbles.

GARRETT: (*in a trembling voice*) Die, Billy!

BILLY: Oh God, Pat . . . an old friend would kill me . . . (*Billy falls. The figure of La Muerte stands over him. There is a scream and Rosa rushes in to gather Billy in her arms. Poe enters. Garrett lights a candle.*)

POE: Did you get him?

GARRETT: I got him . . . (*He holds the candle over Billy and a sobbing Rosa.*)

ROSA: Billy! Billy! Oh, Bilito . . .

BILLY: I love you, Rosa . . .

ROSA: Amor, amor . . .

Billy dies. Paco and three other men rush in. They look at Billy.

PACO: Billy!

ROSA: He's dead . . . Amor, amor . . . (*She holds and rocks Billy in her arms.*)

GARRETT: I had to shoot. He was armed.

PACO: (*kicks the knife Billy dropped*) Armed? It's only a knife! (*He draws his pistol and aims at Garrett.*) ¡Cobarde!

GARRETT: (*wincing*) I had to shoot . . .

The men pull Paco away.

FIRST MAN: No, Paco!

SECOND MAN: He's not worth killing.

Paco lowers his pistol; his head sinks.

PACO: Cobarde . . . Cobarde . . .

The men lift Billy and lay him on the bed. Rosa kneels at the bedside. Women carrying lighted candles appear. They place the candles around Billy's bed and kneel to pray.

WOMEN: Dios te salve María, llena eres de gracia, el Señor es contigo, bendita tú eres entre todas las mujeres, y bendito es El Fruto de tu vientre, Jesús. Santa María, madre de Dios, ruega por nosotros pecadores hora y en la hora de nuestra muerte, amen.

The prayer decreases in volume. Catherine, Billy's mother, rises and walks slowly toward the bed. Dressed in her wedding gown, she appears pale and ghostly. La Muerte backs away into the shadows.

CATHERINE: Billy?

BILLY: (sits up) Mother?

CATHERINE: Yes, Billy, it's me.

BILLY: It's so dark, Mother. I can barely see you.

CATHERINE: It's always dark in the land of death. One never gets used to it. And the wind blows, the cries are the cries of lost souls. . . . But I've found you, Billy. Thank God, I found you. It's time to go.

Catherine reaches out. Billy draws back.

BILLY: But I was goin' to Mexico. Rosa and me—

CATHERINE: Hush, son. That dream is done. Come with me.

BILLY: (*reaches for Rosa but cannot touch her*) Tell her, Rosa! Tell her we're goin' to Mexico! We're gonna start a new life. Get married, raise kids, start a ranch! Just like we planned! (Billy *reaches frantically for Rosa but cannot hold her.*)

CATHERINE: She can't hear you, son. She's full of grief. Maybe with time she'll hear your voice, or dream you are near her. But now the violence of life is ended. Come with me.

Catherine holds out her hand. Billy looks longingly at Rosa, then takes his mother's hand and walks away with her. La Muerte follows them quietly. The women continue to pray softly around the bed. All are frozen onstage, except Paco, who approaches Ash.

ASH: You don't believe that Don Pedro set Billy up—

PACO: How else did Garrett know Billy was going to show up in Don Pedro's room?

ASH: (shrugs) A question that has remained unanswered—

PACO: Until now.

ASH: But it's conjecture, nothing more—

PACO: Hey! You made up what you wrote in your pinche book!

ASH: But I—

PACO: I know! You had Pat Garrett telling you the story. Big deal! Everybody tells the story to suit himself!

Ash hands Paco the bottle. Paco empties it.

PACO: We need a new bottle.

ASH: There's a cantina down the street.

Ash places his arm around Paco and they go off the stage, down one of the aisles, arguing.

ASH: What do you think, amigo? Is there any truth to history?

PACO: There is if you put it in!

Paco laughs. Ash pauses.

ASH: Or is history a myth we write to please ourselves?

PACO: El Bilito is a myth. He had good and bad in him, just like every man. I saw the good, el sharife Garrett saw the bad.

ASH: So you were prejudiced when you wrote about him?

PACO: Sure, I loved the Kid.

ASH: Your love becomes a new element in the myth . . .

PACO: Why not? Those were violent times. You needed a little love to keep going.

ASH: It's sad to see a kid die that young. . . . For a moment he had Rosa's love . . .

PACO: That's all he had, amigo. That's all he had.

Paco places his arm around Ash's shoulders and they go out.

END

Angie

CHARACTERS

CONNIE

ANGIE

JOE

GLORIA

MINNIE

PAT

OTHER RESIDENTS

THE NURSE

DANCERS

JANITOR

AIDES

JUAN

ACT ONE

Scene One

Mid-afternoon in the Joy of Life Nursing Home day room.

The elderly residents sit at tables; some play cards or bingo, while others stare out the windows. A few are in wheelchairs, crutches, walkers. Upstage, the most immobile residents sit in chairs. Gloria sits reading a magazine, Pat plays solitaire, Minnie, dressed as a bag lady, places a boom box in her grocery cart full of junk.

Angie—sitting in a wheelchair, a purse and a flower pot of bright marigolds on her lap—is pushed into the room by Connie, her daughter. Her son-in-law Joe follows, carrying Angie's suitcase.

CONNIE: We can wait for the nurse in here—

ANGIE: Whoa!

Connie stops. Angie stares at the people in the room. Some glance at her.

CONNIE: ¿Qué pasa?

ANGIE: I'm not dead yet!

CONNIE: Of course you're not dead—

ANGIE: Estos pobres están muertos.

CONNIE: Mom! They're not dead.

ANGIE: Well, they look dead.

JOE: (*drops the bag*) Cut it out, Angie. Look, they're playing cards.

ANGIE: They can hardly lift the cards! I don't like it. Take me home! (*Angie turns the wheelchair around.*)

CONNIE: Mom, we've been through this. You can't be home alone. You just can't.

ANGIE: Don't leave me here, please. It smells like disinfectant and death.

CONNIE: You're going to be all right. I can't take care of you right now—

Connie takes the flower pot and places it on a table. Gloria looks at Angie.

ANGIE: I don't need you to take care of me. I can take care of myself. Tengo mi casita, mi carro.

JOE: You can't drive anymore, Angie. When you ran into the police car you didn't have a valid driving license on you, your brakes weren't working, and you were drinking.

ANGIE: I wasn't drinking! I had a beer at the Hi-Lo Club! I'll fix the damn brakes! I'll hire somebody to drive me!

JOE: (sarcastically) Sure, driving Miss Daisy—

ANGIE: I ain't Miss Daisy! I'm Angelina Aragón de Barelas. And don't you forget that.

CONNIE: Please, don't argue.

JOE: You don't have the money to pay a driver.

ANGIE: I'll stay home!

CONNIE: We've been over that, Mom. Your house just wasn't built for a wheelchair. Here you'll have medical attention twenty-four hours a day.

JOE: You can't stay with us—

ANGIE: I wouldn't stay with you if they paid me.

JOE: Have it your way.

CONNIE: Mom, you know what Joe means. We're busy every night—

ANGIE: I know, I know, running around trying to get Joe elected mayor. He doesn't stand a chance.

CONNIE: Mom, what an awful thing to say.

JOE: I'll make it, Angie.

ANGIE: You need the valley vote, Joe.

JOE: And you and Manny control that.

ANGIE: Let's say we don't like your plans for the future.

JOE: Just stay out of my way, Angie.

CONNIE: Cut it out, you two! Let's not talk politics. I don't know why you're always arguing.

ANGIE: Joe knows. Now get me outta here. I've got things to do.

CONNIE: It's not just the hip, mom. You forget things.

ANGIE: So? Everybody forgets things!

JOE: Like not fixing the breaks on your car? Like not paying the utilities until they were shut off?

CONNIE: And not showing up for your doctor's appointment.

ANGIE: I don't like that doctor.

CONNIE: It's for your own good.

ANGIE: I was busy.

JOE: Yeah, stirring up the neighborhood. Come on, Connie, you can't talk sense with anyone as stubborn as Angie. Let's find the nurse, sign the papers, and get outta here. (*Joe pulls Connie away.*)

CONNIE: (*whispers to Angie*) I'll be right back.

JOE: (*as they leave*) She's better off here . . .

ANGIE: (*turns toward the audience*) Joe used to be a nice guy, 'til he got into politics. Now he's hungry. He wants money and power. He uses people . . . uses my daughter.

Ah, I don't interfere in their marriage. I have my own home, my own friends. I go where I want, when I want! When I need a chile fix I go over to the Barelas Coffee House and order the special—enchiladas smothered with onions and red chile. Of course the onions give me gas. All my friends eat there.

We talk about the old days. We were poor but happy. As soon as I graduated from high school I got a job as a waitress at the Sunset. Papá didn't want me to work, but he finally gave in. He would drive me to work in his jalopy. The Sunset. That's where I met Johnny. I remember the night he came in. He was so handsome. He wasn't your run-of-the-mill Old Town pachuco. No, not Juan. He had class. I fell in love with him the moment I saw him.

Gloria timidly approaches Angie.

GLORIA: Hi.

ANGIE: Hi yourself.

GLORIA: I'm Gloria.

ANGIE: Are you alive?

GLORIA: (*laughs*) Yes. (*She takes Angie's hand.*)

ANGIE: You're warm . . .

GLORIA: You too.

ANGIE: It's freezing in here.

GLORIA: It's always cold. I'll get you one of my sweaters.

ANGIE: No, no, I'll get used to it. What about the inmates? (*She motions to the residents who sit staring out the windows.*)

GLORIA: Windows are for daydreaming.

ANGIE: I see. What about my flowers?

GLORIA: They're beautiful.

ANGIE: They're going to freeze to death—

GLORIA: Shhh.

ANGIE: What?

GLORIA: Don't say freeze to death. Don't say "death"—

Minnie approaches. In her eighties and dressed like a bag lady, she is pushing her super-market basket. She whispers.

MINNIE: Can you get me outta here?

ANGIE: I can't even get myself out.

GLORIA: Don't mind her. She asks everyone the same question.

ANGIE: Can't her family get her out?

GLORIA: Can yours?

ANGIE: My daughter? Oh, she only wants the best for me. I fractured my hip, that's why I'm here.

GLORIA: I'm here long-term.

ANGIE: Not me. A few weeks and I'm outta here. Back to my casita.

MINNIE: I burned my house down.

ANGIE: Burned your house down. Why?

MINNIE: My husband was in it.

ANGIE: ¡De veras!

GLORIA: (*pulls Angie's chair closer*) Don't listen to her, she exaggerates. Her husband died of a heart attack while shopping at Costco.

ANGIE: What an asco way to go!

GLORIA: They were arguing over what kind of stewed tomatoes to buy, and he dropped dead.

MINNIE: I won.

ANGIE: I had a friend who was killed at Price Club. A crate of toilet paper fell on him. How can you write a corrido about someone killed by a ton of toilet paper? Bueno, cuando te toca te toca. *(turns to Gloria)* How about you? You look healthy. Why are you here?

MINNIE: She hears voices—

GLORIA: Minnie, go away.

Minnie walks away.

GLORIA: I came to get away from my family.

ANGIE: You don't like your family?

GLORIA: I can't stand my grandchildren's music. Too loud.

ANGIE: Come on, you don't commit yourself to a place like this because you don't like rap!

GLORIA: *(softly)* I had a nervous breakdown after my husband died.

MINNIE: *(from a distance)* He was murdered.

GLORIA: Shut up, Minnie! ¡Entremetida!

ANGIE: Are you better now?

GLORIA: Oh, yes.

ANGIE: You have children?

GLORIA: Yes.

ANGIE: How many?

GLORIA: Let's not talk about them. Where are you from?

ANGIE: Barelas. And you?

GLORIA: Ranchitos.

ANGIE: You have a home?

GLORIA: Yes.

ANGIE: Why not live at home?

GLORIA: The doctor says I have the early stage of Alzheimer's. I forget things.

ANGIE: Damn! We all forget things. What are they going to do, put all the viejos in nursing homes because we forget things!

GLORIA: (shrugs) Some things are best forgotten. I try to remember the beautiful memories.

ANGIE: Like?

GLORIA: My childhood. My parents adored me. Especially my father. He spoiled me. On Sundays he would drive my mother and me to the train station. You remember the old Alvarado Hotel?

ANGIE: Sure I remember.

GLORIA: That's where we ate. It was so fancy.

ANGIE: The train depot. That's where I said goodbye to Johnny . . .

GLORIA: Who?

ANGIE: Juan Aragón. He was from Old Town.

GLORIA: Your husband?

ANGIE: Yes.

GLORIA: Is he alive?

ANGIE: In my heart. . . . Yours?

GLORIA: (nervously) I don't remember.

ANGIE: What do you mean, you don't remember?

GLORIA: He's dead. He was in politics.

ANGIE: Politicians, now there's a species that hasn't evolved in the past two thousand years—

MINNIE: (from a distance) They make too many promises!

ANGIE: They cut too many deals in the back room. So you stayed home, raised your kids.

GLORIA: I don't want to talk about that. Tell me about you and Juan.

ANGIE: Johnny. I always called him Johnny. He was my first love.

GLORIA: You still remember . . .

ANGIE: (*nods*) It was the most beautiful summer of my life. I was eighteen, and the war came. Johnny joined the army. I remember going to the depot to watch him board the train. Hundreds of them. They were in the National Guard, so they went first.

GLORIA: Here comes your daughter.

Connie returns.

CONNIE: I see you already have a friend. Hi, I'm Connie. Angie's daughter.

GLORIA: I just came to say hello.

She backs away. Minnie approaches.

MINNIE: Can you get me outta here?

CONNIE: No.

MINNIE: I gotta get out.

Minnie takes an old black phone with dangling cord from her basket, dials, and speaks as she moves away, pushing her grocery cart.

MINNIE: Hello, 911? This is an emergency! Get me outta here! It's colder than hell here! And tell my husband to quit calling me collect! He's dead!

CONNIE: Weird.

GLORIA: Nobody can hear her.

ANGIE: What's weird?

CONNIE: That woman—

ANGIE: You'd be weird too if your viejo died during a stewed tomato argument.

CONNIE: Stewed tomatoes?

ANGIE: Never mind. Minnie is no more weird than the rest of us. Maybe you remind her of somebody.

CONNIE: Who?

ANGIE: Her daughter.

CONNIE: Does she have a daughter?

ANGIE: Do I?

CONNIE: You're upset with me, I know. But you're going to be happy here. I just know you are.

ANGIE: You're trying to convince yourself, aren't you?

CONNIE: It's not easy for me.

ANGIE: I can take care of myself.

CONNIE: You keep saying that, but you don't realize—

ANGIE: I don't realize my bones are brittle, my back has a hump. I can't drive anymore? Who cares?

CONNIE: I care.

ANGIE: I know you do.

CONNIE: I love you.

ANGIE: And I love you, mi'ja.

CONNIE: (looks around) I wish I didn't have to—

ANGIE: You have no choice.

CONNIE: You're used to doing things for yourself.

ANGIE: Damn right. I've been a free woman all my life. But now— Soy una paloma sin alas.

CONNIE: Don't say that. Here's the Nurse—

Connie goes to Joe, who enters with the Nurse. Angie looks after Connie, then turns to the audience.

ANGIE: Johnny left me with a daughter to raise. Consuelo. She's beautiful, isn't she? The only mistake she ever made was to marry Joe. She raised the kids. Got them through college. Now Joe wants to run for mayor. Got in with Frank Dominic. Ese cabrón wants to build a road right through our barrio. He wants to build casinos along the river! Hotels and casinos! For the poor? No, for the tourists!

Minnie approaches.

MINNIE: Can you get me out?

ANGIE: Later.

MINNIE: Watch out for the Nurse . . .

Connie, Joe, and the Nurse approach.

CONNIE: Mom, this is Nurse . . .

NURSE: Ruth. So you're Angie. Well, I want to be the first to welcome you to Joy of Life. Your new home.

ANGIE: Home?

NURSE: Oh, yes. Joy of Life is not an institution. We consider it our home.

ANGIE: And we're all one big, happy family.

NURSE: (smiling) Yes.

ANGIE: (whispers) Can you get me outta here?

NURSE: (laughs) I see you've been talking to Minnie. No, you won't be leaving us soon. Your daughter has just signed a long-term contract—

ANGIE: (looks in surprise at Connie) Long-term? What's long-term?

JOE: (satisfied) A year.

ANGIE: A year? No way am I staying that long! (turns to Joe) You want me out of the way, don't you?

CONNIE: Mom, nobody wants you out of the way.

NURSE: Believe me, Angie, it's a standard contract. We only offer long-term care.

ANGIE: (looking around) You mean, everybody's here for—

NURSE: (nods) Long-term.

ANGIE: (pleadingly) Connie.

CONNIE: It's for your own good, Mom. I'll come to see you every day.

ANGIE: (nervously reaches for her cigarettes in her purse) I think you're all out of your minds. I'm not staying a year! ¡Ni modo! I've got my girls!

NURSE: What girls?

ANGIE: My dancers.

Four young women in brightly colored Mexican dress appear off to the side. They strike a pose, but do not move. Only Angie sees them.

ANGIE: They need me.

NURSE: You're not doing any dancing for a while— (takes away Angie's cigarettes) Smoking is not permitted at Joy of Life. Not good for the health of the—

ANGIE: Inmates.

NURSE: Our residents. (*turns to Connie*) I see your mother has a sense of humor. That's good. But I suggest no visitations for a while. Give her time to adjust—

CONNIE: No visitations? But—

NURSE: We know from experience all the residents need time to adjust. They meet new friends, and in Angie's case, time to give up smoking.

JOE: (*to Connie*) They know what's best.

Angie struggles to rise. Connie leans over Angie.

CONNIE: Mom, try to be calm.

ANGIE: A year, Connie. You signed the contract—

CONNIE: I had to, Mom. Joe insisted—

ANGIE: Good old Joe. He knows I'll be dead in a year!

NURSE: We don't use that word here. It upsets our family members. (*She starts to pull the chair back.*)

CONNIE: You've got everything you need here. You own room, meals, and most important, nursing care.

ANGIE: And you? Where are you going for your morning coffee?

CONNIE: I'll miss our talks—

ANGIE: My casita will be so sad.

CONNIE: I'll take care of it, Mom.

ANGIE: Promise?

JOE: (*irritated*) We promise.

ANGIE: My casita holds my memories. (*She pauses, looks around.*) This place has only the memory of death.

NURSE: Please don't mention that word.

JOE: This is home, Angie. Get used to it!

ANGIE: I ain't dead yet!

NURSE: She's excited. She needs to rest—

CONNIE: Mom, you'll get used—

JOE: (*to Connie*) I've got an appointment. Come on.

ANGIE: Don't leave me, Connie!

Joe shakes his head and walks away.

CONNIE: You'll be all right. Make new friends . . .

ANGIE: I got friends! My friends at the Hi-Lo Club.

JOE: (*calls*) Connie!

NURSE: She's getting upset. It's quite normal. Don't worry, I'll give her a
  sedative—

ANGIE: A sedative? I don't need a sedative!

CONNIE: Mom, try to rest.

NURSE: Say goodbye—

The Nurse pulls the wheelchair and starts out of the room.

ANGIE: (*resisting*) Connie! Get me outta here!

CONNIE: (*crying*) Mom!

ANGIE: Call 911!

CONNIE: Oh, God . . .

The Nurse pushes Angie out.

ANGIE: (*from offstage*) Con-n-n-n-nie! ¡Mi alma!

CONNIE: Mom, oh Mom . . .

Connie bends her head and sobs as the lights grow dim.

Scene Two

The day room, after dinner.

*The room is dim. A janitor pushes a broom across the floor. He examines Minnie's cart,
picks up the boom box. A loud cry is heard offstage, then the janitor throws the tape
player back in the cart and hurries off. Angie, in a gray robe, enters in a wheelchair.*

ANGIE: I slept all afternoon. Or all night? What time is it? Ah, it doesn't matter.
  I feel like a truck hit me. I feel empty. Connie, Connie, how could you? (*pauses*)
      No, it wasn't her. Joe. He promised Dominic if he's elected they can
  build a road through the barrio. Get rid of los viejitos. Destroy our homes,
  our church . . .

They're going to destroy our way of life! I need to call Manny! (*She struggles to stand up, winches from the pain, then slumps back in the chair.*) I feel useless. (*She pushes toward the table that holds her plants, touches them lovingly.*) Ay mi casita . . . mis flores . . .

Gloria appears, walks to Angie.

GLORIA: Comadre—

ANGIE: (*turns angrily*) Don't sneak up behind me! And don't call me "comadre"! I'm not your comadre!

GLORIA: I'm sorry.

ANGIE: Listen, I need to make a phone call. Where in the hell are the phones around here?

GLORIA: Off-limits.

ANGIE: What do you mean, "off-limits"?

GLORIA: You're not allowed to use the phone.

ANGIE: Not allowed? Why?

GLORIA: It's on your chart. You're DB.

ANGIE: DB? What's a DB?

GLORIA: A Disruptive Behavior patient.

ANGIE: Is that what I am? Who said?

GLORIA: You son-in-law told the nurse a lot of things about you.

ANGIE: Joe? The sonofabitch! What about a pay phone?

GLORIA: In the game room, but you're not allowed in there.

ANGIE: How do you know so much?

GLORIA: I read your chart.

ANGIE: I can't call out—that means my friends don't know where I am! This is crazy!

GLORIA: If you behave, the nurse will let you use the phone in a few weeks.

ANGIE: A few weeks is too late! I'm not going to sit around here and become a vegetable! Not Angelina Aragón! No sireee.

GLORIA: What can you do?

ANGIE: I'll find a phone, don't worry. I'll get to one. . . . But not now. I feel so damn tired. The nurse gave me a shot. Bad stuff.

GLORIA: We all get it.

ANGIE: Is that why the inmates look like zombies?

GLORIA: Some are in pain, some can't sleep, some cry all night. They get sedated. If you're DB you get an extra dose.

ANGIE: I see. Takes the spirit out of you, doesn't it? I feel like I've been sleeping all winter.

GLORIA: You slept through dinner.

ANGIE: I don't feel hungry.

GLORIA: The first night is always the hardest.

ANGIE: I miss my casita, a copita de vino, and a cigarette.

GLORIA: We can't have matches.

ANGIE: No phone, no vino, no music, no nada! The Nurse gives you that drug to sleep and even the memories disappear. I'm cold—

GLORIA: As we get older—

ANGIE: Shut up! I don't want to hear about getting old! I'm not old, I'm . . . (long pause)

GLORIA: What?

ANGIE: Una paloma sin alas.

GLORIA: You love to dance.

ANGIE: It's my life.

GLORIA: What else?

ANGIE: I have a garden. Corn, chile, zucchini, flowers—I even have a fig tree. Small, purple figs.

GLORIA: My father had a farm in the valley. But when he died my husband sold his land to a developer.

ANGIE: (shivers) Esos pinche developers are going to be our death—

GLORIA: Shh!

ANGIE: Sorry. I'm not supposed to mention that word.

Gloria sits by Angie.

GLORIA: Tell me about Johnny.

ANGIE: I was dreaming about him.

GLORIA: He was your first love.

ANGIE: Yes.

GLORIA: Your only love.

ANGIE: (*hesitates*) Yes.

GLORIA: You never—

ANGIE: Hey, quit psychoanalyzing me! What about you?

GLORIA: I never loved—

ANGIE: Not even your husband?

Gloria shakes her head.

ANGIE: How did he die?

GLORIA: He was murdered—

ANGIE: Murdered? How?

GLORIA: I don't remember.

ANGIE: He was murdered and you don't remember?

GLORIA: It's better this way.

ANGIE: I see. And after he died you never had the desire to—

GLORIA: Let's not talk about it.

ANGIE: Why not? It's storytelling time, and everybody has a story to tell.

GLORIA: I don't.

ANGIE: You stuck to one man, huh?

GLORIA: I had everything I wanted.

ANGIE: Sure.

GLORIA: Tell me about you?

ANGIE: Me? I spent half my life raising my daughter. I gave her everything I
    didn't have.

GLORIA: She is a beautiful woman. Just like her mother.

ANGIE: Yeah, a chip off the old block. She could have gone high—

GLORIA: And?

ANGIE: She married Joe.

GLORIA: He's the domineering type.

ANGIE: Yeah. After she married I had time for myself.

GLORIA: What did you do?

ANGIE: One day in my garden, I saw the sunflowers swaying in the wind. I began to dance, and I couldn't stop. After that I took my show on the road, from Taos to Las Cruces. I was Angelina la Danzanta. Now I teach girls to dance.

GLORIA: What girls?

ANGIE: You haven't seen my girls dance? Every spring I teach four high school girls Mexican dances—for the fiesta.

The four girls appear, visible only to Angie.

ANGIE: ¡Muchachas! ¡Un baile!

Angie claps her hands and the girls do a fast folkloric dance. Gloria, astounded at first, seems to see the girls in Angie's eyes.

ANGIE: Aren't they great?

The girls exit.

GLORIA: They're beautiful.

ANGIE: (*trying to get up*) I should be there now.

GLORIA: Angie, you can't!

ANGIE: (*struggles*) No, I can't. Dammit! I can't.

GLORIA: It takes time—

ANGIE: I don't have time!

GLORIA: You're afraid, aren't you?

ANGIE: I'm not afraid! I work hard! Goddammit, look at these hands! I built a home, changed diapers, dug in the earth! I'm a tough mujer!

GLORIA: But you're afraid for your daughter.

ANGIE: (*bows her head*) She still depends on me. Joe, he's a brute. Un diablo. Runs her to the ground. Connie isn't strong like me. Every morning she comes over, we have coffee and donuts—we talk. Connie needs me. She needs—

GLORIA: What?

ANGIE: What we all need—to be loved.

GLORIA: I never knew love . . .

ANGIE: It's easy to forget in here. It's so goddamned cold! My bones feel frozen. Look at me. How can I dance with a broken hip? An old woman is a bag of bones. But these bones still want to dance. (*She hums a tune.*) Johnny used to take me dancing. At the El Fidel. 1940s swing. He looked so handsome in his uniform. I was so in love. There was love in the air. Then we'd walk arm in arm, with the trees shimmering in the moonlight.

GLORIA: How beautiful.

ANGIE: But he was going away to die! It wasn't fair! We were so in love and he was going away—

Gloria holds Angie tight.

GLORIA: I understand.

ANGIE: After Johnny was killed—

GLORIA: You found someone else?

Angie glances toward the shadows, where Juan appears in a World War II uniform.

ANGIE: Don't believe her, Johnny! I loved you! Only you!

GLORIA: (*turns to follow Angie's gaze*) He's here, isn't he?

ANGIE: (*quietly*) Yes. He's always with me. Even when I—

GLORIA: You found another man—

ANGIE: (*now angry*) Shut up! ¿Qué sabes tú? You want to know everything! What about you? Are you an angel?

GLORIA: No.

ANGIE: You had no needs. Is that it?

GLORIA: I buried everything.

ANGIE: Oh, you're definitely from the old school. Marry, raise the kids, work hard for la familia, but keep your desires a secret. Be a mamá, a comadre, a grandma, be anything except a woman!

GLORIA: I sacrificed for my children.

ANGIE: Sure, and you love it here.

GLORIA: You get used to it.

ANGIE: How long have you been here?

GLORIA: Five years.

ANGIE: Five years! ¡Dios mío! It's like being in hell.

GLORIA: No. It's better for me here.

ANGIE: Why?

GLORIA: I'm afraid . . .

ANGIE: Of what?

GLORIA: My husband. He returns to haunt me. Your Johnny is so loving; my husband was cruel.

Angie takes Gloria's hand, waits.

ANGIE: And now?

GLORIA: My family is grown. They ran away from him as soon as they could. Now I have to decide, to sell the house or keep it. Oh, why bother you with all this?

ANGIE: It helps to talk.

GLORIA: I want to get rid of the house. Something horrible happened there, but— (*She pulls away.*)

ANGIE: Go on.

GLORIA: (*anxiously*) When my kids were growing up I used to hear voices telling me to drown them. Take them to the river and drown them, the voices said. My doctor gave me sleeping pills, but that didn't help.

ANGIE: Do you still hear the voices?

GLORIA: Yes.

ANGIE: (*taking Gloria's hand again*) So here we are, two old women with suit-cases full of memories. Some good, some nightmares. And who cares?

GLORIA: I care.

ANGIE: Gracias . . .

GLORIA: Come. It's time to rest.

Gloria pushes Angie offstage. Light fades. Juan walks in, dressed in a World War II army private uniform. He goes to a vase of flowers. A light glows on the flowers. Offstage the music is the 40s swing song they will dance to at the end of the play. Juan walks offstage.

Scene Three

In the day room, the following morning.

Pat, a widower Angie's age, pushes Angie's wheelchair into the room.

ANGIE: Is breakfast always that bad?

PAT: A standard senior citizen breakfast.

ANGIE: ¿Avena, toast y prune juice? What do they think we are, old people?

PAT: I guess they want us to be regular.

ANGIE: Yeah, the orange juice is loaded with Metamucil.

Pat stops the chair.

PAT: After a week or two you get real hungry, then you eat.

ANGIE: Haven't these people ever heard of huevos rancheros con refried beans, smothered with green chile, and hot tortillas? Este oatmeal me va a dar empache.

PAT: Yup, it sticks to your ribs. That's why they give you the prune juice. Don't worry, once a month they bring us tacos from Taco Bell.

ANGIE: And that's supposed to be our soul food!

PAT: I keep a bottle of Tabasco sauce in my room to spice up the tacos.

ANGIE: What else do you spice up in your room?

PAT: (*blushes*) Just tacos.

ANGIE: I like you, Patricio. You've got a sense of humor.

PAT: You need humor to survive old age.

ANGIE: Yeah, especially this place. Why are you here?

PAT: After I lost my wife I started on the pisto. I was lonely, so I drank.

ANGIE: How long were you married?

PAT: Forty-five years. That's a lot of memories.

ANGIE: Yes.

PAT: I used to go to the casinos just to be with other people. I lost my car to the one-arm bandits. My kids figured this was the best place for me.

ANGIE: Is it?

PAT: Ah, you get my age, no wife, friends all dead or in nursing homes—the streets aren't safe. . . . I might as well be here.

ANGIE: But if you had a choice, where would you be?

PAT: In my house down in Los Padillas. I had apple trees. I wonder if they're getting watered.

ANGIE: I planted vegetables for me, flowers for Johnny. (She looks at the flowers on the table.)

PAT: Marigolds are flowers for the dead.

ANGIE: (to herself) Johnny loved flowers.

PAT: I used to have varas de San José around my garden. In the summer afternoons me and my vieja would sit in the portal, watch the world go by. Neighbors came by to visit. . . . I knew all the vecinos— (He stops, wipes his eyes.) Pero todo se acaba. Those were good times. Now we just exist.

ANGIE: We don't have to just exist!

PAT: You got no choice, Angie. You get old and things aren't like they used to be. In the old days when our viejitos got old we took them in. Added a room to the house, or put them in a spare bedroom. We took care of them. Now the kids are too busy. It's better here. I don't want to bother them.

ANGIE: You weren't a bother when you were raising them.

PAT: Yes, but things change.

ANGIE: What did you do for a living?

PAT: I was a santero. Purty good one too, but after my wife died I lost interest.

ANGIE: She was your inspiration.

PAT: You better believe it. When you're married that long you get to be like the other person. All of a sudden she wasn't there to argue with me. I felt empty . . .

ANGIE: Maybe if you started carving again?

PAT: Here? No tools. I have my pocketknife. (*He takes the knife from his pocket.*) Belonged to my father.

ANGIE: It's a beauty.

PAT: I can carve anything with this knife.

ANGIE: But you haven't?

PAT: Ah, the loneliness killed my spirit. I feel my life is over.

ANGIE: It's not over 'til the fat lady sings.

PAT: Maybe I was a coward. I turned to drink.

ANGIE: Maybe you needed a compañera?

PAT: I started seeing an old comadre from Atrisco, but my kids said she was just after my Social Security.

ANGIE: Ah, what do our children know? We're supposed to become saints. No sex, no ganas! Ganas don't die till you're six feet under!

Gloria enters.

PAT: Buenos días, Gloria.

ANGIE: Hey, you weren't at breakfast.

GLORIA: I was busy ironing my dress. How do you like it? (*She shows off the skirt to Angie.*)

ANGIE: You look great. Doesn't she look great, Pat?

PAT: Lovely as a summer rain.

ANGIE: He's a poet.

GLORIA: I hadn't worn this in ages. Today I felt like dressing up.

PAT: Dressed up for the field trip?

ANGIE: What field trip?

PAT: This afternoon we're going to the museum. We've been there three times this month.

ANGIE: How do we get there?

PAT: In a van.

GLORIA: You're not on the list, Angie.

ANGIE: The nurse won't let me outta here. I'm still a DB, according to her. If I could get out I wouldn't go to the museum; I'd head for the Hi-Lo Club.

GLORIA: What's the Hi-Lo?

ANGIE: A bar on Isleta. Lots of us oldies but goodies hang out there on Saturday afternoons. Some nice-looking viejos show up to dance. That's how I broke my hip.

PAT: Dancing?

ANGIE: Yes, this viejo from Belén dropped me. He was blind as a bat and trying to dance like John Travolta.

PAT: Sounds like you've been living in the fast lane.

ANGIE: You bet. Anyway, it hurt like hell, but I didn't know it was broken. The gals got me in my car and I headed home. That's when I ran into the police car.

GLORIA: You ran into a police car?

ANGIE: I forgot I had no brakes. So I blamed the broken hip on the police. I'm going to sue them.

PAT: But your car had no brakes.

ANGIE: Yeah, but his car was stopped at a red light.

PAT: You're supposed to stop at red lights.

ANGIE: Re-e-e-ly?

They laugh.

ANGIE: I need a smoke.

She fumbles in her pocket, takes a cigarette and puts it to her mouth. Minnie appears.

MINNIE: Can you get me out?

ANGIE: Wish I could, honey.

Minnie dials as the Nurse appears and grabs Angie's cigarette.

NURSE: I thought we had a talk about this yesterday.

ANGIE: Sorry, I'll go outside and smoke.

NURSE: You can't go outside!

ANGIE: Can I use the phone?

NURSE: No.

ANGIE: I'm going to call my attorney.

NURSE: I have instructions not to let you call anyone. Now why not be nice and follow the rules?

ANGIE: I don't like your silly rules!

NURSE: The rules are to protect the residents. (*She leans forward.*) Your son-in-law told me about your brush with the police.

ANGIE: Brush with the police? I ran into a pinche police car, that's all!

NURSE: There's a pattern of disruptive behavior. Your family wants to keep you away from a certain club. A woman your age? Have you no scruples?

ANGIE: I left them at the bar.

Gloria and Pat chuckle.

MINNIE: You go dancing?

ANGIE: Yes, I go dancing every Saturday. Have a beer or two—

MINNIE: I'd love to dance again.

PAT: I used to be a pretty good dancer.

ANGIE: You?

PAT: At your service, señorita.

ANGIE: Hey, maybe we can start a dance club.

PAT: This place could use some music—

NURSE: (*loudly*) Pat, you know better. Your problems, remember?

PAT: (*looks down at his trousers*) Oh, yeah . . .

NURSE: There isn't going to be a dance club! Look at her, how can she dance? And all of you are taking medications. If you get dizzy and fall, you could break an arm or a leg. Do you think you'll like that?

MINNIE: No, but—

NURSE: No buts, Minnie. You know the rules.

MINNIE: (*bows her head, whispers into the phone*) Can you get me out of here?

The patients return to their card games or just to sit. The Nurse turns to Angie.

NURSE: We have plenty of scheduled activities for our residents. But a dance club, no. It might prove to be too much excitement. (*She smiles smugly and turns to the others.*) Remember, we have a field trip to the museum this afternoon. All of you get plenty of rest. We want you to enjoy yourselves—

PAT: I'm tired of looking at dinosaurs. We're not kids, you know.

NURSE: (*stares at him*) Is this an official complaint?

PAT: (*looks at Angie*) I used to be a good dancer.

ANGIE: You ain't lived till I've waltzed you around.

NURSE: "Used to be" is right, Pat. You know what happens.

PAT: (*hesitantly*) Yes . . .

NURSE: Let us take care of the activities. Now go sit down. You haven't finished your game of solitaire.

PAT: (*shrugs*) I'm never going to finish that game.

NURSE: (*turns to Angie*) Don't promise what you can't deliver. Dance, indeed. In a wheelchair? (*shakes her head and exits*)

ANGIE: (*imitating her*) "You might fall! Can't dance in a wheelchair! Too much excitement!" Pendeja, don't you know that's what we need? A little excitement? (*She turns to Pat and Gloria.*) ¿Qué no?

PAT: Damn right. The museum is boring. So is playing cards all day long.

GLORIA: And bingo is boring! So is TV. If we could only—

MINNIE: Get out!

ANGIE: We can't get out, but we can dance! Pat, does that radio work?

PAT: Yes.

ANGIE: Turn it to KBAD!

Pat flips on the radio to a station playing "Echale un cinco al piano, y empieza el bacilon."

GLORIA: I remember that song!

ANGIE: Hey, it's party time! Time to dance! Anda, Pat, grab Minnie!

Pat grabs Minnie and a wild dance begins.

ANGIE: Come on, Gloria. Grab my chair.

Gloria pushes Angie's chair to the beat of the music. Other residents may join in the dance or just clap and stamp their feet. All whoop and shout in a burst of freedom.

PAT: Hey! Just like old times!

ANGIE: ¡Ajúa!

MINNIE: 911! This is great!

GLORIA: I'm dancing! I'm dancing!

The Nurse and an aide appear.

NURSE: What's going on here?!

All stop and turn to the Nurse. The aide turns off the radio.

NURSE: (*to Angie*) Are you out of your mind?

ANGIE: No! Just having fun.

NURSE: You call this fun? (*to the aide*) Get these people back to their rooms! (*She takes hold of Minnie.*) Minnie! You know better!

MINNIE: I feel dizzy . . .

NURSE: Yes, and it's a wonder you didn't fall.

MINNIE: No, it's a *good* dizzy!

NURSE: Nonsense! (*turns to Angie*) I warned you . . .

ANGIE: What's the big deal?

NURSE: You. You're the problem.

ANGIE: I don't think so. The problem is this place. It's dead.

NURSE: And you like wild, noisy places, is that it?

PAT: We were just having a little fun.

NURSE: I don't know what's gotten into all of you. Look at Minnie, so dizzy she could have fallen! And look at you, Pat! You wet your pants!

PAT: (looks down) Oh, shit. (He hurries out.)

GLORIA: He always wets his pants when he gets excited. But nobody got hurt.

The others nod.

NURSE: Gloria, you know what you're doing isn't good for your blood pressure.

ANGIE: What's wrong with a little excitement? She doesn't wear a pacemaker.

NURSE: Tell her, Gloria.

Gloria looks confused, searches Angie's face, then bows her head.

GLORIA: I can't.

NURSE: No, you can't. When you get excited the voices return—

GLORIA: Don't tell!

NURSE: I won't. Now go to your room and lie down. I'll be there shortly.

Gloria looks at Angie as if for help, then obeys and exits. The Nurse turns to the others.

NURSE: All of you go to your rooms. You will return for lunch, but I'm cancelling the trip to the museum. You need a quiet afternoon of rest.

All nod and slowly leave the room. The Nurse looks down at Angie.

NURSE: You haven't learned to obey the rules, have you?

ANGIE: I pay my taxes.

NURSE: Funny, funny.

ANGIE: What the hell was I supposed to do with my life? Roll over and die? I'm a survivor! I've done it my way, and I'm not making any excuses.

NURSE: And your way involved dancing in bars and clubs—

ANGIE: Hey, I danced for the kids, too. Don't you forget that. Every year I train my girls to fly.

NURSE: Fly?

ANGIE: Dancing is flying.

NURSE: I wouldn't know—

ANGIE: No, you wouldn't. But I do. It's freedom.

NURSE: Your days of freedom are over. Don't you understand?

ANGIE: I'll understand it when they bury me.

NURSE: No, now! (takes Angie's wheelchair handles)

ANGIE: Hey, what are you going to do? Give me another one of those sleepy time shots?

NURSE: You need to rest.

ANGIE: No, I don't need to rest. (She looks at Minnie, who hangs back.) I need to get outta here!

MINNIE: I'll call 911! (She dials the phone furiously.)

NURSE: (pushing the chair out) You need to be controlled.

ANGIE: (shouting to Minnie) Get me outta here!

MINNIE: Help! Murder! Police! Angie fell in the grease! And all the king's horses and all the king's men can't put her together again!

Offstage we hear the Nurse and Angie.

NURSE: Time to rest.

ANGIE: (shouting) All right! Give me a shot! Show me what you've got!

Minnie crumples to a sofa, mumbling parts of nursery rhymes into the phone.

MINNIE: The nurse has murdered the queen! Now she sleeps, a gentle winter sleep. We sleep like the roses in the garden. But roses don't dream. . . .

Light fades as Minnie falls asleep.

Scene Four

The day room, later that day.

Minnie rises from the sofa, goes to her cart, picks up the phone and dials.

MINNE: 911? Why is it so cold in here? I thought the devil liked warm places. Oh, I see. Winter is coming, winter is coming, sing goddamn, sing goddamn . . .

She turns as Angie, in a gray robe, pushes her wheelchair in.

ANGIE: Oh boy, she really knocked me out this time.

MINNIE: I warned you. *(pushes her cart out)*

ANGIE: I feel like I slept a week. Slept as sound as la muerte. Yes, I dreamed I died. Am I alive? Or dreaming? Where is Angie? *(She pauses.)*
Angelina. Angelina de Aragón. The name of a queen, Johnny said. I was his queen, his Rosa de Castilla.
Now look at me. I smell like caca. Peed in my bed. I haven't taken a shower, didn't wash my hair. No lipstick. I'm forgetting who I am. Forgetting to dance . . .
No! Don't forget to dance! Don't ever forget to dance!

Connie enters carrying a small bouquet of wilted flowers. She rushes to Angie and embraces her.

CONNIE: Mom, Mom . . .

ANGIE: *(smoothing Connie's hair gently)* Hija.

CONNIE: I crushed the flowers . . .

ANGIE: For me? Que bonitas. Gracias. *(She smells the flowers.)* Are these from my garden?

CONNIE: No, it froze last night. I bought these at the flower shop.

ANGIE: How are you?

CONNIE: Fine, I'm fine. And you?

ANGIE: You look tired. You're working too hard.

CONNIE: I'm okay. Were you sleeping?

ANGIE: Yeah, I sleep a lot. Look at me, I'm a mess.

CONNIE: You need lipstick. I went by the house and got your lipstick.

She pulls up a chair, takes lipstick and brush from her purse. Applies lipstick to Angie.

ANGIE: You're a good daughter.

CONNIE: Hold still.

ANGIE: How's my casita?

CONNIE: Everything's fine. Hold your head back.

ANGIE: Ah, feels good. A woman without lipstick is like beans without hot chile. Tasty but not sabrosa.

CONNIE: You used to tell me that.

ANGIE: A woman has to take pride in herself.

CONNIE: You taught me that.

ANGIE: Yes. You dress like a million, you feel like a million.

CONNIE: But inside—

ANGIE: Inside you have to be confident.

CONNIE: Confident. Maybe I've lost . . . (picks up the brush to change the subject) Look at you. Don't the nurses help you with your hair? (She brushes Angie's hair.)

ANGIE: They're too busy. Where's Joe?

CONNIE: He stopped by the front office.

ANGIE: And the race?

CONNIE: Not good. A rumor got out that Joe made a deal to sell out the barrio. It's turning the valley vote against him.

ANGIE: It's not a rumor.

CONNIE: You're sure?

ANGIE: I'm sure. You just don't know Joe very well.

CONNIE: Maybe not. I've learned in politics everybody wants something from you. Dominic wants to build casinos along the river.

ANGIE: Yes, and plow the barrio under. We're in his way.

CONNIE: I'm afraid Joe—

ANGIE: Sold out? Just don't you do it, girl.

CONNIE: (pauses) Maybe I already have.

ANGIE: How?

CONNIE: By bringing you here.

ANGIE: Feeling guilty?

CONNIE: Yes.

ANGIE: Don't—I can jump the fence anytime I want.

CONNIE: Sure, in the wheelchair?

ANGIE: I'll wait a few weeks, then go.

CONNIE: That's not what the doctor said.

ANGIE: Ah, what does the doctor know?

CONNIE: I called his office. You haven't kept an appointment in months.

ANGIE: I told him, there's nothing wrong with my heart. As long as I keep dancing.

CONNIE: You can't dance forever—

ANGIE: Says who! I feel like twenty! But my body! These bones! They're just giving up on me! I feel so weak. I feel so damned old!

CONNIE: You just have to get used to—

ANGIE: Being old? Never. Not me! I'm Angelina la Danzanta. I'll dance into the sunset. It's this place! (*She looks around.*) It's so dull and drab . . .

CONNIE: You have everything you need here.

ANGIE: I miss my casita.

CONNIE: Oh, Mom.

ANGIE: I can dream, can't I?

CONNIE: What do you dream about?

ANGIE: Your father. I dream about dancing with Johnny.

CONNIE: You're a romantic.

ANGIE: Yeah.

CONNIE: (*passes the comb through Angie's hair*) There, that looks better.

ANGIE: I feel better. Thanks, mi'ja.

Joe appears in the background.

CONNIE: Joe wants to say hi. I love you, Mom.

ANGIE: I love you, mi'ja.

Connie kisses her, turns, and exits quickly.

ANGIE: Hello, Joe. How's tricks?

JOE: You got to a phone, huh? Talked to Manny.

ANGIE: We're not letting you sell our neighborhood.

JOE: If I lose the valley vote, I lose the election. You know that!

ANGIE: We want to keep our homes—

JOE: Those homes in the barrio aren't worth a nickel!

ANGIE: But they're ours.

JOE: You're going to be sorry.

ANGIE: You can't make me sorry— (*realizes he means his threat*) Don't you dare touch Connie!

JOE: Not her, Angie. You!

He turns and exits. Angie turns her chair to face the audience.

ANGIE: He doesn't scare me. As long as he doesn't mistreat Connie. Mi'jita . . . It hasn't been easy for her to see her mother grow old. And now she finds out her husband is a crook—Ay, Dios mío.

She hangs her head. Juan appears.

JUAN: Angelina . . .

ANGIE: (*looks up*) Johnny?

JUAN: Why so sad?

ANGIE: Johnny, is it you?

JUAN: Who where you expecting, Fred Astaire?

ANGIE: It's been so long.

JUAN: Too long.

ANGIE: Why did you leave me, Johnny?

JUAN: I had to go, Angie. To serve my country.

ANGIE: I missed you. I remember our last night together. We danced all night.

JUAN: At the Hilton.

ANGIE: You remember?

JUAN: Every moment.

ANGIE: I loved you so much.

JUAN: And I loved you.

ANGIE: I think of you every day.

JUAN: I watch over you, Angelina, mí amor.

ANGIE: I dream of dancing with you.

JUAN: You can. (*He holds out his arms.*)

ANGIE: I can't.

JUAN: Can you hear the music?

A waltz tune plays in the background.

ANGIE: Yes. Yes! I hear it! (*She struggles to rise out of her chair.*) It's our song, Johnny! They're playing our song!

JUAN: You can do it!

ANGIE: Help me, Johnny. (*She pushes herself up, crying his name as she crumples to the floor.*) Johnny! Johnny!

END ACT ONE

ACT TWO

Scene One

Afternoon, in the day room, weeks later.

Gloria, Pat, and Minnie gather to talk about Angie. Pat is carving on a piece of wood.

MINNIE: I think she's flipped.

GLORIA: No, she hasn't.

PAT: She dances at night. I swear she hears music.

GLORIA: Nothing wrong with hearing music.

MINNIE: I bet she has Alzheimer's.

PAT: Old timers. We all have old timers.

MINNIE: Not "old timers"—Alzheimer's!

GLORIA: Don't be silly. Angie doesn't have Alzheimer's.

MINNIE: She's got something.

A patient walks by. Minnie starts toward her, but stops.

MINNIE: Angie's helped me a lot. See, I didn't ask Dolly to get me out.

GLORIA: Good for you, Minnie.

PAT: She talks to herself.

GLORIA: We all hear voices. Voices from the past.

MINNIE: I even answer mine.

GLORIA: Memories. We go deeper and deeper into memories. The body stops, but the mind keeps working.

PAT: Angie can't stop.

GLORIA: She still has a foot in the real world.

MINNIE: You mean out there.

GLORIA: Yes. Out there.

PAT: She still talks about dancing at the Hi-Lo.

GLORIA: She's DB. Only her daughter can visit.

PAT: I know what Angie needs.

GLORIA: What?

PAT: She needs a good stiff . . . drink. When I quit drinking I had this desire to have a drink twenty-four hours a day.

GLORIA: How did you stop?

PAT: I killed the desire.

MINNIE: Angie has to kill her desire?

GLORIA: That's just it, she can't. She still desires the real world.

MINNIE: What are we, virtual reality?

PAT: Yeah. A bunch of zombies. Look at us. (*He looks around.*)

MINNIE: Maybe we're already dead—

GLORIA: I used to feel like that, but not since Angie came.

PAT: She's been good for all of us. I don't know where she gets the wood, but she's got me carving again.

Angie appears, using a cane and walking with a limp.

GLORIA: Shhh.

ANGIE: (*walks up and looks at them*) You were talking about me.

MINNIE: How could you tell?

GLORIA: No, we weren't.

ANGIE: So how come everybody's so quiet?

PAT: We were talking about dying.

ANGIE: How cheerful. (*She frowns and starts to walk away.*)

GLORIA: Wait.

ANGIE: What?

PAT: What do you want to talk about?

ANGIE: (*pauses*) Sex. Let's talk about sex.

MINNIE: Yeah!

GLORIA: Angie, be serious.

ANGIE: I know, I know. We're not supposed to talk about anything that's fun. How about you, Pat, you interested?

PAT: Ah, I gave it up a long time ago.

ANGIE: Why?

PAT: (*embarrassed*) Well you know. I just—

ANGIE: Can't.

GLORIA: Really, Angie. I think this is embarrassing to Pat. Why don't we—

ANGIE: Talk about dying.

GLORIA: Anything.

ANGIE: I want to talk about living. What's the matter, Gloria, didn't you have good sex with your husband?

GLORIA: That's enough, Angie! (*She walks off in a huff, but sits nearby to listen.*)

ANGIE: I touched a nerve.

PAT: It's no good to bring it up.

ANGIE: Why?

PAT: Look, we can dream, but to really do it, no way.

ANGIE: That's because you think you have to do it like you used to. You know what I miss most?

GLORIA: (*perks her ears*) What?

ANGIE: Just being held. That's why I dream of dancing, because in my dreams Johnny is holding me. I can feel his body, his warmth . . .

MINNIE: Ah, that's bee-oo-ti-fool.

PAT: But it's only a dream.

ANGIE: I'm here now—make a pass at me!

PAT: Sure, I'll make a pass. And when my false teeth fall out?

ANGIE: No problem. We'll Fixodent them.

PAT: You mean—

ANGIE: I mean, sometimes just a little cariño is enough.

MINNIE: But who would want to hold me?

ANGIE: (*to Minnie*) Who do you like?

MINNIE: (*blushes*) Pat.

PAT: Me?

GLORIA: I didn't know you liked him.

MINNIE: I do. Do you like him too?

Gloria huffs again and turns away.

ANGIE: So make a movida.

MINNIE: What's a movida?

ANGIE: Make a move on him.

MINNIE: (*confused*) Can you get me outta here?

ANGIE: (*grabs Minnie*) Stop it! The world frightens you, and you revert to your tricks! Snap out of it, Minnie!

MINNIE: Yes, yes, just like you taught me. There is no 911.

ANGIE: That's it . . . you're in control.

GLORIA: Do you like her, Pat?

PAT: Yes, but—

ANGIE: Lucky Pat, he's got two viejas interested in him.

MINNIE: But Pat's got a problem.

ANGIE: What?

PAT: (*shamefully*) I had this prostate operation . . . Now I have to go to the bathroom all the time.

ANGIE: You pee in your pants. So what! Happens to a lot of us. We'll just get you some Pampers.

GLORIA: They're not Pampers.

ANGIE: Whatever. Adult diapers. Keep you dry all day.

GLORIA: He won't use those.

ANGIE: Why?

GLORIA: He's too macho.

ANGIE: Dammit, Pat, you wet your pants and you're too macho to use Pampers.

PAT: I just don't want my friends to know.

ANGIE: We'll keep it a secret, won't we girls? Sure, we fix Pat and we have a dance!

MINNIE: What are we celebrating?

ANGIE: Día de los Muertos.

PAT: I'll try it!

MINNIE: Hooray!

ANGIE: We can build an altar.

PAT: My wife used to light candles for the dead.

MINNIE: Wait! Wait! The Nurse won't let us.

PAT: You're right. They don't celebrate the Day of the Dead.

ANGIE: We'll say we're celebrating Halloween. Light some jack-o-lanterns for them, make an altar for us. We can decorate the day room. Lots of crepe paper. What do you say, Gloria?

GLORIA: (looks around) It would be nice.

ANGIE: We can invite our families!

PAT: Ah, they never come.

ANGIE: They never come because we're no fun! When they visit all we do is complain about our illness. Who wants to hear sick old people complain? Let's show them we're still alive!

GLORIA: I love to decorate. The night my husband was murdered I had decorated the house. It was Valentine's Day . . . Red hearts . . .

They all wait.

ANGIE: He liked to have you waiting for him. Wine on ice . . . you in a negligee.

MINNIE: How lovely—

GLORIA: No! It wasn't beautiful!

ANGIE: It got out of hand.

GLORIA: (*changing the subject*) Look, if we're going to plan a dance, let's plan. We need to ask the Nurse.

ANGIE: There she is. I'll kiss her feet.

The Nurse appears, gathering wilted bouquets of flowers, which she tosses in the trash can.

PAT: I'll help.

MINNIE: Me too!

ANGIE: (*shouts*) Hey, Nurse Ruth! Oh, Rooo-thie!

MINNIE: (*nervously*) For crying out loud, Angie!

The Nurse approaches. Minnie grabs her hand.

MINNIE: Can you get me outta here?

ANGIE: Minnie, cut it out!

NURSE: Don't shout, Angie—it upsets the residents.

ANGIE: Look, we've been thinking—

NURSE: Well.

ANGIE: About having a Halloween party. We can decorate the place, invite our families.

NURSE: (*nods*) Halloween . . .

MINNIE: We can dance!

NURSE: (*to Angie*) Ah, so that's it. I've told you before, a dance is out of the question. Too many of our patients can't dance.

ANGIE: They can do the Viejito Shuffle! Put your little foot, put your little foot—

NURSE: Some are in wheelchairs!

ANGIE: We can dance in wheelchairs!

NURSE: No, it just won't work.

ANGIE: What are you afraid of, that we might actually enjoy ourselves?

NURSE: You want to turn Joy of Life into a fun house, don't you? Well, I won't allow it. I have my responsibilities to the patients and their families. I can't allow the wild kind of parties you're used to.

ANGIE: So, it's me, isn't it?

NURSE: Your son-in-law told me about your drinking.

ANGIE: Good old Joe.

NURSE: And your dancing—

ANGIE: I love to dance.

NURSE: A woman your age should have some dignity—

ANGIE: Dignity! Who in the hell are you to preach about dignity!

NURSE: I'll tell you who I am! My husband left me with three children to support. He couldn't stand the responsibility. But I could. I worked hard to
become a nurse. Where would my children be if I was out drinking and
dancing?

ANGIE: (*to the others*) What she forgot to tell us is that her husband left her for
another woman!

The Nurse slaps Angie.

NURSE: How dare you!

ANGIE: (*rubbing her cheek*) The truth hurts.

NURSE: He was a worthless sonofabitch!

ANGIE: So to survive him you wrapped yourself in rules and regulations.

The Nurse looks around, shocked at her own behavior.

NURSE: I shouldn't have slapped you. I've never slapped a patient.

ANGIE: No, you just put us to sleep.

NURSE: (*drawing herself straight*) You're terrible, Angie. Nothing but trouble.
There will be no dance. I'm in charge here. I don't care how long it takes
for you to learn that, you'll learn.

*The Nurse struts out. Gloria, Pat, and Minnie move toward Angie. Gloria puts her arm
around Angie.*

GLORIA: Are you okay?

ANGIE: I'm fine.

PAT: You could sue her for that.

ANGIE: Ah, she's not worth it. Besides, no loose teeth.

PAT: I guess that means no dance.

ANGIE: We can still do it.

MINNIE: Not without her permission. Not me. (*walks away, talking into her phone*) 911? Can you get me outta here?

ANGIE: Minnie!

GLORIA: Don't talk. Come sit down. I'll get an ice pack for your cheek.

Gloria tenderly leads Angie to a sofa. Gloria and the others exit. Angie sits alone. The four dancing girls appear and dance for Angie.

Scene Two

Gloria returns, sits by Angie, and holds an ice pack to her cheek.

GLORIA: Why do you keep pushing people?

ANGIE: People show their true colors when they're up against a wall.

GLORIA: You should have been a psychoanalyst.

ANGIE: Everybody has a story to tell. If you don't tell it, it festers inside. Like the Nurse—she won't let go.

GLORIA: And you?

ANGIE: I have no regrets.

GLORIA: You sure?

ANGIE: Hey, you're pretty good at probing. (*Angie takes the ice pack from Gloria.*)

GLORIA: I have a good teacher.

ANGIE: Not so good. You haven't told me your story.

GLORIA: Do you really want to hear it?

ANGIE: It's up to you.

GLORIA: What if it's ugly?

ANGIE: We all have our ghosts.

GLORIA: Not like mine.

ANGIE: (*grabs Gloria's wrist*) We all have demons in our hearts. The only way to drive them out is to confront them!

GLORIA: I can't.

ANGIE: What's so terrible you can't reveal?

GLORIA: If you knew I would lose you.

ANGIE: Friends don't run at a sign of trouble.

GLORIA: You're probably the only person I've ever trusted. The first one I can talk to. I don't want to lose you. (*Gloria gently strokes Angie's cheek.*)

ANGIE: You won't. I've got nowhere to go.

GLORIA: (*turns away*) There you go, making fun of everything.

ANGIE: I'm sorry. But you can't put this condition on me, about losing me. That's not fair. You can't be afraid to talk because of that. You either tell your story or you don't.

GLORIA: I want to tell you. I want to be free—

ANGIE: Of your demon?

GLORIA: Yes. (*Gloria nervously stares ahead.*) I didn't want children.

ANGIE: Your husband forced you.

GLORIA: You knew?

ANGIE: I guessed.

GLORIA: He forced himself on me . . . all those years. It wasn't love, it wasn't natural.

Angie nods, waits.

GLORIA: At first I was afraid. . . . I let him do what he wanted. His friends thought he was a wonderful man. He sold real estate, made money, but no one really knew him. When he came home he was an animal. For years he abused me . . . and the kids. They left as soon as they could.

ANGIE: And you?

GLORIA: I couldn't.

ANGIE: You were trapped.

GLORIA: Don't you see, no one would believe me! On the outside we had everything we needed: a big home, money, his reputation. But inside there was a beast.

ANGIE: A beast you had to destroy.

GLORIA: (*surprised for a moment*) Yes . . . I killed him. I thought about it for years. When the time came it was simple. I told the police someone had broken into the house, an axe had been taken from the shed—

Angie holds Gloria.

ANGIE: Ay, Dios mío.

GLORIA: I had to get away. That's why I came here.

ANGIE: Now you're free.

GLORIA: Yes. . . . Thank you. I can let go. I haven't talked to anyone . . .

ANGIE: Rest, mi'jita, rest . . .

Angie strokes Gloria's hair and hums a lullaby. The light fades as Juan appears, dressed in uniform.

ANGIE: Johnny?

JUAN: Angelina.

ANGIE: Oh, Johnny, I'm so glad to see you. (*Angie goes to him.*)

JUAN: I'm glad to see you, amor.

ANGIE: I was talking to Gloria.

JUAN: I heard.

ANGIE: Maybe now she can make peace with herself.

JUAN: You're good for her.

ANGIE: Old women understand each other. We know the suffering—and the mistakes we made.

JUAN: You, too, have a story to tell.

ANGIE: (*nods*) Yes.

JUAN: Some secrets get in the way of love.

ANGIE: I have no secrets from you, Johnny. I loved only you.

JUAN: You were mine, and I belonged to you.

ANGIE: But there's something I have to tell Connie.

JUAN: (*softly*) Yes, it's time.

ANGIE: Ay, que mi Juanito. That's why I loved you. You were always so gallant. So respectful. So cariñoso.

JUAN: We had so little time together. The war came, and we went. "To protect our country," the vatos from Old Town said. Dozens of us in the National Guard went to die in Bataan.

ANGIE: You were so young, Johnny.

JUAN: El destino. Destiny took me from you.

ANGIE: Destiny can be kind, and it can be cruel.

JUAN: I carried your picture with me. It kept me going during that death march. No food, no water. We slept by the side of the road. I shared your picture with my buddy.

ANGIE: The captain.

JUAN: He was a good man. With my dying breath I made him promise he would come and see you.

ANGIE: He kept his promise.

JUAN: I fell asleep dreaming of you . . .

ANGIE: You didn't die, Johnny. You live here, en mi corazón. I feel you near me. Someday I'm going to be with you, forever.

JUAN: I'm waiting for you, amor.

ANGIE: Esta vida es una pesadilla. ¿Y la muerte?

JUAN: La muerte es un sueño.

ANGIE: Is it painful?

JUAN: At first I was scared, but when death took my hand I became a bright light rising into the sky. My soul floated away from my body.

ANGIE: Your soul lives in mine.

JUAN: Yes.

ANGIE: And when I'm dead and there is no one left to remember you . . . what then, Johnny?

JUAN: The memory continues. It expands and fills the trees, the mountain, the sky, moon and sun, the universe.

ANGIE: The memory lives on? I don't understand, Johnny. Don't leave me.

JUAN: I'm always near you.

ANGIE: But sometimes it gets so dark. Memories fade . . .

JUAN: Think of the good times, amor. Our love was like a summer day, a walk in the moonlight.

ANGIE: (*desperately*) Johnny, take me with you!

JUAN: I can't, amor. Not yet.

ANGIE: (*frightened*) I beg you. Take me with you.

JUAN: You still have a few things to do.

ANGIE: (*pauses*) I have to tell Connie the truth.

JUAN: Yes.

ANGIE: I'm afraid to die.

JUAN: The body fears death. (*Juan turns away.*)

ANGIE: (*nods*) We cling to our bodies. We're old and feeble, our bodies fall apart—and still we cling to life.

JUAN: There's nothing to fear, Angelina.

ANGIE: Are you waiting for me, Johnny?

JUAN: (*from the shadows*) Yes, I'm waiting for you . . .

ANGIE: I can't see you, Johnny! I can't see you!

Angie turns and hobbles out. Light fades.

Scene Three

The day room, the next day.

Connie enters with a bag of Angie's stuff. She prepares the Día de los Muertos altar by setting a bright cloth on a table, then candles and a statue of la Virgen. She places Juan's picture next to the Virgin. Angie enters in a wheelchair. There is bandage on her forehead. Connie turns to greet her.

CONNIE: Mom. (*Connie goes to Angie and kisses her.*) Are you all right? Your forehead?

ANGIE: It's nothing. Just a bump.

CONNIE: Thank God. The Nurse called me last night and told me what had happened.

ANGIE: I want out of here, Connie. I have to get out!

CONNIE: I couldn't come last night, Mom. We were at a dinner—

ANGIE: I need to get out!

CONNIE: I know it was a shock. I talked to the nurse—

ANGIE: Esa bruja. She's going to kill me one of these days.

CONNIE: Mom, you know that's not true. They care for you. She called me. She explained how you fell, and how they had to give you a shot. You were wild—

ANGIE: I wasn't wild!

CONNIE: You were screaming, talking to someone. Father—it was Father, wasn't it?

ANGIE: (looks at Connie, searchingly) Juanito . . .

CONNIE: I know you talk to him. I know how much you loved him.

ANGIE: He would have been proud of you.

CONNIE: I'm proud to be his daughter.

ANGIE: I'm afraid, hija. For the first time in my life I'm afraid.

CONNIE: Tell me what happened.

ANGIE: I can't—

CONNIE: What are you afraid of?

ANGIE: Dying. I'm afraid of dying.

CONNIE: Mom, you're not going to die. You fell, so you had a little setback. The nurse said they x-rayed your hip. It's okay. It's going to be sore for a while.

ANGIE: You're afraid to talk about dying, aren't you?

CONNIE: Yes.

ANGIE: Why?

CONNIE: I don't think about it.

ANGIE: Ah, when you're young you don't think of dying. You think you can live forever. Last night Juan came to see me. He told me the soul is a ball of light that goes up into the sky. (*She grabs Connie's arms.*) They can see us, Connie! They can speak to us!

CONNIE: (*nervously*) Mom, it was a dream. You were dreaming—

ANGIE: No, it's real. He's waiting for me—

CONNIE: Mom, I don't want to talk about depressing thoughts. You're not dying! The nurse said you don't even need the wheelchair. You're doing this to yourself!

ANGIE: I had to run!

CONNIE: You only hurt yourself. Your recovery was going great. You were walking, then you try something silly. Where were you going?

ANGIE: Home, to my casita.

Connie turns away.

ANGIE: What is it, Connie?

CONNIE: You can't go there.

ANGIE: Why?

CONNIE: We rented the house.

ANGIE: (*shocked*) Rented my casita! No, you couldn't—

CONNIE: It was empty, Mom.

ANGIE: Strangers living in my casita . . . Joe, it was Joe, wasn't it?

CONNIE: (*nods*) Yes . . . but I agreed. We need the money. This place isn't cheap, you know.

ANGIE: Now there's nowhere to run.

CONNIE: This is your home, accept it. Look, I brought the things you need for the party. And Dad's picture. (*She hands the picture to Angie.*)

ANGIE: He took this picture before he left . . .

CONNIE: And I brought your dancing dress and shoes. (*She takes out a bright Mexican skirt, brightly colored crepe paper, and old records.*) And your old records. Your favorite, Lola Beltrán.

ANGIE: She died—

CONNIE: Mom! Will you get off that dying crap!

ANGIE: Dying isn't crap.

CONNIE: You know what I mean! You've always been so positive. What's happened to you?

ANGIE: I'm tired . . . the drugs tire me. Sometimes I can hardly get up in the morning.

CONNIE: They had to give you a sedative last night. The Nurse said you went crazy.

ANGIE: I ran into the glass door . . .

CONNIE: I'll talk to your doctor.

ANGIE: You have such faith in doctors.

CONNIE: Don't you?

ANGIE: He doesn't believe Johnny visits me.

CONNIE: (pauses) You saw him?

ANGIE: Yes.

CONNIE: What did he say? (She takes Juan's picture and places back on the altar.)

ANGIE: He said to tell you the truth.

CONNIE: What truth?

ANGIE: Why should I tell you? You don't believe the dead can speak.

CONNIE: I can see you're getting better. I've got to go.

ANGIE: What do the polls say?

CONNIE: Joe's losing . . .

ANGIE: You should have run for mayor, hija. With your brains and looks, you'd win. All the vecinos would vote for you.

CONNIE: It isn't that easy, Mom.

ANGIE: It ain't easy as long as you take a backseat to Joe.

CONNIE: It's not a backseat. I support him.

ANGIE: Sure.

CONNIE: You really know how to touch raw nerves.

ANGIE: I know you.

CONNIE: Maybe I have let him direct my life—

ANGIE: It's not too late to change direction.

CONNIE: At fifty-two?

ANGIE: Hey, when I was fifty I took off for Mexico to learn folk dances. I never knew where my next meal was coming from, but I had a blast. The Mexicanos take good care of their artists. They appreciate art.

CONNIE: You were always the adventurous one. Maybe I need to be more like you.

ANGIE: You've been resisting.

CONNIE: You're awesome. Sometimes that's threatening.

ANGIE: Bullshit! I taught you independence.

CONNIE: Yes, you did. But somewhere I lost it . . .

ANGIE: Men like Joe don't like independent women.

CONNIE: (nods) I've got to go. Take care of yourself, Mom.

ANGIE: You too, hija.

CONNIE: (kisses Angie) Your hair needs combing.

ANGIE: (chuckles) I'm a mess.

CONNIE: I wish I had time—

ANGIE: Go on, you've got things to do.

CONNIE: Bye, Mom. I love you.

ANGIE: I love you too, mi'ja. (pauses)
Wait! Before you go there's something—

CONNIE: What?

ANGIE: Nada. I'll tell you later. Cuidate.

Connie goes out.

ANGIE: Adiós. Go with God. When we're in trouble we really call on the Old Man. Tata Dios, ayúdame. ¡Aquí estoy sola y toda chingada! ¡Ayúdame! But does He hear us? Johnny hasn't mentioned God. "Up there the spirits watch over us." That's all he said.

Gloria comes up behind her and covers Angie's eyes.

GLORIA: A penny for your thoughts.

ANGIE: You don't want to know.

GLORIA: Oh, but I do. I've been waiting to catch you alone. (*She comes around and hugs Angie.*) How do you feel?

ANGIE: Sore.

GLORIA: (*looks at the altar*) Oh, this is beautiful. Did you do it?

ANGIE: Connie.

GLORIA: What a sweet daughter. (*She picks up Juan's picture.*) This is Johnny.

ANGIE: Yes.

GLORIA: Oh, he's so handsome. Just as I imagined him. (*She places the picture back.*) What happened last night?

ANGIE: Visitations from the dead.

GLORIA: Pat said you were screaming, then everybody started screaming, and next thing he knew you were smashing down the front door.

ANGIE: 911 didn't answer. How's Minnie?

GLORIA: A little banged up. Like you. They had to put her in a straitjacket.

ANGIE: Damn!

GLORIA: You can't get used to this place, can you?

ANGIE: I never liked institutions.

GLORIA: If only you could learn to be happy here. I'd do anything.

ANGIE: It's not you, it's the place.

GLORIA: The altar and the dance will brighten it up.

ANGIE: I don't have it in me . . .

GLORIA: You have to! Everybody's in their rooms dressing up. And Nurse Ruth is gone.

ANGIE: You mean she actually took a day off?

GLORIA: We're on our own. The aides won't interfere.

ANGIE: (*encouraged*) Yeah, when la gata is gone the ratoncitos play. We can dance all afternoon.

GLORIA: Yes. Everyone's excited. Pat even wants to take Minnie to the dance. He's hanging around her room waiting for her to wake up.

ANGIE: What a lover. Waiting for his amor to get out of the straightjacket. But I thought you and Pat—

GLORIA: I used to like him. He's the only decent man around. But that was before you came. (*She touches Angie's cheek.*)

ANGIE: So, we'll dance together, comadre.

GLORIA: I thought you didn't want to be my comadre.

ANGIE: Hey, we comadres have to stick together. Come on, help me up.

Gloria helps Angie out of the chair.

ANGIE: Ay, pinche hip. Hurts like hell.

GLORIA: Maybe you won't be able to—

ANGIE: Dance? I'll dance at my funeral. I'll get high on Ensure. Hand me those records.

Gloria hands her the records.

ANGIE: Lola Beltrán. God, if every woman could live like her, we'd have no regrets. . . . Anda, let's get this party on the road!

They exit and a Lola Beltrán song plays in the background.

Scene Four

The residents enter and hang bright crepe paper streamers, etc. Everyone is smiling and having fun. Even the aide helps. Connie and Joe enter. Connie carries a fruit punch bowl.

JOE: (*complaining*) I don't have time for this—

CONNIE: I have time for your parties.

JOE: My parties have a purpose—to get me elected. This is crazy.

CONNIE: It's crazy to let the old people have a little fun in their lives?

JOE: You know what I mean.

CONNIE: Maybe I don't. Maybe I really haven't known *what you mean* all these years.

JOE: What are you driving at?

CONNIE: The deal you made with Dominic.

JOE: So that's it!

CONNIE: Joe, it's going to destroy the barrio.

JOE: So we tear down a few houses—

CONNIE: And where do the old people go? We bring them here?

JOE: Why not? They're happy here. Now let's move. I'm meeting with Frank this afternoon.

CONNIE: I'm not going.

JOE: Not going? You're really pissed, aren't you?

CONNIE: You don't need me, Joe. You want me at your side because of the votes the name Aragón represents?

JOE: What's gotten into you?

CONNIE: I want to stay for the party. I've been rushing in and out of here, and I really don't know the place. I don't know what Mom's going through.

JOE: Have it your way.

Joe sulks away to a chair by the window. Angie enters dressed in a yellow Mexican skirt and white blouse, with a bright rose in her hair.

ANGIE: Connie, you came!

CONNIE: (*kisses Angie*) I wouldn't miss it for the world. I brought the punch bowl.

ANGIE: Thank you, mi'ja. Thank you for everything.

CONNIE: Just enjoy yourself. (*kisses Angie and goes to sit by Joe*)

ANGIE: Nothing like a fiesta to lift the spirits. ¡Baile! ¡Baile!

Angie's girls, dressed in Mexican costumes, appear.

ANGIE: ¡Mis palomitas!

The girls dance a jarabe tapatillo; stomping and swirling their skirts, they personify gaiety, freedom, flight. Angie claps during the dance. When it is done the girls bow and exit.

ANGIE: Que bonito. To be young is to dance.

Gloria enters, also dressed in bright fiesta skirt, white blouse, and turquoise jewelry. Her beauty shines through.

ANGIE: Gloria!

GLORIA: How do I look?

ANGIE: Beautiful.

GLORIA: Really?

ANGIE: Really.

GLORIA: (*swirls around*) I haven't felt this good in years!

ANGIE: Atta girl!

GLORIA: We owe it to you, Angie. Look! (*She turns with a sweep of her hand to include the other women, who are all dolled up.*) They're all happy.

ANGIE: Party time! Now if we only had a little brandy to put in the punch.

GLORIA: Angie!

ANGIE: Just kidding! Just kidding!

GLORIA: You'll never change, will you?

ANGIE: Not this old gal!

Pat enters dressed in his Sunday best. He's touched up his thin mustache.

PAT: How do I look?

ANGIE: You look great! Like Gilbert Roland. Ready to dance?

PAT: I'm ready.

ANGIE: Got yourself fixed up?

PAT: Shhh! (*He looks down at his trousers.*) No accidents. I'm in the pampered generation.

ANGIE: All we got to do is accept who we are. Viejitos, pero con ganas!

GLORIA: And if our kids don't like it, que se chinguen!

All turn in surprise at Gloria's outburst.

ANGIE: Gloria!

GLORIA: I didn't mean—

ANGIE: (*puts her arm around Gloria*) Yes, you did. The world may not like us for peeing in our pants, but we like ourselves!

PAT: Ten-four!

He gives Angie a high five. Minnie enters, all dressed up and with a bandage on her face.

ANGIE: Minnie! You made it.

MINNIE: I love parties.

ANGIE: So, you still want outta here.

MINNIE: (*fidgets*) Yes, but I'm not calling 911. I'm going to do it on my own.

ANGIE: That's the spirit! Now before we dance, let's pray to la Virgen. Come on, you don't have to be Catholic. Just pretend she's a kind grandmother you knew as a child. Today we honor our ancestors.

They gather at the altar, and Angie lights a candle.

ANGIE: This is for Johnny, my love.

The others step forward; each lights a candle.

GLORIA: I forgive the demon who abused me. May you rest in peace.

MINNIE: 911. I don't need you anymore. My grandma was a tough woman. I'll call her when I need help.

PAT: For my wife. Que descanse en paz. And my abuelos. I haven't forgotten you.

ANGIE: They live in our hearts, in our dreams. . . . We thank them for the love they gave us when they were on Earth.

All bow their heads in prayer for a moment.

ANGIE: Now we can dance! Here Minnie, you take Pat.

PAT: Con mucho gusto.

MINNIE: (*delighted*) Imagine, me dancing!

ANGIE: (to Gloria) Come on, comadre, let's dance!

She hits the tape player on-button and "Echale un cinco al piano" plays. A wild, stomp-ing dance follows.

ANGIE: ¡Baile! ¡Baile!

PAT: ¡Ajúa!

GLORIA: Oh, Angie, this is great!

PAT: It's great. And look, I'm dry!

All laugh.

MINNIE: I'm the one that feels wet and gushy!

ANGIE: Min-n-n-nie!

Laughter.

MINNIE: Don't get me outta here—I'm having too much fun!

ANGIE: ¡Que viva la fiesta!

GLORIA: ¡Viva Día de los Muertos!

The Nurse enters, scowls, then rushes to the tape player and stops the music.

NURSE: What is going on here? (*She stomps forward, angrily pulling down stream-ers as she goes.*)

PAT: (*weakly*) We're dancing—

NURSE: I don't call this a dance, I call this a travesty! (*She turns to the aide who has been watching and enjoying the dance.*) Did you give permission for this to take place?

Aide shakes her head, cowers.

NURSE: Look at this place! Ribbons all over the place. Someone could trip! The fire code has been violated— (*She turns to Angie.*) You!

ANGIE: (*bows*) May I have this dance?

NURSE: (*fumes*) You think you're so damn smart. Always ready with an an-swer, aren't you? *You're* responsible for this.

ANGIE: Yes.

NURSE: Thought you'd get away with it!

ANGIE: Look, they're enjoying it!

NURSE: You're using them for your enjoyment! (*She turns to the residents.*) Do all of you know why Angie planned this dance?

PAT: To have fun.

GLORIA: We did the decorating ourselves.

MINNIE: (*confused*) I feel a lot better—

NURSE: Angie is using you.

GLORIA: (*approaches Angie*) No, we wanted to have the party.

MINNIE: I think so—

PAT: Angie doesn't use us. She helps us.

NURSE: Oh, she doesn't do this to help you. Angie knows if she does something outrageous her contract will be cancelled. She's using you to get out!

GLORIA: (*touching Angie*) You wouldn't?

ANGIE: Oh yes, I would. Damn right I would. I tricked you into decorating this dull, dreary place, didn't I? For me. So I can get kicked out of here and dance in the streets.

MINNIE: (*anxiously*) Can you get me outta here?

ANGIE: (*grabs Minnie's shoulders*) Damn you, Minnie, don't slip back on me!

NURSE: Aides! Get everybody back to their rooms. Calm them down!

The aides start to lead residents away. Minnie swoons.

MINNIE: I'm dizzy.

NURSE: No wonder. Waltzing around like a fool, knowing you're under medication. Blame Angie if something happens!

PAT: (*jumps forward*) So she used us! Best thing that ever happened to me.

GLORIA: And me!

NURSE: What did you say?

GLORIA: We won't blame Angie.

NURSE: Are you defying me?

GLORIA: (*timidly*) We were just having fun—

NURSE: And this *fun*, as you call it, will bring on your nightmares. Do you really want everyone to know why you're here?

GLORIA: (*backs up*) No . . .

NURSE: No, you don't. You want to forget what happened to your husband—

GLORIA: Don't tell!

NURSE: No, I'm not going to tell. You came here to rest, to forget the past. Now go to your room.

Gloria bows her head and walks away.

NURSE: You too, Minnie.

Minnie follows Gloria. Connie steps forward.

CONNIE: I didn't think there was any harm in this—

NURSE: Maybe it's because you're too much like your mother!

CONNIE: I—

ANGIE: Go ahead, Connie. Tell her you're a chip off the old block!

JOE: Yeah, like her mother.

ANGIE: (*turns to Joe*) And that's why you keep her down. You're afraid she's too much like me. Because women like me like to lead when we dance!

JOE: You stick your nose in other people's business, Angie. Nobody likes that!

ANGIE: (*facing Joe*) The barrio is my business! We're not going to let you tear it down!

JOE: You won't always be around!

ANGIE: If not me, my daughter! Tell him, Connie! Nobody's going to run over us! We're not selling our homes! We're staying where our ancestors are buried!

NURSE: (*to an aide*) She's raving! Get her to her room!

The Nurse and the aide grab Angie and push her into one of the wheelchairs.

CONNIE: Wait!

NURSE: No! She's done enough damage. We have to get the patients settled down. Please leave!

CONNIE: Mom—

NURSE: She needs a sedative!

ANGIE: Okay, give it to me! ¡Viva Día de los Muertos! Don't back down, Connie! Lead!

The Nurse and aide push Angie out.

CONNIE: Mom!

JOE: (*grasping Connie's arm*) Let's go. We can still make the meeting with Frank.

CONNIE: (*shrugs him off, faces him*) You don't get it, do you, Joe?

JOE: I know you're upset.

CONNIE: Upset? I'm not upset. I'm angry!

JOE: She's going to be all right—

CONNIE: We sold her house from under her, and you say she's going to be all right! You cold bastard!

JOE: Don't go blaming me! You agreed!

CONNIE: It's the last time I agree, Joe.

JOE: Look, we can talk about this later.

CONNIE: (*shakes her head*) No. Talk isn't going to recover the years I've wasted—

JOE: I've got to go.

CONNIE: Then go.

Joe shrugs, exits. Connie goes to the altar as the lights grow dim. She lights a candle.

CONNIE: (*whispers*) For you, Mamá . . .

Scene Five

Offstage, 1940s swing music plays. An aide slowly pushes Angie in a wheelchair into the day room. Angie wears a black shawl. The aide exits.

CONNIE: Mom.

ANGIE: (*weakly*) Hija.

CONNIE: How are you feeling?

ANGIE: It only hurts when I smile.

CONNIE: I talked to the doctor—

ANGIE: Ah, ¿qué saben los doctores?

CONNIE: (*holds Angie's hands*) He called the hospital. An ambulance is on its way.

ANGIE: I guess my heart wasn't in too good a shape.

CONNIE: It was the shock. Too much medication. Oh, I shouldn't have let them— (*She embraces Angie.*)

ANGIE: Not your fault, hi'jita. My heart was run down.

CONNIE: And you kept it a secret.

ANGIE: I didn't want to bother you.

CONNIE: (*angry*) It wouldn't have been a bother! If I had known earlier, I would never have put you in here. God, I've grown to hate this place.

ANGIE: Maybe it's part of the cycle of life. We live in the sunshine, then in the darkness, then we exit . . .

CONNIE: The doctor said there's a good chance to repair—

ANGIE: To repair my heart. No, you can't repair the kind of pain I have.

CONNIE: He's sure a bypass operation—

ANGIE: No, no operation. I'm ready to leave the planet.

CONNIE: Don't say that! I won't listen!

ANGIE: You have no choice.

CONNIE: But—

ANGIE: Shh. Él que carga el saco sabe lo que pesa. I know why Johnny came to me.

CONNIE: Dad?

ANGIE: There's something I have to tell you.

CONNIE: What?

ANGIE: About you and me—and Juan Aragón.

Connie sits by her side.

ANGIE: He was so handsome, and a good dancer. I was so worried when my parents met him. Papá was so strict. But Johnny charmed him. (*She strokes Connie's hair.*)

CONNIE: They accepted him.

ANGIE: Yes. He told Papá he wanted to come back and marry me. Papá said yes. We made so many plans. Then he was gone.

CONNIE: But we kept him in our hearts all these years.

ANGIE: Yes. He's been a spirit, guiding us— (*She pauses.*)
Ah, Connie, it's no good.

CONNIE: What?

ANGIE: The secret I've kept from you all these years.

CONNIE: About Dad?

ANGIE: Juan Aragón wasn't your father.

CONNIE: (*calmly*) I know.

ANGIE: You knew?

CONNIE: I knew I was conceived after the war. I've just waited for you to tell me.

ANGIE: I lied to you.

CONNIE: Why?

ANGIE: I loved Johnny so much. I wanted you to be his daughter.

CONNIE: It was a game we played . . . you and me . . . all these years.

ANGIE: Forgive me, hija, forgive me.

CONNIE: (*holds Angie*) There's nothing to forgive, Mom. The past is done.

ANGIE: They say we viejos acquire wisdom, but only we know the mistakes we've made.

CONNIE: Maybe wisdom comes from living through those mistakes.

ANGIE: Yes. At the end we know we made enough mistakes to prove life right.

CONNIE: To prove life right. That's what it's all about. To dance—like you, Mom.

ANGIE: You can't sit in the back seat and let someone else drive you around.

CONNIE: I'm ready to move into the front seat. I never had your gift for dancing, but I'm good with people. I just need to test my wings. Imagine, living fifty years before one tries to fly.

ANGIE: Better late than never, hija.

CONNIE: I let you down, didn't I?

ANGIE: No! No, you didn't! Don't go start blaming yourself for anything. I chose my path, you chose yours!

CONNIE: But we remained good friends.

ANGIE: Yes.

Connie nods, takes Angie's hand.

CONNIE: Are you going to tell me?

ANGIE: What?

CONNIE: Who my father is?

ANGIE: A young captain. Your father's buddy. They shared everything during those months in Bataan.

CONNIE: He came to see you.

ANGIE: It was a promise he made to Johnny. I remember it was a summer day. The captain came to visit. We sat in my parents' porch and talked. The next day he brought me flowers. We went for a walk along the river . . .

CONNIE: You fell in love.

ANGIE: No, not really. Not like I loved Johnny. He knew that. But we shared a common grief.

CONNIE: So it was just a brief affair—

ANGIE: No, it wasn't an affair! Don't you see? Suffering bonded them. They became brothers. One died, the other lived. Johnny returned in the captain to give you to me! Johnny never left me. He's out there, watching over me.

CONNIE: I understand now.

ANGIE: And when I'm gone, I'll be there for you.

CONNIE: You're not dying, and I still have a lot to learn from you.

ANGIE: I'll write.

They laugh softly.

CONNIE: I'll always be the spiritual daughter of Johnny Aragón, the young hero from Old Town. (*She pauses.*) And the captain?

ANGIE: He settled down here, married, has his own family. He never knew you were born.

CONNIE: You didn't tell him?

ANGIE: As far as I'm concerned you're Johnny's daughter.

CONNIE: (*sobs*) God, Mom, you've always been a romantic.

ANGIE: Yes, I have been a romantic. I loved life, and it loved me back.

CONNIE: It still does.

ANGIE: I'm ready to leave.

CONNIE: Mom, no—

ANGIE: Hey, don't argue with an old lady. Ten respeto.

CONNIE: I have more respect for you than anyone on earth.

Gloria, Pat, and Minnie approach with gifts.

ANGIE: Ah, mis amigos.

GLORIA: We don't want to intrude—

ANGIE: You're not intruding, comadre. Come closer. I can barely see you.

GLORIA: How are you feeling?

ANGIE: I'm ready to go dancing.

CONNIE: We're waiting for the ambulance . . .

ANGIE: I'm going to my casita to live with my novio.

GLORIA: I don't know what to say.

CONNIE: (*whispers*) It's her heart . . .

GLORIA: I can't say goodbye. (*She sobs, embraces Angie.*) I love you, Angie.

ANGIE: I love you, comadre. Now it's up to you to take care of the viejitos.

GLORIA: (*nods*) Yes.

PAT: Angie. I carved this for you. (*He hands her a small, wooden cross.*)

ANGIE: It's beautiful.

PAT: I wish I had a bottle of wine, but you know the rules.

ANGIE: The cross is all I need, Patricio. Gracias.

GLORIA: I'll miss you, Angie.

ANGIE: I'll miss you, comadre.

MINNIE: Angie, can you take me with you?

ANGIE: No, Minnie. I can't take you with me. But I'll be watching over you. I'll be watching over all of you.

MINNIE: God bless you, Angie.

ANGIE: I'm so tired . . . so tired.

The muted sound of an ambulance siren is heard in background. Pat, Gloria, and Minnie return to where they stood when they play opened.

CONNIE: They're coming.

ANGIE: A band of angels coming after me . . . I see them, Connie. There's Mamá and Papá waiting for me. And Johnny.

Juan appears.

CONNIE: Rest, Mamá, rest . . .

A light falls on Angie as the stage grows dim.

JUAN: Angie.

ANGIE: Johnny.

JUAN: Are you ready, Angelina?

ANGIE: Yes, I'm ready. I'm so happy to see you.

JUAN: You told Connie?

ANGIE: Yes. I cleared my soul.

JUAN: I'm so proud of you. She's been a good daughter.

ANGIE: Sent by you to bless my life.

JUAN: And you've been a good mother.

ANGIE: You don't think all that dancing and raising hell will be held against me, do you?

JUAN: No, Angie. You've done good.

He holds out his hand. Angie raises from her chair, removes her dark shawl.

JUAN: You look lovely, mi amor.

ANGIE: I feel my soul rising to the heavens. So light I can dance on clouds.

JUAN: Well then, let's dance.

He takes her in his arms and they waltz.

END

AFTERWORD

Engagement with the Human Spirit: Tragedy and Comedy in Rudolfo Anaya's Plays

CECILIA J. ARAGÓN AND ROBERT CON DAVIS-UNDIANO

In that Rudolfo Anaya has been publishing for more than forty years, the absence of most of his plays from print is striking. Only two of his plays have been published previously, so this first-ever one-volume collection is a landmark and will enable a greater appreciation of the totality of his dramatic literature. The full texts presented here are as follows: *The Season of La Llorona; The Farolitos of Christmas; Who Killed Don José?; Matachines; Ay, Compadre!; Billy the Kid;* and *Angie.* The purpose of *Billy the Kid and Other Plays* is not only to share seven plays by an acclaimed novelist, short-story writer, essayist, and playwright, but also to document Anaya's diverse voices of the human spirit. The magical realism, mythology, and cultural themes manifest in these plays are the product of Anaya's work over this period and derive from his creative imagination, sense of humanity, and appreciation for New Mexico culture and folkways.

We both marvel at the depth and breadth of Anaya's ability to capture in these plays the "New Mexican spirit." Anaya is a major figure among twentieth- and twenty-first-century Chicano playwrights and a theater artist who consistently exhibits an inventive and sophisticated imagination for the stage with uncanny insight into the human condition. The seven plays in this volume are part of a distinctive regional dramatic vision that Anaya has developed in New Mexico since the 1970s, and collectively they represent the apex of the Chicano Renaissance and Chicano Theatre. All of Anaya's plays reflect the cultural geography of New Mexico—its history, language, landscapes, religion, mythology, legends, cultural institutions, and politics. In the stories being told on Anaya's stage, it is no wonder that New Mexicans recognize themselves and their grandparents, parents, and neighbors.

Anaya is well known for his novels and short fiction, and no other writer has made as important an impact on Chicano literature. Widely recognized

Cecilia J. Aragón, Chicana director and theater historian, has directed four of Anaya's plays (*Matachines; Ay, Compadre!; Billy the Kid;* and *Angie*) for her theater company, La Casa Teatro, in Albuquerque, New Mexico. Robert Con Davis-Undiano, literary critic and Chicano Studies scholar, has written frequently on Anaya's fiction and nonfiction prose.

as the godfather of Chicano literature, inspiring a national movement of writers dedicated to expressing the culture of Mexican American communities, he has written plays, novels, children's books, essays, screenplays, and poetry, all of which deal with being Mexican American and the cultural commitments and markers of Chicano identity. This volume's plays continue theatrical and performance traditions in New Mexico that connect with mythology embedded in Indo-Hispanic dance/dramas, such as los Comanches, los Matachines, and Spanish *pastorelas* (nativity plays). Before discussing the plays in this anthology, we will briefly trace the playwright's literary career, placing him and these plays in their social, political, cultural, and historical context.

The Playwright

Rudolfo Alfonso Anaya was born in 1937 in the village of Pastura, New Mexico, near the small town of Santa Rosa. Later in his life, his family moved to Albuquerque, where he attended the University of New Mexico, earning master's degrees in literature and counseling. He taught in the Albuquerque public school system and at the University of New Mexico, where he is now professor emeritus in the Department of English Language and Literature.

Anaya's works are filled with images from his childhood and memories of the New Mexico *llano* (plain) and *gente* (people)—the tragedies, the triumphs, and the Spanish and Indo-Hispanic culture unique to New Mexico. Out of these childhood experiences, Anaya forges the themes and questions of his writing, as clearly seen in his award-winning novels, such as *Bless Me, Ultima* (1972); *Tortuga* (1979); and *Alburquerque* (1992). Critic César A. González-T suggests that "at the heart of his writing, we find his intriguing vision of the meeting of our everyday ritual world with the eternal. Literature and myth, [Anaya] tells us, have to do with people remembering themselves, telling who they are so that they will not be forgotten, and about the values that will always matter to all people" (*The Anaya Reader*, xvii).

From the Chicano Movement to the Anayan Theatre

Billy the Kid and Other Plays not only captures this vision of New Mexico but contributes to the larger cultural renewal of the Chicano Theatre movement. While El Teatro Campesino in Delano, California, had Luis Valdez as the father of Chicano Theatre, New Mexicans have the father of Chicano literature, Rudolfo Anaya, as their own father of theater. Beyond Anaya's prolific work with *cuentos*, which are short stories reflective of New Mexican culture and lore, and his New Mexico–based novels, there is the magical realism of his plays and a distinctly Anayan Theatre. His large and diverse body of dramatic literature looks at New Mexican culture to find mythical, historical, and social themes.

We can see from the following list that Anaya's plays roughly coincide with his career as a writer and fit within the larger context of the Chicano Theatre movement:

The Season of La Llorona: 1979 (first performed)
The Farolitos of Christmas: 1987 (first performed)
Who Killed Don José?: 1987 (first performed), 1989 (first published)
Matachines: 1989 (first performed)
Ay, Compadre!: 1994 (first performed)
Billy the Kid: 1995 (published), 1997 (first performed)
Angie: 1998 (first performed)

These plays chronicle the pressing events of Anaya's time—events regarding land use, the nature of the sacred, digital communication and information storage, the weakening of and recommitment to cultural traditions, the loss and restoration of faith—the same themes that run through his fiction and nonfiction prose. These play titles reveal broadly diverse topics and a strong regional inflection that reference the Southwest's remarkable history, *mestizo* (mixed Spanish and indigenous) people and cultures, the Spanish language, and the challenges of dealing with aging and death.

The Season of La Llorona

Anaya's first play, *The Season of La Llorona*, appeared in 1979, just seven years after the publication of his groundbreaking *Bless Me, Ultima* (1972). This play brings to the stage the mix of European and indigenous cultures that flows throughout the Americas. It is the story of the beautiful and intelligent Malinche, who has fallen in love with the Captain. Readers will recognize the Captain as Hernán Cortés, the conqueror of Mexico. He uses Malinche as translator and thus she helps defeat the Aztecs. Once the Aztecs are conquered, he decides to advance his career by marrying a Spanish princess. The treachery drives Malinche to murder her own children before they are murdered by the Spanish princess. Despairing over her act, Malinche becomes the Crying Woman, la Llorona, of the New World. The play highlights the historical and cultural framework in which the history of the conquest and cultural rebellion, as expressed in child-killing, merge into a unique and haunting myth.

Chicano Theatre historian Jorge Huerta suggests that Chicano drama's earliest works and the playwrights' impulse to create them reflect a drive for "a mythos [that] also gives a people a place in the cosmos, describing and recalling their ancestors, giving them a 'from the beginning,' as it were" (*Chicano Drama*, 15). Huerta adds that "for the believers [Chicanos,] these myths are no longer myths but doctrine. . . . Thus when our [Chicano] playwrights began to resuscitate Mexican legendary figures along with Aztec and Mayan gods and concepts, they challenged both the Mexican and North American hegemonies" (15–18). Anaya's use of the archetypal figure of la Llorona/la Malinche has many theatrical functions, as she reflects the Mexican American oppositions of fact/fiction, past/present, oppression/freedom, natural/supernatural, and reality/illusion as well as a "both/and" blended cultural identity.

The Season of La Llorona, Anaya's earliest treatment of la Llorona, is set in contemporary culture to interrogate the problems Mexican Americans face in modern society. Looking back to the history, myths, spiritual thought, legend, and symbols that are part of a collective history in New Mexico and in the Americas, this play offers a summation of la Llorona's persistence in the modern-day legacy of the conquest and her emergence as a palpable reality within Chicano and Chicana consciousness. She is the infamous embodiment of one who is betrayed and the icon of hybrid cultural identity in Mexican *mestizaje* (the nationhood of mixed-race people).

The Farolitos of Christmas

The Farolitos of Christmas, a dramatic adaptation of Anaya children's book by the same name, highlights Anaya's New Mexican childhood through the imagination of a ten-year-old protagonist, Luz. Set in 1944, the play recounts the origin of the Southwestern Christmas lights called *los farolitos*. Luz's father is away fighting in World War II, and her grandfather is too old and sick to chop wood for the traditional *luminarias* (bonfires). So the family is faced with changing the tradition, a sixteenth-century Spanish practice of lighting bonfires along the roads and churchyards to guide travelers to midnight Mass. These fires were also left to burn in case the Messiah should come back. (Luminarias are still used in some pueblos and villages.)

Luz solves the problem by creating los farolitos (small lanterns) for the Christmas celebration. She suggests making los farolitos with small brown paper bags, weighted down with sand, with candles placed inside the bags—an idea that comes to her while visiting the local grocer. Anaya uses the luminar-ias/farolitos as a metaphor for strength, hospitality, and welcome to all who cross our paths, involving community spirit, a gesture of hope for the safe return of a loved one, peace, and the soul of life.

The Farolitos of Christmas brings together an Anayan aesthetic that can be defined as a New Mexican coloring of verbal and visual imagery. For example, in this play Anaya uses a regional dialect of Spanish heard only in New Mexico. The visual elements of the play call for adobe houses, the backdrop of the Sangre de Cristo Mountains, and un altar, a religious altar. From this theatricality, audiences discover Anaya's attitude toward his characters as he reveals the complexities of biculturalism in being both Mexican and American. The culture that is tied to this specific sense of place, the northern Rio Grande, and to these specific artifacts of material culture (adobe homes and a distinctly southwestern Catholic altar) create for audiences the cultural geography of a Mexican American, New Mexican identity. This play also places New Mexicans in a historical context that identifies them as Americans by showing that they, too, fought for American democracy and served valiantly during the war. Anaya tells his audience that Mexican American participation in World War II can be viewed as a renewal of hope, eliciting heroic efforts of bravery and the gaining of new skills. These are the character strengths that Anaya locates in Luz and her mother and father, as they both signal Mexican American values.

Who Killed Don José?

In 1987, La Compañía de Teatro de Alburquerque, one of the oldest Chicano theater companies, produced Who Killed Don José? This production was directed by Jorge Huerta, who stated that he had never before seen "a Chicano play about a wealthy Hispanic" (Jones 1989, 200). And indeed, this play is about a wealthy Hispano, a "rico," a "patrón," who is a steward of cultural traditions. He plans to take his community from the world of slow provincial life into high-tech America to find economic success.

The main characters in this play embody various perspectives on change. The visionary Don José, who says that "to survive we have to adapt," wants to create a local factory for manufacturing the new and improved computer, "the El Patrón A.T.M. 1000 . . . a dream that can become a reality." His daughter, María, has a similar vision, and at play's end she is poised to lead the town into a new era. Tony, an admirer of María and a car salesman focused on quick profits, is overly tied to the past; he murders Don José to settle an old family vendetta. Doña Sofia, the housekeeper, and her son, Diego, are co-heirs to Don José's wealth and focus too intently on capturing it. Don José's confidante,

Ana, wants to acquire a new future by marrying Don José but loses that dream when he dies.

Who Killed Don José? offers the Mexican American community the hope that change and adaptation are possible through bold action. The missing computer disk in the play gives clues about the murder as well as metaphorically represents the Mexican American community's future. Anaya suggests that the future can be bright, as making computers will bring economic prosperity. Anaya's play echoes the work of mystery writer Agatha Christie, as she often used detective mysteries to question the nature of human motives. Anaya shows how the promise of shared cultural knowledge may motivate people, and he calls for his audience to empathize with New Mexican characters whose history is marked by conquest and exploitation, violent politics, intercultural politics, and pressing rural/small-town community conflicts.

Matachines

Matachines premiered with La Compañía de Teatro de Alburquerque in 1992 at the historical Kimo Theater in downtown Albuquerque, where it was directed by Elena Citlali Parres. Eight years later, La Casa Teatro produced Matachines at the South Broadway Cultural Center, where it was directed by Cecilia Aragón. Depicting an Indo-Hispanic ritual dance and drama familiar to New Mexican audiences, both productions were well received.

Matachines explores intercultural and interethnic relationships using the traditional roles of El Monarca (Moctezuma), La Malinche (a young girl dressed in a white dress for first Holy Communion, symbolizing La Virgen), the Matachines (dancers), El Toro (the bull symbolizing the evil one), and Los Abuelos (the grandfathers, or mayordomos), whose roles are to faciliatate and to provide comic relief (Rodríquez 1996, 3). Matachines is Anaya's theatrical exploration of the Indo-Hispanic folk dances of Bernalillo, New Mexico. The play focuses on la Danza de los Matachines, in particular, which takes place during la Fiesta de San Lorenzo. The work reveals close spiritual and cultural ties between European and Mesoamerican ritual dance and drama from las fiestas, and Anaya writes in Alburquerque (1992) that "it was in the fiestas of the people that I discovered the true essence of my people" (9).

Anaya's Matachines depicts young people in a small New Mexican town who perform in an annual dance and drama festival. The climactic scene, set against the backdrop of the Matachines' performance, is a play within a play, one of Anaya's favorite theatrical devices. Matachines gives a portrait of New Mexican youth working through issues relating to love, deceit, betrayal, and friendship. The Anayan aesthetics at work in the play challenge the director and actors with theatrical styles ranging from realism to stylized dancing.

A successful production of *Matachines* must accurately reflect Bernalillo's Danza de los Matachines, a sixteenth-century European and Mesoamerican folk dance. To accurately portray la Danza de los Matachines demands sophisticated choreography of la Entrada, la Bailada de las Promesas, la Marcha de la Malinche, la Matada del Toro, and la Despedida (Rodríquez 1996, 53–54). Further, there are twelve types of music that appear in *Matachines*, including *alabados* (Spanish worship songs) and polkas, and the inclusion of a guitarist and a violinist is also specified (Champe 1983, 17–20). The music accompanies the processionals from church to home or to the performance area of the dance/drama (Champe 1983, 27).

The Matachine dancers wear traditional costumes and use props such as a *palma* (trident), *cupil* (Aztec floral crown headdress), *guaje* (rattle), and white Communion dress, as well as *paños* (scarfs), capes, a cowhide and horns, foresticks, and clown masks (Rodríguez 1996, 3). The cast of characters in the play within the play—El Monarca, El Toro, La Malinche, Los Abuelos, and Los Danzantes—all have special roles. Their costumes and accessories should fit exacting standards. The play within a play requires extensive historical research to produce accurately. Anaya's theatrical techniques in this play remind audiences that the characters portray both the interethnic birth of the Indian and Spanish dance/dramas and the modern complexities of intermingled cultures, what Anaya calls "the true essence of my people" (*Alburquerque* 1992, 9).

Ay, Compadre!

Anaya's most successful comedy to date is *Ay, Compadre!*, first produced in 1995 by La Casa Teatro at South Broadway Cultural Center in Albuquerque, New Mexico, where it was directed by Cecilia Aragón and featured community actors. This play has since been produced in several other venues, from Santa Fe, New Mexico, to the Nosotros Theater in Hollywood, and in 1998, at the Latino Ensemble de San Diego, California, under the direction of Marcos Martínez.

Exploring Mexican American views on midlife crises, this play features two *compadres* (best friends), Daniel and Iggy, and *comadres*, Linda and Helen, and highlights their romantic entanglements, physical/sexual challenges in midlife, and nostalgia for "barrio life." For the *comadres*, the midlife transition means dealing with menopause and rekindling romance with their husbands.

Helen, who comforts Linda about menopause, tells her, "I know how you feel. I lied to myself when I went through menopause. 'I won't let it get me down,' I kept telling myself! 'I look good! I feel good!' Maybe a woman can just hide it better. For a man, if the cosita don't get hard, pues—" Linda and Helen hunger for romantic love, passion, and a sexual renaissance with their partners.

Trying to cope with impotence, the husbands, Daniel and Iggy, transition into middle age in different ways. Covering self-doubt with a swagger, Iggy declares to Daniel, "Look at me. I dress right, I present a good image, I meet a lonely vieja, y vamos! With my attitude I can do anything! Look at you. Look at the way you dress. Sloppy, compadre, sloppy. You think sloppy and you perform sloppy." Caught up in denial and bravado, Iggy imagines himself to be as virile as his attire.

Anaya traverses multiple sexual taboos in *Ay, Compadre!* Iggy has had an ongoing sexual flirtation with his compadre's wife, Linda, and does not readily embrace the fact of his impotence for fear of losing his sexual identity. Daniel reconstructs his identity, challenging Mexican American norms of masculinity by breaking free of the expectations of Mexican American masculinity. He states: "I'm not giving up, I'm just accepting reality. Okay, I'm not as good as I used to be— . . . I have trouble getting it up! Can you hear me? I'm not as good as I used to be! ¡Ahi 'sta! I said it! . . . I'm free. . . . And life doesn't end!" Daniel is the character in the play most open to the possibility of growing and redefining himself in new ways.

The metaphor for Mexican American gender identity in this play is a cactus. In the opening lines, Linda waters her cactus and asks, "¿Cuando me vas a dar una flor?" (When are you going to give me a flower?) She returns to the cactus at play's end, explaining, "You never can tell when it will bloom," as she yearns for love and romantic passion. Through the cactus metaphor, Anaya reflects on the power of sex to bind couples together, and he uses the cactus not only for its regional identification but also for its suggestion of persistence under adverse conditions.

Billy the Kid

Billy the Kid combines *corridos* (ballads) with the legend of a New Mexican bandit. Known as "El Bilito," "El Chivo" (The Kid or Goat), and "El Chivato" (Little Billy), Billy the Kid became an icon of nineteenth-century New Mexico that has survived into the present (Aragón 2011). His legend has special persistence and vitality in New Mexico, and this play provides a forum for critics, audiences, and readers to debate issues relating to how he lived and died.

Billy the Kid first gained fame in the nineteenth and early twentieth centuries through dime novels and other popular accounts. In 1906, the Star Theatre in New York City opened a melodrama entitled *Billy the Kid* by Walter Woods and Joseph Stanley, starring Joseph Stanley as Billy. In 1940, in Lincoln, New Mexico, the community celebrated a folk pageant dedicated to Billy the Kid entitled *The Last Escape of Billy the Kid*, produced by Quatro Centennial. In 1942, the National Theatre in New York opened a ballet production of *Billy the Kid* produced by the Dance Players, Inc. In 1965, *The Beard*, by Michael McClure, opened in an off-off-Broadway production. In 1973, Michael Ondaatje's play *The Collected Works of Billy the Kid* appeared as a performance piece, with poems, historical narrative, fiction, and biography. In 1980, Lee Blessing's *The Authentic Life of Billy the Kid* highlighted the Kid's relationship with Pat Garrett (Aragón 2011).

Rudolfo Anaya's *Billy the Kid* was published in *The Anaya Reader* in 1995, and in 1997 La Casa Teatro produced it at the South Broadway Cultural Center in Albuquerque, where it was directed by Cecilia Aragón. Set in 1881 on the night of Billy the Kid's death in Don Pedro Maxwell's home, this play gives voice to Nuevo Mexicanos through "Paco Anaya," the play's narrator and El Bilito's friend, whose comments remind the audience that Billy occupies a special place in New Mexican consciousness.

In the play's opening scene, in the home of Don Maxwell, El Bilito holds Rosa Anaya, his lover, and speaks to her in a mixture of Spanish and English about plans for the future:

BILLY: Time to settle down . . . give up being a vagamundo.

ROSA: Siempre lo prometes . . .

BILLY: Esta vez lo voy hacer. Mira. A hundred acres, enough land to run a small herd. You should see it, Rosa. There's good grazing, plenty of water, and the beauty of the mountains. It's what I always wanted—

ROSA: Es un sueño, Billy.

BILLY: Tú eres mi sueño, amor. . . . ¿Te vas conmigo?

ROSA: Mi padre no lo permite.

BILLY: Yo hablo con él. Vas a ver. Voy a cambiar . . .

ROSA: ¿Por qué te gusta tanto ese maldado condado de Lincoln? Quédate aquí.

BILLY: Me gustan las montañas, y la gente.

ROSA: Pero los tejanos no te quieren.

BILLY: Qué importa. Anda, cásate conmigo. Quiero hijos . . .

ROSA: ¿Sería posible?

BILLY: Sí, es posible. Ven. Imagina. El Bilito, con hijos. Let the papers write about that. Y después, I'll be a grandfather.

Anaya depicts El Bilito as a Spanish speaker, and part of New Mexico culture. As historian Michael Wallis states in Billy the Kid: The Endless Ride (2007), "[I]t helped that [Billy the Kid] spoke Spanish as fluently as a native, a proficiency that served him well with the Hispanics for the rest of his life" (129). Billy's knowledge of Spanish and his embrace of New Mexico brought him into the Hispano community, as he not only defended Nuevo Mexicano rights but in practical terms became a New Mexican. The primary gesture in this play is Anaya's depiction of the intimate relationship between El Bilito and New Mexicans, with Rosa representative of New Mexico.

In Billy the Kid, Anaya employs corridos and other music, inserting in this play two corridos and a melodía (melody), two important elements of storytelling. The first corrido, for instance—written by Anaya in the category of corridos about bandidos—is delivered by Nuevo Mexicanos mourning Billy's death. Beginning with a description of the fateful night in 1881 when Billy was shot by Sheriff Pat Garrett in Pedro Maxwell's house in Fort Sumner, this corrido tells of Billy's lover, Rosita, crying as the wounded Billy falls into her arms.

Anaya's play ends as it began, with the night scene where Garrett shoots Billy at Maxwell's house. Billy and Rosa sit in a bedroom, and Billy tells Rosa his plans:

BILLY: Espera aquí.

ROSA: No. Voy contigo.

BILLY: We have plenty of time to be together, querida. Tomorrow we leave for Mexico.

ROSA: A new life . . .

BILLY: Don Pedro wants to see me.

ROSA: Why so late?

BILLY: He owes me money. Josefina said he's ready to pay.

ROSA: Josefina? No, Billy, don't go!

BILLY: Why are you trembling?

ROSA: There's no light in his room . . .

BILLY: The old cheapskate doesn't like to burn his oil. Wait.

ROSA: Billy.

BILLY: ¿Qué?

ROSA: I love you.

BILLY: Y yo te amo a ti.

They embrace warmly. Deputy Poe appears.

ROSA: ¿Quién es?

Billy pulls out his knife. Poe backs away.

BILLY: Just one of Don Pedro's vaqueros. Espera aquí. *(He leaves Rosa and softly enters Maxwell's bedroom.)*
BILLY: Don Pedro. Who is the man outside—

Garrett stands. Billy faces him.

BILLY: ¿Quién es? ¿Quién es?
DON Pedro: That's him!
BILLY: Garrett?
GARRETT: It's me, Billy!

Garrett fires once. Billy grabs at his gut in pain, steps forward, reaching for Garrett. The figure of death, La Muerte, appears. . . .

ROSA: Billy! Billy! Oh, Bilito . . .
BILLY: I love you, Rosa . . .
ROSA: He's dead . . . Amor, amor . . . *(She holds and rocks Billy in her arms.)*

Anaya's version of Billy counters the popular Anglo image of Billy the Kid as a cold-blooded killer. John-Michael Rivera explains:

> Billy the Kid became a hero to the Mexican people throughout the terri-
> tory. He became a symbol of resistance and freedom for the Mexican
> population. To the Mexicans, El Bilito was on their side, fighting the
> Anglo regime that had taken their lands and impoverished their lives
> since the end of the U.S.-Mexico war. Because of El Bilito's courage, he be-
> came a weapon that could help fight against the Santa Fe Ring. . . . For
> the Oteros, the death of Billy the Kid symbolized the passing of their
> economic power, and their ability to define the political public spheres.
> (Rivera 2006, 121, 123)

Anaya represents precisely these sentiments as Billy dies in Rosita's arms.

Anaya's Billy is a "social bandit," reminiscent of Robin Hood, working on behalf of New Mexicans. Rivera agrees that Billy is viewed in New Mexico as one who "(1) protects the people from the onslaught of modernity or colo-nialism, (2) is a person who avenges the institutional wrongs the people have felt in the wake of political strife caused by colonialism, (3) is one who im-pedes the civilizing and modernizing mission of a given territory for democ-racy, (4) personifies the marginalization of the people's political and cultural struggles against the encroaching state" (Rivera 2006, 111).

When El Bilito dies, so dies a dream of defending the "political public spheres" of Nuevo Mexicanos, as El Bilito stood for resistance and freedom. To Hispanic New Mexicans, El Bilito was theirs, fighting the Anglo regime that had "taken their lands and impoverished their lives since the U.S.-Mexico War." To this day, El Bilito's death is commonly viewed in New Mexico as a historical injustice.

Angie

Angie (1998) continued an important turning point in Anaya's playwrighting, as with it he began to explore contemporary domestic issues, including midlife themes such as one's responsibility to aging parents. First produced by La Casa Teatro at South Broadway Cultural Center in Albuquerque and directed by Cecilia Aragón, this play focuses on a middle-class Chicano couple, Connie and Joe, who have decided to move Connie's mother, Angie, to the Joy of Life Nursing Home. Connie and Joe have had successful lives, with Joe even running for mayor. The play's major conflict arises when Angie moves to the nursing home and finds everyone there in a near-catatonic state. She complains, "I'm not dead yet! . . . They can hardly lift the cards. I don't like it! Take me home! . . . It smells like disinfectant and death."

In the nursing home, she befriends an assortment of characters. There is Minnie, in her eighties and dressed like a bag lady, who pushes a grocery cart through the home and is always asking, "Can you get me outta here?" There is Pat, a wood carver from Los Padillas who has urinary retention problems. And there is Gloria, who cannot say the word "death" for fear of dying. Angie interacts with these characters, and through her flashbacks we get a glimpse of her *folklórico* dancer period and her relationship with her deceased husband, Juan Aragón, or Johnny.

Sedated with medication on several occasions for not "obeying the rules," Angie is devastated to discover that her daughter signed a long-term contract with the nursing home and plans to rent Angie's casita in the barrio. Angie responds by instigating activities, like dancing, which the nursing home does not permit. The Nurse reminds Angie, "You want to turn Joy of Life into a fun house, don't you? Well, I won't allow it. I have my responsibilities to the patients and their families. I can't allow the wild kind of parties you're used to. . . . You're terrible, Angie. Nothing but trouble." Angie's advocacy of dancing becomes a metaphor for the desire for vibrant life in this play.

Anaya's depiction of Angie as the "disabled, aging body" is accompanied with the irony of her love for dance. When Angie dies, audiences must face the reality of death and also the threat of the disappearance of Hispanic culture. The play depicts the immediacy of an uncertain future in a world that has no patience for the elderly. By helping the audience to reflect on the effects of cultural and physical displacement, *Angie* highlights problems that Mexican Americans with aging parents face.

Angie also sounds a warning about what will be lost as a generation of Mexican Americans slips away. The play's titular character is a colorful reminder of what richness elderly people embody, and her death warns that the loss of that generation could rob Mexican American culture of much substance unless it renews its traditions in the present. *Angie* is about the tragedy of neglecting the aged, but it also sounds an alarm about the failure to renew culture and community through contact with elders and cultural traditions.

Conclusion

There is particular cultural significance in these seven plays as Anaya explores New Mexico's history and social memory. He attempts to contribute to a cultural renewal. The earliest of his plays dealt with mythological references to tragedy, threats to indigenous culture, vengeance, and love. His most recent plays foreground contemporary issues that Mexican Americans face when challenged by mainstream Anglo ideals about aging, health, and cultural activism.

Finally, Anaya's plays use the Indo/Hispano culture of New Mexico as a staging for America and the modern world, and that setting showcases a drama in which traditional cultures are threatened with extinction and in which the forces of commercialism, personal greed, and technological innovation are changing the world in unpredictable and sometimes destructive ways. A critical word describing Anaya's plays could be "engagement" in the sense of having a commitment to the cultural tradition that Mexican Americans are heir to the sacred land beneath their feet, to the community they live in, and to the future that needs a foundation in their lives from which to grow. He implores Mexican Americans and all Americans to engage these forces in their lives and to do so with vigor and the deepest commitment.

In other words, we read or view Anaya's plays because doing so helps us to expand our awareness, and that is essential to what makes us human. The American poet William Carlos Williams once wrote that men and women die every day for lack of what they could find in poetry. The same can be said of Anaya's plays. We read his plays because they strengthen our awareness that we must live with a commitment to preserving and honoring our historical sense of identity and an eco-cultural stewardship of land and place. Anaya urges us to be stewards of our own past even as we must be participatory citizens in local, national, and global communities, responding to the economic and political conditions that shape our lives.

In the twenty-first-century world of rapid change, political instability, environmental crises, and instant communication that can distract people and leave them feeling displaced, Anaya reminds us what being grounded by ties to place and culture can bring—an enriched, spiritual, and immediate connection to each other with a capacity to love that is enhanced through remembering why, what, and who we are. In a word, these plays promise to give us a fuller grasp of the human condition and how we fit into the world around us.

We would like to express our gratitude to Armando Celayo, research assistant extraordinario, for his diligent work in making this volume possible. Muchas gracias. Also, we appreciate the tireless commitment of the University of Oklahoma Press editors to this collection. Finally, we thank Rudolfo Anaya for sharing the vision to bring these plays into the light for the world to read.

Works Cited

Anaya, Rudolfo. 1992. *Alburquerque*. New Mexico: University of New Mexico Press.

Aragón, Cecilia J. 2011. "Politics and Performance: Repression and Resistance in Lee Blessing's *Billy the Kid* and Rudolfo Anaya's *Billy the Kid*." *Western States Theatre Review*, vol. 16.

Champe, Flavia Waters. 1983. *The Matachines Dance of the Upper Rio Grande: History, Music, and Choreography*. Lincoln: University of Nebraska Press.

González-T, César A. 1995. Forward to *The Anaya Reader*, xv–xxiii. New York: Time Warner Company.

Huerta, Jorge. 2000. *Chicano Drama: Performance, Society, and Myth*. New York: Cambridge University Press.

Jones, David Richard, ed. 1989. *New Mexico Plays*. Albuquerque: University of New Mexico Press.

Martínez, Marcos. 2011. E-mail interview. January 19–22.

Rivera, John-Michael. 2006. *The Emergence of Mexican America: Recovering Stories of Mexican Peoplehood in U.S. Culture*. New York: New York University Press.

Rodríquez, Sylvia. 1996. *The Matachines Dance: Ritual Symbolism and Interethnic Relations in the Upper Río Grande Valley*. Albuquerque: University of New Mexico Press.

Wallis, Michael. 2007. *Billy the Kid: The Endless Ride*. New York: W.W. Norton and Company.

Also by Rudolfo Anaya

Bless Me, Ultima
Heart of Aztlan
Tortuga
The Silence of the Llano
The Legend of La Llorona
The Adventures of Juan Chicaspatas
A Chicano in China
Lord of the Dawn: The Legend of Quetzalcóatl
Alburquerque
The Anaya Reader
Zia Summer
Jalamanta: A Message from the Desert
Rio Grande Fall
Shaman Winter
Serafina's Stories
Jemez Spring
Curse of the ChupaCabra
The Man Who Could Fly and Other Stories
ChupaCabra and the Roswell UFO
The Essays

Children's Books

The Farolitos of Christmas: A New Mexico Christmas Story
Farolitos for Abuelo
My Land Sings: Stories from the Rio Grande
Elegy on the Death of César Chávez
Roadrunner's Dance
The Santero's Miracle: A Bilingual Story
The First Tortilla: A Bilingual Story
Juan and the Jackalope: A Children's Book in Verse

CPSIA information can be obtained at www.ICGtesting.com
Printed in the USA
LVOW040923021111

253181LV00001B/4/P